THE LAST QUEEN

Rakesh K. Kaul, whose family hails from Kashmir, migrated to the US in 1972 after graduating from IIT Delhi. In addition to having a distinguished business career as a CEO of multi-billion dollar companies in the US, he has also written extensively for leading newspapers and magazines and been a keynote speaker on the history, politics and culture of Kashmir. He was a founding contributor to the first chair of India studies at the University of California Berkeley, to the Center for the Advanced Study of India at the University of Pennsylvania and the Mattoo Center for India Studies at the State University of New York. He has an MBA from the University of Chicago, a master's degree in electronics from Brown University and holds a chartered professional accountant degree (CPA). He is also the author of *Dawn The Warrior Princess of Kashmir* published by Penguin India.

Praise for *The Last Queen of Kashmir*

'Rakesh Kaul is a gifted storyteller. He does for Kashmir what Sir Walter Scott did for Scotland, and more. In this compulsively readable story of a charismatic, controversial queen, Kaul brilliantly brings to life the beautiful valley of Kashmir.' – **Dr S. N. Sridhar**, State University of New York Distinguished Service Professor and Director, Mattoo Center for India Studies, Stony brook University

'A wonderful story, very touching, inspiring and lively.' – **Theresa Wilke**, University of Halle Wittenberg

'The author has remarkably and felicitously succeeded in weaving together the history of the past and the paradisiacal landscape of his lost homeland with passion and imagination, a narrative that is at once poignant

and evocative, filled with pathos and drama for present-day readers.'
– Dr Pratapaditya Pal, India's foremost scholar, curator, author on South Asian and Himalayan art, culture and history

'A fascinating arc running through one of the most glorious periods of Kashmir's history. Storytelling at its best. The epic tale of Kotarani will leave you mesmerized.' – Rahul Pandita, author of *Our Moon has Blood Clots*, Yale World Fellow

'Speechless...riveting, heart opening...a treasure and testimony to the human spirit.' – Chris Tompkins, Harvard University, UC Berkeley, Kashmir Shaiva scholar

'A brilliant novel that recreates the life and times of Kota in a most compelling narrative. A book unique both in substance and style, it skillfully portrays the complex psychological and historical elements of the story.' – Dr Subhash Kak, Regents Professor at Oklahoma State University and author of *The Wishing Tree*

'Gripping account, it is hard to put down. All Indians should read this book.' – Dr Meena Sridhar, Professor of Linguistics Stony Brook University, New York

'An epic written with intriguing imagination.' – Siddharth Kak, TV producer of Surabhi and Indiadhanush and documentary maker

'What an idea! Combining tradition with the modern novel, fiction with nostalgia, and history with ethics, **The Last Queen of Kashmir** is a reclamation of memory and pride for...the Kashmiri Hindus.' – Dr Shonaleeka Kaul, Reader in Ancient Indian History, Department of History, University of Delhi

'A book for our times. Kaul with his skilled writing has brought forth a masterpiece – a rich historical narrative expressing Shaivite and Buddhist worldview, weaving a rich tapestry of Kashmiri life on each page ...This is a meticulously researched work presenting an authentic, intimate portrait of Kashmir.' – Dr Nirmal Mattoo, co-author, *Ananya A Portrait of India*, 2015 recipient M.S. Swaminathan Changemaker Award

The Last Queen of Kashmir

RAKESH K. KAUL

Second Edition

First published in India in 2016 by
HarperCollins *Publishers* India

Copyright © Rakesh K. Kaul 2016

Second Edition published

globally in 2020 by

Spherenomics

The author asserts the moral right
to be identified as the author of this work.

This is a work of fiction. Names, characters, places and incidents are either the product of the author's imagination or are used fictitiously, and any resemblance to actual persons, living or dead, business establishments, events or locales is entirely coincidental.

All rights reserved. No part of this publication may be reproduced, stored in a retrieval system, or transmitted, in any form or by any means, electronic, mechanical, photocopying, recording or otherwise, without the prior permission of the author.

Rakesh K. Kaul

To
Pushpadanta, who fell from Heaven, for his transgression of invisibly eavesdropping on the divine Great Tale and then retelling it to his wife. Thus was manifested the first drop in the Ocean of the Stream of Stories.

Contents

Foreword ix
Principals xii
Prologue: Battal Balian Refugee Camp xiv

Ekamgrantha (Book I) The Student

Wave 1 The School and the Temple 1
Wave 2 The Fortress 15
Wave 3 The Throne 35
Wave 4 The Damaras 64

Dvegrantha (Book II) The Hostage

Wave 5 The Tourist 74
Wave 6 Close Encounters 106
Wave 7 The Peahen and the Serpent 118
Wave 8 Bonhomie 132

Tregrantha (Book III) The Gambit

Wave 9 The Marriage 154
Wave 10 Lion of Kashmir 163
Wave 11 The World Is One Family 178

Chaturgrantha (Book IV) The Householder

Wave 12 The Love Birds	207
Wave 13 Governance	235
Wave 14 Goddess	256
Wave 15 Epicentre	284
Wave 16 Ascent	305
Wave 17 Polo	318

Panchamgrantha (Book V) Born Again

Wave 18 Descent	337
Wave 19 Avian Flu	344
Wave 20 Parting	362
Wave 21 Forever	381

Epilogue	395
Endnotes	401
Bibliography	403
Glossary of Kashmiri, Sanskrit and Farsi terms	405
Acknowledgements	409
Critical Acclaim	xvii

Foreword

I STUMBLED on Kota by accident.

I was researching the Dhar clan of Kashmir to which my wife belongs. Among the Dhar luminaries is the great liberator of Kashmir, Pandit Birbal Dhar. An influential tax collector serving under the tyrannical regime of the Afghans, who had ruled Kashmir from 1750 to the early nineteenth century, he led a secret appeal to Maharaja Ranjit Singh to take over the Kashmir Valley. Travelling with his son, Birbal Dhar had left his wife and daughter-in-law in hiding with Qudus, his milkman. Judas emerged in the form of a family relative, Tilak Chand Munshi, who betrayed the whereabouts of the women to the governor, Azim Khan.

Troops were sent to bring the two women to the governor's palace. Birbal's wife was a noted beauty and she knew that Khan would dishonour her to avenge Birbal's secret mission. History records that she swallowed poison and that her last words were: 'Know that Kashmir has yet a Kota Rani. Remember me to my Lord!'

Who was this Kota Rani? Who was this inspiring symbol of feminine resistance that was central to the social history that Kashmiri Pandit women carried with them over the intervening centuries? The bare facts were easily accessible but did not justify the banner that Kota represented for Birbal's wife; clearly there was much more hidden behind the veil of time. Thus, began my twenty-first-century journey through the detritus of Kota's fourteenth-century world to try and put the pieces together.

What I found astonished me and would challenge every single preconception that anybody else or I might have about Kashmir. What I uncovered was a treasure that held the supreme secret for humanity. What shone bright was Kashmir's beacon to the known world, and Kota was its queen. What sobered me was that Kota was surrounded by literary geniuses. Ninety per cent of Indic poetry is in Sanskrit, and virtually all of Indic literature in Kota's time, were in the form of poetry and had been written by Kashmiris! The works of these poets were invaluable as I began the sometimes-painful task of reconstructing what had been sundered apart.

In my zeal to be true to Kota, I realized that my writing was synthetic and not true to the great masters of Kashmir. So, I adopted a literary style that would be authentic to the story. Kashmiri literary principles, including Kavya, the poetic expressions, among other things, emphasize that historical stories are first and foremost an art form. The Pandits were the pioneers of storytelling and practitioners of edutainment. A story needed to both educate and entertain, it had to be for all ages and be indestructible. The author had to approach the subject with a love where the very thought would create an emotion similar to that of the mother hearing the cry of her newborn baby. This tug should create an aesthetic experience that builds oneness between the observer and the observed. While the written word could wear ornaments and draw power from suggestion, the end product had to be perfected reality into which the reader gets immersed. There should be multiple levels of interpretation and at the highest levels it should lead to self-discovery and consciousness. There is an ocean there, and this might give you, the reader, an appreciation as to why between the research and the writing of this manuscript it took ten years to craft and complete.

This is the first literary property to be published in the English language that uses Kashmir's formidable literary principles. And just as one experiences exhilaration when driving a performance car and fully appreciates the engineering beneath the bonnet, similarly the global reader should enjoy the reading experience but be aware that the craftsmanship is totally Kashmiri. After the Mahabharata and the *Rajatarangini*, *The Last Queen of Kashmir* is the third and only book to be written in the Virasa rasa style, which is considered to be an impossible style to capture in words. Virasa rasa is very different from the catharsis of Greek tragedies, but instead reflects the bitter- sweet taste of Santa rasa, the peaceful rasa. It is the play of dharma in an imperfect world of moral decay; it is a distasteful inoculation, but one that hopefully leads to a healthier life. In this sense, this book represents a new voice from Kashmir.

Kota was once asked: What is the one thing that you need to know in order to know everything? When it comes to Kota and her Kashmir, this is it, this is it.

Principals

Sharada	Supreme female deity of Kashmir and name of town
Ramachandra	Commander-in-chief of Kashmir and father of Kota
Kota	Queen of Kashmir
Brahma	Kota's love
Ravan	Kota's brother
Suhdev	Deposed king of Kashmir and first suitor of Kota
Rinchina	Immigrant and first husband of Kota
Haider Chander	First son of Kota (fathered by Rinchina)
Udyandev	Younger brother of Suhdev and second husband of Kota
Jatta Bhola Rattan	Second son of Kota (fathered by Udyan)
Dulucha	Turcoman invader of Kashmir sent to capture Kota
Achala	Another invader of Kashmir and suitor of Kota
Shah Mir	Immigrant and final suitor of Kota

Guhara	Daughter of Shah Mir, married to Raja Sapru of Bhringi
Devaswami	Chief pontiff of Kashmir
Kokur	Theatre impresario
Fakir	Wandering Islamic puritan
Yaniv	Jeweler
Naid	Barber
Manzim	Marriage broker
Khazanchi	Financier
Jogi	Hindu fortune teller and practitioner of black arts
Saras	Kota's attendant

Prologue:
Battal Balian Refugee Camp

Udhampur Garrison, Kashmir

I WAS born in a refugee camp, after the Kashmiri exodus of 1990, an exile even before birth. Kashmir was just a latent genetic imprint within me, perhaps a legacy entirely lost when the Kali Andhi, the black storm of militants, had swept through the beautiful, peaceful Kashmir Valley. My world was one of the hutments, next to a polluted industrial centre. Through the small hole in the cardboard sidewall, one could see a greyish haze and dark sediment floating in the air. The heat was stifling at 105 degrees Fahrenheit but there was no electricity in the camp, no running water and the open sewage attracted flies from miles around. I could hear the voices of young girls, studying at the nearby Rishi Memorial School, repeating their teacher's instructions, parrot-like, in a sing-song voice. Repeat eleven times, the memorization secret is left to right, right to left and memorize, memorize, memorize ... just like I had.

My grandmother, my sole surviving relative, lay on a stringed cot clutching in her hands a small birch bark diary, her constant companion. It was the only thing she had picked up when she had grabbed my mother and they had fled from Kashmir that late night of 19 January 1990 in the back of an old truck. 'Hurry, hurry,' the driver, a Mussalman neighbour, had pleaded. 'I can no longer guarantee your safety if they have already blocked the mountain pass. Don't worry, by Allah, I will keep your house and belongings safe until you return.'

My grandmother's milky-white face had wrinkled since that night of horror when the light of my father was stripped away from us. My mother had died shortly after my birth lacking any medical facilities in the refugee camp. My grandmother's hair had turned grey and her voice was a weak whisper but in her proud eyes there was a bright blue fire. In her earlobes, hanging at the end of a chain, dangled the double-star earrings, the *dejhoor*, the most precious possession of any Kashmiri woman.

'Grandma,' I broke the news to her excitedly, 'here is the college admission letter, the full scholarship offer, an airline ticket and, best of all, look at the US embassy letter with the official Great Eagle stamp. I am to go for my visa qualification interview. I will fly in a plane for the first time, just like an eagle.'

She smiled back weakly, kissed the small birch diary and spoke wistfully: 'You are leaving me to go to college and I have very little to give you. Back in Kashmir you would have been in your ancestral home by the bank of the River Vitasta. I would have packed your suitcases with treasures befitting your status. But we lost it all ...'

I pleaded: 'Grandma, I don't need any gifts from the past. Let it go. I am talking about America where money is everywhere, where women can rise as high as the skyscrapers that touch the skies. I will save my scholarship money and return with wondrous gifts. I promise.'

Her eyes seemed to be lost in the past. 'They used to say that about Kashmir too; that when Heaven looked straight up towards Kashmir's royal buildings, its tiara fell upon the earth.'

I was determined to share what I saw through the door that had opened for me, even if my grandmother could not accompany me. 'There is so much I will learn. It is a dream come true.'

'You will learn from America, but will America learn anything from you?'

'Grandma, we are victims but America is not afraid of anybody. It is too powerful, too mighty.'

'If they don't know who their enemy is, if they can't even recognize what shape they come in, then how can America say that it is more powerful?' questioned my cynical grandmother.

'Let us worry about me and not America. I am so nervous about how well I will do in an American college. For the first time there will be boys competing with me. All I want for the future are your blessings.'

Grandmother's mood changed, and she shook her head confidently: 'You were the best student at Rishi Memorial School and you will be the top graduate at this American college. You can learn faster, remember longer and teach better than any of the boys around you. Never forget that any woman can rule the universe by unlocking her Shakti, her inner power. Come closer for Grandma's blessings.'

She sipped some water, ran her fingers affectionately through my long red hair and unconsciously rubbed the birthmark on my wrists. I relaxed under her touch as she blessed me with the Bala, the sacred girl-child's protective mantra:

> OM! I bow to the inner teacher
> Experienced as auspicious illumination!
> OM! It is She whom I honour
> Whose Protective 'Armour' is imbued
> With the omnipotent power of the Supreme Goddess,
> Manifested as the Empowering Radiance of the Young Woman
>   Goddess.[1]

'You have come of age,' she continued. 'If your future makes you leave, then go, but live by what Grandma's stories have taught you. The time has come to hand you the supreme secret of how to achieve the highest pinnacle in life. This treasure map is hidden inside a tale that has been handed down through our lineage, from mother to daughter. It happened in 1313 in Kashmir and it is the true story of Princess Kota, a young girl who was just like you ...'

Ekamgrantha (Book I)
The Student

Wave 1
The School and the Temple

CLOISTERED in her small room in Kashmir's most renowned school, Princess Kota woke up at dawn, and by the light of the oil lamp feverishly completed her last-minute preparations for her upcoming graduation exam. She took a quick look at herself in her hand mirror. Her innocent, milky-white face, rosy cheeks and simple jet-black ponytail betrayed how young she was. Her deep blue eyes were almost black, reflecting her anxiety. The dimples in her cheeks had disappeared because of the tension in her jaw. She clutched the pendant around her neck with both her hands, kissed the woman's portrait on it and nervously pleaded: 'Mother, pray for me!' If she passed, she would begin the arduous ascent to a royal position in the court of Kashmir. If she failed, how would she face her father? Mathematics was her weakest subject and she hastily

2 THE LAST QUEEN OF KASHMIR

skimmed the text beside her bed for the last time. It was written on birch bark, the broad horizontal belts where accurate diagrams had been sketched with great precision. It was all there – Lagadha's painstaking technique on how to calculate an unknown quantity from a known one, Patanjali's measurement of a moment of time, the astronomical importance of the number 108.

She took one last look around the room. It had been her home at the university, as it had been for other female students before her. Across from her, on the stucco wall, was a row of names. The first one, partly erased, read: 'Buddh ... Princess of Sharada'. Next to it was a handprint and the number '1'. The legendary first female graduate from the university had gone on to marry Toramana, the Hun King of Talagana, a town in the Punjab, south of the Hindu Kush mountains. In around the year 495 ad she had consecrated a major Buddhist monastery. Every other female graduate had inscribed her name underneath, but Sharada was at the very top. Kota wondered how many girls had failed to graduate. Their distant memory was stored within these walls.

It was time to leave. Kota placed the palm of her hand over the handprint of 'Buddh ...' and closed her eyes for a moment, drawing strength. Inhaling deeply, she left her room for the short walk to the examination hall. She had worn the simple saffron-coloured cloak that was traditional among the nuns in the monastery with tight cream pajamas underneath and a saffron shawl to cover her shoulders. As she walked, her attendant Saras, who smiled at her encouragingly, joined her. Dressed in white and with striking Chinese features, Saras was Kota's shadow, always discreetly and vigilantly watching her ward. Around the corner came her personal tutor, Guru Gotam Bhatta. Kota offered him salutations and touched his feet as he gave her his benediction: 'Glory to the goddess who is the manifestation of wisdom and who imbues her devotees with enlightened intelligence and understanding.'

'Guru, I am nervous,' Kota blurted. 'My mind has gone blank. I am going to fail today.'

Guru Gotam smiled softly: 'All my students say that before their graduation exam and yet I have not had one fail on me. Koka

Pandit will ask you to do the sun salutation, Surya Namaskar. Do it slowly and with complete control of your breath. Your concentration will return in full force. The toughest question will come from your extreme right where Nagendra Pandit, a haughty and conservative expert, will seat himself. Do not turn to look at him when he questions you; that way his fierce demeanour won't intimidate you. Keep your eyes firmly fixed on the tip of your nose. Let them observe your mind at work, but do not reveal your emotions. Remember that everything is subjective, even if it seems to be objective. The protocol is that Devaswami, the head of Sharadapeeth University and chief tantri of the associated temple, will instruct you in the rules of the examination. He will ask the first and the last question. His first inquiry is always on a core theoretical principle, the last will be on practice. You will pass most assuredly. Kalyan, my blessings are for you.'

Kota felt better after hearing her guru's encouraging words of confidence. She was admitted into the hall and saluted all of the assembled pandits. As the heads of their scholarly disciplines, the pandits were extremely tough examiners. It was not uncommon for them to spend five years preparing for one evening of debate on a scientific subject. The school, which was an adjunct to the temple, was mostly a man's world. Female students were very rare at Sharadapeeth. As Kota was well aware, her female gender and lineage as daughter of Ramachandra, Kampanesa, commander-in-chief of the armed forces, did not grant her any special privilege with these scholars. They were proud teachers attached to the foremost school in South and Central Asia, and maintaining the 500-year-old standard of their graduates was their key to excellence.

Kota saw Devaswami enter the room and all the pandits and Kota rose to greet their leader. Clean-shaven, with a powerful face and a hooked nose, topped by a bald dome and dressed in white linen and a white shawl, Devaswami radiated charismatic energy. His sacred thread was prominently strung around his right shoulder. He had a large vermillion tilak mark on his forehead and on the tips of his ears.

Kota was ordered to sit, and the pandits settled themselves in a half circle around her, with Devaswami facing her in the centre. Placed in front of the confident pandits, with their shaved heads and only a topknot left to grow, Kota felt like a doe surrounded by sharp shooters, the tightness of her lips betraying the tension inside her. Her eyes fell on her father, Commander Ramachandra, sitting inconspicuously in the corner of the room. Her heart leapt that he had come to be with her. She turned her head away quickly and brought her gaze firmly back to Devaswami, who began by addressing Gotam Bhatta, 'Guru, Namaskaram, what courses has Kota completed?'

'Swami, she has studied the core courses and in addition botany, painting, needlework, woodwork, clay modelling, cookery, musical treatises, singing, dancing, art expositions, the Trika scientific shastras and the feminine arts,' the guru replied.

Kota saw Devaswami turn to face her. 'Namaskaram, Princess Kota, let me introduce you to the examination panel. We have Jyotish Pandit, the foremost astrologer; Kumara Pandit, our chief historian and statecraft strategist; Koka Pandit who is dedicated to life sciences; Nagendra Pandit, the authority on our laws and social sciences, and I, who will mostly listen. The exam today will be unlike what you will have experienced in your studies. Traditional tests evaluate the truth of your answers, whether your knowledge reflects an objective understanding of *sat*, the referent reality. We will certainly ask you such questions; however, what we are concerned about today is the truth about you. We will evaluate you just as we would a diamond, measuring your imperfections against your full potential. The difference between the two is the measure of what we will judge to be your performance. Our subjective estimate will determine whether you graduate or not. Are you ready, or do you feel a bit afraid?'

Kota was about to make an honest admission when her Intuition leapt to her aid. It was not a question about her well-being, but instead about a principle. She responded firmly: 'My dharma brings me here and my dharma protects me. There is nothing to fear.'

Devaswami gave a soft smile and then waved his hand towards the pandits on Kota's left. Koka took his turn by asking Kota to recite the invocation mantra, and then he commanded her to demonstrate Surya namaskara. Sun salutations had to be done before sunrise and on an empty stomach. One had to sit firmly planted on the ground as if on a throne. Kota sprinkled some water from the bowl in front of her all over her body, starting from her feet and moving up to her head. Then she did pranayama breathing exercises three times, visualizing the divine firmly on a lion throne inside the lotus of her heart. Finally, she raised her hands in front of her. Even the jaded pandits were impressed as her contoured body rose from her perfectly still, narrow waist. Koka let out an exclamation of aesthetic appreciation when the nimble Kota slowly raised her hands together high into the sky, stretching like a supple reed. Then in long syllables she chanted.

> May our awareness be drawn to the Supreme Soul
> [in the form of the Sun]!
> May we meditate on the wisdom granted by the Sun!
> May the Sun guide our lives!

Koka's questions flew at her like sharp, pointed arrows. 'What is faster than your mind?'
'My desire.'
'Who will be stronger, you or the man in your life?'
'Both are halves of a whole. Man without woman is still. Woman without man is an aimless meteor.'
'What is joyful about love?'
'It is the bliss arising from two souls connecting with the divine and uniting.'
'Between desire for love and dharma, what prevails?'
'Desire – which is rooted in lust, the immediate infatuation of the ten senses or ego or emotions or the gratification of the limited mind – will be incinerated like Kamadeva, the divinity of passion. Desire,

which is a genuine offering of one's true nature to dharma, will prevail eternally because will is then united with purpose.'

'What is so satisfying about sex?'

Kota blushed, but she knew the pandits were as clinical about sex as they were about all matters relating to the human condition. She answered in her most adult matter-of-fact voice, quoting from Abhinavagupta: 'Procreation is the highest manifestation of the creative force. Sex centers one's self into one's true nature.'

Jyotish Pandit stepped in with his gravelly voice: 'True nature could be one's nature at birth. Did you as a child ever think you were someone different?'

Kota was flustered. Her voice sank into a whisper: 'I am told that when I was very young I refused to respond to my name.'

The jyotish was persistent in his examination. 'Who did you think you were?'

'I thought that my name was Didda, but, of course, I had no idea what that meant at that time,' said an uncomfortable Kota.

'Queen Didda, hmm ... As you now know, she was indisputably one of Kashmir's ablest administrators, but Kumara will tell you that she was considered to practise witchcraft to get rid of her enemies. Her paramour was a shepherd, but even he could not fulfil her appetite. If you are her reincarnation what will your karma be? Should you not renounce worldly life and do penance for past misdeeds by staying on in Sharadapeeth as a nun?'

'I believe in reincarnation and I believe in karma. But irrespective of my starting handicap, I also believe that life is a precious gift where everyone has an equal chance to achieve complete fulfilment and experience divinity.'

'An outcome that is granted to very few,' observed the jyotish pandit dryly. 'Life is full of surprises. What does one do if life leaves you with nothing; not even hope, no chance of achieving any fulfilment or of experiencing divinity?'

'If life leaves you with nothing, then you have nothing left to lose and everything to gain. So be the boldest that you can be and do your highest dharma,' replied a defiant Kota.

Kumara sensed Kota's stress and stepped in. In a kind voice he asked: 'When governing his state what is the relationship of the maharaja to his subjects?'

'The maharaja is the mother and the father of his subjects. The maharaja must never tax his subjects more than one-sixteenth to one-fourth of their produce, depending on the land they till.'

'What is the maharaja's duty towards Brahmins?'

'Never take a Brahmin's life and always provide for a Brahmin's welfare.'

'The Brahmins live on bare sustenance. How much wealth should a man have?'

'As much as he needs to perform his dharma. The rest he should be prepared to give away. If not, then the possessions possess the man and not the other way around.'

'Are all citizens equal in the eyes of the law and should justice be dealt impartially?'

'No,' replied Kota. 'Justice should be progressive; the higher the person's stature, the greater the punishment for the same crime.'

'How was the universe created?'

'The universe emerged out of the creator's navel.'

Kota spotted the pandit dart a questioning look at Devaswami. Quickly she added, 'The myth underscores the deeper truth that universal consciousness contracted and manifested into material reality.'

Devaswami signalled his call that the answer was acceptable. Kota mentally thanked the Devi for the near miss. She knew the pandits would not tolerate a memory lapse. She could have failed right there. She had learnt her material well, but she had not expected the questions would be so challenging. The examination had picked up pace and Kota knew she was being tested to see how she would perform under duress. The momentary break had helped her regroup. For hours the questions challenged and tested her. Kota excelled in Ayurvedic medicine and agriculture. Saras was from the Hunza Valley and her informal storytelling of Hunza folklore, in addition to Kota's formal education by Guru Gotam, had really helped. But when it came to mathematics she told herself to slow down and performed the required mental calculations methodically, afraid that she might make a mistake.

Kashmir's society was premised on the principle that the Sword of Truth would always triumph. But truth needed discernment. From the time of the *Panchatantra*, the book of short stories written by Pandit Vishnu Sharma for training royalty, there was a strong emphasis on good judgement. Kashmir had had a spate of immoral and inept kings. This had forced training at Sharadapeeth to emphasize morals, ethics and values. It was the turn of the acerbic Nagendra Pandit to fire his questions.

'You started by saying that dharma had brought you here. What does the word dharma mean?'

'That which sustains eternally what is measureable.'

'You are parroting the respected Guru Gotam's words. In your own words what does dharma mean to you?'

'To do what sustains me forever based on what I desire, what I know about and what is within my grasp.'

'Harrumph!' snorted Nagendra. 'A novel interpretation of dharma indeed but not unexpected from a woman. When Pandit Vishnu Sharma wrote *Vasudhaiva Kutambakam,* the world is one family, was he referring to a way of life or giving a warning to the gullible?'

Kota was prepared for this question. 'The ideal should not blind one to the real, and the real should not blind one to the ideal.'

'When creating women, Manu, the progenitor of mankind and the giver of our ancient laws, allotted to them a love of their bed, of their seat and of their ornament; impure desires, wrath, dishonesty, malice, and bad conduct. Do you agree or disagree with Manu?'

Kota spotted the misogynist trap. ' Manu also said that a perfect man consists of three persons united: his wife, himself and his offspring. How could man be perfect if woman is so imperfect?' she asked sweetly. A pupil answering a question with a question revealed a rebellious streak; it was a dangerous gambit by Kota. The pandit compressed his lips, debating what to do with her answer. Kota's supporters could claim that the gender question had been asked previously, and answered correctly, so she was justified in showing her irritation. This was not the question to rule on, he thought, but this girl's insolence had to be nipped in the bud. Having made up his mind he moved on to his next question.

'Can a motherless daughter connect with the world and have a normal relationship with society?'

Kota was angry and close to tears at the cruelty in his line of questioning. 'Just because I have lost my mother does not mean that I have lost my attachment to her, or that she won't be there to help guide me.'

Nagendra, having struck hard at Kota's vulnerability, moved in for the kill. 'Should a maharaja spy on his own people?'

Kota said she didn't believe so. The pandit then followed it up: 'Should the maharaja authorize the use of poison against an adversary?'

Kota responded back emphatically, 'No.'

The pandit grimaced and, facing Devaswami, made his call. It was a 'Fail'!

There was absolute silence in the examination room as the pandits awaited Devaswami's final decision. Kota despaired. She was going to fail! At Sharadapeeth you only got one chance: if you did not graduate the first time you were done forever.

Kota saw Devaswami staring intently at her as he deliberated. Surely, he could feel the heat in her flushed face and hear the loud thumping of her nervous heart. Finally, he spoke: 'Overruled. The questioner did not state that the maharaja had exhausted all dharmic options of warfare. The student said 'no' but not 'never'. The answer was correct to the question as asked and consistent with the rulings that Sharadapeeth had provided to royalty in the past.'

A much-relieved Kota breathed more freely and mentally thanked the Devi. The pandit stiffly bowed his head at the ruling. He had made the wrong call and would now be disqualified. Sharadapeeth was a meritocracy and the rules were tough on everyone alike.

It now came down to the final test, the experiential exam. Kota knew she would have to get a perfect score to pass. Only Devaswami had the right to ask this last question. He stood up and everyone followed him outside.

Dawn at Sharadapeeth was energizing and exhilarating. Sharada, the goddess named after autumn, whose irradiance was likened to the autumnal moon, was the titular deity, but the pristine beauty of Sharadapeeth was surely proof that Kashmir was a favourite sanctuary for Ushas, the virginal Devis of dawn, as the Sun chased them across the sky. Kota took in a deep breath of the pure, cool air. Today, bright golden rays suffused the landscape. In front and around her, a proud ring of snow-topped mountains framed the school and the adjoining temple, while two snow-fed rivers flowed on either side of it before meeting in the distance. A dense, green pine forest covered the entire land up to the mountains. Kota saw Devaswami stand by the branch of a tree glistening in the morning sun, its leaves moist with dew and bedecked with pearly icicles from the cold night before. He pointed in the general direction of the tree and asked her, 'What do you see?'

Kota understood that this final test was of *Vipashyana*, the ability to see reality as it really is. She sat down on the ground and closed her eyes. Gradually she slowed her heart rate and her breathing flowed at one-third of its normal rate. She focused by silently repeating a mantra.

> I praise She (Usha) who embodies the incandescent auburn light of Dawn
> Glory to She who will last until the end of Time
> To She whose face emanates radiant splendour of a million sunrays
> To She who consists of the pure consciousness pervading the Sky
> As the auburn hue of the rising Sun

Kota's guru had taught her that taking a very short mantra break would settle a restless mind, especially when it was racing, and she had come to agree with him. Now her mind had the clarity of a mirror. She partially opened her eyes and stared at a transparent drop of dew hanging on a branch. The drop twinkled, reflecting the sunlight back to her. She continued staring. Slowly the frozen drop seemed to change, and then suddenly with a flash she saw it all. She saw in the drop the pandits standing behind her, watching her carefully; she saw the temple, the river flowing behind her; she saw the castle, and behind the castle the mountains, and then the blue sky. In the dewdrop was the panoramic view of the entire Kishanganga Valley. She felt overcome with exhaustion. 'I see the macrocosm whole in the microcosm self; I see the microcosm in the macrocosm,' she said in a low voice. 'We are all part of one reality.'

Devaswami smiled at her and proclaimed to all that she had passed.

Kota's heart screamed with relief and joy. 'Thank you mother for answering my prayer,' she whispered silently to herself.

Devaswami was the first to approach her. 'Your father brought you to us eight years ago as a mere child. Today, you are the most fearless princess in the world. Congratulations – you are a Kashmiri *Bhattarika*, a graduate! Here is your *Patra*, your graduation certificate.'

Kota gave Devaswami a big smile, her perfect white teeth, framed by her bow-shaped pink lips, shone in the sunlight. She thanked him and ran over to Guru Gotam to prostrate herself at his feet. She waved over Saras, who brought her a beautiful piece of framed birch bark. Kota placed it humbly in front of her guru. He raised his right hand, palm outwards and slightly curved, then picked up her respectful offering. The bark had been dried and the layers joined together with gum. It had been lovingly oiled and polished until it shone and then placed within wooden covers to make it flat. In beautiful calligraphy Kota had written in brilliant, black ink: *May your blessings always be with me*.

Gotam waved to Kota to move closer to him. She bent her head down as he blessed her, placing his palm gently on the top of her head. 'Kota, from today onwards the universe is your guru. Kalyan.' Then he reached over and gave her a small gift. It was an exquisite Kashmiri carved figure in jade green showing the Devi holding a manuscript in one hand. She clutched it next to her heart, delighted.

The long day had ended well for Kota and it was time for her to be reunited with her father. Try as she would to walk demurely, her feet had a mind of their own as she flew towards him.

'Papa, I am so happy to see you,' she said as she hugged her father tight. Her heart was aching with joy after the long years at the school where no visitors were allowed.

Ramachandra kissed his daughter formally on her forehead. 'Look at you, how much you have grown. You are almost as tall as me. You have your mother's looks, her oval face and dark eyebrows. How proud she would have been if she had lived to see this day.'

'Papa, mother was there with me,' Kota confided. 'During many of the questions I felt that it was she who was answering.'

'Truth be told, I could not have answered half of them,' her father admitted. 'Mission accomplished, I feel on top of the world and so would have your mother.'

Devaswami interrupted them. 'Kampanesa, Kota's mission has just begun. The pandits have done their job, but now she enters the real world. *Sat* is what she has to master, with the aid of the principles she has been taught at Sharadapeeth.'

Ramachandra laughed heartily, 'Swami, I stand corrected, as always. Our first stop will be the *dranga*; a fortress on the front line of Kashmir has a lot to teach about reality.'

The astrologer approached them with a somber expression. 'Commander, I need to privately counsel you on Kota's career and personal future. There are certain aspects that are important for you to know.'

'Sir why am I not included?' questioned Kota confidently, feeling empowered as a new graduate. 'After all, it is my life you are counselling my father about; should I not hear what you have to say?'

Jyotish Pandit was diplomatic and, in his gravelly voice, said, 'Kota, today you are ready for the world, but you are not yet ready for the stars. That day will arrive, and you and I will talk then, but today's discussion is between your father and me.'

'Papa, don't be long,' Kota conceded. 'I will go and share the good news with brother Ravan. Saras, I want to see the expressions of the haughty boys who said I would fail. It is time to make those bullies eat their words. Look out stars, here I come!' With a bounce of her ponytail Kota left to go hunting for her male school friends with Saras close behind her, a victorious glint in her eyes.

Jyotish Pandit turned towards Ramachandra and, with Devaswami watching, spoke gently. 'Kampanesa, I have studied your daughter's astrological chart. There is much to extol in it but there is also a feature that bears watching.'

'What is it, Jyotish? I am not much for stars and as for Kota the youngsters today could not care less.'

Jyotish Pandit's eyes looked intently at Ramachandra. 'She is *Angaraka*.'

Ramachandra staggered as if hit by a blow. Angaraka was the most dreaded of stars that a woman could be born under: the star of Mars that was said to portend the quick death of the first man unfortunate enough to marry her. Angaraka, personified as the fierce form of the goddess without a consort who would take on the power to devour men, was portrayed as the red queen sitting on an angry red lotus associated with the planet Mars.

'It can't be. Not on a day like today. Say it is not true. You are not infallible. Why her?' asked an anguished Ramachandra.

'Kampanesa, I have gone through her astrological chart a hundred times,' Jyotish Pandit replied, 'but in her case Mars in the eighth house is not ambiguous and thus is not to be denied its due.'

Ramachandra turned to Devaswami and asked pitifully: 'Why am I cursed with bad karma? First, I lose Kota's mother when her brother Ravan was born, and then Kota is Angaraka. Devaswami, please do something. You have the power to bless. Spare my innocent daughter of this fate. Which man will want to marry Kota and write his own death sentence?'

Devaswami had been watching Ramachandra with concern and sensed the anguish of a giant among men brought to his knees. He reached out and put his arm on Ramachandra's shoulder. 'Kampanesa, Kota is now my ward. I promise you that I will personally pray for her. I will also teach her a combination of yoga mantras so that she will mitigate the impact of Mars, though it will not be eliminated. But keep this from her until she is old enough to deal with it.'

Ramachandra was not entirely satisfied and quizzed the Pandit insistently: 'Tell me, will she marry? Will she be happy? Will she find love? What is good in her stars?'

'You saw us test her on all her possible imperfections,' the Pandit explained, attempting to balance the misfortune with a nuanced response. 'She is Angaraka, but she also has powerful stars in her heart centre and they will guide her to her true love. She will be ever captivating, but never captive. She graduated because, in our judgement, in spite of her imperfections she has the offsetting Shakti force to power her to unbounded potential. She will be the greatest queen of Kashmir, perhaps the greatest queen of India, and maybe even of the world.'

The three men talked softly, drawing closer together in a protective circle, the first circle that would form around Kota to save her from impending peril as she left Sharadapeeth and entered the court of Kashmir. Devaswami had a few final words of encouragement for Ramachandra. 'It is an imperfect world but even Mars is subject to dharma. May I remind you Kampanesa that it was Kota's heart that answered my first question when she said that she follows dharma, and in return dharma will protect her. There is nothing to fear. If she is Angaraka it is not a punishment, but the goddess's protection.'

Wave 2
The Fortress

THE dranga that Kota and Ramachandra travelled to from Sharadapeeth guarded Shur Ji La (now Zoji La) pass, the gateway connecting Central Asia, Ladakh. It was a notorious trail, its name meaning 'Mountain Pass of Blizzards'. At a height of 11,500 feet it was surrounded by towering, snow-clad mountains that shut down the path for more than eight months of the year. Serpentine rivers flow at the foot of the mountains, paying homage to the deities that reside on the peaks. The gorges are so deep that one would shut one's eyes tight while traversing the narrow trail, praying that the camels would not slip. In this extreme desert during winter there would be bitter cold, freezing winds and perhaps over 60 feet of snow followed by summers of scorching heat. Only bold daredevils would traverse this pathway. Given that the traveller sometimes would have to clear snowfalls that could exceed 35 feet, the trail was also a graveyard for those who had gambled their lives and lost.

Minding the outpost was a demanding job and Ramachandra drove Kota hard, making her do the work of two men. Her father had asked a Chinese soldier to train her in techniques developed by Yue Nu, a legendary female sword fighter. In addition, Kota was to keep track of the traders who came and went and would report back to the maharaja and the treasury. The months at the dranga passed quickly. Ramachandra and Kota worked with the *dvarapati,* the local commander, ensuring he was well equipped and his military forces trained to respond to every challenge. Kota's presence only made

Ramachandra redouble his effort. Conversely, his dawn-to-dusk demands from Kota were no different than from any other young front-line recruit.

One day an exhausted Kota asked her father, 'What is the reason for all of this activity?'

'We need to lay enough provisions aside in case any adventurers take advantage of the improving weather to lay siege,' Ramachandra replied. 'We have to work quickly. There are ten other passes that need my personal supervision: these, and the drangas, are the front-line defence for the kingdom.'

'Whom do we fear?' Kota probed.

'The Turcomans,' Ramachandra explained. 'My assistant, the Sogdian, tells me that there is a Turcoman military commander, Dulucha, plotting an attack. The traders are being questioned about the military strength of Kashmir. We have to be constantly alert, always vigilant: one slip and the kingdom could be lost.'

Kota sensed her father was preparing her for the unceasing state of readiness that this kind of military intelligence necessitated. She had absolute faith in his judgement. Existence in the military world of security had an urgency that was very different from the long cycles of reality the pandits sought to penetrate and decipher. The university was about learning what was known, the dranga about preparing for unknown threats. She was learning by observing and following.

'You are sharing this with me for a reason. Why and what should I be doing?' she asked her father.

'Soldiers teach their sons to become soldiers not realizing that it is their daughters that are more vulnerable,' her father said grimly. 'I want to make sure that as a parent I teach you everything that I know. I am a pretty good general and know a thing or two.'

'Yes, you are the best,' said Kota with pride. 'And I will learn.'

One morning Ramachandra asked Kota to accompany him for a spot inspection. The caravan to Xian was leaving, taking advantage of the early spring thaw to export goods from Kashmir. Their route was to follow the ancient southernmost branch of the Silk Road, through the Karakoram pass and on to Khotan, the city founded by Emperor Ashoka's son. The legendary Italian traveller Marco Polo had visited there forty years earlier. They would stop at the Miran oasis and the fabled Mogao caves, where there were nearly 500 Buddhist temples. Later, Jayuguan fort represented the westernmost tip of the Great Wall and the entrance into China, as the route proceeded towards Xian. The journey covered over 2,000 miles and was fraught with danger and uncertainty at every step.

As they approached the central courtyard of the dranga, Ram and Kota encountered a mass of confusion. Customs duties needed to be finalized – and in Kashmir there were duties to be paid both on imported and exported goods and the traders needed to replenish their supplies for the journey. Invariably local merchants would mysteriously run out of necessities or prices would jump at the last minute. Adding to the tension was the mix of ethnicity, race and language. The air was thick with profanities, camels moaned under their loads and clouds of dust swirled above them. Ramachandra asked the Sogdian, who was multilingual, to order one of the traders to have his camel unpacked.

'I have paid my duty,' the trader protested. 'I am an honest man. Why am I being harassed?'

Ramachandra was gruff in his response. 'I have your paperwork and it only declares half the amount of the others, yet your camel is loaded heavier than everybody else's. Let us see if you are carrying snow out of the Valley.'

The Persian trader's stock was a valuable one. He was carrying *Rankavapata*, the treasured white shahtoosh shawl, large crystal jars and fragrances, and pomades made of saffron, camphor and sandalwood. There was *Costus*, myrrh, and incense for Buddhist ceremonies, spices from the subcontinent, coral prized by the Kashmiris, saffron, and cannabis. Woodwork, artwork, dried lotus roots, dried sardine-like *hok gard* and fish oil. Finally, there were Buddhist scriptures, copies of the *Kama Sutra* and the illustrated *Kok Sastra* and the *Garudatantra* manual, which was used to cure snake bites and other poisons. It was quite a haul, and Ramachandra made Kota reconcile the paperwork with the stock so she could estimate the correct customs duty. As she was going through the inventory a small piece of paper fell out of one of the books. With her back turned to the trader, she opened it and saw a map of the fortress. Everything had been sketched out: the manning of posts, the storage of arms, the food granary and the water tank. There were notes on the timing of the watch changeovers. The trader was a spy!

Shielding the paper in her hand, Kota headed over to her father and showed him the map. Ramachandra instantly understood its implications. He signalled to the Sogdian and moments later the Sogdian had the trader pinned to the ground and Ramachandra had his sword at the trader's throat.

'I have half a mind to hang you,' Ramachandra threatened.

The smuggler whimpered that it was a mistake, but knew that he would not garner any sympathy. The traders respected Ramachandra: he had built a reputation for managing the Kashmir frontier fairly and honestly and was not afraid of dispensing generous doses of tough love. In return he provided security and there was no attempt on the part of his accountants to demand baksheesh payments. The captain of the guard rushed over, arrested the spy and took him away for interrogation.

'What made you suspicious?' Kota asked her father.

Ramachandra let out a hard laugh. 'He was the only Persian in the Chinese caravan. Where was he headed to in China? Clearly he was looking to get out quickly armed with this information. Unfortunately for him he got caught being greedy: his mistake was to try to make extra money from trading. China looks up to our culture for inspiration; Persia looks at us with intention. One has to be ever vigilant of the ambitions of one's neighbours.'

As father and daughter walked back, Ramachandra pointedly questioned Kota, 'What have you learnt so far?'

'My heart wants to trust people but on the front line one's safety may lie in never letting down one's defences,' she replied.

Ramachandra instructed her tersely: 'When we gave you your name, Kota, its meaning – fortress – was to remind you that as a woman you should never ever let your guard down. Open your mind to this beautiful world but always be alert to the dangers that hide in it. Watch, watch and watch.'

Kota absorbed her father's dictum and nodded in agreement.

Turning to the Sogdian, Ramachandra ordered: 'Tell the watchman to take the night off, and have the captain replace him for tonight's duty. Kota take him a bottle of wine from my personal collection and reiterate to him how valuable he is to the kingdom's security. Don't forget his guard dog either.'

The scales were quickly falling from Kota's eyes and she understood why her father had brought her straight from the school to the dranga. She went to visit the watchman, who was astonished to have Kota present him with a bottle of wine. He was even more surprised when she pulled out a big meaty bone for his dog. She played with the animal, rubbing its back as it chewed contentedly on the bone.

'What is his name?'

'Dharma,' replied the watchman laconically.

Kota burst into spontaneous laughter. 'That is funny. When I was at school I learnt about dharma from learned pandits. I thought it was all about doing what sustains you eternally, but I never thought I would meet a dog named Dharma.'

'The dog's dharma is *raksha*. He never fails me on security. Don't forget that in the Mahabharata it is the dog that enters heaven, and not any of the other warriors.'

'Watchman, does he not also keep you company on this lonely job?'

'He is my *bhakta*,' the watchman said. 'My devotee in my tasks.'

Kota picked up on the watchman's one-pointed simplicity: 'You and Dharma make an unbeatable combination. You and my father have both taught me that the first step to reaching eternity is to start with security. I promise you I will return again.' She talked to him for a while and, when it turned dark, left for her hut.

That night while Saras assisted Kota as she prepared for bed, she asked her maid: 'Now that I am getting to spend time with my father I find that he is a tough, uncompromising task master, yet his troops love him.'

'When you strike the bone gently, repeatedly, it hardens,' Saras explained. 'He is toughening his soldiers and they know that. He is also preparing you the best he can for the battles that lay ahead of you.'

'But why is he afraid of his feelings?' Kota asked. 'Sometimes I wish that he would relax and talk to me, even hug me, but he keeps an official distance from me as if not wanting to be seen treating me as special or different. Is he close to anyone? Was he close to my mother?'

'The price that you pay for having to make a life or death decision is that you make them alone,' replied Saras. 'Yes, he would always respect your mother's counsel. After your mother died he had nobody to share his feelings with and became totally absorbed in his work.'

'But what about you, Saras?' Kota inquired. 'You have raised me, but who do you share your feelings with? You don't talk about where you were born and grew up.'

Saras smiled. 'I do not know where I was born, but I grew up as a young girl in Hunza. Then I came to Srinagar and when your father was looking for someone to help your mother, he picked me.'

Kota sensed that Saras was holding back. 'Do you have family in Hunza? How is it that you have never gone back to visit them?'

Saras shifted uncomfortably. 'I have lost touch with them. I did go back once, but nobody seemed to know what had become of them. With the passage of time you became my family.'

Kota persisted. 'You are an attractive woman, why did you never marry? Father would not have stood in your way.'

Saras was quiet. 'I have you, I do not need more company,' she said finally.

Saras was a mystery to Kota; she was a woman who had held her at childbirth and raised her like her mother, but about whom she knew nothing. She was determined to get to the bottom of this and examined Saras as if meeting her for the first time. Saras looked back at her with her gentle smile and brown eyes, her hair covered by a round colourfully quilted cap with beaded cowrie shells. 'Saras, you are like a mother to me. I am growing up and need to feel that I know the people whom I am closest to. Don't you trust me, when I trust you with my life?'

Saras spoke slowly. 'Kota, I will share my past with you if that is what you wish. I did grow up in Hunza. The people there believe that they are descendants of Alexander the Great. They would raid the caravans that would travel from Sinkiang to Kashmir, and on one such raid my father captured my Chinese mother. Hunza is a very harsh land and my mother died young. I raised my younger brother while my father went to herd the sheep. One day my father returned home late at night, drunk on *Chung*. He came into my bed and said that I reminded him of my mother and that I should comfort him, in return for his taking care of me. He started stripping my clothes off. He pushed me down and raped me, his daughter, just a child not yet turned twelve. I could not believe this beast was my father. I escaped from the house, not knowing whom to turn to. Many days later, starving and half dead in the hills, I was found by a Kashmiri military contingent who took me to your father. He brought me from the dranga back to your home to be with your mother, who was expecting you at that time. I have been with you ever since.'

Kota was overcome by Saras's story. 'But why did you not marry, Saras, and start a new life?'

Saras sighed as though her heart was bursting. 'Kota, when I think of a relationship with men I experience uncontrollable bouts of anger. It was much worse when I was younger. Devaswami guided me away from my anger and made me develop an interest in plants. Plants do not hurt anybody which is why I cultivate herbs that heal.'

Saras's pain pierced Kota's heart. She finally understood why Saras spent days wandering in the forests, searching for herbs, but mostly wanting to be at peace. With tears in her eyes, she leaned over silently and took Saras in her arms, hugging her tightly.

'Saras, if you had trusted a man who loved you it would have healed this hurt and anger.'

'Men are weak; they need a woman's strength. I did not find anyone that I could trust. There was no one I cared for enough to share my strength with. I needed it for my own self-preservation. But I found my love, and that was in raising you. Maybe men sensed the injury in me and kept their distance, but for me love never happened.'

The two talked late into the night. For the first time it was Saras who spoke and Kota who was the sympathetic counsellor.

Hunched over a parapet, the watchman and the guard dog peered into the far distance at the mouth of Shur Ji La. The watchman could see a small dark shape as it bobbed up and down moving forward, like a dark sperm. The shape slowly separated into two smaller dots, both scurrying towards the fort. Then the dots became two groups of men. The first consisted of about a dozen stocky men, running as fast as they safely could over the treacherous rock-strewn trail. The men were breathing heavily in the cold air; their breath making rasping sounds and forming wisps of vapour. Chasing them was a larger group of armed men in swift pursuit, their leader on horseback shouting, 'Faster, don't let the traitors escape into Kashmir and the rewards disappear out of our hands.'

The guard dog's pointed ears stiffened in the wind. He snarled in warning, baring his teeth. It was enough for the grizzled watchman: spring was when the Kashmir Valley was most vulnerable to military threats from outsiders. The watchman was sceptical of the intentions of any newcomer – as far as he was concerned they were all bad, these people who traversed Shur Ji La. He picked up the conch shell and blew hard into it. The clarion call reverberated with intensity across the small outpost. The mountains picked up the echoes, dutifully playing their mythical role as the guardians of the valley below. The watchman dropped the conch and picked up the Rama Bow. Pointing it back towards the undulating valley, he shot a burning arrow straight into the sky. The guard dog began barking furiously. Breathing heavily, the watchman ran to a large drum and began beating an insistent cadence with increasing frequency that rolled over the ground and filled the air with its ominous warning. By now the temple bells across the mountains and the valley had picked up the alert and were clanging out their urgent peals. Kashmir's front line was facing an attack from an unknown foreign enemy!

Kota woke to the sound of the barking dog. Slightly disoriented she threw off her heavy blanket and got dressed quickly in the dark. It was bitterly cold and Kota put on several layers of woolens. She slid into the red trousers of the Kashmiri soldiers, quickly put on her boots and then slid into a knee-length padded waistcoat. A round cap covered her head. Grabbing her short sword, Kota hurried outside.

Her father dashed out of the next room. His attendant, the Sogdian immigrant from Central Asia, followed him. Ramachandra was already dressed in battle gear with his chain mail and chest armour. He had protective sheaths on both arms. He acknowledged Kota behind him, and carefully climbed up the wet stone steps to the rampart. He nodded his head at the archers, who had already assumed battle position. 'Stay close to me and be alert,' he ordered Kota.

The sun's pale rays provided sufficient visibility of the ground between the pass and the outpost. Kota spotted the dozen men running towards the outpost. One of them limped heavily as two of his compatriots supported him on either side. From their dress and general mien, she knew they were Bottas, natives of the neighbouring kingdom of Ladakh. They only had a ten-minute lead on the much larger group that was chasing after them.

The three lead men stopped in front of the large, heavily fortified metal gate. The two able-bodied men gently rested their injured companion on the ground.

'Sanctuary!' pleaded one of the men.

'Identify yourselves!' barked Commander Ramachandra with Kota by his side.

'Tukka is my name, my lord. My friend here is Valya. We are lieutenants to Rinchina the Prince of Ladakh.' He pointed to the injured man. 'His Highness has suffered an injury from a fall off a cliff,' he replied in broken Sanskrit.

'Who follows you?'

'They are the evil Kalamanyas who seek to kill the prince.'

'And what is their reason for doing that?' Kota's father asked skeptically.

'To illegally gain the kingdom of Ladakh. We beg you to open the gate; the Kalamanyas are upon us!' beseeched Valya.

Was it an old trick? The outpost could hold off a thousand attackers for more than three months, but if one person entered on false pretences and let the enemy in, it would take only two dozen men to take complete control. Who knew how many others lay waiting beyond the hill?

Ramachandra tested Kota: 'Are they friend or foe? What should we do?' Kota looked below at the injured Rinchina and put herself in his shoes. 'Father, we should not refuse entry to someone of royal blood and who is hurt and of no danger to us. But the others …'

Ramachandra pondered Kota's say. The fortress was the first line of defence for the Kashmir Valley and his standing orders were to never compromise security or jeopardize safety. However, the relationship between Ladakh and Kashmir was of long standing: it would not do if the legitimate prince of Ladakh was denied sanctuary and murdered at the mouth of the valley. Overruling his natural caution, Ramachandra told Kota, 'I agree with you that Rinchina is injured and deserves treatment. Go ahead and give the order but for him alone.'

'Leave Rinchina by the gate. Once you have moved back we will bring him inside and take care of him,' directed Kota to the group below. 'The rest of you must go and face your fate.'

The two lieutenants carried Rinchina to a small door within the larger gate to the fortress, and gently rested his back against it. They touched his feet respectfully, and walked away. Once they had walked a sufficient distance the smaller door opened from inside and two pairs of hands whisked Rinchina in and slammed the door shut.

By now, the Kalamanyas were upon the first group. The man on the horse held up his hand and the rest of the group halted and spread out in a semi-circle. Rinchina's smaller force faced them as they stood in a straight line. Both sides waited expectantly.

Ramachandra and his archers watched the scene dispassionately, but this was the first time that Kota had witnessed combat, and she felt queasy at the prospect. The Bottas were outnumbered five to one; a hand-to-hand sword fight would be one-sided and decisive.

The Kalamanya leader waited patiently without making a move, then pointed to the Bottas with his sword, commanding them to move away, leaving Tukka alone. Unwillingly and slowly the group stepped aside. Tukka stood with his head bowed and his arms folded. Ramachandra explained to Kota that the leader wanted to personally deliver Tukka's punishment; a message to Rinchina that any one collaborating with him would be killed without mercy.

The leader kicked his heels into the sides of his horse, which neighed and reared up, shooting like a rocket towards Tukka. As he gained speed, the rider shielded his body from Tukka as he balanced against the neck of his finely trained steed. His sword glinted in the morning light. The horse thundered closer to Tukka and at the very last moment turned to the side, leaving space for his rider's sword to arc downward and slice through the air in a choreographed move. Kota closed her eyes for a brief moment, wincing at the pain of the mortal blow.

But Tukka's hands had come alive; the rope belt tied around his waist lashed like lightning at the approaching sword, wrapping tightly around its handle. With one snatch, the sword flew away and the rider fell to the ground. The horse darted away.

With both men on the ground, Kota could see that Tukka was taller and bigger: he was at least 6 feet tall, with his hair braided and wound around his head. He was wearing heavy boots and had discarded the encumbrance of his heavy snow leopard skin robe. It was clear that he was a Khampa – the best warriors in Central Asia.

The two men circled each other warily, like fighting dogs. The Kalamanya leader was short and stocky, a Mongol, perhaps a mercenary. If he was disconcerted by the loss of his weapon, he did not show it. Slowly the Mongol approached Tukka and when the gap closed they launched into a fierce flurry of fists. Tukka responded with speed, evading the blows, sometimes using his palms to softly deflect his opponent's blows.

The duel seemed to go on for a long time. The Mongol's breath created clouds of white vapour in the cold morning air, whereas Tukka's breathing seemed effortless. The Mongol became increasingly frustrated, now striking with high kicks in addition to his punches, slaps and grips. With a deafening roar the Mongol launched himself at Tukka, angling his strike at the bigger man's head. Tukka planted his right foot firmly behind him and with his right fist connected with the Mongol's chest, just above the heart. The mighty *Vajramukti* hand strike is known to few and seen by even fewer. The Mongol's ribcage shattered as if it was a bundle of sticks, and he fell to the ground. Kota clamped her mouth with her hand and stifled a scream as she saw the broken figure writhing in an agonizing death.

The conflict ended as abruptly as it had begun. The Kalamanyas fled back to the pass: bereft of their leader, they were no longer a threat. Tukka went down on his knees in a meditative pose, and then after a few minutes stood up and went to his horse.

'Sanctuary for all of us, master?' Tukka called up, humbly repeating his earlier request. Commander Ramachandra stared back at him with piercing dark eyes, then turned his gaze to Kota. 'Father I would be careful with them,' she whispered.

Ramachandra was calculating the benefit Tukka and his companions could be to him in upgrading the native *Sqay* school of martial arts training of his armed forces. 'Are you prepared to take an oath of loyalty and serve this kingdom and me to the end of your days?'

'We will serve you and lay down our lives for you, Kampanesa,' Tukka replied.

'Open the gate and let them in,' ordered Ramachandra. The watchman shot two flaming arrows towards the valley, signalling that the threat had ended. Ramachandra and Kota climbed down the steps to meet the Bottas. They were a scruffy bunch; it was obvious that they had been on the run for a while. Tukka and Valya approached Ramachandra; this time it was Valya who spoke.

'Lord Commander, we have very little to offer except our loyalties and future service, but as a token of our gratitude we want you to have this horse that we have captured from the Kalamanyas.'

The horse was a beautiful golden colour. It was an Akhal Teke, the so-called heavenly horse. It would make for a nice graduation gift for Kota. Ramachandra was gracious: 'We accept this gift from a mighty warrior. When your prince is healthy again I will host a feast for all of you.' He turned to the Sogdian: 'Take our guests to their lodgings and see that they have food and drink, and all their needs are attended to. Have Saras attend to Rinchina's wounds. Tell her that she should spare no effort that he heals quickly.'

It was several weeks before Rinchina had recovered enough to be formally welcomed. A prince from a neighbouring kingdom, however down on his luck, was still royalty: they had a way of bouncing back, and it was during the tough times that one could build lasting relationships. Ramachandra organized for the feast to take place the night before Rinchina's departure.

The dinner for Rinchina was a formal affair, and Ramachandra and Kota dressed accordingly. Kota was proud that her father was such an imposing figure, and with his *safa* – the white turban – he was even more so, standing a full 6 ft 2 in. In true Hindu tradition, he wore a long achkan coat over narrow pants, which accentuated his slim hips and broad shoulders. Kota teased him about his long nose and fair skin that was pink from too frequent exposure to the cold. It made him smile. But it was his penetrating aristocratic stare, accentuated by the big red tilak centred on his forehead, which made those who met his gaze wish that they were elsewhere. He wore a *navrattan* necklace, accompanied by his sacred thread draped over his right shoulder outside his topcoat. Though he was a Hindu, and everything about his cultural influences and his behaviour bore testimony to that fact, among his soldiers he had men of all faiths and none had ever felt they were treated differently for it. Kota was dressed very simply: she had not yet been to the capital city and had only purchased a few clothes from the traders.

There were two dining halls at the dranga. Ramchandra and Kota made their way through the public hall, which served excellent food to reach the hall where the feast was to take place. The traders were a picky bunch and would share stories as to which fort offered the best food. When one travelled for months at a stretch, such details were very important and the rest stops competed to provide the best amenities. Similarly, the soldiers wanted hearty food – and lots of it. It was one of the few diversions available at an outpost. The hall was full of raucous traders from China, Ladakh, Mongolia, Persia and other kingdoms on the Silk Road. They greeted Ram respectfully.

The cook met Ramachandra and Kota in the private dining room and talked them through the meal he was planning to serve. Kota had arranged to have the room dusted and the walls washed. An artist had painted the mud walls with highly imaginative frescoes to give the room a feeling of luxury in the midst of military austerity: there were lifelike images of a Hindu sage holding the *Vajradhata*, the thunderbolt; there was a Trimurti of Brahma, Vishnu and Shiva; on one wall there was a Bodhisattva in serene contemplation and next to it a wild-eyed ascetic with red hair and beard and blue eyes. Ramachandra's final instructions to the cook were to make sure that the guests were served first and that the largest portions were to go to Rinchina. Saras, who was working in the kitchen with the cook, did a taste test of some of the dishes and pronounced them perfect.

Rinchina arrived with his people and after the customary exchange and draping of shawls, both groups sat down on the carpets for dinner. Ramachandra was accompanied by Kota and the captain of the guard. Rinchina had brought Tukka and Valya. Kota was surprised to see how strong and handsome the young man was. He was of medium height but stocky and certainly had a princely bearing. His skin was leathery from exposure to the sun at high northern altitudes. With his crinkling eyes and infectious grin, he was altogether charming. His hair was rough and tangled in knots and gave him a rugged look. Kota was glad that she had made the right decision on the ramparts. She had been following up with Saras regularly on her treatment of their guest and was glad that his healing was complete. The Ladakhis showed proper respect to Kota, and Rinchina greeted her with a big, warm, engaging smile.

The opening course was *maish krey*, a fermented cheese fried in ghee; the strong flavours and slightly chewy texture stimulated the taste buds. This was followed by *tabakhnat*, braised goat ribs cooked in milk, then fillets of river fish cooked in a hot sauce made with *gordolos*, wild sour plums. To finish, the guests were offered rice with kidney beans and turnips along with leafy green *hak*. Kota watched Rinchina tear into the tender meat and reach out for more and more. He had quite an appetite, even by the generous standards of the well-fed Kashmiris.

The serious business of food over, the company now turned to conversation. Kashmiri tea was offered as Kota heard her father apologize for the poverty of the meal, given the conditions at the outpost. Rinchina burst into infectious laughter. 'My Lord and Princess, you are apologizing for the meal, when you should know that for the last four weeks before we arrived here we lived on a diet of nothing but Tibetan *goji* berries and dried meat.'

Ramachandra chuckled, 'Goji berries – the army ration used when everything else runs out during winter – are considered an exotic health food for the aristocrat ladies in the capital! I tell them: Spend a winter at the dranga and you will never look as skinny, come spring. But nobody takes up my offer!' Everybody laughed and the ice was broken. 'My father was Raja Sangram Chandra of Nagarkot and my grandfather was Bala Chandra,' continued Ramachandra, explaining his lineage. 'It was my father who made me a warrior, but he also taught me that the greatest warriors die grievously, wounded in the back.'

Ramachandra's words struck a hidden spring of emotion within Rinchina. 'My father Bakatanya too died that way, and at the hands of his own kinsmen, the Kalamanyas, who he had protected and fed and nurtured as his own blood.'

'Then what happened?' Ramachandra questioned gently.

'I was determined to take revenge,' said Rinchina with his jaw set. 'I sent a message to the Kalamanyas through Tukka and Valya that I would meet them unarmed by the riverbank. I told them that I would drink the peace chalice. I would indenture myself to them as a servant as long as they brought my wages in advance so that I could pay my father's debts and clear his name. Tukka is known among the Ladakhis for always speaking the truth but the unobservant Kalamanyas did not realize that he was mostly silent and that Valya did all the talking. They took the bait. We asked them to drop their arms and bring our wages. They saw that it was just the three of us and there were twenty of them; laughing at the success of their own plans, they dropped their weapons and approached us. But as they came close to us we took up the battleaxes that we had hidden in the sand and dispatched them to their ancestors. Their last words were that Tukka and Valya were traitors,' Rinchina said with a cruel laugh.

Kota had been focusing on Rinchina intently but with her eyes to the ground. She could well imagine what must have happened: Tukka with a battle axe in his hands would have been lethal. She guessed that the endless cycle of vendettas would not end, the surviving adversaries would not spare Rinchina; hence his decision to seek greener pastures.

The captain spoke. 'Rinchina, you have suffered a lot. But revenge is part of your past – from now on you are a part of Kashmir where dharmic justice is the law of the land. Within Kashmir the common people are wedded to non-violence. If you drop a sesame seed anywhere here, it will fall on holy, sacred land. Words and debates are the only weapons inside Kashmir. A Kashmiri's identity and actions are driven not by religion, not by race, not by ambitions of empire, but by our culture, and our culture is shown by our civil, harmonious behaviour. Our word for it is *lihaz*.'

Ramachandra nodded in agreement. 'Rinchina, there is much truth in those words. We Kashmiris are fearless to outsiders, but we are fearful of the imperfections that reside inside us. Learn more about us because we believe that ignorance is the root cause of any bad outcome in life. I will treat you as one of my own and to get you started I am going to give you the jagir and administrative control of the villages in Gagangir where my family has a fortress. The people there are much troubled by the Khasas: you and your band will provide welcome protection.'

'I will protect the people with my life,' Rinchina responded.

'Bind your people together,' Ramachandra continued, 'and over time I will make sure that you progress in our kingdom. My family has served our maharajas faithfully for generations, so much so that we are now referred to as "Maharaja Makers". You can make a name for yourself in serving me, and you will not be disappointed in the rewards that will follow. Someday when you return to your homeland you will look at this period of exile kindly and it will strengthen relationships between Ladakh and Kashmir.'

Rinchina bowed deeply in gratitude for the chance that he was being given. 'My lord, you are more than a father to me because you have given me a new life. Come what may, I will regain my kingdom and when I do, Kashmir will see that it has a loyal friend in me forever.'

He turned towards Kota. 'Please accept a small gift from me. I hope that you will treasure it as much as I have treasured your father's and your generosity.'

Kota was taken by surprise by the small box in Rinchina's palm. 'It seems to be a personal gift,' she uttered. 'We hardly know each other and it would not be appropriate.'

Rinchina betrayed no sign of rejection. 'I am a prince and now a guest in your kingdom. Yes, it is a personal gift but it is the only gift that I have to offer. Will you turn me down?'

An unsure Kota accepted the box with both hands. Ramachandra signalled to the captain, who presented Rinchina and his followers with gifts in return: silk robes for the prince, *Kauseya* robes woven from a combination of silk and muslin for Tukka and Valya. For the rest of the Botta guard they gave garments of *Ksauma*, linen manufactured from flax and hemp. The grateful Bottas bowed and took their leave.

Ramachandra and Kota left the dining hall to head back to their sleeping quarters, the full moon was out and seemed almost within their reach; the millions of smaller stars studded every point of the sky and joined the moon in shining their silvery light on the snowy Himalayan peaks. In the centre of the sky and blazing with their incandescent light were the seven *Saptarshi* stars pointing true north and providing their watchful eye on Kashmir. Combined with their glow, the Valley of Kashmir was lit in a purity of snow white.

As they walked back Kota asked her father, 'What did you think about Rinchina?'

'He is a fighter but not a warrior.'

'What is the difference?'

'He is driven by passion whereas a warrior acts solely with detachment.'

'As it says in the Bhagvadgita?'

'Yes but more as we are told in the *Mokshopaya*.'

'*Mokshopaya?* My teachers did not teach me it at Sharadapeeth!'

Ramachandra laughed. 'Yes, they would not teach you that because it emphasizes the pathway of practical knowledge over the attainment of samadhi consciousness. It is the epic, secret doctrine of the Kashmiri warriors, which makes them fearless and fierce in what others would see as a cruel profession. It is 8,000 shlokas longer than the Ramayana and the largest war doctrine in the world. Every aristocrat warrior is trained in it by his father. It protects you from bad karma arising from your military actions. It promises the warrior fulfilment and liberation on earth while one is alive. When we return to Srinagar I will take you under my charge and teach you, the way my father did.'

Kota was amazed at the revelation and so proud. 'You are the greatest military commander that Kashmir has ever had,' she proclaimed.

'No, the greatest minister of war of Kashmir was Hrasvanatha in the tenth century,' Ramachandra said objectively. 'When one reads and practises his techniques, the very clanging of the swords with one's adversary recharges one's energy with that of the opponent's; then one is humbled by those who preceded us. What empowering secrets they have passed on to us!'

Kota filed the name and remembered her gift; out of curiosity she reached for the box and opened it. To her enormous surprise, inside lay a blue stone the size of a pigeon's egg – a Kashmir sapphire! Resting in the palm of her hand, the sapphire radiated its cool light, bathing everything around it in a steady luminosity. She gasped when she saw the gift and showed it to her father.

'You have the perfect item to wear when you are presented to the maharaja at the upcoming New Year celebrations,' observed Ramachandra dryly to a very overwhelmed Kota.

Later that night in her room Kota asked Saras: 'Why me? What does Rinchina expect in return for this gift? I do not feel good about him giving this to me.'

Saras was also suspicious. 'A gift that is accepted must be reciprocated on the spot or else later it can prove to be very expensive. Only time will tell what is in Rinchina's mind.'

'His mind is like muddy water,' Kota said. 'When still it was clear but when agitated very dirty. He gets stirred very easily. I feel he has suffered a lot, and hopefully Kashmir will represent a new beginning.'

Saras was not won over by Kota's assessment: 'Yes, the mind is like water. It can float a boat. It can sink it also. Let us see which way Rinchina goes.'

Sensing Saras's caution, Kota changed the subject. 'What do you think our guests are saying about us right now?'

Saras smiled. 'They are talking about how beautiful you are. They are also probably talking about how your father is fair and considerate, a rare quality in a military officer.'

'Why do you say that Saras?' asked Kota, picking up on her implicit criticism.

'Maybe I do not trust men, but to me he should have first taken time to verify that they are trustworthy before giving them charge of a jagir.

'I will advise father to not be so giving right away to unknown strangers, even if they are fellow royalty,' said Kota in a determined tone.

'It is advice that you may well take for yourself,' said Saras, sensing that Rinchina was the first, young, attractive man that Kota had seen at the outpost. 'When I tended to Rinchina's wounds he paid no heed to me. But in his unguarded conversations with his men he revealed that he is an opportunist. Kota, never forget that even if infatuated with desire you should never let yourself be captured.'

Kota nodded, but her mind was on Rinchina and if he was wondering about her reaction to his gift. The two talked some more about Saras's cautionary assessment. Finally, Kota could not stop yawning; it was time to go to bed. 'If one dranga could have so many surprises, what must the court of Kashmir hold in store for me?' wondered a drowsy Kota. 'It is so hard to know whom to trust, yet I know that with you and my father next to me I feel safe and can face anything,' she said, before finally falling asleep.

Wave 3
The Throne

'MOTHER, I am home!' shouted Kota with delight, running from room to room, feeling her mother's presence and expecting to bump into her at any moment. Then she felt someone shaking her shoulder. She awoke and saw Saras's caring face looking down at her. At once the realization came rushing in and a tear coursed down her cheek. It was just a dream.

'Saras, I felt my mother's presence. She talked to me,' said Kota in a choked voice.

Saras wiped Kota's face. 'You have come home after many years. Your mother is part of this place and in this very bedroom she would tell you children's stories when she tucked you into bed. Your favourite tale was of the four friends and the hunter and you would always ask for it before going to sleep. Now get up because someone has showed up bright and early and is waiting downstairs for you.'

Kota heaved a heavy sigh, freshened up and got dressed. But when she ran down the stairs to see who it was, there was nobody in the room. She walked past the drapes towards the kitchen.

'Tadpole,' a voice whispered in Kota's left ear. She spun around. *Oh, it is Brahma, the brat!* 'Brahma!' she screamed, hugging her friend with all her might. Kota could feel Brahma's muscular body, flexible and strong. After all these years he still had an impish grin and the devil-may-care handsomeness that girls found maddening. Now in his early twenties, he was tall and wore his hair in a loose topknot. The bunched hair fell down his back while a long wavy lock fell on each shoulder creating a tripartite division. He had called her Tadpole since a young Kota had followed him unquestioningly into a river and nearly drowned, thinking that one was born knowing how to swim. In her eyes he looked noble and magnificent.

'You left as a caterpillar and have become a butterfly,' Brahma cooed. 'But I hear that you barely scraped through your examination at Sharadapeeth!' said Brahma, smiling at Kota.

'Brahma, you mischievous rascal!'

'At least she passed school,' Ramachandra said as he entered the room. 'I still remember having to accompany your father to apologize to Devaswami for all of your misdeeds when you were at Sharadapeeth, and then failed to pass!'

'*Toth Kak*, uncle, how was I to know that I was not supposed to go fishing in the rivers around the temple?' protested Brahma. 'The mahseer fish there grow up to 6 ft long! Catching them was the most exciting sport I've ever known. Nagendra Pandit threatened me that I would end up as a fish in my next life if I did not repent.'

'If only that was the all the trouble that you got into,' Kota countered, her eyes bright blue with the pleasure of seeing Brahma. 'Your exploits are still used by the Brahmins as a warning for all future generations of Bhatta students. Have you forgotten how you hid in the temple and at midnight, in a fake woman's voice, ordered all the Brahmins to hold a yagna and pray unceasingly for one whole week?'

'What was wrong with that? I still don't get it. The Brahmins are constantly telling everyone to pray to the Devi. When I told them to pray I was just paying them back.'

'How is your bottom now?' teased Kota with an impish smile.

'Fine, fine,' said Brahma turning beet red, having been reminded of the sorry ending to the whole episode. The pandits were forbidden from holding anything which could be construed as a man-made weapon but that did not stop them from using the most draconian practices. Brahma had been ordered to strip his trousers off by Nagendra Pandit and was given a *Soi Shallak*, a light thrashing with a bouquet of local Kashmiri nettles. His bottom was so sore and red that he had to rest facedown for one week, unable to move.

'I hear that you used to throw my name out to your class fellows to keep them at bay.'

Now it was Kota's turn to blush because Brahma was right. If the schoolboys were unbearable Kota would threaten them that she would ask Brahma to come and set them straight. He was well known and it was enough to make even the biggest bullies retreat.

'Run away, both of you,' said Ramachandra, 'I am sure you both have a lot to catch up on.'

Kota and Brahma fled outside into the garden. Brahma Bhatt became Kota's best friend after her mother died and her father went away on long military expeditions. Saras was good for adult advice but it was Brahma with whom Kota had got into all her childhood scrapes. There was little in her life that he had not been part of. Ravan, her younger brother, dutifully tried to keep up, but Kota adored Brahma, and the fact that he was a few years older than her made him the ideal companion. Brahma updated Kota on the gossip on everybody at court; with him around she did not feel so lonely any more. The two talked until Saras had to force them to come in for breakfast. Ramachandra joined them briefly and then left to attend court.

'What kind of a man is the maharaja?' Kota asked. 'I am going to be presented to him at the New Year party in the spring. I do want to make the right impression.'

Brahma was about to answer, then had a madcap suggestion: 'Do you want to see the maharaja at court?'

'How would we do that?' Kota asked, puzzled. 'Father said that it is closed doors only and they have important matters of state to discuss.' Brahma grinned. 'Silly, no wonder you failed the question on spying!' Brahma grinned. 'Thankfully, Devaswami saved you because you are a girl. A year ago, while I was walking through the hills, I found a small cave. I went inside it and to my surprise it had a passageway. I followed it only to discover it led me to a little opening in Suhdev's palace that overlooks the room where he holds court.'

38 THE LAST QUEEN OF KASHMIR

Kota could not believe what Brahma was telling her. 'You mean this secret passage was an escape route that some maharaja had built in the past and now nobody, including Suhdev, knows about it?'

'Correct. He does not deserve to know about it. He is a pompous fathead, but you will find that out for yourself. Just remember that you cannot sneeze!'

An hour later, Kota was squeezed into a narrow passageway, peering through a peephole to watch events down below. Sitting side by side with Brahma she was being pressed uncomfortably against his left thigh, but there was no space to move. She saw eighteen ministers; each one was briefing Suhdev, the Maharaja of Kashmir, in turn. Kota saw that Suhdev was of average height, barrel-chested, with stout limbs and forearms, and had a round face that was topped with a large turban. His topcoat, bursting at every seam, served nicely as a showcase for his necklaces. His fingers were encrusted with rings and jewels. His forehead was marked with sandal paste; next to him were lit *dhoop*s and Kota could even sense from up high that a fragrance surrounded him.

Maharaja Suhdev was preoccupied. Out of the corner of his eye he was looking at himself in the large mirror at the end of the hall. He was resting his chin in the palm of his hand, his forefinger at the point of the nose and his expression fixed in abstract contemplation as befitted a maharaja deliberating on weighty matters. Chewing betel nut was the only recreation permitted during the meeting and to Kota he looked like a cow chewing the cud. The meeting dragged on through endless reports on the trials and tribulations of Suhdev's subjects. The good news was that finances were strong and the treasury receipts were flowing in. This would help bring down the considerable debt that the kingdom was burdened with.

'He is not paying any attention to what is being said,' Kota whispered to Brahma. 'The Brahmins would have tweaked his ears for doing that.' 'He is sterile and it has vexed him to the point of madness,' Brahma whispered back. 'For a maharaja to not have sons is the ultimate failure. Even an ass rates higher than him. At least it can reproduce!'

Kota nodded her head in agreement with Brahma's analysis. Impotence in a maharaja would create crises in the kingdom. She examined Suhdev with greater interest given his handicap, but was distracted by Brahma, who had moved even closer to her and had taken hold of her hand and was playing with her fingers. Squeezed into the tight space, not knowing how to respond to Brahma, she kept her eyes on Suhdev. The maharaja was yawning with disinterest and called an end to the meeting. He ordered his chamberlain to bring in the supplicants who had requested an audience with him.

'My Lord, may I first have a word with you?' It was Commander Ramachandra, and Suhdev waved to him to proceed.

'Maharaja, security conditions outside Kashmir are degrading badly. There are indications that an attack is imminent. We must take decisive pre-emptive action if we are to forestall any such threat.'

Suhdev rolled his eyes and cut him off: 'Ram, don't scare everybody in court. We Kashmiris are turning into chickens. If this is a ploy to get more money to spend on the army there is simply none. In fact, you should change the army to a voluntary one and mobilize it when needed. Who is next?'

Kota could feel her father's public humiliation. Had Suhdev ever visited the dranga? Did he even know the watchman whose entire existence was dedicated to protecting Suhdev's miserable skin? Suhdev angered her, but the chamberlain announcing, 'Yaniv, the jeweller, with a party from Rajasthan, is here,' interrupted her thoughts.

Yaniv was in his late thirties, wearing a skullcap denoting his Jewish roots. He was of medium height, with loose clothing and dark eyebrows that framed his bearded face. His pointed nose fit in with that of the Kashmiris, many of whom were similarly endowed. Standing by him were two tall, swarthy men with handlebar moustaches and a regal bearing. Yaniv, dressed in his foreign attire, made a sharp contrast to the men next to him.

'What do you have to show me, Yaniv, that this meeting is so urgent?' Suhdev asked.

'Your Highness, once in a millennium, a maharaja has the opportunity to show the world that he is truly the anointed one. Your

Highness, that opportunity has presented itself today to you, and it is not to be missed.'

Suhdev could see through the opening sales pitch, but Yaniv was good at what he did.

'As you know, My Lord,' continued Yaniv, 'the Rajasthani nobility is locked in a life and death struggle with its Persian enemy. Today, we have with us two emissaries from the Rajputana royalty, and they have brought the Suryavansh diamond. I have personally inspected the diamond for its clarity and its colour. I can confidently state that there has never been a stone like this; there will never be a stone like it again. Great power will undoubtedly be conferred upon him who holds this stone: the emperor of China, the sultan of Persia and the maharajas of the central kingdoms will know that they are declining and it is the kingdom of Kashmir that is the ascendant centre of the world.'

Yaniv signalled to the two Rajputs to advance. One of them opened his shirt and pulled out a bag that was hanging by his neck. Kneeling before the maharaja, he laid a silk cloth gently on the carpet and spread the contents of the bag on the cloth. The sun shone through the latticed window, and then there was silence. The Rajput gently reversed the stone to show its signature: it had a six-star formation on each side, with pink rays radiating from the centre. Suhdev let out a spontaneous whistle when he saw the diamond with an intense watermelon colour coming out of it. If he were not seeing it he would not have believed that a stone like this one existed in the world. His courtiers were still and Ramachandra's face was so grim that to Kota it looked like it would burst.

The maharaja nodded at the astrologer who knew it was time for him to do his evaluation. The Rajputs were prepared: one of the men reached into his pocket and pulled out a dried palm leaf, on which was drawn the astrological chart of the stone based on the exact date when it had been found at the Golconda mines. The astrologer looked at his *nechpatri*, his brow furrowed.

'The stone is restless, but it is destined to bring great goodness to its owners,' he announced decisively.

'This stone will benefit you and your descendants forever, and you will always be remembered for having brought it into the dynasty. What other stone can one say that for? A permanent acquisition, Your Highness,' Yaniv exulted.

The allusion to Suhdev's descendants was not lost on him. This stone would give him unparalleled power and punch through whatever was restricting his fertility. Gemstones were reputed to have that power and Yaniv was not just brokering any stone. This was royal supremacy and immortality in a single package. 'What is the price?' Suhdev asked. 'Your Highness, as you know a stone like this has no equal, and the price cannot be truly set for such a piece. However, given the extreme difficulty that the Rajputs face and the cordial relations that have long existed between the two great kingdoms, the price has been set at the ridiculously low figure of one lakh dinars.'

The courtiers gasped, a hundred thousand dinars! There were few kingdoms in the world that were worth that – no more than a handful – and here was a stone that was being valued at such a price. Suhdev shushed them with a wave of his hand. 'Yaniv, you have gone way beyond being a hard bargainer for the Rajasthanis. If I don't buy it, who will?'

Yaniv was unmoved; this was business, and a chance to make the deal of a lifetime. But Suhdev was not done yet. He played his last trump card: 'Yaniv, in the Valley there is one temple that all the Jews go to and pray alongside the Kashmiris. It is sacred to you; the Temple of Mammasvamin. When it was consecrated, eighty-five thousand cows were donated along with five thousand dinars for each cow. I ask you by what you hold sacred in the temple: Is this a deal that I should do?'

Yaniv choked. The price was high but not unfair for the stone, yet the king had asked the question in a manner that was a test of his conscience and character. He knew about Suhdev's debts and the precariousness of the kingdom. Slowly, and to the surprise of the Rajputs and the king, he answered: 'If I were you, sir, I would not do this deal.'

Taken aback but tormented by his desires Suhdev thought about the New Year's party that he was holding in a few months' time. He had wanted a nice new piece of jewellery, but he'd had no idea that the price would turn out to be this large. He thought: *Yaniv is right; there is a time to act, and this is the time to buy, when the central kingdoms are being stripped of their gold, their women, and their land. I can fund half of the purchase out of the treasury surplus. As for the other half, the spending on the new social programmes will have to go. Ramachandra will have to use the indentured labour system for his army. It will have to be a military order, or Ramachandra will be stubbornly resistant to it. Plus my test of Yaniv was just to see if he would lower the price and he did not. He simply insinuated that I could not afford it, not that the price was wrong. If I don't buy now, this story will get out and nobody will ever trade their precious gemstones with me.*

To Yaniv's astonishment, Suhdev picked up the silk bag, signifying his acceptance of the deal. Casually he addressed the Rajputs: 'Would it be acceptable if you went to the treasurer tomorrow? He will make arrangements for the payment.'

'Maharaja, your word is good enough,' the Rajputs replied.

Suhdev asked them if he could make arrangements with Commander Ramachandra to give them security on their journey back, which they graciously accepted. There was a spirit of bonhomie in the group, the result of a deal successfully closed.

Suhdev turned to Yaniv. 'So, you have closed the biggest diamond deal ever. Are you happy you migrated to Kashmir? What first brought you here?'

'I am very happy that I was able to be of service to you, My Lord,' Yaniv replied. 'As for me, my interest in Kashmir began because there was always a belief that our ancient people, including Ruth, wore Kashmir shawls. There was a feeling that the Jews were connected with the Kashmiris because of the similarities of language and some dietary customs that were peculiar to only these two groups. The Jews learned the secret of dyeing from the silk trade, and many settled in Persia, including my family. My fascination with Kashmir led me here, and in order to make a living I focused on the coin and jewellery trade, which has been kind to me.'

'How interesting, the New Year's celebration is in a few months. Do come,' Suhdev suggested.

Yaniv bowed his head in appreciation for the royal invitation and then departed with the Rajasthanis in tow.

Kota was speechless at what she had seen. Did Suhdev know that if his front line soldiers had witnessed the scene that could have provoked them to rebel and kill him on the spot? They already had to scrounge for provisions, their armament was aging and rusty and the dranga was badly in need of repair. She could see that her father was furious. The other courtiers were equally disturbed but did not know how to express their dismay at their king's profligacy. But the court was not yet done. 'Shah Mir from Dwarkasil requests a short audience with you, My Lord,' the chamberlain announced.

Brahma leaned close to Kota. 'Shah Mir is an immigrant who arrived in Kashmir from Swadgabar in 1313 with a band of followers and relatives,' he whispered.[2] 'On hearing his story of persecution by Islamic zealots, Suhdev, who is extremely liberal, was terribly moved and went out of his way to receive him. He wanted to demonstrate that Kashmir was a home to those who were persecuted elsewhere. He was lavish in his hospitality and gave him gifts, including 5 kg of precious jewellery of which half was gold and half silver. Your father was irritated to no end and the word spread that Suhdev attracted supplicants like leeches were drawn to blood.'

Shah Mir entered the chamber. Of medium build with a small face, round eyes and a short, pointed beard he presented a fastidious look. His arms were stout but what was striking was that his hairy eyebrows met in a tuft giving the impression that he had a dark, closed, third eye. He was wearing an embroidered *Qaba*, a calf-length coat open in the front, over a kameez. His baggy trousers were held up with a thick girdle, and, with his upturned shoes, he stood out. He was accompanied by a woman who was completely covered by a veil; in the Valley of Kashmir the women were free and participated fully in all walks of life. Even the ministers did not quite know what to make of it.

'Aadab Maharaj. Allah is great and may his greatness always be on you, oh greatest of maharajas,' spoke Shah Mir, presenting himself with a graceful, sweeping bow. Kashmiris believed in equality and only prostrated themselves to divinity, so the court watched Shah Mir with bemusement.

'Aadab haz,' Suhdev hailed. 'What brings you to us, Shah Mir?' he asked.

'My Lord, does the flame ask the moth why the moth is drawn to it?' responded Shah Mir rhetorically. 'You welcomed us into Kashmir when you said that Kashmir was like *vasudhaiva kutumbakam*, the world is one family. You are the one who said that a tree gives its shade even to the woodcutter that approaches it. It is spring, when Mother Earth blesses us with new gifts. I wanted to present the maharaja with a small gift in appreciation for what he has given me and my family in our new life in Kashmir.'

Suhdev responded gaily: 'Shah Mir, if you be the moth, then we will have to watch out for your activities at night. Yes, diversity is as much a necessity for society as it is for nature or biology. What gift do you propose to give us, sir?'

Shah Mir turned to the woman who had accompanied him. 'My Lord, you gave us sanctuary in Kashmir when we were victimized for violating canonical purity. Just as you have given me and my family more happiness than we could have dreamt of, I would like to present this slave for your pleasure and happiness.'

Shah Mir drew away the woman's veil and the onlookers gasped, both at the audacity of the action and at the woman herself. She was no more than sixteen with long blonde hair down to her waist; a beauty of perhaps Georgian extraction. 'Tatiana is her name, My Lord. She is something different and will be the perfect addition to your seraglio.' Suhdev smiled; the day was getting better. Just as he was about to speak, Commander Ramachandra interjected: 'My Lord, Shah Mir is to be thanked for his gift, but he is an immigrant in our land. In Kashmir, unlike the world of the Mussalmans, we do not have slaves. Your seraglio has free women in it. Even if the Turushka come and seek to sell slaves we cannot set a precedent in accepting this girl as a slave. The Kashmiris expect the maharaja to set high moral standards; this would not be tolerable to them.'

Suhdev stopped in his tracks at Ramachandra's admonishment. The vein in his forehead throbbed; the silence in the room grew thicker and the atmosphere more awkward. Then a slim, androgynous-looking figure stepped forward. It was Kokur, the court dramatist and jester. 'My Lord, to not accept the gift from Shah Mir would be to insult him. But to accept a female slave as a gift would be misunderstood in some quarters, even though your motives are most noble. In such a situation it seems the right thing would be for Shah Mir to set the girl free and for Your Majesty to gift her as a devadasi where she will serve the gods. Devaswami does not subscribe much to that practice in his temples, but I am told that there is a jogi at the abandoned Shiva temple who is accompanied by a bevy of young women; matters might be satisfactorily arranged with him. The world will see that the maharaja upholds the highest principles, as befits a direct descendant of the gods.'

Suhdev was mollified by the references to his divine origins. Kashmir was a Hindu kingdom and royal authority was ultimately rooted in its lineage being descended from the gods. He understood the benefits of the arrangement and what could be worked out privately with the jogi and Tatiana later on.

He said, 'Kokur, the world has gone mad, and in a mad world only a mad person like you can make perfect sense.' The jester bowed his head to the maharaja. Turning to Shah Mir, Suhdev announced: 'I am pleased by your gift. How can I reward you, and what reason did you seek the audience with me?'

'My Lord, to have an audience with you is reason enough. However, if Your Majesty sees fit, the girl was brought to the Valley by a Sufi who is originally from Herat in Persia and is on a mission to obtain herbs and medicines from the mountains of Kashmir. While he is doing his work I would like to start a small charity in the village of Malchmar, where this fakir could be gainfully employed in supporting your causes. As you know, the village houses the Muslim butchers who perform a service for their Hindu brethren since they do not want to slaughter animals. But they lack someone who can give them religious and moral guidance.'

'I would like to interrogate the fakir before he is let in,' Ramachandra interjected again. 'Prospect immigrants are masters of dissimulation and represent potential threats to Kashmir.'

'Kampanesa, you see threats everywhere even in works of charity of a fakir,' Suhdev chided irritably. 'Don't you see that by showing the world that Muslims are welcome in Kashmir, and have more freedom here than elsewhere, we pre-empt attacks from Islamic zealots? Shah Mir, let the fakir stay in Kashmir as long as he needs to and work for your charity. He will earn a great name for you, who already has a good name in the Valley. But be careful – there must be no propaganda in the charity centres. If your man perchance finds the magical extract *Salajeet* bring him to us. Now the audience is over. Commander Ramachandra, we are told that you are presenting your daughter at the New Year celebration and we look forward to meeting her. Let me know if she wants a job at the palace.'

The maharaja stood up to leave; all the ministers bowed their heads. Shah Mir bent his head the lowest.

Kokur took the Georgian girl's hand to lead her away, but before leaving he brushed by Ramachandra. 'My Lord,' he whispered, 'in court we may carry sheathed swords, but as you can see unsheathed tongues can be even more dangerous.'

Ramachandra permitted himself a wry smile. 'Kokur, you rascal! You saved me and your master from overstepping our boundaries.'

Kokur was respectful with his answer: 'It was my duty. There is something about Shah Mir that I do not like. He is not genuine, a man who claims to be pious and yet also of royal descent. His gift corrupts the court.'

Ramachandra was pragmatic. 'If there was no corruption, Kashmiri society would come to a halt. I agree that Shah Mir is up to no good here. The request for the fakir's stay could have been done through the normal course and judged on its merit. It did not need an expensive slave as baksheesh. He will need watching over. But much as I don't like what happened here, Suhdev has a point that his policy of admitting Muslims and treating them favourably creates goodwill for us. By the way, how have Kota's practice sessions been?'

Kokur smiled. 'You will soon see that your daughter will make us both proud.'

The courtiers dispersed, and when all was quiet Kota and Brahma, who had been watching the whole scene from above, slowly withdrew into the passageway. Brahma was holding Kota's hand tight as he led her out.

'What did you think of Suhdev?' Brahma asked when they emerged from the cave and it was safe to talk again.

'The fool,' said Kota vehemently. 'Suhdev is oblivious to reality and obsessed with his insatiable, degenerate desires. For him to purchase that expensive stone is to bankrupt the kingdom. I also did not like what happened between him and Shah Mir. That young girl deserves better. He is debauched, a corrupt squanderer. My father would make a better maharaja than Suhdev any day. Tell me more about who this Shah Mir is?'

Brahma was slightly taken aback by the uncharacteristic vehemence in Kota. She had grown up in more ways than one. He nodded his head in agreement.

'Shah Mir is an enigma to many but your father got him checked out. He is from Swadgabar, a suburb of Gabhar in the Rajauri area south-west of Kashmir. One of his ancestors, a Hindu named Partha, founded the town, but the family line then converted. Yet, when he presents himself to the world it is as if he is from Persia and he puts on all those airs and graces and relays the persecution story that was just a sham to gain asylum. He is nothing but a converted Muslim Khasa who are a very troublesome people for the Kashmiris.'

Brahma wanted to distract Kota from her thoughts as she absorbed what she had just heard and invited her to go swimming. They headed to a nearby lake and Kota waded in the water fully dressed, but Brahma went for a swim bare-chested and only wearing a loincloth. He was showboating his moves to Kota as she relaxed by the shore.

'How is Ravan doing at school?'

Kota's younger brother was in his first year at Sharadapeeth and she had kept a watchful eye on him. 'He is very quiet and shy and the other kids overpower him. In some ways it is good that I was there, but in other ways he would have been better off if he had to fend for himself without his older sister watching out for him. But overall, with father mostly away, he is enjoying being with so many boys his own age.'

'Did you develop a crush on any of the boys while you were at school, or were you a crashing bore?' Brahma suddenly showing strong, spontaneous interest in her. Kota was not sure where it was leading. She smiled back sweetly, and said playfully: 'Now, why would I tell you? Do you tell me about your flings with those spoiled oligarch girls?' 'Bet you, nobody could do what I am about to do,' said Brahma as he climbed up a tall tree and then proceeded to do a straight dive, splashing water all over Kota and bursting out of the water holding a fish. It was flapping madly as he tossed it into Kota's lap making her scramble madly away screaming and laughing at Brahma for surprising her so. She sensed that Brahma was trying to kindle a fire, but she was blindside by his next statement.

He was direct: 'You have grown into an extremely beautiful woman, Kota. I thought that I was going to be revisiting an old friend but the moment I saw you I have been love-struck. I want to make you mine.' A nonplussed Kota reacted awkwardly, 'Brahma, please don't say that. I have only just graduated. What I remember about you and us has been frozen in an eight-year-old time capsule. We are good friends and I look up to you. I need time to adjust back to my world and discover my own feelings. To find out whom I desire.'

He came closer to Kota and sat beside her with his arms folded across his broad bare chest.

'Need time? Silly, in our world we have arranged marriages with strangers. By contrast, you and I have known each other since childhood. Our families have the same social status. You lost your mother. I lost my father at an early age. Your father is the one that I look up to just as you do. We have so much in common. It would be perfect.'

Kota looked at Brahma's noble, attractive face. He was strong and masculine. Her sons would be handsome like him. She quickly arrested the thought before it carried her away. 'Brahma, I have not forgotten what Nagendra asked me. Can I form a relationship with anyone? I did not have a mother to teach me how to bond. Both Saras and my father have led their lives with their feelings buried so deep inside, that their hearts have lost their way. Sometimes I feel that I will be too needy because I was not nurtured and will not be able to give love to my partner.'

Kota started sobbing, feeling very inadequate and unable to deal with a man whom she trusted, who was her first and only male friend and who had now professed his love for her.

Brahma was tender and understanding. 'Maybe it was too much too soon. We are young, and time will clear everything up like a mirror. Our love will bloom. Come, let us dry up and head home.'

Kota felt so grateful to Brahma for not laughing at her. Compared to the sophisticated oligarch girls that Brahma must be used to, she felt so naive. She spontaneously hugged him and rested her head on his shoulder for a long time with her eyes tightly closed, feeling the sound of his heartbeat next to hers.

For Kota the dance rehearsals for the New Year's celebration took her into a new world. She had no female friends her age, and being surrounded by the giggling, dancing girls from the maharaja's troupe with Kokur as their choreographer made her realize how little she knew of the fairer sex. The girls were respectful towards her, but Kota would often catch them whispering to each other and then bursting into shrill laughter for no ostensible reason. They had been trained to smile and be pleasing in word and action and every movement of their eyes, lips, hands and hips was graceful and entertaining. Time passed swiftly when they practised and all too quickly the New Year party was upon them.

When Kota's palanquin reached the entrance to the palace for the party she felt like she was entering a fairyland. At six storeys high and with fifty rooms on each floor, Suhdev's palace was an aesthetic wonder. For the maharaja's grand New Year soiree, the guests were first greeted at the outside gates by twin elephants in full armour. As Kota, along with the guests in their palanquins accompanied by the mounted troops on horseback (themselves escorted by bearers with parasols), came down the drive, the royal guards flanking both sides of the access road saluted them. The royal guards wore the standard red trousers. As the infantry regiment provided for these ceremonial occasions by Commander Ramachandra, they carried broad, heavy, double-edged swords suspended from their left shoulders and long bucklers of undressed ox hide; each man also carried either a javelin or a mace, and long, double-edged knives hung from their belts. The fully armed and uniformed men certainly brought flair to this party, Kota thought; the atmosphere was positively charged. Attendants standing on either side of the steps swung large fans over her. It was still chilly and Kota wore a shahtoosh shawl around her shoulders to keep warm. At the door, the maharaja's own female attendants welcomed her, swinging diyas around her creating a magical light. Upon entering the hall she was illuminated with a thousand more brightly lit diyas, which reflected the paintings and the colours of the frescoes on the walls, bringing them to life, so that the painted images seemed as much a part of the party as the painted people themselves.

Kota entered the hall with her father. There was a crush of bodies inside; men and women in excited conversation. The women had adopted a new style, wearing brilliantly embroidered, tight half-jackets with short sleeves, while the hanging trains of their skirts swept the ground. A line drawn with collyrium from the eyes to the ears enhanced the beauty of the women's faces. The men were competing like peacocks for their attention with jewellery and gold necklaces. The attendants were serving snacks along with wine in mother of pearl, jade and bejewelled glasses. The delighted guests held their glasses in their left hands and joyfully toasted, 'Bom Shiva!'

One look at the assembled crowd made Kota realize how simple her outfit was compared to that of the nobility; even the style of her hair was monastic compared to the fashionable women. She had done it up as befitting a recent graduate from school – long and tied back, but at the very end knotted to hang on the front of the left shoulder. This exposed the back of her swan-like neck without the need for a plunging backline in her bodice. Held by a thin gold chain, nestling just above her breasts, lay Rinchina's sapphire pendant, a glamorous touch in an otherwise unadorned look. Ramachandra was stunned to see how blind he had been to his daughter, who was growing up into a woman in front of his eyes.

'I feel so plain among all these beautiful women,' Kota whispered to Saras.

'Shush! You do not know your own beauty; it is natural rather than artificial like these women,' Brahma interrupted, languid and lithe and unaffected by the glitter around him. Kota's eyes sparkled. She held Brahma's hand and squeezed it slightly. They had been seeing each other regularly for the past few months after their swim together. Every time she saw him something lit inside her. Her feelings for him were strengthening, going hand in hand with her rising confidence, as she started interacting with her peers in the upper circles of Kashmir's society. But what had crazy Brahma done now? She questioned him, barely able to suppress her laughter, 'Brahma, when did you go and get yourself diamond earrings?'

'Women make earrings dangle with every move of theirs,' Brahma replied with mock seriousness. 'This is a memento of how I am a slave now to your every move.'

'Stop it, behave, we are surrounded by gentry!,' said Kota, but she could not resist smiling.

Brahma pointed out the powerful merchants and traders to Kota. 'They are being invited in greater numbers as their importance has increased. Their leader, in the cream outfit, is Khazanchi. His wife

Manjari is next to him. She was born in a house of ill repute and is illegitimate, but courtesans have always had direct access to the kings. She has become an equal partner in Khazanchi's deals, and is considered to be the most powerful woman in Kashmir. Suhdev is deeply in debt to them and they are the real owners of Kashmir. But their one worry is that he has no descendants; what would happen to them if Suhdev had an accident? They have money, but are searching for security.'

Congregating in one corner, the moneylenders stuck together in their own exclusive circle. Kota's eyes crossed Manjari's. Much younger than her husband, she was clearly proud of her firm, curvaceous figure which she had swathed in tight-fitting, imported Chinese silks, befitting her husband's role as a trader. Manjari swept over to Kota, her presence preceded by a seductive fragrance that enveloped her. The cloying aroma of honeysuckle wafted from her; she must have lined her clothes with flowers the day before. Her lower face was covered with a light veil of white gauze that added to her mystique; her eyelashes and eyelids had been darkened with collyrium. The tilak marking in the centre of her forehead was multicoloured in gold and silver matching the colour of her outfit; it was vertical and slightly wavy, unlike the dot bindis worn by traditional women or that of the men, who wore horizontal tilaks on their foreheads. She had done her hair in a large vertical bun ornamented in front with a string of jewels.

'Kota, we had heard that you had graduated and were being presented at court. There are always rumours that your father will lead a coup, but seeing your beauty he obviously plans to capture the throne through kama. You have your mother's looks, so there is clear precedent. I am looking forward to what the king thinks of you when he sees your dance recital.'

Kota curtsied to the woman, whom she instantly disliked. 'My father is loyal to the maharaja and to the kingdom. He has no designs on the throne.'

'Your father spurns the throne? Ha! In this room everybody pursues power through patrimony, profit, principles, peace or pleasure, but your moral father plans to stick to providing protection? Maybe he follows your foolish mother who once had her chance. Will the daughter follow her parents or does her desire have greater ambition?'

Kota sensed she was in deep water. Manjari had chewed betel nut to redden her lips, which were shaped like Kama's painted bow of desire. Her scrubbed bare arms were smooth like ivory; her skin gleamed with a tawny glow in the lamplight. She wore a single choker of large pearls around her neck, matched by conspicuous earrings that drew attention to her prominent lobes. Kota saw that Manjari's trimmed eyebrows had been darkened. Her feminine armour did not permit a chink in it. She was lethal all round.

Kota spoke in a sweet voice: 'Our birth determines our stars and our stars and karma determine our destiny. I will have to see what direction life takes me in.'

'Royal blood always brings up birth. Birth means nothing, money means everything,' sneered Manjari. 'The oligarchs politic, thinking that they are all maharaja makers, but I own the throne. I look forward to your dance recital and becoming friends.' She stared pointedly at Saras's Kalash wicker shoes, with her front tips curling up and she spat out: 'Have your attendant come and visit me. I may have some footwear that I can donate to her so she can attend a royal function in appropriate attire.' Then she was gone, her flashy peacock shoes strutting away.

Kota turned to Brahma. 'What did this whirlwind mean with her reference to my mother?'

'Suhdev badly wanted to marry your mother,' he whispered, 'but she was in love with your father and refused him. It is the only time a maharaja of Kashmir has been turned down by a woman. Had it not been that your father was commander-in-chief her life would have ended very quickly.'

Kota absorbed this finding. 'Mother was even more of her own person than I had ever imagined. I am determined to show the same strength that she showed in her actions.'

As she finished ruminating on the latest revelation about her mother, she saw Suhdev, surrounded by his courtiers, including Yaniv, approaching the small, elevated pedestal where a majestic chair had been placed for the king. By his side was a youth in his twenties who looked like Suhdev but was lean, attractive and scholarly-looking. The crowd parted to let the parasol-bearing attendants move through. As Suhdev seated himself, those nearest to him started murmuring. Suhdev was richly bedecked with ornaments, pearl and diamond necklaces draped on his chest, as befitted his kingly status, but instead of a turban he was wearing a diadem with five crescents. At its centre was the Suryavansh diamond! Manjari rushed to approach the maharaja. 'My Lord, today the sun's journey has ended. From now on it only graces your divine presence. He who seeks the sun will now have to seek Lord Suhdev's audience. You are the superpower amongst lowly mortals.'

'Manjari, your wit stands you in good stead,' Suhdev said with a wide smile. 'If we are now the sun, it is only to shed light on the beauty of our subjects. If we are the sun it is all because of Yaniv who has brought it to our land.'

Yaniv bowed at the credit that he had been given. Courtier after courtier vied to step up in front of the maharaja to exalt him in the most mellifluous of words and extol Yaniv's contribution. Kota saw that only her father held back. Sensing that his daughter was concerned he spoke softly: 'What an idiot! He is still in debt to the moneylenders. Yet, he has further mortgaged the kingdom and its future for that stone.'

Kota understood the stress her father was under and she tried to get him to relax. 'Everything will be fine. Please forget your worries for tonight for my sake.'

Ramachandra grimaced but nonetheless he took Kota and introduced her to Suhdev, who glanced at her with interest. When they were out of earshot Kota asked her father who the young man was next to Suhdev?

'It is Udyan, Suhdev's younger brother. We don't see him in court generally – he detests coming here. He is more scholarly and prefers to stay at the fort in Kishtwar,' Ramachandra explained.

Kokur stepped into the centre of the room and clapped his hands. The New Year's Eve gala dinner was about to begin. The servers lay down clean sheets in front of the sitting guests before bringing pitchers of water and a basin for everybody to wash their hands. Large lotus leaves had been laid on the ground as dining plates; these were then washed lightly with a sprinkling of water. The guests that were high security risks, such as the maharaja or Commander Ramachandra, were served on silver plates that would reveal any known local poisons by changing colour in reaction to the toxins. Even the poorest family would feed their babies with a silver spoon to protect them. The servers used wooden spoons as they distributed a dizzying array of dishes, one at a time, walking in between the guests, who were facing each other as they sat on carpets and leather cushions.

First came the rogan josh, the signature goat or lamb dish cooked in red Kashmir chilli gravy. The mighty *Markhor*, the world's largest goat, grazed in great numbers in Kashmir and provided the base meat stock. For a cooler dish there was *yakhini*, meat cooked in a creamy yoghurt sauce. Each course had been slow-cooked in local *degchi*s, clay pots; the meat was so tender that it melted in the mouth. Consistent with Kashmiri dietary laws, there was no garlic or onion in the food.

Then there were the royal dishes that the maharaja had a monopoly over – partridge, venison, roast duck and two different types of fish. Fruit-based dishes, starting with meatballs filled with apricot stuffing, followed. There were vegetable and cheese-based dishes, kohlrabi and other greens such as hak, lightly blanched and then cooked with hot green chilli. The crowning glory was the saffron pilaf with huge pieces of black morels, aromatic and fragrant, covered with a thin silver foil that shone in the light.

The spices gently teased and seduced the palate, and the aromas completed the heady intoxication so that one was literally drunk on the food. As the evening wore on it became a battle between diners and serving staff: the guests would beg the waiters to hold off, guarding their plates with both hands, but the servers would show no mercy and continue to ladle more food on to the lotus leaves.

'Watch the Fat Boy,' Brahma whispered to Kota. Manjari had seated herself strategically next to Suhdev and was feeding him with her hands as if he was a baby, mixing the rice and meat like a chef to create taste sensations that hinted of more pleasures to come. Khazanchi was on the other side, unperturbed by his wife's attentions towards Suhdev. Kota wondered where Suhdev's wife was.

'Banished or in self-exile with her parents,' Brahma explained. 'Having failed to give a son to her husband she is better off there, where she will not be subject to humiliating stares and whispers about her inadequacy.'

Kota did not like hearing that, and changed the subject. 'Don't expect me to ever feed you like that Fat Boy,' she told Brahma flirtatiously.

'You do not have to lift a finger,' Brahma responded. 'Just looking at you tonight is all the food that I need.'

Kota blushed. Tonight, his interest made her feel wanted and special and gave her confidence to face the oligarchs. She felt that she had power over Brahma and she liked the feeling. When it came to being possessive, maybe she was no different than Manjari. She smiled playfully at Brahma.

Meanwhile, the head chef came by inquiring whether the guests were satisfied with the meal. When he came to Kota he stopped and greeted her: 'My attendants tell me that you ate very lightly. Did you not like the food? The morel rice pilaf is my speciality.'

Kota hadn't eaten such opulent food at school or at the outpost and was amazed by all that was being served.

'I have to perform soon, so I will eat later,' she replied politely.

The chef smiled. 'Our food binds the Kashmiris to each other and to our land. The more one eats Kashmiri food the more I know they are true Kashmiris.'

The guests laughed at the chef's food-centric view of the world. Pleased to have a captive audience he continued: 'The lesser chefs over-spice the food so that it burns the palate. Only the master chefs are able to create taste through the explosive release of flavours; they understand the dying of cognition that triggers an awareness so acute that it settles the mind. As the taste of the spice lingers, the dying notes bring the awakened mind back to rest. It is there that one experiences sublime joy. That is why I am the royal chef.'

The crowd smiled appreciatively. He was right, there was none other like him and he was a star performer in his own right. The chef ordered the last dish to be brought in, *shufta*; small cubes of cooked cheese mixed with roasted nuts and raisins, a slightly sweet confection. It was served with salty, red tea boiled with milk, the perfect ending to a royal repast.

Fully replenished, the guests were now ready for the night's performance. After Suhdev was carried by his bearers through the sliding doors his distinguished guests filed into the adjoining *Natyamandapa,* a hall within the palace dedicated to dancing and theatrical entertainment. The seats were fitted with leather cushions, for the entertainment could stretch into the early hours of the morning. Many of the guests would often doze off for a while before waking up to partake in more of the entertainment. The Natyamandapa had been decorated even more imaginatively than the reception hall. There were carpets on the floor, the walls were painted with murals, the lamps were brighter near the stage and dimmer farther away, and the air was heady with incense to intoxicate all the senses. Kokur, as master of ceremonies, said a short prayer and announced that gifts, including black antelope skins, were to be presented to a select group of Brahmins who then gave their blessings. Musicians filed on to the back of the stage, carrying lutes, flutes, drums and the vina, a stringed instrument. There was the *hudduka*, the bagpipes, the conch and the cymbals, and finally the highly regarded santoor.

When Kokur escorted Kota to the centre of the stage there was complete silence as the nobility watched the stunning young woman being presented to the maharaja. She had changed her outfit and was wearing a diaphanous silk dress with ribbed folds. Her long hair had been drawn upwards from the sides and piled above the head in a double-looped, heart-shaped topknot. It was held in place by a narrow fillet headband while loose tresses with tightly twisted ends fell over her left shoulder. Her beautiful oval face and slightly raised cheekbones gave her the look of an aristocrat. Kokur had applied some make-up on Kota for the first time and her natural innocence was replaced with an alluring glamour. When Kota bowed towards the maharaja, her neck was as graceful as a swan's as she serenaded him with a verse:

> A wonder it is that being one
> You dwell in the hearts of three:
> In enemies, in scholars and in women,
> By your bravery, humility and grace
> You bring severally their suffering, their affection and their love[3]

Suhdev waived his hand indulgently. Dance was considered to be a more important offering than flowers or food and the Devi would be pleased with tonight's performance.

Kota moved to the front of the stage and introduced the theme of the recital: 'Tonight's production by the royal troupe is The Dance of the Honey Bee, befitting spring. The accompanying *Chakri* music will be to a fast beat.' As she exited the stage the curtains came down to reveal a group of beautiful ballet dancers.

Kota watched from backstage as four women stepped forward in turn to perform a dance indicative of their individual personality. The egotistical bee, who wiggled her legs with dazzling coordination, was all about her steadfast courage in battling a headwind and an encounter with a predatory bird. The second bee was duty personified as she danced with mechanical, technical precision with her nose to the ground making figures of eight until she slumped down, a spent force. We live to work and finally to die; we exist to do our dharma, her movements sang. The third bee was the young, rebellious one who did not want to dance in figures of eight and was not sterile, like all the other worker bees. Ideas that should have been exterminated had somehow stayed alive in her. The drones rushed in to control her, eventually stinging her into submission. She slowly expired, never quite knowing what was wrong and why she did not fit into the regimented society of the hive. The fourth bee was the clown; her short, loopy dance had everyone peering and scurrying around, uncertain of the direction to follow. What did it mean that the food was within us, she thought.

It was her time now, and on to the stage came Kota. With gestures that evoked nature, she conjured up the fragrance of the meadows and the colour of the blossom, illustrating the angle to the sun that her trajectory had taken. The audience saw her viewpoint as she came in for a graceful landing on the pistil of a flower. Kota's sinuous pelvic movements kept the audience in thrall as the drones swayed rhythmically in the background.

Suddenly, the wicked flowers invaded the stage. They were sensual dancers with undulating hips and taut breasts thrusting proudly towards the bees as if to say 'We are one'. Covered with fabric as soft as petals, each one carried a colourful scarf over their heads. It is not about work, it is not about food – it is about the pollination that connects us and the interdependence that keeps us both alive, the dharma of our beauty is to create desire; so come, let us pollinate and propagate.

Each flower trapped one bee and, holding each other with crossed hands, they moved in ever-decreasing circles. But as the bees sucked the nectar from the flowers, they fell down one by one. Kota saw the drones drawing closer, forming a circle around her. They sensed her irresistible power: they wanted to mate with her, they wanted to die for her, while the worker bees wanted to be her swarm and start a new life with her. The heavy smell of the incense, the gentle hum of the music, and Kota's hips thrusting in tune with the rhythmic movements of the Chakri dance moves was hypnotic and the audience was spellbound. The drones clasped Kota's slim waist, pressing against her back in a tight lover's embrace, and spun her round and round. A fire was raging within Kota; every nerve ending was screaming at her to let go. This was not the dignified performance that she and Kokur had rehearsed. Her breasts, full and ripe, were ready to burst out of her shimmering dress. She wanted to tear her clothes off and her lithe body wanted to dance free of all restraints. Each move spun sensuous curves that promised sweet pleasures as she clasped the drones with fierce fervour.

She was the honeybee yogini retaining the sweetness from each flower. Her body's heat ignited their libido and as each drone fell it was replaced by the next one, their last thoughts of love requited and nature's mission accomplished. When the last drone had mated and expired and she was free of the flower's bindings, Kota the Queen was anointed and ready for creation. The worker bees swarmed behind her, leaving the stage to start the cycle of life anew.

The background hum had transformed into the primordial sound of the universe, AUM, and enveloped the audience. At precisely the same instant midnight struck, ringing in the 4,000th New Year of the ancient Kashmiri calendar. All across the Valley, in over a thousand temples, bells began to peal joyously. The mountains echoed back their blessings. The audience hugged and embraced one another, wishing each other Navreh blessings. They started thumping the floor with all their might and the actors and actresses returned to the stage, their faces flushed and the heat radiating from their bodies towards the audience. They were showered with silver and gold coins. The wine, the food, the incense, the passion of the poets, the Chakri dance, and the frenzy of the musicians, which threatened to break the very strings not only of their instruments but also what bound the people to rationality and decorum, had had their desired effect. Kota had aroused a primal sensation of desire that the audience did not want, nor could let go of.

Kota saw Suhdev remove Manjari's hand from his thigh; stand up and, in an unprecedented act, walk up to the stage. He took off one of his own necklaces and placed it around her neck, letting his fingers linger on her nape before brazenly brushing her breast with his elbow. Kota quickly withdrew from the stage to escape the lascivious sovereign, but everyone in the audience had witnessed the king's move.

Kota was still breathing heavily from her energetic performance when Brahma and Saras joined her. As they walked over to her father together, Kota felt embarrassed about the daring entertainment she had been a part of.

'Papa,' she said shyly, 'Brahma has asked all of our cousins to come over and sleep at his home tonight. Can I please, please go with them? It has been eight years since I have seen them and I very much want to be with them tonight. May I please?'

Her father knew that his daughter's days as a young woman were rapidly approaching an end.

'Kota, you may go but Brahma, I do not want you and your *gagar* gang burning the house down. Be careful.'

Brahma bobbed his head energetically, knowing full well that sometimes things just happened when he and his cousins got together, but also realizing that Ramachandra meant every word that he said. Saras returned home leaving Kota to go with Brahma.

Brahma's friends had already gathered for the late-night revelry. He was the lucky one who did not have a father supervising, so his party was the one to get invited to. They were all young, and their very private party had got off to a good start with wine, and even opium, being passed around. It was spring and Kota was not surprised that many of the aristocrat girls were topless. Nudity was not a big thing, but what was surprising for her to see were the ancient artist designs and Gilgit hot pants that were the new fashion. Gilgit men were notorious for their drinking binges and illicitly seducing their daughters-in-law. They were gold panners adept at prospecting in the bed of the River Kishanganga. The Gilgit carried a hint of transgressive possibilities and the girls knew how to tease the minds of the young men. The young Kashmiri girls, with their long, strong white legs, swayed tipsily across the floor, laughing with each other and mischievously conversing with the men. Clearly, society's rules on the outside meant nothing to the decadent privileged!

Kota stopped herself from staring like a country bumpkin, and was reminded about something that was bothering her. She turned to the person who would always tell her the truth.

'Brahma, what is the connection between Suhdev and Manjari?'

Brahma observed Kota intently. 'Let us walk out in the garden where we have privacy.'

Kota followed Brahma and when they reached a secluded grove, Brahma whispered into her ear: 'Some people say that Manjari is half-sister to Suhdev.'

Kota was shocked at first and shook her head slowly. 'No, that cannot be true.'

Brahma continued. 'People say that that is the real reason why Ramachandra would not permit Suhdev to marry the young Manjari when he was besotted with her. It was the second time that your father thwarted Suhdev. Khazanchi married Manjari knowing full well that she was close to Suhdev, and perhaps because of it. Suhdev comes from very low stock and in spite of his pomp and show his actions are those reflective of a humble birth. He is always very insecure because of that.'

Kota grimaced. 'Why did Manjari hate me at first sight?'

'She has never forgiven your father for blocking her plans. Now you have emerged as a threat to her hold on the maharaja. By the way, who gave you the sapphire that you are wearing?'

Kota shared the story of her encounter with Rinchina.

Brahma reacted badly. 'Take it off! I do not want you to wear it. Do you know that wearing sapphire can be very bad for you, unless the jyotish has examined your horoscope? Nor do I want you to wear the necklace that that dotard Suhdev gave you.'

Kota was surprised at Brahma's reaction. 'Why?'

'They are trying to own you and they don't deserve you,' Brahma pleaded. 'Besides, you know I have developed feelings for you beyond those of a friend.'

'Brahma, I know how you feel, but it is all moving too fast,' Kota remonstrated. 'There is a part of me that is still a child. Give me some time to think it through.'

'Kota, thinking will tell you nothing, feeling each other will,' Brahma said forcefully.

'Hush with your double meanings,' begged Kota. 'The parrot in the tree will repeat everything you said in the morning and the world will spit shame at us both.'

Brahma moved closer to Kota and, holding her at the waist, gently but firmly pulled her inside the privacy of the grove. Kota did not and could not resist. That entire evening her body had been functioning outside of her mind. She found herself drawing closer to him, her breasts pressing hard against his chest. Their lips met, then their mouths, then their tongues. She tried hard to bring her mind back to dharma, but her rebellious mind kept telling her that the dharma of beauty was to create desire, that the dharma of desire was to procreate, and that the dharma of procreation was dharma itself. Her rampaging desire was uninhibited by dharma, and Brahma instinctively knew how to free her of all her inhibitions. Kota's feeble protest carried no meaning; she was as lost as everyone else in Suhdev's Kashmir. Brahma licked it all: the place of touch, the inner touch, and the erotic touch that felt as light as the touch of a butterfly. The wicked girls who danced with her would tease each other about who the master of *sparsh*, the art of touch, was. They would arch their eyebrows and sing in coded words, 'No insertion, only immersion; no perversion, only pervasion'. Soon Kota's exhalation merged with Brahma's inhalation and they were breathing in cadence. How much of her time at school had been spent thinking about him, imagining what he was up to, and weaving dreams of them together? Brahma was her true love and they would be soulmates forever. Their bodies were locked together, straining to fuse as one. Kota let out an involuntary cry. There was a faint humming sound in her ears and then she felt her body dissolve and her consciousness float away.

Wave 4
The Damaras

KOTA and Brahma spent more and more time together and for Kota it was a bliss that she had never experienced before. It also gave her a chance to observe Brahma more closely; orphaned at a young age, he had matured in some ways but in others was quite impetuous.

'Nobody has ever put any controls on Brahma, but he complements me because I am a homebody. We are going to be the happiest couple,' she declared to Saras. 'I will be the ideal wife for him. You and father will be part of it, because I will ask Brahma to move in with us. I don't want to stay at his place, where he used to hold all of his parties.' Saras would smile back, happy for her ward.

'How many children will you have?'

'Three at least. I want two boys and one girl. Daughters are better. They remember their mothers.'

'Will you send them to Sharadapeeth?'

'Of course, but I will want to tutor my daughter first. I want to teach her everything that I have learnt, so that she has a flying start. I want her to see the Kashmiri girls' wall of fame. To think that this young girl 'Buddh…' from the village of Sharada became queen and made her birthplace into a major city and centre of learning is inspiring for any woman. As for the boys, they will learn from their father. We will be the perfect couple, and the perfect parents.'

'Really?' queried Saras with a deadpan expression on her face.

'Yes!' Kota said with determination, and then stopped and started laughing hard. 'I now understand you. No, I would not want our sons to be like Brahma at school. He is not the best role model. I will start them at the nearby school at Ishber and then transfer them to Sharadapeeth where Guru Gotam will be their tutor. He was inspirational for me.'

'A perfect couple from two imperfect parts,' counselled a cautious Saras. 'So far, how well do you know Brahma? He did not have a father when he was growing up; he was rebellious when he was at school. He may not take well to a wife who tells him what to do. But he is very kind-hearted and loyal and certainly has the classic Kashmiri handsome looks.'

'I will make him perfect,' Kota said confidently. 'Just you wait and see. He told me that he would be like my earring, ready to dangle with every move I made.

'Love may be blind, but marriage needs the eyes to be wide open. Marry in haste and repent at leisure is an old proverb. Make sure that you get to know Brahma really well before you take the final step.'

Kota accepted Saras's admonishment to keep her in good humour. Once she was married, Saras would accept Brahma and everything would be fine. The young couple was inseparable, and soon Brahma announced to Kota that he was going to approach her father to seek her hand in marriage. The next morning, Kota was informed that Brahma had entered their home and had requested an audience with Ramachandra and herself. Kota's heart beat fast as she stood before him with her father as Brahma announced that he was there to propose marriage.

Kota's heart was bursting with happiness, until she saw the reaction on her father's face. It was as if a rock had been hurled at him. What was he thinking?

'I know that Kota likes you and I think of you as my own son but I cannot give approval for this marriage,' Ramachandra proclaimed.

Kota and Brahma froze; the possibility of a refusal had never entered their heads. Unaware of her Angaraka curse, Kota moved closer to Brahma holding his hand in hers.

'Uncle, why not?' Brahma pleaded. 'What is wrong with me, or this proposal? Kota and I would be very happy together.'

Ramachandra was firm. 'You are a bit immature, but that is part of your fun-loving charm. However, that is not the reason for my turning down your proposal. Marrying Kota would be the worst thing that could happen to you and her. My decision is final.'

'Are you saving Kota for a strategic alliance?' Brahma demanded. 'Perhaps marriage to Suhdev?'

'Suhdev did have the gall to approach me after the New Year's party but I snuffed that idea quickly,' Ramachandra explained. 'The man is impotent, physically and mentally.'

'Father, what is going on that I do not know about that lecherous Suhdev?' Kota asked angrily.

'What good would have been done by your knowing about Suhdev's interest in you? We nearly came to blows.'

'If not me and not Suhdev, then who?' Brahma asked pointedly. 'Are your plans to ship Kota out of Kashmir?'

Ramachandra was emphatic. 'Kota is Kashmiri and will not go anywhere. That is my promise.'

Brahma was not to be denied. 'Perhaps you are plotting a coup against Suhdev!' he cried. 'People say that you are holding out Kota as the trump card for the person who would be maharaja. Kota would become queen and you would be kingmaker.'

'You are questioning my integrity and duty of loyalty,' he said with pursed lips. 'I serve the maharaja for who he is and in spite of who he is. Whosoever Kota marries, only the stars will decide.'

Brahma pulled his hand away and turned to confront Kota. 'You have to decide, not your stars! Are you with me or with your father? He can't bear to lose you and obviously wants you to end up a spinster.'

'Father, you have been a bachelor for most of your life,' Kota stated. 'If I have found the person that I want to be with, what objection could you have?'

Ramachandra was cornered, but as a military man it did not mean that he would surrender. 'No, it is precisely because of my loss and the pain that I have lived with that I cannot approve your marriage.'

Brahma had always lacked patience. 'Enough of this. Kota make up your mind; are you with your father, or are you with me?'

Kota looked uncertainly at the two men. 'I don't know what to do or whom to turn to. I don't have my mother to tell me what to do. I am not going to choose between the two of you just as I am not going to choose between my two eyes. I need my father to say yes before I can say yes to you, Brahma.'

Brahma was unsatisfied. 'So the answer is no! It is the last time that either of you will ever see me in this house.'

He swung around and marched out of the front door.

Kota confronted her father. 'Why? Why not?' she pleaded.

'I will tell you when you are ready for it,' was all Ramachandra could say.

'Papa, I am not a young child anymore. I am a grown woman who has to have control of her own life.'

Ramachandra stayed silent and refused to respond.

Kota turned and ran after Brahma, shouting his name and imploring him to wait and not do anything impetuous. Brahma did not pay any heed to her and sped away. Soon he had disappeared into a crowd that was heading towards the cremation ground. A tempest was raging inside Kota's mind as she raced after him, reaching the cremation ground desperately out of breath and with her chest heaving. A large crowd had assembled and, not wanting to be noticed, Kota found a secluded spot in a grove of trees from where she could watch the proceedings unseen as she tried to spot Brahma. Small groups of men and women were seated quietly on the ground. Each group had a feudal head, the *Damara*, who was accompanied by his village people. It was almost as if a sheepdog had brought his flock of animals with him. The moon was bright, and Kota could see its reflection in the Vitasta. The temple was next to the riverbank, with steps down to the water where pilgrims performed ablutions for the departed accompanied by the family priests. Kota spotted Brahma standing back in the shadows. His face was red and, uncharacteristically, his grim jaw was set firmly. She wished she could reach out to him and pull him away from this dark cremation ground, but there was nothing she could do.

The jogi lived in the ancient Shiva Temple, which had always been used for cremations, and had become the most visible face of the tantric practices in the Valley. The assembled crowd of devotees believed wholly in his powers, bringing simple offerings with them. A bouquet of flowers, a pot of ghee and a bag of rice, fruits and other food baskets, all waited to be offered to the Devi.

A small group appeared from the banks of the river and Kota could see the jogi surrounded by a group of eight women. His sooty black dreadlocked hair was matted and hung down to his shoulders, and he wore only a g-string with a thin cloth flap that barely covered his private parts. His body was dripping wet as he sat down cross-legged on a large flat stone. The women stood around him and, after drying him, rubbed ashes all over his body. They were wearing tight waistcoats and lungis, a light cloth folded and then tucked into the front of the waistband so that the edge meandered in folds above the knees revealing bare legs. Kota had her first look of the striking jogi: he had no facial or body hair, had a sharp nose and jaw and wore earrings in both ears. He was short, and his body was boyishly thin, reflecting his abstemious lifestyle. His member was long and restless, swaying from side to side like an elephant's trunk under the loincloth. His fingers had long, untrimmed nails. His sacred thread was made out of human hair. He was adorned with bracelets on his upper arms, earrings, a necklace made out of human bone and a small sickle moon nestled in his hair. He opened his mouth and started drumming his cheeks with his fingers, making the sounds of Hu Duk. The crowd was enthralled. When he finally stopped and spoke, Kota understood his power. The jogi's inflection involved his whole body, the air rising up the windpipe from the abdomen and then like an accordion expanding in the space in front of him. The words came fast. His bony frame vibrated with the intensity of his speech. He talked about the Devi in the most intimate of terms.

'I am without inhibition,' he declared. 'I have conquered the fear of death. I have mastered the 112 secret techniques from the ancient *Vigyan Bhairava Tantra* that can grant any and all desires. Gautama practised just the first technique and it made him into the Buddha. I bow to Shiva who is the grantor of all. For you I will invite the Devi to temporarily reside within one of the yoginis. The Devi will answer any question and solve all problems. The Devi is angry and hungry because the people have forgotten her ways. Suhdev's punishment is around the corner and the decadent ruler will fall, but the Devi will be fed and propitiated and then she will give her powers and blessings to her clan.'

Kota recognized that the jogi had the audience in the palm of his hand. These were simple, impoverished farmers and herdsmen: their lives were subject to forces over which they had no control, no better than the animals that they raised. To exist they had to believe in something that would give them instant relief from their existential sufferings. Faith would carry them during good times, but now the times were threatening to turn bad and they needed a miracle.

'No one has the magical powers that I do,' the jogi concluded. 'I can fly, I can become invisible, I can see into the future. I can eat excrement and drink urine with the same pleasure as the best meat and wine. I can find buried treasures, exorcise spirits and cure seizures. All experiences are the same to me. I can solve all of your problems; grant you all your wishes.'

By now, the eight yoginis were sitting in a circle around him and had started to sing. The crowd sang along with them. Kota could see that one of the girls was different and realized it was the Georgian girl Tatiana, dressed in the simple Kashmiri clothing of a loose red lungi. The lead woman was dusky by Kashmiri standards and seemed to shake as she sang. Kota recognized her as Hanji a washerwoman who was often seen on the streets carrying laundry in a basket on the top of her head. The crowd understood that she was the chosen one and their song grew louder:

Now she's come, the Lion rider
Now she's come, the Lion rider
Now she's come, the Gracious One
Now she's come, the Gracious One

Get darshan now devotees
Now she's come, the Lion rider
Now she's come, the Lion-rider
Now she's come, the Lion-rider
Say: Jai! Victory to the true Mother[4]

The dusky woman was now in a complete trance and had begun to speak in a deep voice. One by one the devotees approached and asked her a question about an issue they were facing: health, crops, a neighbour's evil eye, a pregnant mother wanting a safe delivery, the failing rains. In each case, the yogini would recommend prayers at a certain shrine, a fast on a certain day or donations to the Mother Devi.

Kota recognized Kokur sitting with two other men. One was the barber, Naid, and the other was Manzim, the marriage broker. Naid stood up. 'I am an unmarried barber and the razor is my only companion. My non-existent livelihood depends on tonsuring young boys for their sacred thread ceremony but nobody cares any more about their religious obligations. Can the Devi grant my wish that I have a change, any change from this living hell?'

The yogini chastised him. 'All are born healthy but none die healthy. Let not your desperate desire lead you astray. Tonsure your own head first so that you are what you want the world to be.'

Naid sat down, nonplussed. Finally, after almost an hour, the jogi called an end and the yogini came out of her trance. The yoginis passed around small cakes as prasad and Kota wondered what was in it. The crowd began to thin, satisfied that their prayers had been answered and that they had not been subjected to the expensive demands of the temple priests. All that the village folk needed was hope and caring and they had been provided that and more.

Kota shivered slightly. Was it the chill or was it the cremation ground? The jogi was no different to Suhdev, manipulating people's emotions and playing with their minds. These were the have-nots – the people whose life had rejected from its favours. But what troubled Kota deeply was how wide a chasm there was between the palace and the public. While Suhdev was wastefully acquiring unique diamonds for the centrepiece of his diadem, his destitute people were clutching at straws. Suhdev was not acting as the mother and father of his people and his throne was resting on quicksand that could swallow him up. But Kota had her own pressing heartache that the jogi could not heal; she had to talk to Saras. Her head was throbbing as her attention was drawn back to the jogi.

The yoginis had made a small circle around the jogi and the fire, and for some reason Brahma had joined them and was seated in the centre. The flames were reaching for the skies, the logs growling with hunger, spitting and crackling. The jogi was repeating an invocation mantra, 'Agnivetala, Agnivetala, we celebrate the *Viramelapah,* the gathering of the *Vir* brave-hearts'. He had poured red wine into a skull that was strewn with flowers and was sitting in front of him, offering more prasad to Brahma. Kota could not understand why the yoginis had selected Brahma to join them. They began to dance in a ritual circle, moving three times right to left, slapping their left thighs, and then reversing their direction and slapping their right thighs, and then reversing direction again. Then they broke out into individual dance. One was leaping and gamboling, another was going through the various mudra hand gestures, and a third went up to the skull and drank wine copiously from it. A fourth had gone up to the fifth and had stripped her skirt off and was licking her anus crooning: 'Pichu, Pichu, Pichu.' The dusky woman's countenance had changed; she seemed ravenous from her dance exertions. As if she had made up her mind, she moved towards Brahma and grabbed his arm, leading him to the centre of the circle. The prasad must have affected Brahma's faculties: he followed passively as the jogi chanted:

> *Through the practices revealed to me, the liberation Guru, this assembly of yoginis is honoured. The yoginis have assembled into one circular gathering for the 'Great Yoga Celebration'. In their Tandav dance some are surging into the sky, while others remain on the earth. The Divine Power of all beings is experienced as the Auspicious One (Mangala) the Goddess who Presides over all.*[5]

With a swift move, the dusky woman removed her waistcoat and dropped her red lungi to reveal a firm body, glistening under the moon. On her back was a snake tattoo with alternate red and black rings stretching from the base of her spine and rising in a coiled pattern up to the very top of her head where it was lost in her hair. As she lay down gently on the earth, the yoginis seemed to know what to do. Taking the jogi's skull bowl, they poured water from it in a slow steady stream between her thighs. The jogi intoned slowly: 'You are the original male, the bestower of semen, place semen in me.'

Kota watched in horror as the yoginis held Brahma then, swiftly removing his clothes, laid him on the ground. 'No, Brahma. Stop, fight!' Kota screamed without a voice, but there was no resistance on his part. What alchemy was in the prasad he had eaten? Had he told the jogi about what had happened between them and Ramachandra? Just because he had experienced rejection from her father did not mean that she loved him any less. What did it say about him or his love for Kota? Brahma had no one to blame but himself for being in that place. Kota had no one to blame except herself for watching him.

To Kota's revulsion, the dusky yogini mounted Brahma and her face brought nearer to his. She kissed him on the mouth and Kota saw her transfer a piece of betel nut from her mouth to his. She slowly began to ride him; her breath long and deep as her body began to writhe, the snake undulating along its entire length. Brahma was energizing the yogini through her *Padma*, and then the yogini was lifting him, speaking softly: 'I draw nourishment from you like a lotus stalk from the lake. You are flying through the air. Higher and higher we go until the village, the city, the valley, the continent and the very earth has receded to a mere pinpoint.'

The yogini's rhythmic breathing became short and fast, the snake's movement hypnotic to the few viewers. She seemed transformed by the experience and gradually she slowed down.

'You are my darling and I am a thousand tongues licking you from inside, massaging every nerve ending in your body with my cool silver flame,' she whispered to him. 'My sweet nectar flows now. You are my *Vira*, my hero forever!'

The jogi walked over and, with a betel leaf, collected the pair's secretions. Kota was crying silently; she was nauseous and could have retched at any moment. Could Brahma not see the face of the yogini contorted into ugly intensity during her climax? Brahma was hers, how could he do this to her? Why was he not willing to be patient? Were all men like this, like animals on heat at the first woman who tempted them?

Kota backed out of her hiding place. Unnoticed she ran back home as if all of the ghouls were chasing her from the cremation ground. She fell into her bed, so distraught that she could not stop her teeth from chattering. When Saras heard the loud sobbing coming from Kota's room she found her heartbroken ward holding her face between her hands and crying.

'I was a fool. I meant nothing to Brahma. He seduced me and used me. When papa said he could not marry me he threw me away.' She choked for a few moments and then sobbed: 'I have lost everything. Every part of me is broken into a thousand pieces. Mother, what will become of me?'

Without saying a word, Saras forced a mixture of hot wine spiced with cinnamon into Kota's mouth. The herbal potion sedated her, and Kota drifted away from the cataclysmic end of her first love and into merciful unconsciousness.

Dvegrantha (Book II)
The Hostage

Wave 5
The Tourist

AFTER Brahma's act of debauchery, Kota sulked in silence, alternating between self-pity and repugnance for him. Her appetite had disappeared and she began to waste away. Saras attended to her while her father left her alone to avoid any outbursts. The hardest part for Kota was waking up in the morning when her first words were that she did not want to get up.

'Why did he do it to me? Did he ever love me? We had not broken off yet. Was this the way to leave me? Did the jogi put a spell on him?' Saras was also angry with Brahma, but showed him more understanding. 'This dog is not the Brahma we know. Let us wait and see. Someday you can confront him and then you will have your answer. If he exhibits shame, then you have hope.'

'I never want to see his face again. He has ruined my life. I thought that Brahma was special, pure and different. He turned out to be either a dirty cheat or stupid. You said that you could never trust men. I now understand; I hate them!'

It was the first time that Saras heard Kota use the word hate. Alarmed, she tried to mollify her ward.

'True, he was not faithful to you. But it is he who has to change, not you.'

'Even if I think I know a man inside out I will not trust him. This is the first and the last time that I will let a man hurt me,' announced a determined Kota with finality.

Kota was unexpectedly jolted out of her malaise by the sight of a flaming arrow shooting up in warning from the vicinity of the dranga guarding Varahamula. She, along with everyone else, nervously awaited the second arrow, but it never came. Instead of the usual all-clear signal there was only silence. Kota climbed up to the highest spot on the top of Gopadiri hill with her father to determine what they could see. A very alarmed Suhdev was already there with a small group. They could see all the carrion birds in the valley heading towards Varahamula as if they were welcoming a new visitor, who was seemingly reciprocating by throwing a giant feast in their honour. As if to guide the birds there was a pall of smoke rising from the vicinity of the dranga. The smell and stench had begun to permeate the valley air. Within a few hours the first of the refugees started to arrive. The column of people with barely the clothes on their back seemed unending. Stunned women, crying children, the old and the infirm in a state of shock, the men bitter and angry but afraid, they seemed like the shattered logs of wood that an angry Vitasta river occasionally tossed on its banks as it sped around its curves.

Commander Ramachandra's spies began reporting in; it was not unexpected, the signs had been there all along that Dulucha might attack. What was unexpected was the scale, the severity and the savagery of it all. Dulucha and his Turcoman troops had clearly been lying in wait across the mountain passes and had moved with the first sign of thaw, even before the traders. Their timing was such that they had not permitted the locals to even plant their spring crops – so that come autumn, there would be no food left in the Valley.

'The dranga has not just been captured, it has been annihilated,' one spy reported. 'The guards, even those who surrendered, have been brutally hacked to death and butchered.'

Kota's trauma at the horrific reports of the attack was the shock that transformed her into action. She forgot her own pain in the midst of the real suffering of everyone around her and became highly visible as she consoled the refugees. Reports said that the dranga had been put to fire; the wooden structures had reportedly gone up in flames like tinder. Its stone walls had crumbled in the fire and the red-hot stones trumpeted a message of crazed hatred. It was not an attack to conquer and subjugate, as the rest of the central kingdoms had seen: it was an attack to end Kashmiri civilization forever. Like locusts, once Dulucha's men had had their fill, they had destroyed the remaining foodgrains. It was not enough that they had access to food to continue on their murderous way; it was equally important to them that the locals died. This doomsday machine had set its sight on the Kashmiris, and nothing could stand in its way.

Confronted by unprecedented evil, Kota's assessment was that the Turcomans were determined that not just the humans, not just the livestock, not just the blades of grass, but that each and every stone would have to be rearranged and a fresh start made in the Valley.

Suhdev's cabinet was called to an emergency meeting. Rejecting court protocol, Ramachandra asked Kota to accompany him. When he arrived he found the ministers in a state of deep shock: Suhdev was so unstrung that when he spoke his teeth chattered. The reports were piling in of the numbers of the dead and the refugees streaming into the capital. There were also rumours circulating of the temples in Varahamula being desecrated, of the stone idols being taken out and shattered, stripped of their gold and jewellery by the howling mob of raiders. Kota corroborated the rumours based on what the refugees had told her.

'Ram, who is Dulucha? What do we know about the attackers?' Suhdev asked in a trembling voice.

'Dulucha is the leader of an army of 75,000 Turkic Mongol warriors,' Ramachandra explained. 'He has 60,000 horsemen; one hundred for each village in Kashmir. Their interests have converged with those of the Ghazis, the zealot warriors. It is this group that has attacked Kashmir.'

'Ramachandra, I command you,' said Suhdev, his speech halting and unsteady. 'Throw these barbarians out of our kingdom.'

'My Lord,' responded a composed Ramachandra, 'that is the worst thing that your majesty could ask for.'

'Explain yourself, sir,' said Suhdev, nearly overcome with tears.

'Militarily, the takeover of our dranga is nothing; psychologically it is everything,' said Ramachandra. 'Dulucha is using terror to provoke us, to draw us into battle. He knows that he has the advantage of surprise, the benefit of a well-armed and well-equipped fighting machine. This is a standard Turcoman tactic. By contrast, we are undermanned. We have our strengths, but we cannot take him head-on in battle. Defence is our strongest offence.'

The foreign minister interjected. 'What good is our military, sir, if it is not there when it is needed? Once again, we have been the victims of a surprise attack on the kingdom of Kashmir. Once again we suffer for our lack of alert generals.'

'The military is ready, but where was the intelligence alerting us to this attack?' Ramachandra retorted.' We anticipated an attack on Fort Loharkot, which is where Mahmud of Ghazni came twice. Nobody in the Foreign Office alerted us to the fact that Dulucha would come via Varahamula and catch our undermanned dranga by surprise. Thanks to the indentured labour that was introduced by this court, the peasants have now fled. The army is immobilized and we are now cornered into defensive positions within our forts.'

'What do we do now?' Suhdev asked bleakly. 'Wait until Dulucha decides to move upon us and destroy us?'

As if to answer his question, an attendant came into the court and whispered into the ear of the foreign minister. An emissary from Dulucha was demanding an audience with the maharaja.

The man, styling himself as an ambassador, was a military officer. He strode in, staring insolently at everyone, and leered at Kota. He was bestial in his appearance: he had a long beard, a straggly unwashed turban, baggy pajamas with an unkempt waistcoat, all covered with spots of blood and food stains that he had not cared to wash off. The menace of his curved scimitar was there for everybody to see. He spoke in the Turcoman language, so the Sogdian was brought in to translate. His brief was simple: Dulucha demanded unconditional surrender and ownership of everything – *zan*, *zamin* and *zenana*, the three 'z's, which stood for gold, land and women. He also laid claim to the tip of the small finger of the maharajah, which he wanted to add to his collection from the kings that he had defeated. The maharaja had one week in which to deliver his answer or else ... The emissary spun around like a scorpion and was gone, leaving Suhdev and his courtiers in a catatonic state of shock.

Ramachandra had observed the ambassador closely. He knew that the ruthless Turcoman invaders were a seasoned military machine honed over many fighting campaigns. They were killers, and their lack of respect for life and its virtues was the key to their success. Fuelled by religious fervour, they were sweeping across Asia and had been making increasing inroads into the subcontinent. Ghazni had repeatedly invaded India after failing in Kashmir, and had taken so much booty that he had become the envy of the Islamic world. Kashmir was the fabled treasure that no outsider had been able to conquer. Ramachandra had neither the money nor the manpower, and this battle was going to require all of his strategic skills. He may have been the underdog, but he had the home advantage, which counted for more than numerical superiority and military prowess. The Turcomans could count on a very stout fight; Kashmir would not yield easily.

'What will satisfy this Dulucha?' Suhdev asked frantically of no one in particular. The foreign minister, who sat closest, chose a direct approach.

'My Lord, the invader has obviously heard about Suryavansh. He recognizes that Suryavansh stands for everything, and it is Suryavansh that he lusts after. I am sure that if you gave up Suryavansh he could be made to leave the kingdom.'

'I will not give him Suryavansh!' Suhdev shouted petulantly. 'We will give him the monetary equivalent. Chief minister call a meeting of the council this evening and have all the Damara chiefs and the Brahmins come. We will speak to them and confront this invader together!' Gemstones had power: Suryavansh was going to deliver an heir to Suhdev and he was willing to sacrifice anything, but not his immortality.

Confronted with the maharaja's proposal to raise money by taxes that would in essence ransom Suryavansh, the Brahmins and the Damara chieftains rebelled, cursing Suhdev that his rule and lineage would end. The businessmen, led by Khazanchi, were plain-spoken in pointing out that they would prefer to run away with their money than hand it over to Dulucha.

The chief of the Damaras said, 'We came to find out what plans you have to protect us and our people'. 'At this crucial juncture you should be paying us to stand by your side, not the other way around.'

Kota could see that Suhdev had failed to rally his people: he was more concerned with protecting Suryavansh. The Damara chiefs filed out, the worst fears about their selfish King confirmed. A desperate Suhdev had said that he would even tax the Brahmins to raise money. He lost their support, and some of the more vocal ones could be heard cursing him: 'Rakshasa, you demon! On the pretext of protecting the country you have devoured Kashmir for nineteen years and even now when you face doom you cannot stop.'

It was now every man for himself: the divided kingdom had been overpowered even before the first battle was fought. Kota whispered to Ramachandra that he needed to take control and he asked for private counsel with Suhdev. Ramachandra was direct with the king: he was in imminent danger of being killed by his own people rather than the enemy. After the short meeting the men emerged and made a brief announcement to the waiting ministers. Ramachandra had been vested with martial powers and had been appointed to run the kingdom on the maharaja's behalf. Kota was appointed to take charge of the refugees and attend to their humanitarian needs. The maharaja would be unavailable: he would stay in the palace with the elite guard, and needed to prepare to fight the invaders if negotiations at the end of the week did not yield satisfactory results. What was most surprising was that Khazanchi and the ever-perfect Manjari had done a complete about-turn.

'Finally, the kingdom has the leadership that it needs and deserves,' they congratulated Ramachandra. 'I always liked you and have looked up to your father as the very epitome of nobility,' Manjari told Kota. 'We are in good hands now.' Kota's nostrils flared at the woman's hypocrisy; she wondered whether Manjari woke up in the morning in the same skin that she went to sleep in at night.

Ramachandra and Kota drew up a list of the protected forts that had been heavily fortified and provisioned. The poorest people, including the Dombas and other weaker sections of society, and the extended families of the army were all directed to go to the main Gagangir fort in Lar. Ramachandra sent a large group to Rinchina with a note thanking him for the revenue increases that he was generating and giving him instructions for the future. The friendlier Damaras were placed by Kota in faraway safe places. However, there were many Damara chiefs who stubbornly decided to fortify their village defences and fight it out, while others decided to flee to the inaccessible caves in the mountains. The capital saw a steady exodus of people who took only the scantiest of belongings with them. Ministers were also shipped out to the furthermost forts in inaccessible locations.

These were times for reconciliation, and Ramachandra asked that Brahma be sent for. They met privately, and it was the first time he had seen Kota since he was refused her hand in marriage. He could not look her in the eye. He had lost his mischievous smile, and seemed to have become more serious. There was a chill between them, but times were perilous and required the setting aside of personal differences.

'Brahma, my son, as you know we are facing a determined enemy,' Ramachandra said. 'Even the bear needs to hide from winter in a cave until the sun comes around. I need you to accompany the Sogdian and stay with him until this is over.'

'What does it involve?' asked Brahma.

'You will go and stay with Shah Mir in his village, that is all.'

'Then why do I need the Sogdian, and why does he need me?' asked Brahma, mystified.

'Brahma, there is no knowing what may happen now. Our best chances lie in all of us separating. The Sogdian will assist you. One real need is from Shah Mir. I do not want the Mussalmans in Dwarkasil village to feel that we are deserting them, but I cannot give them military protection. Brahma, while you are ever so quick to risk your life, you are not trained as a fighter. Your weakness is the Sogdian's strength, and he will guard you. I know that Kota and I will sleep better knowing that you two are together.'

'I would rather be here but I understand that the Mussalmans need to feel that we have not abandoned them,' Brahma said, still not quite understanding his mission. 'When do I leave?'

'The Sogdian has to pack a few belongings, and then you can go,' Ramachandra instructed. 'Do not tarry – the roads will become death traps. Start growing your beard and blend in with the Mussalmans in the village. And follow whatever advice the Sogdian offers you, he was once himself a Mussalman and can be trusted implicitly. Say goodbye to Kota and until we meet again, may the Devi protect you.'

Kota had been watching Brahma carefully. She accompanied him outside, but it was difficult to speak to him, especially since they had only met to part again.

Brahma spoke first. 'Irrespective of what has happened, and irrespective of what is happening, my feelings for you have not changed.'

A sea of contradictory emotions swept through Kota. It was the first time she had seen Brahma after the horrible night in the cremation ground. She wanted to hurt him as much as he had hurt her and she had a hard time restraining herself.

'Brahma, you may not have changed but I have,' she said with a clenched jaw. 'You need to know that I was at the jogi's *melan* the last time we were together.'

Brahma's face fell. 'It was a mistake. I was out of my mind and the prasad the jogi fed us was laced with datura.'

Kota's eyes flashed fire as she shouted in Brahma's face: 'Is that all you have to say for yourself. Do you know I have not been able to sleep or eat after that horrible experience? I used to look up to you so much. I would dream about our times together. I would crave for your company because you were one of the special few that I have in my life. But now I always see you with that witch and hovering over both of you, the jogi!'

Her wounding words satisfied her after all the injury that she had suffered.

Brahma backed off slightly. 'Kota, when your father turned me down, I had nothing to live for. I was mad and, in that state, did not care whom I hurt, even if it was my own self. Life mattered nothing without your love.'

'We may never see each other again,' he continued. 'One or both of us may not survive this attack. I take an oath by my late father's name that what I am telling you is the truth.'

Kota heard him and felt the sincerity of Brahma's words. A little calmer after her outburst, she considered that Brahma did love her after all, but like all men in matters of the heart he was weak and needed a strong woman to protect him and guide him. He could be forgiven for his first mistake. When she finally spoke Kota was gentler and optimistic. 'We will not only survive. We will win.'

'If we don't?' questioned Brahma.

'Then I am released from my obligation to my father, and you and I will be together eternally.' Kota embraced Brahma tightly; she ran her fingers through his long hair caressing it as if to memorize each strand. Brahma's body was rigid but slowly he let it relax.

'Never fail again or fall again,' Kota whispered. 'The jogi has his place but he is not the role model for society. Remember Devaswami's dictum that freedom is ours after we graduate but only to be exercised when moving into the householder phase. Goodbye Brahma, may the Devi protect you and our love.' As she turned away from Brahma to return to her father, he could not see Kota's quivering face.

'Can we prevail when every town and city is falling?' she asked her father.
Ramachandra's expression was grim and his jaw was resolute. 'I am not sure that we will prevail, but I am sure that we will never give in to his terror. Our history teaches us that if the maharaja spares the thunderbolt, the snake will rear its head. Based on his actions, Dulucha deserves no mercy or consideration.'

'He deserves death. I will go to the hills with Saras and collect my weapons,' Kota promised. 'We will start with a few spies of our own also and teach him a lesson.'

From the look that her father gave her Kota could gather that he had picked up the change inside her. It was the first time that she had experienced the hardening of the heart that precedes an act of predetermined cruelty. Brahma and she had ended in a good place. Her hate had morphed towards the foreign invader. Brahma deserved another chance but Dulucha deserved not a moment more of existence. Her feminine maternal instinct having been aroused by seeing the suffering of her people, Kota was willing to lay down her life and even attack it if needed. She left to find Saras, her trusted partner in her secret mission.

The deadline brought every activity in the Valley to a halt. The butterflies had fled, the leaves were still and the breeze was paralysed by an invisible force. Time had run out to meet Dulucha's demands and the unenviable task fell on the foreign minister. Ramachandra handed him a box containing Suryavansh, commandeered from Suhdev as ransom for the kingdom. Based on Kota's advice, Kokur went with him as his attendant. The two left with Dulucha's emissary, who had promised them safe passage. The public was told that Udyandev was leading the negotiations in order to build their confidence: there was no way that Dulucha could be given another negotiating advantage. Death has a smell all of its own. Kokur could see that the foreign minister, used to court life, had never been on a battlefield. As he approached Dulucha's camp he knew that this was different, that there was something horribly wrong with the people that he had to face. Stuck on pikes along the road were the heads of butchered cows; Kashmiris, whose hollowed faces seemed familiar; and even a few Turcoman soldiers who had been insubordinate. All of the horror stories of the middle kingdoms of India who had been conquered were now being repeated in Kashmir. The carrion birds were parked on their thrones of skulls, ripping out pieces of flesh and pecking into eye sockets. In death, the birds ruled over humans. The foreign minister was beginning to have real misgivings on their chances of success, and he shared his insecurities with Kokur, who was of little help.

They reached Varahamula, where Dulucha had made his base camp. The River Vitasta, swollen with the melting snow, lashed angrily at the banks with its waves. Logs that were carried by the swift currents crashed into the river bends sometimes with such force that they would crack and shatter loudly. The river had a blood-red colour from the hundreds of bodies that were floating silently, mute witness to the wholesale murder that was occurring on shore. The party had just reached the central tent, when the ambassador came out. Without saying a word he caught hold of the foreign minister by the scruff of his neck, and with his head pushed down to the ground dragged him in front of Dulucha and his court.

Kokur followed meekly. The short, squat Turcoman with a goatee and a weather-beaten, leathery face, appraised the foreign minister. Dulucha's nose was squashed, perhaps an early boxing accident; his cheeks were scarred, he saw the world through slit eyes and he had the pugnacious profile of a bulldog.

Staring down at the foreign minister, Dulucha spoke coldly and with great intimidation. 'What do you have for me?'

Straining at the collar, with his head turned upwards at an angle so that he could see Dulucha, the minister eagerly tried to present himself in the best manner possible. 'Everything, My Lord, everything that you wanted. I have brought you Suryavansh, which is everything and more.'   Dulucha took the box and opened it. His narrow eyes widened with pleasure when he saw the jewel nestled inside. But when he looked up he shook his head in disagreement. 'I do not see everything. Where

Is the treasury? Where are the people who are now my slaves? Where is the rat Suhdev's amputated fingertip?'

Gesturing to his ambassador with an expansive wave of his hand, Dulucha asked, 'Do you see everything?'

The ambassador grinned wolfishly. 'Absolutely not, My Lord. As the guests of the Valley, our hosts have insulted you.'

With great regret on his face, Dulucha pronounced his verdict.

'Foreign minister, your brief is over. You neither have the ears to correctly hear the message that we delivered nor the tongue to apologize for your failure to deliver our requirements.'

'My Lord, I am merely a messenger,' the minister croaked. 'Give me a chance to go back. I will make sure that everything else is delivered to your satisfaction.'

Dulucha spoke in a low, steely voice. 'In war, when there is a failure to communicate, very bad things can happen. There are no second chances in war. An example must be set to the Kashmiris that we mean what we say, and we say what we mean. Take care of him,' he said, waving the minister away.

Kokur watched in horror as Dulucha's guards pounced on the foreign minister, pouring boiling oil into his ears and mouth. As the dying wretch screamed, they solicitously inquired as to whether the wash was cleansing the passages. The screaming ended with a piteous whimper, and then mercifully the horror was over.

Dulucha turned to Kokur. With years of practice, Kokur fell face down on the floor and prostrated himself. 'Get up on your knees, you pervert! Don't show your ass to me,' Dulucha commanded. 'What is your name?'

Kokur nearly fainted, that damned question to which there was no answer, at least none that he could give Dulucha. He mumbled.

'Interpreter, did he say chicken, he could not have said cock?' demanded Dulucha. 'You do not even know how to say your own name. Maybe you meant hen. What should we do with you? Hang you by your balls or stuff my pubic hairs up your nose and suffocate you?'

Dulucha continued through the interpreter, his menace laced with poisonous charm. 'Tell me, where has that rat Suhdev holed himself up?' Kokur replied reluctantly. 'He is hiding in the palace and Commander Ramachandra and Kota are with him guarding the treasury.'

Dulucha examined Kokur alertly. What use could he be? Should he have him beheaded? No, he would have him lead his men to the target. Dulucha laughed. 'You worm. If you have lied, you will pay for it. Ambassador, take your men and bring back Suhdev's head. Also, bring me back Ramachandra's daughter who you saw in court and reported to be a prized mare. Breaking her will and then riding her bones with her neutered father as witness should provide good sport.'

Having spent a lifetime with the powerful, Kokur had learnt that the great acquirers of power were fundamentally unable to feel pleasure: the greater the acquisition, the less the satisfaction. With the powerful, the safest survival strategy was to be a shadow, as if one did not even exist in their world. Dulucha, having shared his thoughts out loud, ended the session by instructing his ambassador to not fail in his task and that he would see him again in a couple of days.

The return trip was a sombre one. Kokur was alone, surrounded by the platoon accompanying the ambassador. Nobody anticipated that the palace would offer anything more than light resistance, so it was just a question of time. Kokur wondered where everybody had scattered; where were his friends Manzim the marriage broker, where was Naid, the barber? What would happen to everybody once Dulucha took the kingdom? Clearly, there would be no future for him. He wondered if he would see the end of the day once Kota was brought back to Dulucha. It was the women and children that suffered the most when men went mad. Kokur silently prayed for her safe deliverance from the hell of Dulucha's cat-and-mouse game. Kokur was leading the platoon, and as they got closer to the palace nobody saw him take his actor's vanity mirror and reflect the shining sun three times at the palace. Inside, a waiting Kota picked up the signal and gave the command to prepare for the imminent attack.

When the Turcoman expedition approached the palace, the emissary arranged his men in battle formation of units of ten. The captain was the lead followed by two vanguards, then three middle guards and four rear guards. The units moved towards the palace, bloodied swords drawn and still hungry for more. They charged through the front doors of the palace, fully prepared for the guards within: they were met with nothing. Kokur watched as the swordsmen raced through the maze of the palace rooms, each man wanting to find the royal harem first, where presumably the maharaja was hiding. To the victor would go the spoils. Then the cries changed to expressions of frustration, and finally the sinking sensation as the party realized that the birds had flown the coop. Their anger rising at having been deprived of their prey, the party entered the kitchen quarters where they found a fully cooked meal. The residents must have been about to sit down and eat; they must have fled just a few steps in front of the advancing party. Somehow, they had received advance warning. In the confusion, Kokur managed to hide himself in one of the many rooms and then slip away.

Through a peephole in the secret passageway, Kota watched the ambassador sit down with his men to take stock and regroup. Her face was expressionless as she studied the ambassador, whose attack had not gone as planned. The swordsmen took advantage of the unexpected break to consume the abandoned meal – small consolation for their failed mission. While eating, the ambassador thought over what his next steps should be. How far could the royal family be? Where in the world could the treasury have been taken so quickly? The spies had all returned detailed reports; nothing had prepared them for this. The plan had to be revised, but his master Dulucha did not like being surprised.

Kota silently observed Dulucha's men taking generous helpings of the Kashmir black morel pilaf. It was understandable since it is one of the tastiest dishes in the world. The aromatic perfumed rice, the saffron colour and flavour, the slightly nutty notes of the Kashmiri morels with their delicious chewy texture, the lightest of light silver foil wafting in the slight breeze like a veil covering the beauty that lay behind it, all ensured that one could not eat enough. It had taken the meticulous eye of the *waza* chef to ensure that within the morels there was no diminishment of the gastronomic pleasure by cheaper sister mushrooms getting mixed in. Poisonous mushrooms were a time-honoured weapon in internecine royal politics, but the great wazas' code of conduct forbade them from adding a known poison into food. Kota had secured a martial command from Ramachandra to give clearance for the highly poisonous mushrooms that Kota and Saras had picked in the hills to be used. Dulucha had followed a scorched earth policy in seeking to destroy the food supply in Kashmir; Kota had returned the favour, but she had used temptation, not fear, to deliver the coup de grâce. The writhing, dying soldiers on the floor were her just revenge for the innocent women and children that had been violated. Kota felt no sense of guilt; this was justice and small recompense for the suffering the Turcomans had caused.

Kota and Ramachandra, along with a few trusted followers, left for the fortress of Lar. Kota would reward the waza and the helpers who had stayed behind to take care of the last supper. The secret passageway from the palace, through which Kota guided her father's party, had eluded Dulucha's spies. Her father was pleased that the death of his men in the dranga was avenged. This was just the opening round and the score between Ramachandra and Kota vs Dulucha was one all and round two was about to begin.

The good news was that they had received a report that far away from Srinagar, Suhdev had entered the safety of Kishtwar fort, his wife's ancestral home. It was inaccessible except by narrow, dangerous trails referred to as either *ajapatha* (goat tracks) or *sankupatha* (nail and spike tracks) and guaranteed his safe passage. Suhdev was welcomed warmly by his wife and father-in-law. His younger brother Udyandev had also camped with them, squashing any rumours that Suhdev's family had abandoned him.

When Dulucha heard the news about his ambassador, his anger knew no bounds, according to Kota and Ramachandra's spies. Kashmiri resistance to his forces was unforgivable, and he vowed that these rebels would be eradicated and exterminated: *I will turn Kashmir into a graveyard – the only thing that will grow when I am finished is the iris. Even the birds will be so traumatized that they will remain silent forever. Kota, you will experience such pain that with every breath you will beg to be put to death.*

The Kashmiris who had chosen to hide behind their village fortifications were wiped out; their belongings put to waste and their lands set on fire by the Turcomans.

'Slaughter the older people; keep the young ones for slaves. We will sell them in the markets of Turkistan and elsewhere. Massacre anyone who resists.'

There were so many dead Kashmiri bodies floating in the Vitasta that it overran its banks. Anyone who survived had their collar bones pierced and were strung together with a single strap of leather so tightly that they could not even turn their heads to look into each other's eyes. The Ghazis were even crueler, forcing their hapless victims to take off their sacred threads and repudiate their faith, making them repeat: 'I am not a Kashmiri Bhatta; I am not a Kashmiri Bhatta.' Then they would give him a choice: die as a Mussalman or as a Bhatta. Either way they would cut off the men's penises – a single step for the Bhatta, two steps for the instant convert who opted to be circumcised first. They would then stick the severed organs in the mouths of the Kashmiri womenfolk and use the sacred threads to strangle them. Others would be kept alive and starved for sport. They would then be offered urine to drink and leftover beef bones to gnaw at. In the darkness that had befallen the Valley, demons and ghouls now reigned. It was all spoils of war for Dulucha, for the Ghazis it was their chance to exercise their ordained licence to kill. From the boundaries of Kamaraj to the extreme end of Maraj, the destruction was complete and final: 1319 would prove to be the year of the apocalypse for the Kashmiris.

In all of the destruction, Kota had been praying for Brahma's welfare. It seemed that the fire that had burnt inside her because of the jogi's séance had only burnt the impurities away leaving her heart stronger and her love for Brahma even purer than before. Much later she learnt from him that only one village was saved, by the providence of Allah, and that Brahma had been given a warm, obsequious welcome by Shah Mir and his family.

'I am humbled by the honour you had given us. You are my treasured guest. Kashmir gave us sanctuary and I offer it to you in return,' Shah Mir had said while holding his right hand on his heart. 'You have my full protection, and as long as I am alive no harm will come to you under my roof.' Shah Mir had introduced Brahma to his two sons, Jamshed and Ali Sher, and to his three daughters and wife, who all wore the veil and were very shy.

A few weeks later, the Turcomans approached Dwarkasil. Shah Mir boldly went out to meet them. He bid salaam to the invaders and spoke to them in Turkish.

'Who lives in this village?' demanded the Turcoman general, sitting erect on his horse.

'All 500 or so of us are from Swadgabar, Malik, and of Turkish ancestry, like you,' said Shah Mir. 'My father's name was Tahir and my grandfather was the devout and religious Waqur Shah. We came here to build a life for ourselves seven years ago. Spare us, Malik, we have no quarrel with you. We are simple folk; as you can see from the village, we have little in the way of money or goods.'

The Turcoman was suspicious. 'Order everyone to come out of their homes and let me inspect them.'

Shah Mir did as he was ordered. All of the villagers emerged; the men in beards and skullcaps, the women in their chadors, proving the truth of Shah Mir's words.

Dulucha spotted a young girl with an uncovered face and questioned her, 'What is your name, child?'

'My name is Gulbehara, Huzoor. My parents call me Guhara,' the girl answered respectfully while pointing to Shah Mir.

'Rose of the spring! What a beautiful name, Guhara. You have the most striking green eyes. Now you must tell me the truth if you don't want any harm to come to your parents. Are there any strangers in the village here?'

'This is my own family, Huzoor,' said Guhara in a slow, sweet voice. 'I have three brothers and two younger sisters.' Guhara held Brahma Bhatt's hand tightly as she spoke. With his new beard and his long hair covered by a skullcap, Brahma stared at the Turcoman without fear. The Sogdian sat quietly along with the others in the background.

'You have a beautiful daughter,' the Turcoman said to Shah Mir. 'Is she a virgin or is she married?'

Sensing that he had passed the test, Shah Mir was all tact. 'Malik, my daughter is still a maiden. How I wish as I get older that her responsibility did not weigh on my shoulders!'

'We will come back again. Guhara, wear the veil and stay indoors with the other womenfolk, as befits a virtuous Mussalman girl. Keep everybody inside the village,' ordered the Turcoman. 'If anyone passes in or out, you will all be put to the sword.' Patting his horse, he licked his lips at Guhara and then signaled to his followers that it was time to move on. Shah Mir rushed to kiss the hem of the Turcoman general to thank him for sparing the village. Brahma could feel Guhara's hand clench tighter as the general stared at her. As soon as he left, it was time to return to the safety of Shah Mir's home.

Besides the carrion birds, two other things flourished in Dulucha's reign of terror. First were the merchants: Dulucha's huge army needed vast provisions and the camels groaned under the loads they carted across the mountains during the summer to support the invaders. Dulucha and his band had gained enormous gold and silver and there was wealth for all. Sometimes the Cathay merchants would make an offer for a comely Kashmiri and the Turcoman would have to decide whether to wait for a better price in Persia or back in Turkistan; some chose to take the cash now, and so the slave supply slowly started trickling out of the Valley. But the choicest captives were held back, and even after all the carnage, Dulucha still had 50,000 young men and women, the flower of the Valley, waiting to be transported over the mountains to one of the largest slave markets in the world.

The second thing that flourished was the grass. With none of the land being tilled, the grass had grown all spring and was soon higher than the tallest man. The wailing prisoners lamented that Dulucha had become the master of the turf; the grass seemed to be covering the shame that mother earth felt at the pillaging of this sacred land.

Inside the protected fort, Kota had organized community life with strict discipline so that the people would not give in to despair. There were morning prayers at the small temple, followed by rigorous yoga. Then there were the tasks that needed to be done by both men and women. The women worked on oiling the hemp ropes, assembling first aid kits and growing the herbs and vegetables. Then they taught the children, because education could not be interrupted. Afternoons were time for fun and play: games that had a strong history in Kashmir, such as chess and the cowrie shell game, were very popular. Kota organized contests in which both men and women played to forget their immediate problems. It was a distraction for her, but at night her dreams would revolve around Brahma. Would they make up, would life ever get back to normal for them? Sometimes she would panic; her mind would worry about his well-being and she would agonize about how he was.

At night the Kashmiris all gathered to sing songs, tell stories to their children from the *Katha Sarit Sagara* and recite prayers that would dispel fear. Simple marriages took place and all of the major festivals were celebrated. Kota was determined that irrespective of the circumstances, the social fabric of Kashmiri life would be maintained, and the spirits of the survivors would stay high. She was indefatigable, and her positive disposition lifted everyone's morale. Ramachandra had also arranged for the distribution of a daily dose of a saffron-laced drink: the spice had a mildly euphoric effect on the people. Kota had freed her father from worrying about the morale of the people, enabling him and his commanders to focus on preparing for battle.

It was in the midst of this that Yaniv approached Kota one day. He had taken sanctuary in the fortress and Kota was surprised to see that Tatiana accompanied him. Their story soon tumbled out: they had decided to get married.

'What faith do you belong to?' Kota asked Tatiana.

'I have no faith,' she replied bitterly. 'When I was a child I belonged to a Christian family, then one day two horsemen came and abducted me while I was playing. They took me to the town of Oswiecim and sold me. My new owners raised me in their household. They did not convert me, but I was too young to know my own faith and could only watch them. They then sold me to a Persian who in turn sold me to the fakir. His first words to me when he converted me to Islam by making me recite the *Kalima* were that he owned me, but that it meant nothing. Now I am in Kashmir, in the company of the jogi. Words like faith and hope have no meaning for me.'

Kota turned to Yaniv, 'What connection do you feel to Tatiana?'

'Princess, I came to Kashmir as a young man seeking my fortune,' Yaniv replied. 'I am from the family of Rashid-al-Din Hamadani, the eminent Persian Jewish physician, historian and statesman, who converted from Judaism to Islam so as to advance in court. I heard that he was beheaded in 1318 on false charges of trying to poison Oljietu. The crowd carried his head around for several days as a message to the Jews, who were forced to wear a distinctive mark on their foreheads. My family was so frightened they did not venture out for months. It was at that time that I decided that one could not live with this evil and that I would reside permanently in Kashmir, a beacon of tolerance and harmony. Princess, it is the shared horror of our experiences that brings Tatiana and me together. The world may end tomorrow for us with Dulucha waiting to attack, but whatever time remains for us we want to find happiness together.'

Kota nodded her head in sympathy and agreement.

'The most beautiful flower in the world is the lotus because it teaches us that sublime beauty can exist surrounded by mud. The Devi stands on the lotus flower and gives us hope in our darkest hour. Saras, bring my golden lotus brooch; Yaniv and Tatiana, please accept it as my wedding gift to you.'

Yaniv and Tatiana thanked Kota profusely for the unexpected gift and then left for a small ceremony, followed by a private celebration.

Never before had Kashmir experienced such ferocity; the historian Jonaraja wrote that the burnt land seemed to be as if before creation. Autumn had come, but there was no fruit because there were no trees, no crops because the land was not tilled. Stories were passed down about the existence of secret caves, with pigeons as watchful companions and where families brought goats and raised kids; the stalactites and stalagmites providing water and the occupants leading a life of primitive survival, hoping the threat would pass.

Dulucha launched expeditions into the mountains that occasionally captured a few Kashmiris who had ventured forth from their caves out of desperation. In many cases they would smoke them out by setting fire to the mouth of the cave. Piles of skeletons were later discovered in these caves, alongside telltale black marks at the entrance to the grottos. However, slaves had started dying of starvation, and even the army, fattened by over seven months of unmitigated plunder, was beginning to feel pinched for supplies and necessities. Dulucha knew that with winter approaching it was time to mount the final assault on Lar fort and beard Ramachandra in his own den. His military preparations were complete and it was time to strike.

To the sounds of trumpets and pipes, the Turcomans worked on bringing their arms and personnel forward to the base of the hill. The military camp was moved to the east of the hill on which Lar fort was perched, and the supply chain for the replenishment of the ammunition was established. The night before the battle, the Turcomans rested, preparing themselves for the day ahead.

Kota walked over to the innermost sanctum of the fort where the children had been sequestered. She found them very aware and afraid of the impending attack. They moved close to her, seeking protection and succour. She hugged them tightly, and in the faint light of the moon she could see on the young faces the struggle to understand why this was happening.

'Why does Dulucha do bad things? Did his mother and father not teach him the right things?' asked a girl.

'He believes his gain lies in hurting us,' answered Kota simply.

'You told us once that one has to love everybody, even those that do not agree with you.'

'Shiva teaches us that only love can change severely distorted people like Dulucha and help them learn but this love has to be given by someone more powerful than them. That is not us.'

'I am afraid to sleep because Dulucha will scare me in my dreams. Please spend the night with us tonight,' requested a young boy piteously.

Kota agreed, much to the joy of the children. They snuggled up to her on the bedding spread out on the floor, some resting their heads on her legs. Soon they were clamouring for a bedtime story. Kota was tired but she agreed.

'At school I had to study the *Panchatantra*, written by the Kashmiri Pandit Vishnu Sharma. He is the one who gave us the Kashmiri motto *Vasudhaiva Kutambakam*; my favourite story is of the hunter and the four friends.

'Once upon a time a great fear had spread through the forest. A vicious hunter had entered the jungle and he had been heard to say that he was going to capture every animal in the forest. The four friends: a deer, a crow, a tortoise and a rat were terrified, but they had to eat. One day, the hunter spotted the deer in a field and laid a trap. When the deer returned to feed, he was caught in the trap. His friends were distraught, but the tortoise calmed them down and said that they should join hands to save the deer. His plan was put to work; when the hunter returned to check on his trap the deer lay down as if it was dead. The crow started poking into its eyes the way crows do to dead animals. Then the tortoise crossed the path in front of the hunter. The hunter thought the deer to be dead so he turned his attention to follow and catch the tortoise for its succulent meat. Undetected, the rat cut the net that had trapped the deer with his sharp teeth. The crow started cawing and making a loud noise. The hunter saw the deer moving and ran back, but the deer was already free and bounded away. In the commotion the tortoise quietly disappeared in the bush. Thus, all the friends, by standing up for each other, defeated the hunter.'

The children were fast asleep, their peaceful breathing and warm bodies lulled Kota to sleep as the moon gazed upon them benevolently. Morning dawned. Inside the fort the warriors had spent a restless night, knowing full well what awaited them. Ramachandra and Kota assembled every man, woman and child and addressed them gently:

'Today we will win. We will win today just as Lohar fort withstood, not once but twice, against the pederast, that despicable slave of a slave, Mahmud of Ghazni. Our enemy is bereft of his senses; Dulucha has embraced violence as a way of life and become a messenger of death. His karma will catch up with him today. Howsoever dark it may seem, we will be victorious because of our superior intelligence and secret weapons, aided by the Devi.'

Kota spoke next, her voice firm and inspiring.

'You fight for your families, for your children. You fight for Sharada land. You fight to protect Devi Sharada's gifts to us. She is the Devi of a just war, just speech, just knowledge and wisdom. Hovering over the battlefield will be countless apsaras. Any warrior who falls will be approached by these cloud dancers and escorted directly to heaven. They will say: 'Great warrior, be my husband!' Now, let us pray together, 'and the gathered audience repeated after her:

'Jai Ganesh!'
'Jai Ganesh!'
'Jai Shiva!'
'Jai Shiva!'
'Jai Shakti!'
'Jai Shakti!'
'Forever Bhatta!'
'Forever Bhatta!'

The Kashmiris blew their large conch shells, which thundered their defiant message in unison across the fort to the Turcomans assembled below: the mountains echoed back the challenge.

Ramachandra and Kota were told that Dulucha had assembled his entire army of 75,000 men at the foot of the hill for the final assault, and had ridden through the ranks so that each soldier could be charged by his commander's presence.

'According to Islamic custom all soldiers will be given three days to pillage the fort, dividing the royal treasure stored there fairly between them,' his heralds announced. 'The first to scale Lar's walls will be given the added incentive of land grants and fiefdoms for themselves and their heirs. The slaves will be divided according to seniority up to a maximum of twenty per person. The fort, the buildings and the land will belong to Dulucha; the only other thing that Dulucha wants is the live capture of Ramachandra and his daughter Kota to complete his conquest of Kashmir.'

'The plan of attack is simple,' Dulucha announced to his cheering army. 'We have the numerical advantage over the idol worshippers: wave upon wave of attackers will assault the fort, eventually breaching it, and then the infidels will be overwhelmed. The attack will be initiated by the irregulars who will be followed by the Ghazi mercenaries and finally finished off by the Turcoman sipahis.'

Dulucha had clenched his fist and cracked a walnut that was inside. He slowly extracted the kernel and chewed it visibly for all to see.

'There is no God but Allah, and Mohammed, Peace be upon Him, is his Prophet.'

The assembled soldiers responded in kind, cheering: 'There is no God but Allah and Mohammed, Peace be upon Him, is his Prophet.'

When Dulucha gave the signal for his assembled formations to move forward, Ramachandra, watching from the ramparts thundered the code word *'Shivoham!'*

'Hari Om Shiva,' responded his warriors. Each of the assembled archers drew an arrow and pulled at his bow, one end of which had been implanted in a hole in the ramparts. The mighty bows strained and absorbed the stupendous tension, in some cases of up to 200 pounds, without curving. Next to each archer stood his wife, who held Agni to fire the arrow: inside each bow Shiva manifested himself as potential energy, and then transformed into his consort Shakti, whose

kinetic energy unleashed the flaming arrow. They flew so high that it seemed that they were headed to the sun – but it was an illusion. The blazing missiles, having left their conscience behind within the bow, saluted Surya and obtained his blessing for their dharmic duty, then turned downwards and sped towards their targets. In an instant, the theatre of war turned into mayhem as the attacker's tents caught fire; the horses started screaming and stampeding and the arms and armaments exploded into a prairie of burning grass.

'Shoot back at the infidels!' screamed Dulucha. The Turks were also equipped with burning arrows, and he certainly would repay the Kashmiris in kind.

'Sultan,' said his field commander, 'given the height of the fort, our bows are not in range. We must be within 1,200 yards of the fort to use our weapons.'

'Then march forward and grind them as you would ants!' Dulucha shouted.

The highly disciplined Turcoman force did not break stride and kept moving up the hill. Inside the fort, Kota watched the dark column move like a monstrous slug up the hillside. It was her first battle and she was scared. Her body was trembling although her spirit was strong. As they got closer, the moving attackers set aside their sword and shields and picked up their bows. The falling arrows were the trigger that turned fear into boiling anger. Kota, supported by the women, directed the replenishment of arrows and tasked the stronger ones to pair up and carry the injured warriors to a safe place where Saras and the Brahmin doctors could treat them. As secret painkillers alleviated their pain, the wounded Kashmiri warriors would not cry, even if in their death knell, because they did not want to trouble their compatriots.

The attackers' arrows were falling with increasing regularity inside the fortress. Ramachandra signalled to Kota, who cupped her mouth and screamed the next coded command: *'Bumro, Bumro!'* In the hands of a skilled archer, the longbow could fire up to ten arrows a minute when replenished quickly by a loving spouse. When a conventional arrow hit its target, the energy would generally dissipate itself within the tip. The Turcoman warriors were well protected in their leather jackets, and at worst the victim would get one small injury. But Bumro, the bumblebee, was a different strategy: these were half the size of a regular arrow and were poisoned darts. A thousand archers could fire ten arrows a minute each, and in a ten-minute period let fly 100,000 missiles that sped so fast that the attack was like a blur. The practised hands of each spouse would dip the arrow into the poison and hand it to the archer as if one person was orchestrating the shooting. The sun went dark and the hail of arrows turned the day into dusk.

The attackers tried to avoid the unending swarm, but the Bumro kept coming; stinging the face, the hands, the thighs, anywhere they could reach with their poisonous sting. It was lethal firepower that turned the slopes into a killing field in a matter of minutes. The irregulars were completely decimated; the Ghazis were writhing on the ground like dying porcupines covered with darts, and the sipahi column came to a shuddering halt. The Brahmins knew of the antidotes to the poisons of their day, but Dulucha had killed them all: the Turks had excelled at archery and to have these tiny arrows destroy them at their own game was too much to bear.

Dulucha charged his horse up the hill, screaming. With the flat of his sword he began to hit at the sipahis on the edge of the column.

'Fight or face the hellfire of *Jahanam*!' he cried.

They started again, this time pushing from the rear rather than pulling from the front: better to face death than retreat and run into Dulucha's wrath. The invaders drew closer to the ramparts and soon they were within a hundred yards and closing in on its walls. Within the fort the archers moved back and the Chandalas moved into a defensive position. The Chandalas performed all the thankless tasks for society. Ramachandra had sent the wealthiest in the Valley far away; alongside him he kept as many of the poor folk in the fort as he could – in a fight, they were the group that you wanted on your side. Cooped together in the ramparts they had bonded, tossing aside all social barriers.

The Chandalas took out their ancient weapons, simple but deadly slings armed with knife-sharp flint stones and rocks: the long siege had given them ample time to stockpile their arsenal. As the invaders advanced singly towards the ramparts, the Chandalas would target each invader. Their aim was unerring; the smooth motion of the pitch reflecting years of practice, the flints sliced through leather, skin, bones and the victim was generally incapacitated for life. The poor man's weapon, stone and sling, was deadly in short range.

Stepping over the dead bodies and shielding themselves against the stones, the column came ever closer to the fort and it was time for the trident spears to come into play. The weapon that the Damaras used to hunt boar was now turned on the attackers: thrown with great strength and propelled downward by the force of gravity, the tridents penetrated everything in their way and pinned their hapless victims to the ground. Kota went hoarse, cheering her troops, shouting to the women in the supply chain, directing them as to where the Kashmiri army needed replenishment.

The lead Turcoman reached the top of the rampart and faced Ramachandra. Wide-eyed, Kota watched her father grip his sword and then release it, picking up a mace that lay within reach.

'You are mine!' he shouted, and with a massive swing he shattered the Turcoman's head; the cracking sound ricocheted around the valley. An inadvertent cry escaped from Kota's open mouth. The severed, grotesquely mangled head started rolling down the hill with increasing momentum. Down and down it rolled, faster and faster until it came to a stop at Dulucha's feet, its frozen eyes staring reproachfully at Dulucha.

Dulucha's vanguard soldiers teetered on the hillside. The pressure from behind pushed them up and the rampart would have been breached at any moment by the sheer force of numbers. Kota could smell the filthy Turcomans, breathing heavily as they sought to grasp the prize that was so close. Then suddenly she heard a loud war cry, 'Ayo Botta!' and turned her head to see over a thousand men emerge from the nearby forest. As the Turcoman army swung awkwardly to face the new attack, their forward momentum was broken. Hand-to-hand fighting was the Ladakhi Botta's specialty; they were merciless, slaying everyone. The Turcomans broke rank and then fled downhill in the direction of their base camp, desperate to escape. The retreat turned into a stampede, the Ghazis and Turcomans clambering over the corpses of their comrades in an effort to get out of harm's way. More soldiers die in a retreat than in battle: this was no different. Kota had never seen anything like it. Dulucha's army was retreating and fleeing the enemy; his commanders directing their beaten soldiers to go back to base camp so that they would have time to regroup and come up with a new battle plan.

Ramachandra and Kota were giddy with joy. It was Rinchina and his men counter-attacking savagely and showing no mercy, slaying all stragglers and anyone who sought to put up a fight.

'Good man!' Ramachandra cried. 'Rinchina followed his instructions: in the last few years he has come along well managing the people whose charge I gave him. The day's battle is over.'

Kota and Ramachandra could see Rinchina waving the flag of Kashmir at the bottom of the hill. Kota picked up the flag in the fortress and waved it madly at Rinchina. The two flags fluttered proudly in the wind, the Kashmir troops blew their conches loudly and triumphantly and the mountains cheered right back. Kota impulsively borrowed a bow and arrow. On top of the rampart she plucked a flower, kissed it and pierced an arrow through it. Then she fired the arrow that landed at Rinchina's feet. He picked up the flower and pressed it to his lips. Overcome with relief and joy Kota asked her father, 'Are you happy that we admitted Rinchina into Kashmir?'

'Yes. He will prove to be a great ally of Kashmir.'

Kota smiled, feeling warmth spread inside her. She left her father to attend to the children, like a lioness returning to her cubs. They had all been hiding in the safety of the innermost rooms in the basement in the fortress. It was time to give them their freedom. Sadly some would emerge as orphans having lost their father or mother, or both, in the attack.

As night fell, Kota watched the Turcomans strengthening their defensive positions in their base camp. The late autumn air carried an ominous chill, as if to signal that after eight months the invaders had overstayed their welcome. Kota returned to her room and prayed to the Devi for deliverance for all. She performed the *Rudram Chamkam* mantra, the most potent mantra known to the Kashmiris. The little jade green figure of the Devi that she had received as a graduation gift was in front of her. After her prayer she felt strength and hope. There was a small chance that perhaps now they could win!

Inside Dulucha's tent a fierce discussion was going on as to the future course of action.

'Sultan, our normally obedient captains are themselves facing mutiny from their men,' Dulucha's key commander reported.

Dulucha screamed, his mouth foaming and spitting poison. 'Tell me who they are and I will ram my *kir* up their ass hole. Only then will the others learn their lesson.'

The key commander refused to be intimidated and he pushed forward.

'We had calculated that the fort would fall in a day or two and all of its supplies would be ours. It hasn't, and our army has run out of food supplies – the Valley is now merely a giant grass bowl. The caravans have stopped bringing in the provisions because winter has set in the high mountains. We cannot return and we cannot stay here because it can snow any day. We have to leave the Valley quickly with what emergency rations we have.'

Dulucha was forced to accept that the commander was being pragmatic. He put on his best face.

'We can return next year and finish the job that we began with these *Kuni*s; these fags will not be able to recover and offer us any resistance. We have the slaves and we have Suryavansh and enough booty to make it worthwhile.'

But the way out was an unknown. Dulucha ordered his men to bring the leader of the Kashmiri captives to him, a man who had been captured at the Bumzu cave temple. He seemed to have some stature in his community and Dulucha demanded to know whether there was a faster way out of the Valley. The man answered that there was a mountainous trail via Brinal, but the path was known only to one person, a mendicant named Ishaan. Dulucha did not know what to make of what seemed to be a young drug addict with long tresses and wearing a deerskin. His body was fair as camphor, and he had ashes smeared all over it and on his forehead. He had a trident in his hand that he used for walking. When asked whether he knew a path out of the Valley, he replied that the paths out of the Valley were numerous; when asked what the shortest path was, he grinned and pointed up. The Kashmiri leader interpreted that Ishaan was indicating that they should take a path up the hill through Devasar Pargana and go through Tarbala. Dulucha's commanders fiercely resisted following this unknown navigator, but when it was pointed out that the 50,000 Kashmiris captives would hardly gamble away their lives, they calmed down. Preparations started in earnest that very night and the next morning Dulucha and his Turcoman invaders started the march out of the Valley.

The long line of horses, slaves, carts full of treasure, Suhdev's prized elephants, the Ghazis and the Turkic warriors, slowly started wending their way out of the Valley, watched carefully by the circling vultures. It took two weeks of forced marching to get the troops to the pass, and the climb up the hill was steep and tiring. The Kashmiri slaves were made to carry the loot that the invaders had plundered in their eight months of terror. Dulucha was feeling better as they traversed the pass, knowing that once they crossed it they would be going downhill and then on to level ground. He was looking forward to leaving this accursed land: not for Dulucha were the charms of Kashmir – he longed for the steppes, where a man could ride his horse fleet as the wind. In Kashmir the horses would go lame traversing the hills, valleys and gullies. Nothing was straightforward here. By the same token the Kashmiris' steps became ever slower, as each one taking them away from their motherland forever. When they camped that night Dulucha could see them lighting a campfire and their leader laying simple offerings on the fire. The Kashmiris had assembled in large concentric circles, sitting closely together and quietly chanting:

I meditate upon Lord Shiva who is dear to Shakti
Who is Lord of the three worlds
Who is dear to his worshippers
Who removes all fear and hardship
Whose flag bears the mascot of a mighty bull
Who is known as Rudra
And is beyond the concept of time.

As their singing grew louder, Ishaan jumped up in front of the campfire, obviously intoxicated. He had a jug of wine and was drinking from it; obviously someone had managed to brew some new alcohol. One of the Kashmiris presented some of the new wine to Dulucha and his officers, explaining that it was a local custom to celebrate. It was strong and fruity and they asked for more. Ishaan put the jug aside and started dancing with his trident in one hand and a small drum in the other. He moved round and round with his left foot raised and his right foot planted firmly on the ground, his hands spread out maintaining a steady vertical balance. As Dulucha watched it seemed that Ishaan's body was starting to glow with a bluish grey colour. Then the long hair on his head came loose and began to stream behind him.

Something did not seem right to Dulucha; he stood up and started walking towards Ishaan, but it seemed that the closer he got to the dancing mendicant the farther he seemed to be. The night also seemed to have suddenly darkened. Then the wind began to pick up and the low whistle slowly began to turn into a howling sound, as the very world seemed to be coming to an end. The Kashmiris seemed to be oblivious to everything around them. They were holding one another's hands and calmly chanting '*Om Namah Shivaya, Om Namah Shivaya...*' Ishaan spun faster and faster and yet seemed to be so finely balanced that it appeared as though he might take off. A cosmic fire emanated from his radiant body; the long hair radiated like meteor tails across the sky, the drumming rattled faster and faster as if speeding up the universe. Dulucha was hypnotized by the sight and quickened his step, determined to get to the crack head *Mafangi*. The wind started blowing harder and then the snow started falling: it was Rudra, in the shape of an unprecedented early winter storm, the snowflakes falling gently at first and then heavier and heavier until the darkness of the blizzard was utterly blinding. Dulucha was almost upon Ishaan and he reached out to catch him, to make him stop, not knowing quite what was happening. Ishaan seemed to be a mirage, a spectre that was visible but not of this physical world.

As Dulucha moved even closer he felt his foot slip. Somehow in the darkness he had reached the edge of the cliff even though Ishaan was just ahead of him and seemingly standing on solid ground. Nobody heard his cry as he fell from the mountainside: his fall, head first, was peaceful. Only Suryavansh, which was strung around his neck, separated and fell alongside him; a hard diamond, the jewel landed on the granite rock and survived the fall without a scratch. With a gentle bounce Suryavansh rolled into a crevice. As for Dulucha, the man who had intended to turn Kashmir into a graveyard ended up being buried in it.

Kota was in deep sleep when the dream appeared. She tensed slightly but for the first time it was not the jogi she saw, but Ishaan, who had come once before to Sharadapeeth at the consecration of the shrine. He had caused a minor sensation with the monks running helter-skelter saying that Lord Shiva had come personally. In her dream Ishaan was telling her that he had toasted the first snowfall with *nava madya*, the new vintage wine, as per local Kashmiri custom. The wine had been offered to Dulucha, ignorance had been slain and everything was going to be all right. Now he had to head to Amarnath cave where his consort Devi Shakti awaited him, and he was missing her. He knew that his spouse had a soft spot for Kota, who was one of her loyal devotees and his intercession on Kota's behalf was by her express wish. Kota relaxed in her sleep; the figure of Ishaan faded away and instead was replaced by the sweet, ever-serene face of the Devi. Kota felt warmth entering her body seeking and healing the hurt of her heartbreak. Slowly the hate was cleansed away. A blissful relief from terror and fear flooded her and love and optimism sprouted again.

Wave 6
Close Encounters

KOTA walked through a section of Lar fort that she had never been to before: it was where Saras lived. She had received a message that Brahma was alive and her first reaction of joy that her prayers had been answered was followed by an uncertainty as to what to do next. She needed counsel and had informed Saras that she would come and visit. Saras was uncomfortable to show Kota her quarters, but the invitation was as much command as request and could not be refused. Her chamber was high up in a tower, and Kota was breathless when she entered the small room in the turret. It had a small hole, which served as a window to let air and light in. Since it was her first visit, Kota brought a small gift, a woolen shawl, which Saras would benefit from in the coming winter. She had also brought a few pomegranates that she had saved during the long siege. Saras was very precious to Kota, and she knew she had a passion for fruits. Kota let her eyes stray around the room and was surprised to find a monkey staring at her from the corner. There was also a bird in a cage, a bustard that watched Kota intently. Given their interest in Kota it was obvious that Saras had few visitors.

Saras had kept a samovar ready on a small charcoal fire and poured tea into two copper cups. The urn was bubbling with a hot nourishing drink made from a few tea leaves, cardamom, powdered almonds and some cinnamon, honey and saffron.

The women sipped the tea quietly, savouring the aroma and the lift that it provided.

'This is the first moment that I have had to think about myself,' Kota admitted 'and I feel that I need my mother to better understand what she may have expected of me and what would be right for me. You are my bridge to that understanding, Saras.'

'It is natural that you would seek her support,' Saras soothed. 'In some ways you are no different from an orphan, having lost your mother so young and your father being absent during your formative years. But you have to look to new relationships now, to new loved ones, because those will heal the injury that you suffered from losing your mother.'

'Saras, I have to confess that when it comes to injury I do not know whether I still love Brahma or whether I am past him. When my father sent him on his mission, I thought for sure that it was the last time we would see each other alive. If it had come to that I did not want us to think that we died hating each other. But a message has arrived that he is alive and well. When he returns what should I do?'

'What exactly happened that night? I saw you sobbing in bed and assumed that it was something terrible.'

Kota recounted the episode of the séance to Saras. At the end she spoke with her eyes closed and left out much of the detail, not able to bring herself to describe what had actually happened. Saras perceptively filled in the gaps as Kota sobbed through the end of the story. Saras calmed her down.

'The jogi was once a good man, but he has fallen off the razor's edge. He gained power through his meditations, but power for him became an end in itself rather than a means for goodness. What he did that night has been banned in Kashmir for the last 360 years. King Yasaskara branded Chakrabhanu, an ascetic, on his forehead with a dog symbol for leading a group to commit such a transgression. His uncle, Viranatha, took revenge by performing a ritual of chastisement that led to the king's death. Ever since then, kings have turned a blind eye to these practices. The jogi must have told Brahma that he would get rid of his love for you, but that he needed to undergo the rite with the yogini to do so. Secretly he must have planned to use Brahma to make inroads into the aristocracy – these yogis inject their body fluids one way or another into their victims to implant their seed. Once they take control, the person loses free will and becomes the jogi's agent, just like the yogini who reputedly had no control over her actions.'

Kota sobbed. 'Will I ever be able to love Brahma again? I know it all depends on him, but he has to convince me that being in love means constancy and fidelity through any and all adversity.'

Saras reassured Kota instead of searching for fault.

'He loves you but needs your strong hand to hold his reins so that he does not go astray. Come, let us eat now or else the food will get cold. We can continue talking.'

Saras had cooked a meal quite different from what Kota was used to. It started with dried apricots and goji berries, and then there was a shake made from roasted and ground apricot kernels, honey and fruit juice. Then came the real surprise: the entire meal was composed of edible flowers. The first course was squash blossoms with pumpkin flowers dipped in chilli batter and then fried. The second course was curried day lilies with water chestnuts. The last course was lotus roots in a creamy velvet sauce accompanied by dense, chewy maish krey. The sweetener was chilled apricot custard followed by candied apple and plum blossoms, which Saras had made in the fall and stored in an airtight container.

Kota had never eaten a meal like it. It was light with textures that she had never experienced and the flowers had a subtlety of taste and aroma that was exquisite. She felt the food giving her energy, the body gaining warmth without being overindulged, the organs more sensitive and the mind alert and in harmony.

'I now know the secret to your beauty!' Kota exclaimed. 'You have this secret diet that keeps you looking young and gives you the waist of a fifteen-year-old girl. Wherever I go, people stare at me, yet I never worry about growing old. Will they say, "There goes the old hag!" I want to be beautiful every day of my life and yet I want my beauty to be simply being me.'

Saras gave Kota an enigmatic smile. 'You will always be you, but start on the apricot kernel fruit shakes with pomegranate seeds. It will keep your skin baby-soft and the colour of saffron milk naturally for the rest of your life,' she promised Kota. 'Since you are not vain in your youth you will not be afraid of old age.'

Kota wrinkled her nose at Saras's observations. Saras must have seen some changes in her; she had begun enjoying looking her best and made sure she always presented herself attractively. Sometimes she wished she were thin like the harem girls, who would snigger and derisively refer to themselves as meatless bones filled with sinful marrow.

Kota changed the subject back to Brahma. 'What if Brahma was to think that all is forgiven and forgotten between us? What if he was to ask me to marry him on my return? I still don't understand Papa's rejection of his proposal.'

Saras was reluctant to comment, but Kota pressed her. She could not keep the secret from Kota any longer.

'Kota, do you remember the day that you graduated from Sharadapeeth?' Kota nodded in agreement.

'When Jyotish Pandit approached your father to speak to him you left them. I followed you, but not before I caught some of what Jyotish Pandit told your father.'

'What was it?'

Saras broke the news gently to Kota.

'He said that your stars predicted that you would be pre-eminent but they also showed that you were Angaraka.'

Kota felt her world die within her. Her face crumpled and tears coursed down her cheek.

'I carry a curse,' she sobbed. 'To think that Brahma could be dead because of me. To think that I wronged my father. What is left for me?' she wailed

Saras was serene. 'Hush, do you remember that you said you were not afraid of Dulucha because you would pray to the Devi for strength and victory. You also said that your prayers were answered and you believe that Ishaan appeared in a dream to tell you that. If the Devi could do that for you why would she not respond to your prayers for marriage, love and happiness?'

Kota was unconvinced and not willing to be consoled.

'Saras, I did not pray for myself but for the Kashmiri people. What should I do? I loved Brahma, then I hated him. We made up and now I want to hide from him. Here I am worrying about what to do when Brahma returns, when all along I have had no choice in the matter.'

Saras was stubborn.

'Well then, pray for Brahma to find his love and achieve your end that way. I will also give you a potion that you can give to Brahma so that he is rid of any influence that the jogi may have over him.'

The two women talked late into the night. Kota lightly touched upon Rinchina and how he had come through for the Kashmiris. That night when Kota went back to her room she pulled out her birch diary and started writing.

Dear Mother, I know that what I write in this diary you get to read what is in my heart and mind. I am ready for love, marriage and children, but today I learnt that my stars will that I am destined for nothing. I now understand the pain that my father has lived with all his life, first in losing you and then knowing that I am Angaraka. His love for me and his loyalty for you will never be equalled by anyone. I cannot, in fact I must not and will not, sacrifice my dreams even to the stars, but it is so hard. It seems that my stars are mocking me saying that whatever I love I cannot have. I cried all day today and turned to Saras for solace but mother even she was helpless. I will confess to you that I have experienced ecstasy with Brahma. I cannot imagine life with anyone else than him. Yet, if I cannot have him, I cannot also become Saras, a spinster for life. Mother, even though your presence is with me and you are my greatest inspiration, sometimes I wish I could curl up and rest my head in your lap and be without a care in the world knowing you are watching out for me. Love 𝒦

Meanwhile in Dwarkasil, Guhara was shrieking with delight as Brahma tossed a snowball at her. He caught her younger sister and squeezed snow down her back, sending the young girl into a delirium of laughter. Brahma had taken Shah Mir and his entire family out and was introducing them to the Kashmiri custom of celebrating the first snowfall of the season. Brahma had been accepted as a part of the family, and he had reciprocated by making himself useful wherever he could. Somehow the Sogdian had managed to procure a bottle of wine and Brahma had drunk from it gleefully to the utter embarrassment of the Mir family who were strict teetotallers. They had walked together to the nearby spring and the girls squealed when Brahma boisterously jumped in for a dip.

In spite of the early and unexpectedly heavy snowstorm that had fallen the previous night and had deposited over three feet of snow, the day had dawned bright and sunny. An early snowfall after two years of drought spelled joy to the Valley, presaging flowing rivers, refilled groundwater, a bumper paddy crop, abundance and prosperity. Dulucha's departure from the Valley followed by the snowfall was a good omen that the bad times had come to an end and life could grow again.

'You are drunk and *mot*, totally crazy,' Guhara said to Brahma. 'Who in the world would go and take a dip in the freezing spring, the day of the first snowfall?'

Brahma chuckled. 'Guhara, we celebrate our roots when we do that. More than 4,300 years ago King Nilanaga agreed to teach the Kashmiri Bhattas what rites to perform so that our people could stay all year around even during the bitter winter months. He had certain conditions, one of which was that we should pray to him when the first snow falls. All the Brahmins also get to drink the new wine on this day. As new immigrants, we honoured those who preceded us.'

Shah Mir's expression stiffened, and he questioned Brahma: 'Praying to Nagas, who were half-humans, half-serpents and lived underwater, hmm ... we don't have that in Islam. We don't have alcohol either. These primitive ways are those of backward people.'

'I will share the deeper yogic meaning of what snake worship means to Kashmiris someday,' Brahma countered. 'We worship our springs, because water is life.'

Guhara sensed that Brahma had become serious. 'Brahma, my father was only teasing you.'

Shah Mir's face had relaxed.

'Brahma, we are new to this land and we want to learn and honour its customs, history and people; my daughter is curious, and I meant no offence.'

'None taken, Shah Mir. I do not pick fights. Guhara saved my life, and you and your family have protected me – for that you have my eternal gratitude. But the time has now come for me to leave. I must find out how Kota and Ramachandra fared, and everybody else. Let us return to the house. I need to warm myself on a *kangri*, or else Guhara is right, I will freeze to death here.'

Guhara was silent on the way back. When they returned home, she went to make Brahma a hot cup of tea as Shah Mir left to arrange for horses for Brahma and the Sogdian. As she returned with the tea, Guhara asked pensively: 'Brahma, what will I do after you leave?' He understood what she meant. Her brothers would go to the Madrassa, a local school that had been recently opened in the village, but the girls were not allowed to go there; beyond a few household chores, there was very little to do. In the months that Brahma had spent in the house, he had been a window through which Guhara had seen a whole new world, and it was now closing on her.

'My father says that he wants to marry me to somebody back in Persia or Turkistan so that I can start a family,' she continued. 'He says that Kashmiri society is far too permissive. But I told him that if he feels that way, why did he come here? It is he who should go back. I do not want to leave Kashmir, Brahma. I have grown up here for the last seven years and this is my home.'

'Why don't you tell your father that you want to go to school?' he suggested.

Guhara sighed. 'The local school in the village is run by the elders, and the Mussalman custom is that it is only for boys. In any case they mostly study the Koran, and I want to learn to sing and draw.'

Brahma knew of Guhara's interest. She had a delightful voice that never failed to cast a spell on the listener. It was a mix of little girl and vixen with a slightly breathy overtone. But he also understood her father's fear: Guhara was maturing into a beauty, and so it was important that she be married quickly before she invited unwanted interest. Her enormous green eyes and long thin face gave her a haunting mysteriousness. Her lilting voice was intoxicating with just enough theatricality. She could be the object of male fantasies, not a welcome thought for a protective father.

'There are many fathers in the Valley who have the same needs for their daughters,' Brahma told her,' but they get private pandits who come home for them so that their education does not suffer.'

'Then that is what I will do. I will ask my father for a private pandit. Tell me Brahma, who is this Kota? When you spoke her name, I sensed you had feelings for her. Do you like her?'

Brahma was surprised at the question. 'Of course I like her,' he responded. 'She is very dear to me.'

'You have deep feelings about Kota. What is it about her that you like so much? After all Kashmir is full of women each more pleasing than the next one. What is her secret?'

Brahma was perplexed.

'Kota does not have any secret power. Her greatest quality is that she will sacrifice anything and everything for the people that she is loyal to.'

'What makes her like that?' wondered Guhara.

'I think she inherited many of her qualities from her mother. Her mother died giving birth to Kota's younger brother. Ramachandra was on the front line. Her mother made the decision on her own when the midwife told her that it was a choice between her and the newborn son.'

Guhara was persistent.

'Kota has not sacrificed anything for you but there is a special bond between you two. What is it Brahma?'

Brahma felt the intensity of Guhara's inquiry.

'When Kota was young she told me a story that perhaps explains it best. She said that every relationship was a triangle between two persons and the Devi. The best relationships were those where both parties steadily moved closer to the Devi and without realizing it moved closer to each other. When I am next to Kota I like myself better and I feel myself to be alive and energized by her. I think I have the same influence on her which is why we are the best of friends.'

'How about it if the triangle is the three of us?' Guhara asked cheekily. 'We each have so much in common. There is nobody that is perfect for you, Kota or me.'

'It is not about perfection. It is about connection. In any case I made a mistake once and I cannot ever permit a three-way human triangle to happen again.'

'You must love her deeply if you feel so strongly that you have regrets.'

'My feelings have proven to be an untamed horse perhaps best left rider less.'

'I am not sure about that. You are covering your feelings up. Don't give up. Don't you wish that you were Mussalman like us? Then you could marry her, and you can marry me also and I could be with you.'

Brahma shook his head.

'Guhara, there is no cover-up. I will always love Kota. However, Kota's father has rejected my proposal. Much as I find it impossible to understand, he must have a very good reason as to why I should not marry her. Nor can I marry you: it would violate the trust that your father placed in me when he took me inside your home and gave me protection.'

Guhara was not to be denied.

'Society is always in the way. I want to go to school, I want to lead a free life, and be able to sing and paint. I want to experience the free love that you have for Kota. I want her independence. What a precious thing!'

Brahma heaved a sigh.

'Guhara, our ways attract you and that is good. However, you have migrated here with your own culture; don't rip your family apart as you adapt to this land and benefit from its virtues. Give yourself and your family the time to assimilate – eating rich Kashmiri food too quickly will cause indigestion.'

Guhara was unwilling to give up.

'Will you introduce me to Kota someday so that I too can be her friend?'

Brahma agreed easily.

'Silly, she will be delighted to have you as a friend.'

After her uncharacteristic outburst, Guhara fell silent. Brahma sensed that the conversation had ended and he went out of the house. Shah Mir was most solicitous and his sons stood in the distance, respectfully watching Brahma prepare for his departure. It was time to bid goodbye and leave. Shah Mir hugged Brahma tightly and kissed him on both cheeks and the expression of affection brought a smile to Brahma's face. The Sogdian brought out their belongings, and with the horses loaded the two men headed back to Lar fort.

A few weeks later Kota heard a commotion at the gates. Against all odds, Brahma and the Sogdian had managed to work their way through the snow-covered roads to reach Fort Lar. On their way they had gone through a village that had been totally burnt down and come across a creature skulking in the shadows: it was Kokur, half dead from hunger and hiding in the village all alone. They had shared their provisions and revived him. The joy in the fort was unbounded: Brahma was everybody's darling, his spirit and ability to take risks energizing to all.

Kota ran to hug Brahma, tears of happiness in her eyes. Ramachandra followed close behind.

'Thank the Devi,' she cried. 'I used to pray every day for your welfare.

Not knowing was even worse than facing Dulucha.'

Brahma was taken to the private quarters; there was so much to share. He recounted his stay with Shah Mir and confirmed the man's loyalty and support for the local cause. He went to great lengths describing his conversation with Guhara as an illustration of how well the family was integrating with the Kashmiri ethos, but also mentioned the momentary episode where Shah Mir had revealed a disdain for the Kashmiri's history and religion. When he came to Guhara's suggestion that he marry her, he could see Kota choking back her laughter.

'I think Guhara has found the right answer for you and all the women who dote on you. Convert and become a Mussalman. You do look very handsome in your beard,' she deadpanned.

The only negative that Brahma mentioned was that the Sogdian seemed to be worried about the newcomers who had recently arrived in the village, especially the fakir who ran the charity kitchen in Malchmar. According to the Sogdian, while the fakir was no friend of the Turcomans he had been making highly inflammatory speeches against Suhdev and said the Mussalmans were losing their identity in Kashmir. The local Mussalmans had labelled the fakir as an extremist, but he was getting a small following among the youth. So far Shah Mir had been able to keep the fakir under control.

'Brahma, I can now tell you the real reason for my sending you to Shah Mir,' Ramachandra explained. 'In the trunks that the Sogdian took with him there was part of the royal treasure because Suhdev could not carry it all. Dulucha had his people searching all over, including the caves in the mountains. I wagered that the Turcomans would not hurt Shah Mir and his followers, and the gamble paid off.'

Kota and Brahma looked at Ramachandra in amazement. He had bluffed the Turcoman and run rings around him, with the loyal assistance of both the Sogdian and Brahma, and supported by Shah Mir and his family.

When Ramachandra left them, Brahma had a surprise for Kota. He took out a wrap and draped it over Kota's shoulder: she had never seen anything like it before. Unlike the simple *Uttariya* wraps this was made of shahtoosh wool and the master weaver had put the wefts pattern on the warp threads to create an autumn full moon against a black sky.

'There is a Persian weaver in Shah Mir's village and he has joined hands with a Kashmiri,' Brahma told her. 'Kota, you have to see how they use small sticks to insert the thread and make the most incredible patterns. This moon reminded me of Sharada, and I bought it as a present for you.'

Kota's heart melted. In the midst of all of the danger Brahma had been visiting the shawl maker watching it patiently being woven. The shahtoosh was so soft that it kept slipping through her fingers.

'Whenever I will wear it its warmth will remind me of you,' she promised.

Kota considered sharing with Brahma what she had learnt from Saras. But not tonight, it could wait just as her father had waited for the right time to share the secret of the treasure with them. Tonight she wanted to make up for the eternity that she had been separated from him. Kota pulled Brahma to her and they were in each other's arms.

'It has been too long. In a way the separation was good because it helped me do a lot of thinking. I was angry when you left but now I am at peace.'

Brahma, who had long dreamt of this reunion, embraced his desire. 'I still don't know what to do about rejection,' Brahma confided. 'It is not something that as a man I can come to terms with easily.'

Kota kissed him softly. 'Your marriage proposal was rejected, but not you. We women are used to marrying men that we do not love and love men that we cannot marry. Perhaps women can come to terms with the unfairness of life easier than men can. Maybe it comes from staying connected to one's self rather than to whom the world attaches you to.'

'When one stares at the future and sees only the unfairness of death each morning, the self also becomes more uncompromising with the world. After all, why live if not on your own terms?'

'Shush' said Kota, gently but hungrily running her fingernails down Brahma's chest. 'The world of fear has released us, so let us enter a shahtoosh world, soft and warm, tender and beautiful. Enjoy the moment for the present it gives you.'

Wave 7
The Peahen and the Serpent

KOTA was overjoyed when her brother Ravan came to Fort Lar through the melting snows to report that Sharadapeeth had been saved. None of the marauding bands had any knowledge of either the temple or the school and so both had escaped destruction; they were in a different valley and did not have any wealth or resources of the kind that the Turks were after. Ravan had been given an exemption from the school to ask on behalf of Devaswami if the Brahmins could be of service to the Valley in its hour of need. Kota hugged Ravan tightly. She observed interestedly that her brother was now in his early teens, an awkward time. His gangly body and pimpled face attested to his budding adolescence and his behaviour oscillated between a desire to please and a need to assert his adult individuality. Holding him tightly by his hand the way she used to when they were younger she took him to the kitchen to feed him the choice delicacies that he was fond of. With the weather improving, Ramachandra decided that he would take a small platoon to see what had happened to Dulucha's army. News had come in that they had all been wiped out in the terrible blizzard that had struck Devasar Pass. Accompanied by Kota, Brahma, Ravan and Yaniv the small group climbed up a trail that was still covered with snow in parts. It was a daunting expedition and the trees were mute warnings to not proceed further. Still heavy with fall leaves when the premature snowfall had struck, the branches were weighed down with snow. Mighty limbs had come crashing down, the trunks bearing fresh gashes. Arriving at the pass Kota saw a gruesome sight, black and blue bodies frozen in their last act as far as the eye could see. The Kashmiris were gathered in concentric circles holding the hands of those next to them. They had obviously been praying until their last breath froze. The Turcomans had run around vainly trying to escape but there was no avoiding the terrible wrath of Rudra in his form of a blizzard. Death had spared neither the Ghazis nor the innocent Kashmiris, but the Bhattas had faced Yama with full faith in Shiva and their faces were calm and in repose. In contrast, the scattered Turcomans had horror written on their faces, twisted in agony and fear. The sight of 120,000 men and women frozen to death was a horrendous spectacle that Kota would never forget. She recognized distant relatives and young cousins with whom she had played and studied, and for whom time was now still. Instead of weakening, her heart hardened and she walked purposefully through the corpses, righting them, trying to honour their memory in any and all ways. The group decided to immediately head to Sharadapeeth. Yaniv stayed behind with a few attendants to retrieve the personal belongings that could identify the corpses. He was interested in identifying Dulucha's remains, which could not be found with the others. Devaswami conducted a Maha Shraddha, a mass funeral rite of passage for all of the 50,000 Kashmiris who had died in Dulucha's invasion. Devaswami asked Kota to end the prayers with a short address. She was acutely aware of her audience, both visible and invisible, since it was believed that the dead people were still in the transitory phases awaiting the proper rites.

'Fifty thousand innocent Kashmiris achieved liberation at this spot,' she said, sobbing as she spoke. 'They invoked the Devi's wrath to enjoin Rudra to hurl destruction at the evil that was amidst them. Their great collective sacrifice to ensure that not one of the 70,000 Turcoman invaders escaped alive from Kashmir will forever be etched in our collective memory. I will never forget this sight before us where 120,000 beings lie dead. After today I will never be the same, but I will

120 THE LAST QUEEN OF KASHMIR

be the Kota whose voice will ring out the message for posterity that we will not be subjugated, nor do we fear death. The Virs will rejoin their ancestors whose names they have brought great glory to. *Jai* Shakti! *Amar* forever Bhatta!'

The priests ended the ceremony by sprinkling water on a few objects donated to the Brahmins, such as money, shoes, mirrors, knives, needles, threads, soap, dry fruits and a cane. Everyone stood up holding an oil lamp and prayed for the departed souls. Devaswami left to go back to the temple. Ramachandra, Kota, Ravan and their contingent returned home, rejoined by Yaniv. Despite the horrific tragedy, everyone's heart felt lighter now that they knew that these 50,000 souls would attain peace.

On his return, Ramachandra invited Shah Mir and Rinchina to Fort Lar to thank them for their support during the invasion and for their loyalty to the kingdom. Rinchina was accorded great accolades by everyone. Kota was the hostess and she had seated Rinchina on one side of her and Brahma on the other. Shah Mir was next to Brahma and then Commander Ramachandra. In Rinchina's honour, Kota wore the sapphire he had given her and to match it, a daring blue silk dress that hung very low on her hips, revealing her midriff and falling gracefully to the floor in pleated folds. She saw a smile of recognition in Rinchina's eyes on spotting the sapphire. She had worn a *channavira*, a cross-belt golden ornament that proudly jutted her prominent breasts inside a waistcoat that had a concentric conical ring design. Her boots, hidden underneath the long dress, gave her added height so that she was almost as tall as Rinchina, who could not keep his eyes off her all night long. Ramachandra presented Rinchina with a *zanjir* sword made out of wootz steel and with a beautiful chain damask pattern. There were many presents for Rinchina's followers. Kota gave Rinchina a small ivory box and when he opened it his smile widened with pleasure. She had given him an ornament: two crossing swords with a golden heart in between. He put the box to his lips and kissed it. Kota must have had too much wine before the meal because she gently brushed her foot against Rinchina. With a start, she realized that Brahma was watching her. Was he jealous? He had no reason to be. After all, Rinchina had been their saviour.

'This evening brings back memories of when my father would hold court,' he told Kota. 'If fate had not willed it otherwise I would have invited you to our kingdom and you would have seen the pomp and the glory. But now I, a Prince, live in a hut that does not befit even a pig farmer.'

'Nobility shines even more when it is not surrounded by false glitter,' Kota answered. 'The bards will sing of your heroic actions. We are indebted to you forever. Anytime you miss courtly life, you can come and visit us.'

Rinchina bowed his head at the open invitation but was firm about his aspirations.

'The time has come for me to reverse my fate. At some point the mulberry has to begin its journey to become silk.'

Shah Mir had come alone. In his stiffly starched clothes he was a formal, striking figure. Brahma was especially attentive to him, Ramachandra accorded him all honour and Kota gave him an array of gifts. Shah Mir was quite overcome and thanked everyone for their recognition of a humble immigrant. He was most lavish in praising Kota on her beauty, and she was reminded of the first time that she had seen him fawning over Suhdev. He made her uneasy, in spite of his charm and attention to her and cordiality to Brahma. Rinchina addressed the crowd, sharing in their tragic losses. Having lost everything, he had been given a new beginning: what was lost could be regained and he would show that he could become king of Ladakh. On hearing these words, Shah Mir rushed up to Rinchina and kissed his robe. Making a personal promise to Kota that he would return soon, Rinchina departed the fort receiving a hero's ovation from the people living there.

That night Saras came to Kota's room with a most odd request: Yaniv had asked for a private audience with Kota in her chamber. He had been extremely specific that nobody should know about it or could be present. The women discussed what could possibly be behind this bold and unprecedented request. Was Tatiana pregnant and in some trouble or did Yaniv want a pass to leave the kingdom? Having exhausted all the possibilities Kota overruled her natural instinct to be cautious, and gave permission for Yaniv to come and see her.

Yaniv entered Kota's chamber and made sure that he did not come too close to her, putting his fingers to his lips in a gesture of silence. Walking slowly to the middle of the room he placed a small box with a single lotus flower on the floor and then withdrew to the door. Kota looked at the box. It was obvious that it was for her but why was Yaniv behaving so strangely? She walked to the case, picked it up and opened it. Nestled in its silk throne lay a resplendent Suryavansh!

A thousand questions flooded Kota's mind. How had he found it? It must have been when they had left him to go to Sharadapeeth. Why had he not quietly decamped with the diamond that could buy a kingdom? Why had he offered it to Kota and not to Suhdev? What did he want in return that Kota had to offer? Perhaps Yaniv sensed her questions and, as quietly as he had come, he left the room leaving Kota with a secret and a heavy responsibility. But no answers.

It was only in the morning when Kota woke up and was discussing the previous night's celebrations that things became clearer. She said to Saras, 'It is the lotus flower that holds the key to the answer,' she said to Sarah. 'Remember the wedding gift that I had given to Yaniv and Tatiana, and what I had said to them about the Devi who stands on a lotus flower. Yaniv clearly accepted Shakti that day and become a Kashmiri, pure in thought and action.'

'Yes, I am inclined to agree with that,' Saras concurred. 'Yaniv's act is one of supreme loyalty to you and to Kashmir. However, Rinchina is not a supplicant any longer but instead feels secure enough to reveal his true character.'

'You are always suspicious. After all, he was merely voicing his longing for his own world where he was a prince.'

'Nostalgia is one thing; ambition to rule is another. He will bear watching.'

'In any case, you agree that Shah Mir was really spreading it thick on anyone he could lay his ghee on?'

'He reminds me of poppy seed smoke, sweet-tasting but in the long term, bad for your health.'

Kota burst out laughing. Saras could be harsh with her catty remarks but there was always a kernel of truth in her observations and, unfortunately in this case, it wasn't long before Saras was proved to be right.

Ramachandra had invited Shah Mir to move his family to the capital where his role could be expanded and he would be more in touch with court matters. It was decided that Shah Mir would start building a new home for himself in Srinagar, there being no available housing. Brahma and he jointly negotiated with an reputable builder a fair price for contracting the construction of a simple but comfortable three-storey home. Shah Mir's move was part of a broader confidence-building strategy to get the common Kashmiris to return. Kota, accompanied by Brahma, travelled to the outlying areas to reassure the public that Dulucha was finished, that the threat was behind them and that they should return to the capital city to rebuild a new life.

It was no small challenge that the Kashmiris faced when they came back down to the Valley from the mountains where they had fled to escape massacre: there was simply nothing left. No homes, no relatives, no food – and most importantly – no law and order. The Kashmiris emerged like mice, staring in bewilderment at the world that had come crashing down around them in the villages where the Damara feudal chiefs reorganized their defences and made themselves the masters of their principalities. Others began to prey on the weak: the Khasa hill tribes raided vulnerable residents, carrying them off as slaves and plundering whatever slim pickings were left, like jackals.

Ramachandra and Kota had been discussing what would be an appropriate response to the increasing lawlessness when they started receiving disconcerting and disturbing reports that Rinchina and his followers had stepped into the vacuum. They had begun to take increasing control of the villages around Gagangir, encountering little resistance from other Damara chiefs. The more aggressive they were, the more they were rewarded. Rumours began to circulate that Rinchina and his gang were also trafficking Kashmiri women to merchants from Cathay. It seemed that a newly manifested greed had made Rinchina rapacious in his attacks. The Kashmiris described Rinchina as the kite who was swooping on the unfortunate fledgling bird that had fallen from its nest. In this he was aided by the Ghakkar community, a despised group from Punjab, who served as middlemen in the export of slaves to the Central Asian markets where they were exchanged mainly for war horses. Rinchina's changed behaviour was perplexing. Ramachandra sent a stern message to him, demanding an explanation but alarmingly received no reply in return.

Matters came to a head when one fateful morning the watchman let a dishevelled, wounded soldier into the fort. He was one of Suhdev's personal guards and the attendants revived him with some hot spiced wine. When he came to his senses, he recounted the story of what had transpired with Suhdev during his stay in Kishtwar. The childless Suhdev had proposed that Udyandev, who was still single, marry and that Suhdev would adopt his brother's first son as the heir to the royal throne. But his younger brother had stubbornly refused the offer. Nobody knew of any vice that his brother had except that he was very religious minded; so there was no explaining his staying unmarried. Suhdev's sagging spirits had lifted when he heard of Dulucha's departure and demise. He had decided to return to the Valley at once, now that the snow had thawed and spring had arrived in her full glory. The Kashmiris had already celebrated Shiva Ratri, the wedding night of Lord Shiva, the most important festival in the Valley. Most of the survivors had also returned to the capital city or their villages, and it would be a good time to re-establish the old order.

Suhdev had departed for the capital during the lawless state that was prevailing in Kashmir. On the way they faced many desperate attempts by roving bands, and matters worsened when Suhdev and his party encountered Rinchina's followers as they were heading to the palace. The guard observed that Suhdev had always been impetuous by nature. He did not have the benefit of his advisers, and had left the fort with only a small contingent headed by one captain. Rinchina's followers, led by his lieutenant Valya, encountered the royal party and demanded to be paid money to grant the maharaja the right of way. The outraged Maharaja shouted at the rag-tag band of Bottas: 'Get out of *my* way. I will have you thrown out of the kingdom for your insolence. Captain, take them prisoner.' The captain and his small group advanced on the Bottas who prepared to counter-attack. The captain and his men skilfully fought a rearguard action, the sounds of their mortal cries intermixing with the thuds of swords landing on leather shields. Inspite of his soldier's best efforts Suhdev was badly injured in the battle. His captain died, along with his men, but they had bought valuable time for the maharaja to escape. A few guards managed to rush the mortally wounded maharaja into the Pramandala cave where they sought to protect him until reinforcements could arrive. However, Rinchina got to him first. Remarkably, the injured king shook off his fright and stood up to do battle with his new enemy. When Rinchina's sword pierced him, Suhdev's followers saw him die as a warrior king bravely fighting off a traitorous immigrant. His body was carried back to his family, who could barely hold Udyandev back and they wept over their erstwhile larger-than-life maharaja. Udyandev spoke with solemn determination to the gathered audience.

'By my brother's dead body, I swear that I will avenge him and recover his honour. His treacherous attackers will not evade me. I will be relentless, like Yama, and will not be denied. Suhdev, you protected Kashmir for nineteen years and four months, less five days. Rinchina will not live to see one sixth of that. '

Together, the family members took a blood oath of revenge against Rinchina. The guard had been tasked to return to court and inform Ramachandra and Kota about the tragic development.

Kota saw that the news of Suhdev's death and the instability that it created, were a blow to Ramachandra who immediately dispatched the Sogdian and Brahma to Kishtwar to offer condolences and succour to the royal family. Previously ignored rumours that Rinchina was stealing from his land taxes on behalf of the maharaja, and that he had indulged in trafficking Kashmiri slaves to Cathay merchants, reasserted themselves. Ramachandra knew that this situation had to be dealt with firmly: he sent a messenger to Rinchina, given the powers vested in him by Suhdev, ordering that he present himself at Fort Lar, or face his wrath.

Kota arranged a family dinner for her father and invited her brother to join them. Having both Ravan and Kota with him at the same time was a luxury that her father had not had for six years. The conversation revolved around family memories.

'I wish that your mother were alive, to see how our son and daughter have grown into fine adults,' Ramachandra said. 'Yet destiny had different plans; there is always something incomplete in everyone's lives. Does anyone truly find total happiness in life?'

'You miss mother every moment of your life,' Kota observed. 'What do you treasure most about her?'

For once her father made himself vulnerable to her and her brother.

'From the first moment we met, her mission in life was to please me. She would find virtue in every part of me. I would tell her that just her presence was sheer joy and that comfort was not a soldier's lot in life but she would not hear of it.'

Kota asked the question that had always been uppermost in her mind.

'What did she think of me?' quickly adding, 'and Ravan?'

'She adored you and would pray to the Devi that you be a leader of the Kashmiris. K for Kashmir and K for Kota meaning the chieftain or fortress. She only knew Ravan inside her and for him she would pray that he be the greatest devotee of Shiva but obedient to Ram. Of course she never lived to nurse Ravan.'

'What do you regret the most about mother?' Kota asked.

'Sometimes I wonder if duty to the kingdom made me blind to her and her needs. She was always there for me but I was not there for her when it mattered,' he said softly, before retiring for the night.

The next morning, Botta peddlers appeared at the fort's gates. The watchman was in a quandary: merchants and their caravans did not usually arrive before midday; having to travel from the camps they would have struck the night before. For the last few days there had been a steady group of Botta merchants who had arrived to sell fine cloth. Under normal circumstances he would have called the Sogdian and asked him what to do, but he had gone to Kishtwar. It was still too early for Ramachandra and his household to be awake. This watchman did not have a dog, so there was no one to give him a second opinion. The watchman was alert, however, and Ramachandra had rightly placed confidence in him. He quizzed the peddlers as to what they were selling. They answered that they had brought much-needed wood kindling and charcoal, opening several of their bags to show the watchman. Deciding that they spoke the truth, he opened the gates and let them in. As soon as they were inside, they set upon the watchman with ferocity. It was Rinchina and his followers who had hidden nearby, sending the peddlers ahead with their cargo to gain access to the fort.

Kota was in early morning prayer in the Thokur Koth, the meditation room, and Ravan was still sleeping when they were taken prisoner by Tukka and Valya. Grabbing the two, and with the advantage of surprise and treachery, they swooped into Ramachandra's quarters with wild, loud war cries. He had barely risen and was still unarmed when Rinchina and his followers stormed into his room.

'What are you doing here, unwanted and uninvited?' he challenged Rinchina.

Rinchina averted his face from Ramachandra's piercing eyes, hiding it behind his raised left hand as he silently plunged his sword into the commander's chest.

The brave man's last words hung in the air: 'O traitor, by your own hand you stab your name forever,' as the last great military defender of the magnificent civilization of Kashmir died. Kota fainted when she witnessed her father's assassination and it was several days before she regained consciousness under the skilful ministrations of Saras. She went into a state of deep trauma and refused to eat or drink or communicate with anybody. Having been imprisoned, Kota could only just see and hear the Bottas celebrating in the courtyard of the fort from her cell. Rinchina sat by the campfire with his lieutenants. Tukka was speaking; a rare thing for him to do but the battle had excited him.

'Rinchina, there was disorder after the great Chinese emperor Kublai Khan died. Your father's enemies, the Kalamanyas, took advantage and killed your father. You were doubly orphaned: you lost your father and your kingdom. If we had stayed where we were, we would have been sentenced to death – there was nowhere to retreat to, we had to move forward. Here the situation is the exact opposite.'

Valya expressed his misgivings.

'Tukka, the Kalamanyas had the benefit of numbers. We are just a small band of Bottas in this valley; we have no local support. And we gave our word when we sought sanctuary that we would be loyal to Ramachandra.'

Tukka was confident in his assessment.

'Valya, words are mere words – only worth the air that carries them. Winds of chance that had gone against us seem to now be turning in our favour. Life is precious and comes first. We must look out for ourselves. As far as local support is concerned, there is nothing to fear – Dulucha decimated the locals, we can blow them away like so much chaff.'

Rinchina grudgingly agreed with Tukka.

'Valya, we are doing nothing that we have not suffered ourselves. What does a hawk do when it sees a piece of meat but swoop on it? Do not forget that I am a prince, and the only mission of a prince is to rule and to expand his domain.'

From her cell window Kota watched them, as did the cowering Kashmiris: the Bottas were drunk and started singing songs. First, Valya stood up and pretended to be a Kashmiri warrior:

Guardians of the teachings of Kashmir:
Watch over me and direct my hero-song.
I am gYulag, the leader of the army.
Armies that come, I throw into the depths.
I am a hero who can grasp the Garuda bird!
You can chase away little dogs with stones,
But it won't work with the red tiger.

You can catch little birds with a sling,
But it won't work with the high-flying Garuda.
You can despise weak little princes,
But it won't work with the Maharaja of Kashmir.[6]

Tukka stood up next. There was a clay plate nearby and he stomped on it, reducing it to tiny shreds before scooping up the remains and throwing them into the fire, which crackled as the flames licked at the added fuel. Holding his fists up to the sky and in a loud oratorical voice, he sang the song of the defeat of the Kashmiri army:

> The red of Chinese coral and of rose-hips
> May seem Alike in being red;
> As time passes, they are unlike and separate.
> The yellow of gold and brass
> May seem Alike in being yellow;
> As time passes, they are unlike and separate.
> The army of Kashmir and that of white Gling
> May seem Alike in force and ability to win
> As time passes, they are unlike and very different.[7]

Finally, Rinchina stood up and, flushed with alcohol and victory, he sang of the omens of greatness that the shaman presaged in the *Gesar* epic:

> Behold! As a presage of greatness
> [The thread] falls first on the life-knot of the heavens
> You will have dominion like the blue sky covering all.
> The second falls on the life-knot of the earth.
> An omen that you will be established on a firm unshakeable foundation,
> An omen, that if you take the throne, you will occupy the leading place
> An omen, that you will be enthroned for the good of all beings.[8]

With power surging within him, Rinchina let out a war cry.

'The prince of Ladakh has unfurled his flag and planted it on the mountain peak of Kashmir: the turquoise fortress of Kashmir is mine, just as the epic *Gesar* predicted. I know that I am going to be a good ruler: my reign will be great and enduring. I have equalized my father's loss; I have re-established my father's name; I have laid the foundations of a new dynasty. This is only the beginning. The fierce Tibetan warriors combined with my Ladakhi fighters will be unbeatable. After the Great Khan, China is now complacent and weak, waiting to be conquered. I have scaled the mountain top and truly now the sky is the limit.'

His followers joined him in a circle and proceeded to do a Tibetan warrior dance until late into the night, filled with the delirium that attends ultimate success.

In her cell above the courtyard, Kota watched the proceedings with heart-rending sobs. Her father, the great general of Kashmir, had fallen at the hands of an opportunist to whom he had extended a hand of friendship. Fort Lar, which had not fallen to Ghazni or Dulucha's military prowess, had succumbed to treachery: the immigrant band who had only a few years before sought sanctuary and received mercy in Kashmir had now usurped the place of the man who had given them life and showed them only kindness. She took out her diary and wrote as the tears fell unabatedly.

Dear Mother,

The first man I loved; the stars have decreed that I cannot marry. The first man I extended a kind hand to has ended up taking Father's life. My judgement of Rinchina failed me catastrophically. He earned a place within our family and then betrayed it. I am now sustained by only one mission: whatever it takes, I take a vow that I will avenge Father's death, re-establish Father's name and win back the kingdom from these usurpers. I will use whatever weapons come to my hand, but I will not be denied. My stars had willed my life but now my dharma will lead the stars. Dulucha did not escape and neither will Rinchina. Let the world see the cruelty I am capable of when I lose my loved ones. I pray for my father's soul, the noble Kampanesa Ramachandra, I pray to the Devi to grant me Shakti and may my heart be glacial cold in seeking justice for treachery. Yours and Papa's loving daughter. ℵ

Wave 8
Bonhomie

KOTA was left undisturbed in her cell and Saras was allowed to minister to her needs, including slowly weaning her back to normalcy with food. Even Brahma, who had left the Sogdian behind and rushed back, was permitted free access to her. The Sogdian had joined Udyandev to seek allies and both had left for Kandahar, which had historically been under the suzerainty of Kashmir. Brahma told Kota that the Damaras were watching and waiting to see how events would turn out. There was a groundswell of sympathy and support for Kota after the murder of her father and everybody was waiting for her to give the signal through Brahma for an uprising.

Meanwhile, Kota received a report from Saras about an incident that surprised the public about the astuteness of Rinchina's mind. Two neighbours had taken their livestock to the grazing grounds in early spring. It so happened that two mares gave birth at the same time to colts of the same colour, but one of the two colts died. The survivor suckled from both the mares, and became attached to both of them. A dispute arose as to who owned the survivor. The word of the herdsmen was not accepted in this dispute, so they referred the matter to Rinchina. He ordered that the colt and the two mares be taken to a bridge and the colt be thrown into the water. Since animals are endowed with love and affection for their offspring, the colt's real mother threw herself into the water while the other paid no attention. Thus, the difficult dispute was solved.

Rinchina had appointed Tukka as his prime minister and commander-in-chief and gave Valya the job of treasurer. Valya immediately reversed the taxes that Suhdev had imposed on the Brahmins, which proved to be extremely popular and they likened it to the flood in their eyes being replaced by a drought. Rinchina established a dialogue with Brahma and tried to reassure him that he meant Kota no harm, but Brahma took scant comfort from his assurances. Rinchina also visited Ravan frequently in his cell. The young man was contemptuous of his father's murderer but Rinchina attempted to be kind, respectful and considerate, speaking loudly and emphatically knowing that Kota could hear through the wall that separated the two cells. She figured out that Ravan was merely a conduit and that the message was for her. With Kublai Khan's death, Kashmir was the perfect launching pad to carve out a larger empire and reclaim lucrative silk trade routes, he told Ravan. Rinchina sought to expand the empire – but he needed a trustworthy partner to run the kingdom while he was away. It would not help to further disturb matters in Kashmir, and it needed a strong hand: Tukka and Valya were foreigners in Kashmir and would not be suited for the job.

On one of his visits Rinchina presented a specific proposal that Kota could hear clearly.

'Ravan, as I travelled these last few days, I saw that the Valley needs to be stabilized – it cannot wait any longer. I come to you with an offer, which I hope reveals my good intentions and my desire to start a new beginning with you: Join me and I am prepared to put you in charge of Fort Lar.'

'Sir, you give me what is mine already and make a virtue out of it,' Ravan retorted.

'Then you agree that you are not the lesser for it. Instead of answering to Suhdev you will answer to me; objectively, you cannot say that it will be any worse.'

'Suhdev had his faults as a person, but as a maharaja he obtained his position legitimately. You, sir, will always be seen as a usurper.'

Unfazed, Rinchina advanced his move. 'Even admitting that I am a usurper it only means that I am all the more dependent on you – and from your point of view, what is so wrong with that?'

'Illegitimate power always ends badly. I have no wish to be part of a failed enterprise – I would rather bide my time and be on the right side.'

'What time you have is determined by me.'

'If you believe that, you don't need me. Are you the new Yama, Lord of Death, more powerful than Shiva?'

Rinchina then played his trump card. 'Ravan, I will do this for you. I plan to marry soon and when my son is born, I will place him in your custody to be raised.'

Kota's ears pricked up: it was news that Rinchina was planning to get married. Her curiosity was aroused as to who he had picked for his mate. She would have to ask Saras and Brahma to immediately find out who would be the new Maharani of Kashmir! She recognized that Rinchina was invoking an old tradition in Kashmir among noble families. In order to mitigate the risk of something happening to Rinchina while his son was a minor, Ravan would in effect rule the kingdom until the son was old enough to take over. Rinchina was intimating that minors very rarely inherited their kingdoms; their guardians were in effect the successors, first in line to the throne if anything happened to the ruler.

'Matters of state can be dealt with objectively, but you killed my father when he gave you sanctuary: at a personal level I am duty-bound to kill you,' said Ravan vehemently.

'Ravan, right now I hold the power of life and death over you. Think about it. You want to take revenge because I killed your father, what you fail to see is that I am giving you the gift of your life – not just for you but for Kashmir, so that its people may experience peace rather than continuing war.'

'What you call the gift of life is no gift! Peace without victory is no peace at all. You take my respect and honour in the same breath. How will I face my family, my community?' questioned Ravan.

Kota could hear Rinchina take in a deep breath and then speak carefully.

'Ravan, what you call murder – I call pre-emptive self-defence. Circumstances caused a clash between my people and Suhdev. Your father was a brave man and loyal; he would have killed me dispassionately in the cause of duty. We are warriors and rulers. We can agree to disagree, but look at the future, there is a lot at stake. If not for your own sake, then for the sake of the Kashmiris and your country let us agree to a path forward. I need you and you need me. With no agreement there will be anarchy in Kashmir – and whoever comes after you and me will make Dulucha look like an angel.'

Ravan spoke defiantly.

'Rinchina, if there is one thing that Dulucha should have taught you, it is that Kashmiris do not compromise on their core principles at any cost! Your way forward is simply base expediency, and for me that is the way backward. What you think is pragmatic – it is not acceptable to the son of Ramachandra. Anarchy or no anarchy, each and every Kashmiri will understand that.'

'Ravan, there is no hurry,' Rinchina replied. 'Think it over for the next few days. I want you to know that Khazanchi and his wife Manjari have come on board and will provide the money that I need. With time more people will fall in line. For those who don't, their future will be dim.'

Rinchina left but to Kota, whose ears were now pressed against the cell wall, it was clear that Rinchina had recognized that he needed help to stabilize his rule, and he needed it fast. The gambit with Ravan had failed for now but her brother was young and Kota wondered how long he would hold out. By the same token Ravan was merely a foil. She was the person for whom the message was meant. It was clear that either one had to join Rinchina or face death. She had to calculate and plan her next steps quickly. She called out to Saras to come and see her and briefed her on what she had heard.

'*Huli Jing* is the name that my mother used to give to fox spirits,' counselled the pragmatic Saras. 'The spirit enters into a young woman and she uses it to seduce men. She would tell me the story of Daji who married the Chinese tyrant Zhou Xin and ultimately led to his downfall. The lesson is that for women to conquer men they have to engage with their enemy. We are most powerful at close quarters. We are most lethal when we are most intimate. Locking up yourself will not get you anywhere.'

Kota had transitioned from the university to the fort and understood that the secrets of success differed from the world of books to the world of warfare. Now she was learning what it took to succeed in the world of the court. The scales were quickly dropping from her eyes.

'Kashmiri stories are also about the wily fox, but I never thought that they were addressed to the woman reader. Saras, are you telling me that I have to form a premeditated and deliberate plan that is based on deceit, intrigue and intimacy?'

'A woman needs both compassion and cunning to counter and conquer men. I never conquered my injury and thus remain a spinster, which as a princess cannot be your choice. With Dulucha you used poison but he was an outsider. The Devi shows the way – dharmic always yet sometimes seemingly diabolic. This has to be your secret weapon against Rinchina. Take it from my Chinese mother who had to live with an animal,' concluded Saras firmly.

It was at that moment that Brahma walked in and Kota shared her dilemma with him.

'On one hand, I ask what Sita would have done if her Ram had been killed and she was a prisoner of Dashanan Ravana? On the other hand, how can I live with myself?'

'There is no right answer,' Brahma replied. 'It comes from what will lead to the greater good. And that comes down to how important Kashmir is to you.'

Kota had ample time to think about Saras's and Brahma's advice. Rinchina had received an extravagant invitation from Shah Mir, who had offered to host him for a day. Rinchina was extolled as the ruler of the skies, and Shah Mir wanted to pay his humble tribute. His new home in Srinagar had recently been completed, and he had invited Rinchina to grace it with his presence and to join him in his favourite sport, falconry. Knowing that Shah Mir was close to Brahma, Rinchina welcomed his offer of hospitality. It was his first visit to the capital and he was struck by the contrasts: completely burnt out buildings stood alongside new homes still under construction. Merchants plied their trade from boats on the river, hurrying around the banks with vegetables, fruits and other daily necessities. A new Srinagar was rising from the ashes of the old, and Rinchina understood how important it was to be a part of it.

When Rinchina arrived at Shah Mir's residence, it stuck out like a rose among the thorns. Newly built, it combined the best traditions of the local Kashmiri artisans with the Persian style that the Mussalmans favoured. Shah Mir excitedly took Rinchina into his pride and joy, the hamam, where they could laze in the hot tub while servants scrubbed their skin until it glowed. After the journey on horseback, it was highly relaxing. They were then led to the outside garden, where they were served sherbet. Shah Mir was a devout Mussalman and did not drink alcohol; the sherbet was refreshing, cool and sweet, but left no aftertaste. Rinchina was cosmopolitan enough to recognize and respect his host's wishes. Then, after some snacks, Shah Mir took his guests out of town for sport, accompanied by his pet falcons and their handlers.

'Mubarak, Shaheen, Tufan,' Shah Mir cooed to his peregrine falcons. He had names for each one and was stimulating them to prepare them for the hunting. Two of his falcons were nearly white and one was jet black: they were rare and priceless, and Shah Mir's most valuable assets. One of his helpers brought out a pigeon tethered with a rope. As the frightened bird attempted to fly away, the handler swung it round and round with the rope, the falcons chasing the pigeon and making trial attacks. Once practice was over it was time to hunt.

Circling high over the valley the falcons spotted the *teetar*, the partridge, and the wily houbara bustards, and hunted them down. A houbara tried to hide on the ground, but the falcon cajoled and frightened it to take to the air; then the falcon came diving down with an immeasurably fast speed, the fastest speed of any living animal. The bustard did not stand a chance: the falcon broke its neck with one strike. When the bustard fell to the ground, Shah Mir's helper cut its throat in one swift motion – now the meat was halal. He gave its liver to the waiting falcon. Shah Mir turned excitedly to Rinchina.

'My Lord, the meat of the bustard is highly prized for its aphrodisiac properties. Tonight, we will feed first and then experience the pleasure of real men.'

'A beautiful young woman should be sufficient to arouse a man,' Rinchina laughed. 'What need is there for an aphrodisiac?'

'Spoken like a true man in the prime of his youth,' Shah Mir responded quickly, 'but for those of us who are getting on a bit in years our search for miracles is unending.'

Everybody laughed at Shah Mir's admission of vulnerability. Much older than Rinchina, he was deferential and pleasant, but in his hunting, he had revealed a side of himself as cruel and sexual. This was not the bravery of a warrior who faced his adversary, man or animal; it was that of a person who hunted through proxies while keeping his own hands clean.

There was a full day of hunting to occupy Rinchina and by evening the hunting bags were full; given the risk that the falcons would tire and get hurt, the party headed home for dinner. On the way, Shah Mir took Rinchina on a detour to the charity kitchen that he and his helpers had opened. Rinchina was surprised to see how many people had lined up for the free soup and food that was being provided: it was nothing fancy, but it was Shah Mir's way of showing Rinchina that while he may have been an immigrant he was a man of the people. The fakir, dressed in a coarse, black, woolen shirt, was in command and had trained his young assistants to respond to his every order. It was hard not to notice the fakir. His head was bald and his forehead was broad as if to store all of his religious knowledge. His face was pale white and his eyes were red. When he looked it was with his eyes downcast as if the light hurt his eyes. His beard was dyed yellow, as were his eyebrows and lashes. His speech was rough and guttural; the gruffness belied his charitable activity. On each of his forearms were three marks where he had gouged himself in an act of Sufi religious self-mortification. In contrast, next to him was one young boy who stood out with his comeliness and pleasing manners. Rinchina was struck by Shah Mir's ingratiating style, the older man showed the same respect to the down-and-out peasants who had come to the charity kitchen as he did when he welcomed Rinchina to his own home. His palpable bonhomie was highly infectious.

But an unpleasant incident embarrassed Shah Mir even more than Rinchina. An old Kashmiri woman recognized Rinchina and hobbled up to him, hissing:

'Murderer! You don't deserve to stay in Kashmir. Why don't you and your Botta peddlers go back to where you came from? Free Kota quickly. She only has to give the signal and all of you will die a swift death!'

The women's outburst triggered a burst of wild anger on the part of the fakir who felt that she had insulted their royal guest. He cursed the woman and asked his followers to throw her out and beat her up.

Shah Mir hastily intervened and spoke in a soothing voice.

'Mother, don't be so harsh. Rinchina defended the Kashmiris from the evil Dulucha. Nobody knows what happened in Fort Lar, and there are always two sides to every story. Rinchina has not harmed a hair on Kota's head.'

The other Kashmiris dragged the old woman away, but the episode left its mark on Rinchina. As they prepared to leave he announced that he was donating money from the treasury to expand the soup kitchen. Shah Mir was delighted that Rinchina was publicly willing to become a patron and support his effort.

Shah Mir's family had arranged a traditional dinner for their guests and had also invited a few respected Mussalman elders. All of the food was arranged in utensils that were covered by a long broad cloth, the *dastarkhwan*. When the guests were seated the dishes were uncovered with a grand flourish and the dastarkhwan went flying to be spread on the floor. First there was shurba, the meat soup. Then Razaq, the cook, came and served one meat dish after another. Shah Mir's household had a strong Persian and Turkish influence – his cook knew many exotic recipes and had pulled out all the stops. There were four different types of kebabs, and then there were seven lamb, game bird and fish courses. There was yoghurt set in an earthen bowl and walnut chutneys on the side. Each guest was served on their own individual Trami metal plate since Shah Mir had adapted the Mussalman custom for his Tibetan guests. Interestingly, when the Mussalman guests had eaten half of their plate they stopped and the platter was covered with spread cloth and handed to their assistants to take away. Rinchina observed this and asked as to why the Mussalmans had stopped eating.

'In our culture we eat and enjoy but in small quantity,' Shah Mir explained. 'The rest is sent to the womenfolk. Our women thus share equally and also get to know how their males were honoured by their husband's hosts.'

Rinchina laughed. 'I suppose we can eat the whole portion since we have no womenfolk at home to share with.'

'My Lord, when one has travelled a long distance in life, as I have, one finds that a companion can ease the journey,' Shah Mir said respectfully. 'Have you thought of taking a wife?'

'They say that single men want to get married and married men want to become single, Shah Mir, I have been a warrior so far and I have been only married to my sword.'

'My Lord, you are now ruler of Kashmir and it is not simply personal pleasure that should persuade you to marry but the needs of the state; you must have an heir – a son – for the kingdom to be stable and safe.'

'I only control Fort Lar – there are many forts in Kashmir held by those who oppose me. I have control of the treasury, but I do not have the Kashmiris with me. Ramachandra's death still rankles with them. They have reportedly sent their oath of loyalty secretly to Kota and she has links with them that I don't. But you are right: when I first came to Kashmir somebody else made the same point to me, so I guess I will have to ask some Damara chief to give me his daughter.'

Shah Mir's round eyes widened.

'My Lord, you are the ruler of Kashmir; you can do better than a Damara chief's daughter. They are all now your subjects, slaves to your bidding. You need somebody who can be an equal to your magnificent persona, somebody that the world will see as the very embodiment of beauty and virtue.'

Seeing that the flattery was having its effect, Shah Mir continued. 'What are your plans regarding Kota? You have imprisoned her and as you saw, she has become a martyr in the eyes of the people. It would be best to dispose her off in a human manner.'

Rinchina eyes widened, 'What do you have in mind?'

Ever obeisant, Shah Mir offered, 'I will be happy to help out and to take her as my wife. She will convert and move out of public life. At the appropriate time I will ship her out to Persia and sell her. She will fetch a good price. There will be peace in the Valley and you can rule without interference. In exchange, I will offer you my daughter Guhara in marriage and that will bond us forever.'

Rinchina was totally caught off-guard by Shah Mir's servility, which had masked a brazen plan. He had not anticipated that Shah Mir would switch sides so quickly but like Khazanchi and Manjari he was clearly tying his future with Rinchina. Shah Mir's narrowed eyes stared intently at Rinchina and for a moment Rinchina was reminded of a crocodile.

'It would not sit well with the Kashmiris to force Kota into a situation which is not voluntary,' Rinchina explained. 'Power in Kashmir now flows through Kota. This will take time to resolve.'

Shah Mir let his suggestion rest.

'My Lord, I am but your humble servant and your calculation on Kota is correct. My daughter Guhara will now be pleased to entertain you.'

Shah Mir clapped his hands and the evening's entertainment began. Shah Mir had instructed Guhara that she should sing for the royal guests and be at her best. He had opposed his daughter's interest in music considering it haram but now saw opportunity in it and was not averse to putting his daughter's talent to work.

Rinchina, resting on pillows piled on the carpet, could not believe the slim dazzling beauty that shimmered before them. Still in her teens, Guhara had matured into a fully developed woman; she wore a tight upper garment with long diaphanous sleeves and with narrow white pajamas underneath. Her refined face, with delicate features and dark eyebrows, served to showcase her striking green eyes and thick lashes that she had accentuated with black kohl; her jet-black hair hung loose over her left shoulder, but she had covered her head with a scarf which framed her face like a portrait. She had brushed her teeth with walnut bark that had left her lips with a pink glow. There was a sleek, suppleness to her movements like that of a cat. Compared to the voluptuous rosy-cheeked girls of Ladakh and Kashmir, she was exotic in her skinny sexuality. A santoor player and two other musicians accompanied her.

Guhara salaamed Rinchina shyly, and then after a few moments she started to sing a Qawali. She opened the evening with a tribute to the great Amir Khusro, who was born of a Turkish father as she was and whose poetry was the most popular in her times. The Qawali was an ecstatic form of repetitive singing that Khusro had pioneered and it had become wildly popular with the Sufis.

> Khusro!
> The river of love has a reverse flow
> One that avoids, drowns
> And one, who drowns, gets across.[9]

She then served up desire and total submission:

> You've taken away my looks, my identity, by just a glance.
> By making me drink the wine from the distillery of love
> You've intoxicated me, by just a glance;
> My fair, delicate wrists with green bangles on them
> Have been held tightly by you, with just a glance.
> I give my life to you, Oh my cloth-dyer,
> You've dyed me in yourself, by just a glance.
> I give my whole life to you, Oh Nijam
> You've made me your bride, by just a glance.[10]

Rinchina was mesmerized by Guhara. The first words were as if sung by a nightingale, tremulous but steady; then, gaining confidence, Guhara's voice and her subject matter became bolder by the hour. He could see that Tukka and Valya were in the same state, having never encountered anything quite like this before: it was not the stuff that warriors sang around the campfire. Guhara was singing to each one of them, filling the aching void in each man's heart. Even though women were considered the emotional sex, it was men who needed love. For hours the hypnotic singing continued relentlessly; it seemed as though while the men weakened with the passage of the night, Guhara became stronger, wringing out any and all feelings buried inside the deepest recesses of the men's hearts.

Give me yourself one hour:
I do not crave for any love,
or even thought, of me.
Come, as a Sultan may caress a slave
And then forget me forever, utterly[11]

The conversation's full implications now dawned on Rinchina. Shah Mir was hunting, Guhara was the falcon and they were the prey and with that, the invitation, the aphrodisiacs, the night's entertainment all fell into place. They were all foreigners in this land of Kashmir and each one of them, like creepers, was trying to cling to whatever provided security and strength at that moment. Rinchina smiled at Shah Mir with empathy for a fellow opportunist. Even though Shah Mir was nearly twice Kota's age it had not constrained his rapacious thinking. Yet, he had given Rinchina the germ of a plan. He unobtrusively pulled out the ornament that Kota had given him and looked at it. She was the reason he was admitted inside Kashmir. She had liked him and sent him the flower from the ramparts. She had gifted him the heart memento. How could events have gone so wrong between them? What was her relationship with Brahma? What was the way forward? Guhara intuited that Rinchina had not fallen, that her father's plan to entrap an alliance with Rinchina had failed and she sang her last song for the night.

> Farewell, it was not mine to fold you
> Against my heart for any length of days
> I had no loveliness, alas, to hold you
> No siren voice, no charm that lovers praise
> Yet I, even I, who am less than dust before you
> Less than the lowest lintel of your door
> Was given this breathless night, to adore you
> Fate, having granted this, can give no more.[12]

Then Guhara salaamed Rinchina, stood up and was gone, a vision of exquisite beauty, the slight sway to her hips bidding the men goodnight and sweet dreams.

The next morning Rinchina and his group left, after giving Shah Mir and his family valuable gifts. Shah Mir had placed his hand on his forehead and then on his heart and closed his eyes as if Rinchina's departure was more than he could bear. It was definitely a most successful trip. While an alliance had not been consummated, an understanding had been established. By the same token the incident with the old lady had made Rinchina realize that he had to come up with a gambit to resolve the stalemate between him and Kota.

At the same time as Rinchina was visiting Shah Mir, Brahma had come to visit Kota in her cell. Ramachandra's rejection of his marriage proposal was eating into him.

'Kota, it is not the best of circumstances, but I need to know whether you will ever make a commitment to me.'

Kota knew that she could not hold the truth back any longer and in a level voice she revealed her cursed handicap.

'Brahma, the reason my father did not give his permission to you is that I am Angaraka.'

She saw his shoulders sag and his speechless face sank. He did not need to be told more. She was taboo in the worst way. He now understood why she had been affectionate but had held back. Brahma struggled to absorb the news and yet maintain his hold on normality.

'Kota, why do you believe in that superstitious stuff? Don't let it ruin our lives?'

Kota was stubborn, 'Brahma, I cannot pick and choose based on convenience what we have been taught about our traditions. I do yoga every morning. I believe in reincarnation and astrology. You may laugh at it but I have to go with what I know today, true or false.'

Brahma knew Kota too well.

'These are your personal truths and I cannot make you deny them. In my heart you will always be my true love. I am prepared to die to marry you.'

'I have thought this longer than you have Brahma,' Kota explained. 'You will also always be my true love but I will not be the instrument of your death. Even if it was only by chance could I ever forgive myself? This is what my father was trying to prevent. Our true love should not lead to death but instead death should lead to our eternal love.'

'I cannot continue in this state of limbo,' Brahma said sadly. 'What is our future?'

Kota knew that this day would come, that she could not hold on to Brahma forever.

'My love carries a curse so I cannot follow what my heart desires,' she said tearfully. 'Stand by me as a friend. I need you more than ever. The Devi will not desert us and deprive us of happiness.'

As Kota embraced him lightly, Brahma could not bear it any more. He turned around and departed without saying another word. Kota paced her cell alone. This pain she could not share even with Saras. That night Kota wrote in her diary, sadly:

Dear Mother,

I did today what I think you would want me to do. I did today what Devaswami would want me to do. He taught me that dharma means to do what sustains eternally that which is measureable, namely existence? Do I feel doubt, anxiety and heartbreak at what happened between Brahma and me? Yes, but I am also beginning to get a sense that there is a purpose that I have to pursue and the first preparatory step in that pursuit is to be able to make a personal sacrifice. For me the most valuable possession I had was my love for Brahma and today I have sacrificed it on the altar of dharma. Mother, Saras says that I have to bring the foxy spirit inside me. Pray to the Devi that she be ever watchful that as Huli Jing enters me she may not completely take over dharma and that I may be strong in the mission ahead and ready to make any sacrifice.

Love 𝒦

On Rinchina's return he sent a message to Saras requesting her to tell her mistress Kota that he wanted to meet her. It would be their first meeting after her incarceration, and in his message, he referred to her as Kotarani, the queen of Kashmir. Saras responded that Kota would meet Rinchina in the afternoon. The sun was slanting through the narrow window when he walked in alone, carrying a simple gift of a basket of fresh fruit with him. When he entered, Kota had her back to him and she did not do him the courtesy of turning around. Rinchina chose not to acknowledge the insult.

'Kotarani,' he said. 'I know that we meet in the most unfortunate of circumstances, but I want you to know that we have more in common than you think. Today is the anniversary of the day that my father was killed. It has taken me a long time to come to terms with that, and I know that the injury that you have suffered is still fresh.'

Kota remained silent, so he continued. 'I have come to give you your freedom, and I am recognizing you as the maharani of Kashmir. I ask you if you will accept me as your commander-in-chief, your Kampanesa? If not, then I am ready to take my followers and go into exile.' Kota still did not respond, her back was motionless, she had accepted a gift from Rinchina before and she had lived to regret it, but Rinchina was not to be denied.

'Kotarani, sometime back an old Kashmiri woman accosted me and told me to my face that I am a murderer. I have learned that to rule one needs legitimacy and the love of one's subjects. I have neither in Kashmir: this is your land and nobody can take it away from you. If you will turn and face me, you will see that I am on my knees and ready to swear eternal fealty and loyalty to you.'

This time she responded, in a voice colder than the glacier on the Harmukh peak.

'You gave your oath to my father and then you murdered him, and now you plan to swear the same oath to me. How are you different from the Ghazi murderers who go around masquerading as holy warriors to cover their plunder and destruction?'

'Kotarani, I am different in one key way. I believe in justice. As the prince of Ladakh I dispensed it, and I am equally willing to submit to it. We Bottas owe a lot to Kashmir as the beacon of knowledge and spirituality; I do not want to go down in history as the person who was responsible for the destruction of Kashmir. If you judge fairly that I must die for the death of your father, I am willing to submit to your decision. I have not reached this conclusion lightly and will not fight it.'

Kota turned slowly to face Rinchina and confronted him with her fearless eyes flashing lightning. She had grown since he had seen her last at the celebration; her face had the firmness that comes from strength of character. Rinchina dropped himself, prostrating to the natural-born maharani of Kashmir and showed that Kota was one woman he would always look up to. She could not be won through fear: no force on earth would have made her submit. She was not a woman that one could deceive; her intelligence was far too great for that.

When she spoke, her voice was the icy wind blowing through Shur Ji La.

'From that window I watched you dance around the campfire celebrating my father's death, my father who gave you sanctuary. First, go pray to the Devi, then you and I will talk. You need forgiveness from the Devi, not justice from me, least of all the hollow title of Kampanesa. One does not give the jackal the job of guarding the chicken coop.'

'I hear you and obey, Rani.' Rinchina turned around and went straight to the courtyard where his horse was waiting, and then with a few of his followers he left for the Buddhist monastery overlooking the Valley. Was it his imagination that Kota was watching him from the window as the horses descended the trail? Rinchina's father had once told him that appeasement was the key to sex and politics: the same word was used for talking around an offended woman and conciliating a nervous political enemy. Rinchina was under no illusion that the seat of the ruler of Kashmir was merely rented to him – at any moment it would be pulled away from him by Kota. He could not return to Ladakh if Kashmir became inhospitable. China was already closed and there would be nowhere to turn to. Kota may have been imprisoned but she had boxed him in. As Ravan had said he had to return back to Kota what was hers, the kingdom and its treasure and hopefully only then could he get what he wanted: to be king.

Rinchina rode to the famous Buddhist monastery in Srinagar on Gopadiri Hill. It was built on the crest that joins the peak to the massif that rises above Srinagar towards the east. The location would catch the first rays of the rising sun. Here in the monastery was a miraculous tooth of the Buddha; even the Chinese pilgrim Hiuen Tsang had commented on it. There had once been over 700 Buddhist monasteries in Kashmir, and Buddhism was now experiencing a slight revival, the final flare of a dying candle. As a Buddhist, Rinchina knew where he had to go and the monastery that he had chosen was the most sacred in Kashmir.

As a Buddhist prince, Rinchina was received with honour at the monastery. Rinchina was surprised to find out that the abbot here was an abbess. She was an old lady and she said that she was the follower of *Pandita* Lakshmi, a famous Buddhist preceptor of Kashmir. She listened to Rinchina's story and asked him several pointed questions.

'Do you admit to the sin of killing Ramachandra?'

'I do.'

'Was it anger, greed or power that drove you to that act?'

'It was all three. Anger at the loss of my father and my birthright to inherit his kingdom; greed that I could have what I coveted, a new kingdom; power, that I had the cunning and the strength to commit the act.'
'Do you commit to repent and do penance?'
'I do.'
'Even at the expense of your ambition?'
'Yes, I have achieved all that I wanted. From now on my only ambition is to follow the just path, and whatever dharmic fruits result from it, those alone will satisfy me.'
'Do you commit to never taking a life again and following the path of the Buddha?'
'I do.'
'Rinchina, you are going to embark on a dangerous journey where you can end up mad. Your hot-headedness will be your bane but if you are committed to the change, I will put my life as surety that you will be cured of your weakness.'

Rinchina and the abbess talked late into the night about the Great Ashoka, whose renunciation of war and adoption of ahimsa was the beginning of the golden age of Buddhism in Kashmir. The next morning the abbess instructed him as to what he had to do. He was taken to a small cell where his penance began. It was bare except for a small crystal statuette of Avalokiteshvara, the Buddhist deity of compassion. He had to fast until the Great Compassionate One made his appearance – or until he died. For forty days Rinchina stayed in the cell: his body shrivelled, his limbs became like sticks, he started hallucinating, and in his hallucinations he had nightmares, the recurring theme of which was that the world around him sought to assassinate him; because he had broken the trust placed in him, he in turn could not trust anyone around him. He died a thousand times, a victim of assassination each time. He grew weaker and weaker and finally fainted. When he awoke, the abbess was dabbing water and juice into his mouth. She saw his eyes open and she smiled. 'You are reborn, Rinchina. Welcome to the world.'

It took another month to nurse Rinchina back to health. He seemed to have aged in some way, and there was a new deliberateness in his movements. He weighed every word that he said and he seemed to be much more tolerant, as if he saw the world through new eyes. From that day on Rinchina became very interested in religion, all religions: any path to sacred experience intrigued him. On his return to the capital he invited learned scholars to debates and the discussions would go on late in the night. On one occasion he had a local play *Much Ado about Religion* staged in the palace. His sense of justice, honed by his own personal experience, became even stronger and he would brook no injustice to the poor and weak. When he would visit Ravan his discussions with him would be on spiritual matters and very rarely did he talk about his political vision and grand plans. He had already removed the guards on Kota's chambers, and she was free to receive whomever she chose.

Brahma went to visit Kota on Raksha Bandhan day, an important festival for all unmarried Kashmiri women. Kota was waiting for him; their last conversation had been a difficult one when he had informed her that he was going forward and looking for someone else to marry. But today was a new day and both of them put on a brave face. Kota tied a simple red thread around Brahma's right wrist.

'*Sarva asha mama mitram bhavantu*! May all the solar realms be friendly to me!'

In return Brahma reiterated his commitment: 'I will provide raksha, security to you when you need it for your safety, honour and dignity. And I have an announcement to make. I have arrived at a decision for which I need your help.'

'What is it? You seem so serious.'

'I was walking through the small market by the riverbank in Srinagar when I saw a girl selling fruit from a small stall. I bought some fruit from her and we started talking. Her name is Sharika. When I asked why she had no help she opened up and revealed that she and her family had hidden in the caves near Loharkot, for over a year – the rest of her family had all died in the cave, leaving her the sole survivor. Her only income is the little she makes from selling what fruit she can gather from the uncultivated wild orchards. I have made up my mind to marry Sharika, but I want an intermediary. Now that you are free – although so far you have chosen to not emerge from your room – would you go on my behalf to ask Sharika for her hand?'

Kota was surprised. 'I would never have expected something like this Brahma. You are marrying a homeless girl! What about all the women in court who would follow you to the end of the earth?'

'I think the world is changing. The old order does not exist. Sharika has handled great tragedy without becoming a victim to it. She does not know who I am and yet she was trusting of me. She believes that when life is threatened one should live as fully as possible. I felt connected to her and trust my instinct that she will be a good life partner to me.'

Kota fought back her negative reaction to losing Brahma to another woman. The Devi had sent a signal through Brahma that one could not become a prisoner to the tragedy of the past. She was curious as to who this woman was who would possess what she had been cruelly deprived of.

'I am happy for you and agree to your request,' she said in a level voice. 'I will approach Sharika on your behalf.' A relieved Brahma ran to make preparations.

Kota's horse was giddy with excitement. His mistress had not ridden him in nearly a year, as she had sequestered herself in her cell; the crowd gathered around her, kissing her skirt and touching her riding boots. The people were in rapture at the sight of her, following her out of the fort, not caring where she was going so long as they didn't lose sight of her. As Kota reached the outskirts of Srinagar the crowd had turned into a *jaloos*, a veritable procession. Kota smiled at Brahma, his proposal was going to end up being the most public event in the Valley over the last twelve months.

Kota looked over the refugee camp, despairing that her Valley had been brought so low. The proud Kashmiris were now living in conditions that even their animals would have found objectionable:

the squalor, the filth was abominable to the Kashmiris, who were so fastidious in hygiene and matters of pollution. They had no leader, no one who cared for them; they were no different from the gangs of stray cows that foraged in the Valley. After Dulucha, the Kashmiris, who had offered sanctuary to everyone for millennia, were bereft of anyone willing to extend a helping hand to them.

Kota entered the hut the girl shared with another family. She was surprised and scared when Kota came in, not quite knowing what had happened or what she had done wrong. Kota could barely conceal her astonishment at what she saw: Brahma was so unpredictable – he had never said a word that Sharika was completely bald. In order to protect their womenfolk from the foreign scourge, many of the Kashmiris had either disfigured their daughters by cutting off their noses or ears, or scarring their faces: death and disfigurement were preferable to dishonour by the Ghazis. This girl had escaped but she had voluntarily kept her hair shorn. Kota could see that she was a calm young woman, attractive in a sweet way. She had obviously suffered great tragedy in her life, the loss of all her loved ones, and it showed in her face.

Kota gently explained the purpose of her visit.

'Sister, I come here on behalf of my brother Brahma. He wants to have you as his life companion. I can vouch for Brahma's character. He would be the best husband any woman could have and I would be overjoyed to have you as my sister. Will you please entertain our proposal?' The girl nearly fainted in disbelief, but Kota then insisted that Brahma enter and speak to her himself as well.

Sharika assented to the marriage, but she had one request. She had promised herself that if she ever married, the ceremony would have to take place in the cave where her family had spent their last days: she wanted their spirits to witness her new life and bless her with their good wishes. Brahma consented to the unconventional condition, and they both agreed to consult the jyotish on the most auspicious date for the marriage.

When Kota and Brahma came out of the hut the news spread like wildfire: an oligarch's son was marrying a homeless orphan girl. It was too good to be true! Nobody could have asked for anything better. Surely, great karma would accrue to Brahma in his next birth for his ground-breaking decision. This time a homeless orphan, next time he would marry a Devi!

Sharika returned to Lar to stay with Kota until the marriage. The crowd accompanied them all the way back to the fort exhilarated and singing with happiness. They had pulled out the *Kutagrha*, a processional temple chariot constructed of wood in which the Kashmira Devi was kept with sumptuous decorations. Kota was struck by Brahma's choice. Her mind made up, she said as much to him.

'You have made a personal decision to lift up one life – and here I am, wallowing in my personal grief while our people are crying for help. I have to act quickly and decisively, irrespective of the personal sacrifice, if our people are to be saved.'

'What do you intend to do?'

'Brahma, you are going to marry Sharika and I am going to marry Rinchina!'

'Are you out of your mind?' Brahma was shocked. 'Is this an emotional reaction to my decision?'

'No, it is our people that are asking me to do this. By his treacherous, heinous act Rinchina has raised the stakes and made it personal. I promise you that treachery will be met with deception. I will respond in kind and justice will be delivered by karma. Brahma, you and I are going to take the leap separately but trust me we will land together!'

Tregrantha (Book III)
The Gambit

Wave 9
The Marriage

THE heralds went to every village: in the year 1320 Kashmir was going to be reborn! Kota and Rinchina's wedding theme was a return to roots, and Kokur had evoked earth, water, fire, light and sky. It was a river wedding, and the biggest flat-bottomed boat to be found was decorated and sent to bring Rinchina. He wore a long, high-buttoned coat with narrow crinkled drainpipe trousers, a pink turban with a tongue of hair peeping out in the front, and a saffron tilak adorned his forehead. On his feet were embroidered cloth shoes. He was received on the boat to the loud sound of the conch, the singing of ladies and a shower of petals, dates and sugar crystals. He had a floral parasol covering him and accompanying him was the after-groom, a young boy.

Kota had told Kokur that she wanted the wedding at the small but ancient Shiva temple at Pandrethan, the hallowed site of the ancient capital of Kashmir. As a young girl Kota had always wanted to be married in this temple, where the flying figures holding garlands on the walls represented to her a celestial wedding: their effortless flight to a distant honeymoon on a star was a romantic fantasy that she had always dreamt about.

Rinchina's boat, rowed with heart-shaped oars by fifteen pairs of willing hands, reached the bank. He stepped off the boat with his entourage, including Tukka, Valya and Shah Mir and his family and formed a wedding procession on horseback to the temple. Tukka looked out of place in his fine clothing, but Shah Mir was distinguished and powerful in his embroidered *jama* coat and crisply starched salwar pants. He was the broker that had made this alliance and was given due deference. His family – particularly his daughters – attracted everyone's attention: Guhara was radiant, her eyes glittering and sparkling with excitement. She was amazed when a pack of forty young women accompanied by an equal number of young men arrived on horseback to attend the party, the women with their hair flowing in the wind, the men chasing them hard and the animals neighing with excitement and adding to the clamour. The beautiful aristocrat girls flirted with the young men, while the older folks watched observantly to see what future matches could emerge.

Saras was the first one from Kota's family to formally welcome Rinchina. She held *isband*, dry seeds, pinched between her thumb and fingers and pressed them on Rinchina's forehead, saying a blessing for prosperity and health. The isband was then put in the kangri, the fire pot that she carried: it produced a crackling sound and there emerged the most fragrant of aromas, spreading good cheer. Saras was followed by Kota's side of the wedding party, starting with Brahma and then her cousins and other family members. They all welcomed Rinchina and embraced as the groom's entourage was given garlands. White silk *kataks* were hung around each other's necks, a nod to the groom's Tibetan heritage and as they kissed on the forehead the outpouring of bonhomie and affection was clear. Everyone was determined to exchange pleasantries, the young women making an extra special effort since these impressions would go a long way in determining their marketability. When talking to the boys the Kashmiri girls all stood in the stylish manner prescribed to them, chest up with one foot flat on the ground and the other foot raised with the knee slightly bent so that only the toes touched the ground. This was to signal that they could stay or flee away depending on whether the boy's attention pleased them or not.

To the sounds of the santoor, Kota made her grand appearance from the other side of the temple, supported by her elder maternal uncle and Brahma. She was an ethereal vision: her hair was plaited in cornrows and she wore a brocaded silk dress of virginal white. On her head was a *taranga,* the headdress of Kashmiri Bhatta women dating from antiquity when the Saraswats had fused with the local Naga people. First was the *kalaposh,* the cap, then the *zoojy,* the net flowing to the back; then the taranga, wrapped three times around the head and held in place with a pin set with a gemstone. Finally came the *poots*, which extended from the top of the head almost to the heels, starting with a hood and ending with a pair of intertwined snake bodies tapering into a double tail. The bride was Shakti, and the taranga symbolized the secret supreme force. Only now, married to a woman, could the man, Shiva, hope to unlock his force through union and with the grace of the Devi Shakti.

Kota's arms jingled with gold bangles; on her ears she wore an extremely traditional dejhoor, the six-pointed star worn on each ear with the help of a long chain made of gold or thread. A famous sculpture of the Buddha's mother nearby was adorned with the dejhoor and Kota had asked the jeweller to reproduce the antique design, given that Rinchina was Buddhist. She was adorned with heavy necklaces and her fingers were loaded with rings of various designs. Kota's hands and feet had been decorated with intricate floral henna dye patterns the night before; she had a saffron tilak, and her body had been drenched with oils and perfumes so that she left a trail of sweet fragrance.

It was her face, though, that caught everybody's eye. Saras had used the Ladakhi technique of *shoglo* to colour Kota's natural complexion: she smeared the juice and seeds of ripe belladonna berries on her cheeks and forehead, and the yellow seeds made her pink, radiant face and fair complexion look as if it had been polished and then sprinkled with grains of gold. Rinchina could have been looking the girl next door from Ladakh except that this was a princess with Kashmiri features and Kashmiri beauty.

Everybody could see that this was Kota's night, her show – there was something extraordinarily charismatic about her. Was royalty truly something separate from the ordinary? Fair, radiating a wholesome aura of innocence, Kota was the picture of loveliness. Next to the bride was Ravan: he had the same features as Kota but what was pretty in her indicated weakness in him, a lack of strength of manly character.

Brahma guided Kota as she was led to the mandap. The hooded canopy, supported by four pillars, had been decked out with flowers. 'It is the saddest day of my life,' Brahma whispered to Kota. 'I cannot believe that I have to hand over my prize to a stranger that came out of nowhere. Are you still confident that you want to go through this Rakshasa marriage, forced by a demon?'

'Brahma, I married my people today,' she whispered back. 'All that Rinchina is going to get is Huli Jing. I did not jilt you, and Sharika is a beautiful loving person. This is the only way to go and you would do this if you were me.'

'You are a woman, and given what you are faced with I agree I would not do anything different,' Brahma conceded.

'Pray for the Devi to keep me strong,' said the bride.

'Your soon-to-be husband does not seem to be a bad human being,' Brahma offered,' but if one crosses him, better watch out. He can murder. Yet, I have truly never seen the strength that I see in you today as you prepare to sit on the chest of the murderer.'

'Yes, I know he is a murderer,' Kota replied serenely. 'I learnt that about him the very first day I met him. We have that in common. Don't worry, I am in control here.'

Saras instructed Kota: 'Stand next to Rinchina under the mandap. I am going to take a piece of sugar candy and place it first in Rinchina's mouth and then in yours Kota, alternating three times.'

Kota made a slight face as Saras smiled at the awkwardness of this first and very public union of their bodily fluids. She held them tightly and kissed both of them on the forehead, giving them her blessings. Rinchina had a broad, triumphant smile on his face: his wedding night represented the crowning of his ambition.

The crowd separated to let Devaswami approach. As the family priest to noble clans, he had personally come to attend this most important of weddings. He started the prayers and placed a six-strand sacred thread around Rinchina, signifying three for himself and three for Kota. He gave Rinchina a consecrated drink and then escorted the couple to the fire outside the main structure of the temple. A bevy of priests already stood before the sacred fire. Brahma sat close to Rinchina to guide him through the priest's instructions. First, Kota's uncle placed a mirror between the couple: it represented their first glance at each other and confirmed that each party was marrying the intended partner. Then both parties introduced themselves in terms of their lineage. Then Kota's uncle, who had Kota sitting on his knee, gave her as a gift to Rinchina by placing her hand in his. The priest then laid out the key condition of the marriage.

'In the attainment of piety, wealth and desire, she is not to be transgressed.'

'Transgress her I will not,' Rinchina vowed.

Guhara whispered to her mother, 'Kashmiri women rule their marriages. How exciting and different they are!' Shah Mir understood the contract completely. This was a royal wedding and while Rinchina would rule publicly, Kota had complete power of veto and privately was the ultimate authority.

Rinchina eulogized Kama, the God of Love, and then pronounced a eulogy to Kota, who offered a tribute in kind to Rinchina, before they both took the seven vows of marriage.

'Cross your hands, one over the other and hold each other's hands tightly,' Brahma interpreted for the priest who covered their hands with a cloth.

'Go for the ring!' shouted Brahma, but it was too late. Kota slipped Rinchina's engagement ring off his finger and with a triumphant wave showed it to the crowd.

'What was that all about?' Rinchina asked.

'That was *aathwas*,' Brahma replied, laughing. 'Whoever gets the others' ring off first dominates the marriage. Welcome to the world of being a henpecked husband.'

'Brahma, you never warned me!'

'You never asked! In any case, Rinchina, we are all henpecked husbands after marriage, ring or no ring.'

'What else have you not told me about this wedding?'

'Pay attention to the priest,' Brahma whispered back. 'Priests can be irascible, and you do not want them losing their temper on your wedding night.'

The couple was made to stand and walk the seven circles around the sacred fire. Rinchina led Kota, holding each other's hands tightly. The first circle was made as they stepped over seven silver coins; the next six rounds were done to the chant of mantras seeking the Devas' blessings. At the completion of each round, the groom had to commit that he would not transgress his wife. Devaswami took the left feet of the bride and the groom, one upon the other and placed both on a stone used for grinding grain. Kota firmly rolled the pestle with her right foot as Rinchina recited: 'Oh wife! May you stand firm on the stone kept in front of you. May you acquire the samskara of this stone and be steady and firm like it is. This firmness may help you tread the foes down and overcome enemies.'

'This firmness may help me tread the foes down and overcome enemies,' Kota repeated.

Saras picked up the stone and placed it in her bag for safe keeping as Tukka and Valya congratulated Rinchina: 'Now you have achieved everything that you wanted in life.'

'I owe it all to you,' Rinchina replied. 'The three of us are one forever.'

Devaswami congratulated Kotarani: 'From today you are queen, rani. May the Devi give you strength, Kotarani, as your marital clock starts ticking. Remember the special mantras that I gave you, and chant them every day.'

Kokur assisted Kotarani and Rinchina on to the cushions under the canopy placed over their heads, symbolizing their bridal chamber where they would create ideal progeny. Outside, a flood of people surrounded them – courtesans, vagabonds, women singing *wanwun* marriage songs, dancing girls, musicians thumping the *tumbakhnar* and the *nutt*. It was happy bedlam and all were joyfully celebrating the queen's marriage. Inside was a crush of guests congratulating the bride and the groom and two groups formed, one around Kotarani and the other around Rinchina's whose group had started drinking hard, with each round of toasts leading to more noisy merriment.

Guhara blushed when Brahma came over and squeezed her tightly; his new wife Sharika was an attractive girl but no great beauty and Guhara idly wondered what Brahma saw in her.

'You had always wanted to meet Kota,' Brahma said, 'and tonight is the perfect night to do that. Come let me take you to her.'

'Thank you for taking care of my brother Brahma when he was with you,' Kotarani told Guhara after they had been formally introduced. 'We owe you and your family a lot. Brahma had told me how beautiful you are, but it seems he was holding back.'

Guhara blushed. 'Maharani, I look up to you. I wish you all the happiness in the world. I want to be like you.'

Kotarani smiled. 'To be like me, just be yourself.'

'Maharani, at one time I dreamt of marrying Brahma and at another time my father tried to match me with Rinchina,' Guhara blurted out. 'Now they are both taken. I think I will end up staying single forever.'

'The right man will come and I will be there to celebrate with you,' Kotarani smiled.

'Does Rinchina have brothers?' Guhara asked naively. 'Brahma was telling me that you would have to serve as the wife of all of Rinchina's brothers. It seems to me that having multiple husbands is even worse than being one out of many wives.'

'Brahma is just being humorous. Kashmiris have one husband and one wife and that is all Rinchina is going to get. The days of harems are over.'

Guhara was firm: 'Then I want a Kashmiri wedding just like this one. I have never seen revelry like this. Kashmiris are the happiest people on earth.'

Kotarani laughed: 'Once you have your man, I will make sure that Kokur will organize a Bhatta wedding that any princess would be proud of. Now circulate, or else people will look at us and will be drawn to your beauty and not that of the bride.'

Guhara bonded instantly with Kotarani at her admission of feminine vanity and knew she had found her role model.

Ravan came over to Kotarani.

'Sister, I want you to know that while this is not what I would have wished for you, I will always stand by you.'

Kotarani gently placed her hand on her brother's arm.

'We have lost our father, but we have not forgotten him, and we have each other.'

Ravan was unconvinced.

'I will play along but I don't know where I belong in this new order.' A concerned Kotarani watched him walk away, alone in his thoughts. Kokur had arranged for the royal couple to be transported for the night to a private island in the middle of the lake. Rinchina was very drunk on the local beer that the Tibetan Bottas had pumped him with and had to be supported to the boat. He slumped against his new wife as the gathering sang moving hymns and showered flowers on the new couple. Soon they looked like the divine couple Shiva and Shakti, buried under the blooms. The mountains and the rivers, the very sacred geography of India, were invoked in the *Posh Puja* and mapped on them to bless their union. The *Hanji* boatmen slowly started moving the oars and the boat glided out, away from the temple. The women had tears in their eyes and their singing grew more poignant: Kotarani had bid goodbye to her own world and was entering the new one of her husband. A Kashmiri bride would only return as someone else's wife and not as a daughter of her parents.

Through a small opening in the flowers and the hem of her headdress, Kotarani saw Brahma, Saras and Devaswami standing together and looking at her. Saras's lips moved silently blessing her. Kotarani's eyes moistened with tears. Her mother and father were not alive to be at her marriage. She remembered her father telling her that when he went into battle he placed Shakti in his heart and then felt no pain doing his dharma. Kotarani shut her wet eyes and meditated upon the Devi, to grant her people victory in the dangerous journey she had embarked on. All along the Vitasta the river folk had gathered in their boats to salute their new maharaja and maharani. The Hanjis were proud that it was their people who had escorted the royal couple: with lit lamps in their hands they showered the pair with yet more flowers, giving them their blessings and auspicious wishes. The oars gently and rhythmically paddled in the water. The liquid river, effortlessly bearing the weight of the boat, slipped in and around the firm oars, propelling the long boat to its destination, the bridal chamber.

When they arrived at the cottage a drunken Rinchina pawed at Kota in his hurry to remove her clothes: she stiffened at his awkwardness. He fell on top of her like a deadweight, oblivious to her presence. Her body turned ice-cold. Whether it was nerves or dysfunction he was not quite up to it. Kota distanced herself mentally, and when Rinchina came quickly it was as if she was far away. Rinchina was no Brahma and for that she was grateful. She turned over to the other side and as a satiated Rinchina started snoring she slowly got up and went to sleep in the neighbouring room.

Wave 10
Lion of Kashmir

As Kotarani began her rule she was vigilant with the kingdom's affairs and, since she was one of their own, the Kashmiris were content. While there were lingering questions as to her motivation for marrying Rinchina, these were not uppermost in the minds of the people. She was happy that the people described her husband as 'The Lion of Kashmir'; he ruled alongside her with intelligence and justice, and never forgave the wicked. He roamed the land restlessly seeking anyone who was malignant. Once again there was security and festivity in the kingdom: Valya was made prime minister and Tukka commander. They were new to the Valley and so was Shah Mir, but the ministers were impartial, knowing that Kota was watching them and that Rinchina would not tolerate misconduct. The usually accommodating Shah Mir surprisingly proved to be a strong disciplinarian and brought a firm hand to the Kayasthas, the tax collectors, much to the relief of the public. Even Khazanchi and Manjari had changed their moneylending practices and were careful to not be seen as too unscrupulous and so end up on the wrong side of the new maharani. After their initial differences, Manjari had kept her distance from Rinchina once he married Kotarani.

The administrative matters of the state requiring Kota's attention were numerous and kept her pinned on court matters. It was a rude awakening to find that while the ruler had the panoply of power, it was the vast state officialdom that ruled, and royalty was merely a figurehead. She now had some sympathy for the deceased Suhdev who, while an inept and indolent ruler like other Kashmiri kings before him, had been shunted into irrelevancy by the powerful officials. She let Rinchina handle most of the public engagements since it gave the community and him a chance to get better connected. Then one day, Rinchina asked Kota to accompany him and Yaniv: he had a surprise in store for her. Yaniv led both of them to the home of the *Saraf*, the goldsmith. The mohalla he and his family lived in had served as Kashmir's royal mint for generations.

Yaniv had been commissioned by Rinchina to create a new bronze *kesarah*. He had played it safe with an emphasis on calligraphy; the only innovation was the incorporation of Persian script on the back. One side stated 'With the Grace of Shiv Nath-ji' in Sanskrit, and the other side honoured Sher-e-Kashmir, who was a lion when it came to justice. Kashmiri coins were always known for the beauty of their engraving, and Rinchina and Kota could see that Yaniv had excelled in his task.

Rinchina liked the prototype design instantly, but Kota demurred.

'This is a new design and it will not be accepted quickly by the traders,' she said when pressed. 'We cannot put pressure on the money system when the kingdom itself is under so much stress. The public will be suspicious of this change. This coin will not be popular instantly – it will drive up demand for older coins, which means that they will be hoarded and trade will freeze. I would continue the production of the traditional designs.'

Kota could see Rinchina was disappointed that she had thwarted his idea. Had she felt threatened that the coin gave Rinchina the centre stage? Coins were one way for Kashmiri rulers to gain immortality and global recognition. However, even Yaniv had to concur with her logic and the Saraf was instructed to make no change in his production. He thanked the king and queen for their visit. He made more money with the traditional coins since his production was already set up, so he was not unhappy with the decision. Although Kotarani sensed that Rinchina was upset, she had no interest in pandering to his ambitions: she was queen, and as the ruler she had the final say.

A few months later, Kotarani had some exciting news and asked Saras to come and see her. She stared at her with a smile on her face, but did not say anything. Saras waited patiently, but Kotarani kept grinning. Finally she announced, 'I am pregnant.'

'Maharani, I am so happy for you,' a genuinely happy Saras exulted.

'Saras, the Devi has answered my prayers. Now it had better be a son.'

'Maharani, it will be a boy and the kingdom will now be secure.'

'Not a word to anybody. I will announce it when the time is right.'

Saras nodded her head in assent. Ill-wishers of Rinchina could cast evil spells. She advised the maharani to take more rest and eat well. She warned Kotarani that she would experience mood swings and should be especially careful around her husband. But Rinchina was restless: he would often spend a sleepless night tossing restlessly in his bed. Kotarani had suggested he take a trip to Achchhoda lake and Rinchina agreed. However, he found no charm or peace in the serenity of the lake surroundings.

'I am bored and need to do something challenging,' he told Kotarani one day. 'You are running the kingdom and my day is wasted drinking with Tukka and Valya. This is no way for warriors to spend their life.'

Kota observed Rinchina carefully. 'What interests you?'

'Kotarani, at one time Tibet ruled the Silk Road. Today we have become prisoners bound by the mountains. What happened, how could things have gone so bad?'

'You think that with the death of the Great Khan there may be an opportunity, but Kashmir is ill-equipped to take advantage of it. As to why things turned bad nothing is permanent, especially power. The Buddha taught us that.'

'Power stays in the hands of the person who has the grip – and we lack that might.'

'The people are the might, Rinchina, and the people will give their strength to the leader that they have faith in.'

'Our people are weak, Kotarani. Most till the land; the rest spend time in their religious schools and become lamas or priests. We are like sheep in a world of wolves. At one time the Tibetans were the fiercest warriors! Now look at us, vassals of the Chinese. Look at the Ghazi warriors. They are today what we were.'

'Nature's prime directive is to survive,' Kotarani argued, 'so how can one adopt thinking that is premised on causing death. As for the Ghazi warriors, my father showed them whom to remember. My Lord, was Ashoka strong when he slaughtered hundreds of thousands on the battlefield at Kalinga or was he strong when he embraced Buddhism and built an empire whose messages remain on the Silk Road for posterity?'

'I do not know the answer to that – both were important to him. He had to win his military battles first, and only then he could establish universal order. I am a Buddhist myself and I do not understand its relevance to our daily challenges.'

Kotarani laughed lightly so as to not come across as disagreeable.

'My Lord, think before you say that. It was the abbess who taught you not to use the sword and instead to share power and co-opt people: has that not worked well for you? Are you not through winning your battles yet? Is Kashmir and Ladakh not sufficient?'

'But there is no guarantee that there won't be another Dulucha hiding behind the mountain pass,' Rinchina countered. 'I want to understand what it is that gives Mussalmans strength? Is Islam the answer? It seems to give all – might, material success and finally rewards in paradise.'

'My Lord, we are back to square one,' Kotarani stated. 'What force unifies the individual with the limitless generative universe? Devaswami will tell you which way of life has found the answer and can provide mastery of all – but I can tell you that the lesson of history is that at one time or the other we can fall prey to our weaker selves.'

'But how do you make this connection and become one with the universe?'

'If you want to become one with Shiva, you must visit Devaswami.'

'I am inclined to do that. Maybe I should convert and become a Hindu,' Rinchina suggested. 'It will make me more acceptable to the

Kashmiris. In any case, when we were married I was very intrigued by what Devaswami said. I will go and visit him and maybe he will teach me how to become the master of the universe.'

Kotarani could see that Rinchina was testing the waters: if he went along with her and converted to her faith she would be obliged to consent with him, but there was no way that she would agree to a military campaign. Rinchina was looking for a diversion to overcome his frustration at being a king in name only. Maybe if he focused on the war within he could be weaned from his obsession on waging a war without.

'Do that,' Kotarani agreed. 'Devaswami will be happy to see you, and once you take him as your guru, you and I can celebrate our festivals with even more understanding.'

'You mean you won't come with me to visit Devaswami?'

'I think that he will want to be alone with you – and there are things that he can only share directly with you, the maharaja. I would only get in the way. In any case, I have things to do; when you are with Devaswami, I will have time to work on them.'

'What things?'

'It will be a surprise,' said Kotarani with a secretive smile, 'so come back quickly.'

On his return to the capital, Rinchina attended to pressing matters but his conversation with Kotarani was at the forefront of his mind. He sent a messenger to Devaswami informing him that he wanted to pay a visit to Sharadapeeth and received a formal invitation, handwritten with exquisite calligraphy on a patra, in return. The pandit messenger read it aloud to Rinchina and Kotarani; the trip had all the trappings of a formal state visit. Thousands of Brahmins had congregated to see their titular head before Devaswami claimed him.

The canonical arrogance in Devaswami did not change, even though he was talking to the Maharaja.

'Rinchina, with regard to men you are majesty; with regard to me, the representative of the Devi, you are all humility.'

'Can I convert and become a Hindu?' Rinchina asked directly. 'And if I do, what is my relationship with you?'

'Yes, you can become a Shiva. The *Shivadharmottara* makes it abundantly clear that this worship will benefit not only you, but also your lineage and all Kashmiris.[13] There are rituals, such as your commissioning the transcription of a manuscript of scripture donated to your guru. I would personally lead the *lingoddhara* ceremony and couple myself to you, extracting all of your past faith marks and vows to drown them in water; your merits and failings would be consigned into the fire. You would be a newborn. I would install your personal Devi in you and give you your sacred mantra: as your guru I will integrate the real world with the divine world for you. I will assist you in guarding the kingdom of Kashmir from all of its enemies and in maintaining cosmological order.'

Rinchina was an intelligent person and he had to evaluate carefully.

'Devaswami, how do you do this? You Kashmiris are so proud of your lineage, your *gotra*. Would you truly accept me, a Ladakhi? I cannot give up what I have earned so far that easily.'

Devaswami spoke slowly, as if Rinchina was a small child.

'Maharaja, you will be reborn in the ceremony, and at the time of your rebirth the jyotish and I will recreate your future. You exist in many parallel universes and I will pick the one that will give you a far happier and liberated life than you are destined for now.'

'How do you do that?' Rinchina persisted.

'With our scriptures, our codes, our prayers, rituals and mantras,' replied Devaswami. 'The *Mokshopaya* scripture is our guide to parallel universes.'

Rinchina was not convinced.

'Devaswami, when I was young, shamans came to my father's court with their black magic and performed incantations too. But it did not do much good. Is it really necessary?'

'Maharaja, this is not black magic or blind faith; these are precise shastras, technical knowledge which encompasses economics, politics, warfare, architecture, medicine, dance, chemistry, biology; every aspect of human existence. While the rest of the central kingdoms have fallen, Kashmir is a beacon of independence. You tell me if it is necessary.'

'Devaswami, would you give me the mantras and let me study and think about it on my own?'

Devaswami was aghast at the sceptic's request.

'My Lord, the Brahmin should give his knowledge freely but the Brahmin's power is integrally tied to his morality and can only be given sparingly. These mantras are not words to be spoken mechanically but instead are *spanda,* divine pulsations; they must be approached with study and reverence.'

'Devaswami, we are all equal human beings. I should be able to understand and work these mantras just like you. After all, they are only letters and words. This is merely song, chants and rhetoric.'

Devaswami was appalled.

'What you call words is *vac* to us, the very articulations of universal consciousness which comprise incandescent light and vibrations and can manifest all of reality. My Lord, we are all equal as humans but not equal in training, karma or our talents. You are a warrior: what may seem an innocuous handshake or hug in your world may be a death grip in reality. Similarly, you must be trained to generate and absorb these mantras; you must have a noble purpose sanctified by me to invoke them.'

'So you would refuse the request of your maharaja?'

Devaswami faltered in the face of the direct challenge.

'We meet to bind so that the generative force can flow. I connect with you and grant you *Shaktipat* and it is through that union and synergy that I am an agent of empowerment. If you are not unconditionally open to me, I cannot see evidence inside you that Shiva is descending on you. In such a case, I cannot give, you cannot receive and I am not the right guru for you.'

Rinchina adopted a new strategy.

'I had asked the maharani to accompany me, but she said that she was preoccupied. Had she been here with me would you have refused her if she had made the request?'

Devaswami responded easily.

'No, because women have been the custodians and set the highest values of Kashmiri society from times immemorial. All that I know has emanated from a woman, Ardhtrymbhaka, from the days of the rishis. Men are not the equals of women when making a spiritual request.'

Rinchina was frustrated.

'Devaswami, I came to visit you because my mind was troubled, and I have trouble sleeping. I fear that I will return to Kotarani with little to show for my journey.'

'Your Majesty, seeking conversion without self-recognition will only yield bad outcomes. If you return back with little to show, it will also mean that I have failed to accept you. On the smaller matter of sleep, I can certainly try to help. When you lie in bed, take three deep breaths, My Lord, try to wind your mind in reverse: think of your last act of resting your head on the pillow, then the preceding act of lying down, then changing into your night garments, and so on. Perhaps that will work for you.'

'Will you share with me as to why it will work or is that a Brahminical secret also?' Rinchina asked sarcastically.

A humbled Devaswami did not take offence.

'The technique teaches you to observe your own mind. The moment the mind is observed it becomes still. Please try it.'

Rinchina departed and after some time Devaswami, with a great effort, lifted himself up and walked towards the quarters of the jyotish. Along the way, he could see the accusatory eyes of the grim-faced Brahmins on him. They had guessed at the failure of his meeting: the maharaja had come to visit Sharadapeeth and was returning without visiting the temple. When Devaswami reached the jyotish's residence he was sitting hunched over his charts. He did not even look up when Devaswami walked in.

'It went as I predicted, did it not?' the tired voice of the jyotish asked.

'He has a strong heart but a weak head,' Devaswami protested. 'The penalty of being uneducated and illiterate. The Botta is no Bhatta.'

The jyotish nodded affirmatively. 'Yes, he has a weak head but posterity will also say that it was you who were headstrong. Your inhibition will carry its own implications.'

'I did not give or give in. How bad will the consequences be?' the chastened Devaswami asked.

'The extreme form of being headstrong is Rahu, an immortal, bodiless, head-only demon. Rahu can destroy a person, swallow a people – nay, even the sun and the moon, and cause an eclipse. So the consequences are grave, we could perish. The antidote to arrogance is to expand one's heart and give and only then can one be saved. You need to do that,' advised the jyotish dismissively.

Rinchina broke his return journey in Srinagar where Shah Mir came to receive him: Rinchina recounted his frustrating discussion with Devaswami to his host, who exhibited his usual empathy and pragmatism.

'My family's history is that we are descendants of the Pandavs. Partha founded the town of Garbhara within the limits of the Pancagahvara district in Swadgabar. He was a second Arjun. His son was Babhruvahana, from whom sprang Kuru Shah, who sired my father, Taharaja. Honestly, I have also given serious thought to converting back and becoming a Hindu. It would be easier socially for my sons, and my daughters would be happier. Yet, today I am a devout follower of the Prophet, Peace be upon Him. To Muslims, my grandfather was the pious Waqur Shah and my father Tahir: Kuru becomes Wakur and Taharaja becomes Tahir. My Lord, your faith is between you and your maker – but for a ruler to publicly vacillate in his faith is not good for the kingdom, especially when you are faced with uncertainty on all fronts.'

'Shah Mir, you are a wise and trusted friend. I don't believe in blind faith but do not have the patience for the shastras. Tonight I rest and sleep; tomorrow when I wake up and step out, I will adopt the creed of the first person I spot. Brahmin, Buddhist or tantric sects that fill our streets will be mine from tomorrow. It will be a new day.'

Rinchina bid his friend goodbye. But when he sat on his horse, Shah Mir whispered an urgent command to his servant. The servant whipped his horse and sped away. Shah Mir had given explicit instructions and the task had to be done that night. Luck had come Shah Mir's way and he was going to grab it. As Rinchina lay in his bed that night he remembered the suggestion that Devaswami had given him. Impulsively, he decided to try it; it seemed so simple and although his mind flitted slightly, he began to retrace his day...

Morning dawned and Rinchina woke up refreshed and with a sense of purpose. He had to tell Devaswami when he saw him next that maybe there was something to his technique. It was then that he heard the first cry: 'Allah-u-Akbar, Allah is great!', followed by 'Hayya al-as salat! Hayya al-salat! Come to pray, come to pray!', and finally, 'As-salatu khairul mina 'n-naum! Prayer is better than sleep.'

Rinchina went outside. The sun shone with a bright intensity; each ray sought to illuminate every dark corner, hunting any shadows that might darken the landscape. Rinchina immediately saw a dervish prostrating himself in namaz: he watched the man patiently who began to sing in the most haunting of voices:

God
There is no God but He,
Living and Everlasting.
Neither slumber overtakes Him nor sleep.
To him belongs what is in the heavens and what is on earth.
Who shall intercede with Him except by His leave?
He knows their present affairs and their past.
And they do not grasp of His knowledge except what He wills.
His throne encompasses the heavens and the earth;
Preserving them is no burden to Him.
He is the Exalted, the Majestic.
There is no compulsion in religion.
Right guidance has been distinguished from error.
He who repudiates idols and believes in God
Has grasped a handle most firm, unbreakable.[14]

Rinchina took the dervish by his hand and invited him to come to his palace, asking an interpreter to join them.

'Who are you?' asked Rinchina.

'I am a *garibam*, a stranger,' he replied through the interpreter.

'Tell me your name, what faith you profess and what community you belong to?' ordered Rinchina.

'They call me Bulbul Qalandar. I belong to the sect propagated by Shah Nemat-Ullah Farisi Shirazi who in turn looked to Zia-ud-Din-Ul-Najeeb Abdul Qahiri. I am a Mussalman.'

'Where are you from? Why did you come to Kashmir?'

'I come from Tamkastan in Persia, via Baghdad and Turkistan. The Mongols were persecuting our Suhrawardy Order, so we left. I am accompanied by a thousand souls and among them are other pious believers such as Kamal-ud-Din, Jalal-ud-Din and Kamal Sahib.

'Tell me more about this faith,' said Rinchina.

Bulbul talked at length about the Prophet, the virtues and superior qualities of Ali, the imam, and lastly, the extraordinary feats of spirituality performed by Shah Niyamat Ullah Wali, a khalifa of the Suhrawardi Sufi sect. His face radiated love and peace. As Bulbul talked, Rinchina's heart opened wide. It had called out and its call had been answered: a preceptor had appeared. He recited the *Kalima* and accepted Islam: the seeker had united with the sought and there was sanctuary in their union. Islam's simple message of brotherly love and universal peace had resonated with Rinchina, who bid a final goodbye to his roots and embraced his future as Sadar-ud-Din, the first Shia king of Kashmir.

Kotarani was shocked to hear about Rinchina's spontaneous conversion to Islam on his return trip from Sharadapeeth. She observed his gratitude towards Bulbul closely; it knew no bounds. He ordered a *Khanqah* to be built for Baba Bulbul Qalandar, now known as Khanqah-e-Bulbul Shah, in the neighbourhood of his own palace. He conferred upon him a jagir, an annuity, from which he could draw expenses for his followers, kinsfolk, the mendicants and visitors to the Khanqah. Rinchina also built the Awala mosque for Friday prayers, and joined them at the five prescribed times of prayer regularly.

'He has converted because he found out that by marrying me he neither got control of me nor did he get Kashmir. He wanted to become Hindu and get Devaswami to perform the coronation because he figured out that legally he is not king in Kashmir. Now he is trying to line up with the Mussalmans, the foreign immigrants and mercenaries, and build a military force which is loyal to him,' a fiery Kota told Saras.

'He is an opportunist, so he will go where he smells that he can gain something. He wants desperately to regain Ladakh and Tibet. It must be because he thinks that he will get respect there. He may be king in Kashmir but for society he is just a murderer and usurper. Lining up a Mussalman army is his only way forward. The Mussalmans are small in numbers, so I am not sure as to what he gained by his conversion. It will bear watching.'

Kotarani kept her counsel private on the change in her husband and accompanied Rinchina on Fridays to listen to Bulbul Shah. At first she was cautious, but soon she saw there was no issue with her, a Hindu, going to a Mussalman Sufi: their message of love, not just that found in a mystical union with God but for all living creatures, was one that resonated with her own intuitive feelings. While Kotarani stayed true to her faith and her Devi, there was much that she liked about Bulbul. The Sufi adherents were vegetarians, practised non-violence and planted trees; Kotarani herself had become vegetarian after her dinner discussion with Saras.

Lol, love, was in the air and the Kashmiris celebrated Madana Trayodoshi, Lovers Day, with gusto. Husbands would put aside a pitcher of water with flowers and herbal essences in front of a picture of Kamadeva the night before alongside his conch and the lotus. In the morning, before sunrise, the husband would wash his wife with the fragrant water. Then he would worship both her and Kamadeva. Husband and wife would gaily decorate themselves and the entire family would go to the gardens to celebrate and enjoy a picnic. That night wives dressed themselves in delicate, enticing underclothes and transparent nightgowns to await their husbands.

Rinchina was unaware of the custom, and Kota must have been the only woman in the land who did not celebrate Madana Trayodoshi. In order to lift her spirits it was on this happy day that Kotarani broke the good news to Rinchina that she was expecting their child. Rinchina's delight knew no end: when Kotarani saw his reaction her ambivalent feelings towards him softened. It reminded her of the infectious smile he had when they had their first dinner at the dranga. There was a good side to Rinchina, she considered. Maybe the birth of their child would reconcile her to him and bind them closer. It was a slim possibility, but nonetheless it was a possibility.

In honour of the upcoming birth, Kotarani and Rinchina introduced a new ritual. A large number of Kashmiris, led by Kotarani and Rinchina, joined the small Mussalman community and went to visit Mohalla Bulbullinko, where Bulbul resided, and tied coloured ribbons on the wooden planks. When Bulbul came out to give his benediction the Mussalmans greeted the Sufi saint.

'*Salaam alaikum*! Peace be with you!'

Bulbul responded, '*Vaalaikum salaam*', with a beatific smile on his face, evidence of his divine joy. 'And unto you be Peace!'

The Kashmiris recognized that in Bulbul they had a Sufi mystic who was in touch with his deepest inner self. The Kashmiris honoured Bulbul for his divine insights and in return they were the beneficiaries of his grace. Being in his presence, just thinking about him, talking about him would put one in an exalted state. There were stories of how people had been cured miraculously by visiting the saint; there were stories of how people had gone into a trance of ecstasy contemplating Bulbul. It did not matter what faith you were: Bulbul's heart was the universal receptor, and the Kashmiris marvelled that Islam had produced such a luminous being.

Shah Mir's wife Layla had taken her daughters to see Bulbul. She had just given birth to another child and she wanted the Baba's blessings. When she approached him with her family, the saint gave Guhara, who was first in line, a small amulet and a cube of sugar.

Bulbul had murmured a benediction: 'You are unto me like my daughter.'

Guhara's mother was ecstatic as she helped her daughter tie the *taviz* around her neck.

'It will ward off evil. May the saint always protect you,' she whispered in her daughter's ear. Her silent prayers had been answered.

The daughter that she worried about so much was under the protection of Baba Bulbul – now nothing could go wrong.

Guhara returned home to her father, her face flushed with excitement.

'The Kashmiris are a wonderful people. They have not only given sanctuary and a home to the Mussalmans but also are willing to adopt our spiritual leader and celebrate their faith with us. Kotarani was there and she greeted me.'

'Yes, the Kashmiris have freely accepted us and made us part of their community,' her father agreed. 'Every Mussalman is filled with gratitude for their generosity.'

To add to the joy of the royal household Brahma had come to visit Kotarani to inform her that Sharika had given birth to a baby boy. However, Sharika was not able to lactate and the midwife had tried desperately to find a wet nurse, but to no avail. There was real danger that the baby would die: the children's female demon *Putana* would give her breast to the baby at night and the starving baby would drink of her and die immediately. Shah Mir's closeness to Brahma had led to Sharika and Layla becoming great friends. Layla was older and motherly and it was to her that Sharika had reached out for help. Layla had recently given birth to a baby herself: her breasts that had suckled several children were overflowing with milk.

'I will feed him,' Layla had offered firmly.

'But what about your own child?' protested Sharika weakly. 'I need you to find me somebody from your village, not do this yourself.'

'I will feed your child first. When he has had his fill, whatever is left my child will have. They will grow up to be brothers, bound by my milk.'

Layla had decisively picked up the baby and rested his mouth on her breast, guiding her nipple into his mouth. The baby could barely fit her pink nipple in his mouth, but once he had hold of it primal instinct took over. He started sucking, and the nourishment flowed into his starving body. With each pull Sharika felt her heart and mind lighten at the great sacrifice of her true friend.

When Kotarani heard Brahma's story, as an expectant mother she could especially relate to it. She addressed the subject in court.

'Sacrifice and gratitude are the rare great twins of human emotions! Hail Layla and Shah Mir's family. Hail Bulbul! All honour to Baba Bulbul who through his thought, word and deed has inspired Kashmiris to come closer to the divine, and in the ultimate Shaivite test inspired the Kashmiris to come closer to each other. May Hazrat Sharaf-ud-Din Abdul Rehman Bulbul Shah always serve future generations of Kashmiris as the eternal reminder of the ultimate triumph of peace and love. May the nightingale's song always fill the Valley with its sweetness. Kokur, you may read the verse to the court:

Every spring and each spring
    Mashalla
May our new desires bring
    Blessings from the enlightened Bulbul
the Kashmiri Sufi king
    that Shiva
May give his bliss to every being.'

Wave 11
The World Is One Family

THE birth of Kotarani and Rinchina's son sent the Valley into a whirlwind of celebration. Kotarani had taken advantage of Rinchina's absence to decorate the nursery. Maharani or not, any woman approaches childbirth as if going into battle and Kotarani understood how to be battle-ready. Nothing had been left to chance. She had personally supervised the decorators and the nursery walls had been painted with Gandharvas, the celestial granters of fertility. The ceiling had been painted with clouds and pictures of protective Devas and Devis, most notably Kartikeya, the son of Shiva and Shakti and the victorious general of the Devas' army as also Shashthi, the friendly goddess of the sixth night after the birth, after which everyone could breathe easier. In one corner on the outside wall was a small painting of *Putana*, the dreaded Devi of smallpox who had to be placated. Since she had already been represented pictorially outside there was no need for her to come inside the nursery in person.

All arrangements had been made. To ensure completely that the Bhutas, the Pretas, the Pichashas and the Vetalas, all belonging to the demon fraternity and all foes of conception, did not attack the baby, Devaswami had arranged for a round-the-clock contingent of Brahmins to sit outside the lying-in room and chant defensive mantras. Guards had been posted to be on the lookout for cats, as it was well known that *Jataharani*, the female robber of newborns, prowled in the shape of a cat.

The biggest risk was that of Kotarani dying during the birth: not only would the kingdom be left without its leader, but Kotarani could suffer the greatest of misfortunes – according to some of the primitive superstitions, a woman who died in labour would turn into a *churel*, one of the doomed spirits who wander about with their feet turned backwards. Kotarani had turned to Saras for support; she advised Kotarani to sleep on her left side only and fed her until she gained so much weight that her plump cheeks looked like they would burst. Saras promised repeatedly that she would be personally present, that the birth would be fine – and that, based on the left kick of the fetus, it was a boy.

The jyotish had sent a similar prediction to Kotarani, but he seemed to be increasingly cranky and out of sorts of late. Kotarani's horoscope had favourable stars, but those of Kashmir were beginning to move into dangerous territory with Shani, Saturn, in transit. The uncertainty created by Rinchina becoming the titular Maharaja of Kashmir and the jyotish having no knowledge of Rinchina's stars – since nobody had kept track of when he was born – was also an unsettling variable. What was worst was that he had sent a highly cryptic message to Kota that he had found out that Shah Mir had entered the kingdom in 1313. The name for the number 13 was *Terah*, or yours, in Kashmiri. A double number 13 appeared to be a very serious threat: could it all be his? Kota did not know what to do with this strange warning, but right now she had more pressing matters to attend. The lying-in room had been decorated with auspicious white wreaths, and *hurrilegs*, earthen vessels, filled with water stood everywhere facing the different quarters of heaven; there was incense, melted butter and mustard seeds, and uncooked rice had been sprinkled around the bed. A fire was kept burning night and day to ward off dark powers.

When the baby was born and let out his first cry, to Kotarani it was a cry of her victory and a celebration of the Kashmiri people. Devaswami was the first to place the boy on a straw mattress of *Durba grass*, which had been rendered holy with incense. He murmured protective mantras in the boy's ears and then handed the baby to a relieved Kotarani. The Devi had granted her first wish and Kotarani's heart swelled with gratitude. With the future assured, she could face her next challenge. Finally, the baby was taken to Rinchina, who joyfully held his son in his arms.

'You who were born of my heart, may you live for a hundred years. May you see a hundred autumns, a long life, bright and happy, to be the next Maharaja of Kashmir,' he declared proudly.

The jyotish noted the exact time of birth. Inside the lying-in room an exhausted Kotarani fell asleep with the watchful Saras by her side.

On the eleventh day a baby shower, *sundar,* was held for the newborn and his mother. Huge pots were filled with water and herbs, which were boiled, creating a strong aromatic smell in the air. When the water was scalding hot, a wet cloth was used to scrub the baby and the mother until both were pink. The hot water was allowed to cool and then poured over them in a continuous stream. Mother and child were towelled dry and dressed in new clothes. The women were singing and calming the baby after his first shower. Food was served on seven plates and a prayer offered before the dishes of meat and fish were distributed to close family members. Finally, everyone could eat. From that point on, Saras fed Kota rigorously with meat and fish so that she could rebuild her strength. On the fortieth day, both mother and child were given another bath; Kota was ready to emerge into the world with her 'unclean' phase behind her and with her son in front of her.

Rinchina was the first to visit Kota and he was effusive in his excitement at seeing the baby next to her.

'Rani, I am the happiest person in the world. I have spoken to Bulbul and I have decided that the boy's name will be Haider, the Lion.'

Kota was shocked and highly resistant.

'My Lord, when the baby was conceived you were not Islamic. In any case in Kashmir the baby is referred to as belonging to the mother. In consultations with Devaswami I have chosen the name Chander for him.'

Rinchina was defiant.

'He is my son and he will be named for the future that I have picked, not for my past.'

Kota was fierce, like a lioness.

'This is a ploy to grab control of my son the way the kingdom and the Kashmiri people have been stolen. I will not let you make my son a pawn of court power politics.'

'Your son? You are merely the earth. I am the farmer that planted the seed. I am the one who gets to harvest the crop.'

Kota sprang up in bed and shouted back at her husband: 'Don't talk like an illiterate peasant. He is mine and he belongs to Kashmir and he will be raised as a Kashmiri and not in a Mussalman household.'

The marriage alliance, which many had questioned, was now an open battle line drawn around Haider. Courtly niceties, which masked murderous intent, were stripped away. Finally, a difficult compromise was agreed upon: the baby would be addressed as Haider Chander or Chander Haider depending on one's preference. It was agreed that the boy would be raised with teachings in all three faiths: Islam, Shaivism and Buddhism, this being the Kashmiri way. Ravan was designated as his tutor since he was acceptable to both sides. Kotarani was bitter about the naming compromise and took a mental oath to take all steps to protect her son.

As Haider's designated protector and mentor, Ravan started spending time with Bulbul to learn more about Islam so as to bring up the boy properly. In one of his meetings he had questioned Bulbul about a particularly vexing episode. Just a few years before, a Buddhist monk had returned to Kashmir from Persia and shared the reason for his return. Ilali Ghazan had converted to Islam as a prelude to ascending the throne of Persia. He had told the Buddhists: 'Those among you who wish to return to Kashmir, to Tibet and to the countries whence you came, may do so.' Those who stayed behind were made Mussalmans and their temples and images destroyed. What was even more troubling was that earlier there had been a dialogue between a Buddhist monk and Shaykh Ala-al-Dawla Simnani, a key Sufi figure with connections to the Persian court. The Buddhist monk had made the case that violence against any living creature was against the Buddha's teachings. He forbade violence even to the grass on which one trod. The gist of the Sufi's reply was that he was familiar with the teachings of Buddha but the killing of those who were non-believers was like the action of gardeners who prune the branches of fruit-bearing trees in order to improve their yield. By the act of jihad, mankind was made more obedient to God's will.

Bulbul's reassurance and kindness assuaged Ravan's fears and confusion about what the Sufis really stood for. He explained that jihad was the inner struggle of the soul that one wages against egotistic desires from achieving inner peace. Explained in this way, it was no different from what the rishis had been preaching in Kashmir since time immemorial: there was no compulsion in religion or coercion in Islam, and freedom of religion was laid down in the Koran itself. Rinchina would often join Ravan and Bulbul and they would talk late in the night discussing how Haider would be educated and brought up. Soon Ravan had bonded so closely with Rinchina that his initial reservations were not even a distant memory.

During these settled times, the fakir went to see Shah Mir in his black gown and his black turban. Shah Mir had not seen the man exert himself at all on his stated mission of searching for herbs but had comfortably ensconced himself in the charity kitchen. He had built a strong following, with many youngsters preferring to listen to him over Bulbul. Once the pleasantries were over, Shah Mir asked the fakir for a report on the charity kitchen.

'Every day 400 kilograms of rice is cooked,' the fakir said proudly. 'One ram is slaughtered for the soup. Sixty kilograms of flour is used for baking bread. We alternate beef and cereals since the costs have risen, but most importantly there are group prayers five times a day,' he concluded triumphantly.

'No, don't worry about the costs,' Shah Mir overruled. 'Feed the Sufis meat every day. They have to be strong for the mission ahead of them. Are their women producing children? We need to grow our numbers beyond our 800 to be safe and secure.'

'Yes, the families range from six to eight. I have told them nothing less than a dozen and they should take wives from the local women who are freely available. Of course the permanent solution is that we have to bring in our Shia brothers from Persia in greater numbers.'

'You are right. We have to get to at least 10,000; so, send the word to Persia that Kashmir is hospitable to the Mussalmans,' counselled Shah Mir. 'Is there anything else that you would like to discuss?'

The fakir brusquely came to the point: 'Word has it that Layla is suckling a Hindu baby who is not of the family. There is no such thing as adoption in this situation, and so this is haram, a sin. The baby will grow up to be a man and Layla's nudity will have been exposed to a man other than you. There is really very little that can be acceptable about this arrangement.' Shah Mir studied the intense man carefully. The fakir had appointed himself to the role of conscience keeper in the small Mussalman community. The charity kitchen had embedded him with the weaker section of society while Bulbul was seen as the preceptor to the king and families. Clearly, the fakir was of limited theoretical intelligence, but ambitious.

Shah Mir spoke pleadingly: '*Wali*, we would be lost without your watchful guidance. This suckling ensures that my family cannot enter into any marital relationship with Brahma Bhatt's family. Given our frequent social intercourse this protects us and segregates us from the Kashmiris.'

The fakir, while not entirely satisfied, was mollified by Shah Mir's response. Shah Mir had addressed him as Wali, the spiritual protector, and shown respect even though he was not entitled to the honorific. The wet nurse issue was really designed to test Shah Mir, who had now shown that he was willing to be respectful and considerate.

Encouraged, the fakir pressed on.

'There is concern that certain leading Mussalmans have started accompanying Rinchina and Kotarani to temples to celebrate the festivals of the Kashmiris. While the Mussalmans are not admitted to the inner sanctum, they see the idols from a distance and watch the Kashmiris engage in their rituals. I enjoin you in your duty not to support idolatry.'

Shah Mir sighed at the man's impracticality.

'Maulvi,' he said, 'Rinchina is maharaja, and he must be present with his people. He rules with the consent of the Kashmiris, not in spite of them. Kotarani is Hindu and she accompanies him to the Mussalman congregation at Bulbul's and he reciprocates. I attend as an observer, not as a participant: for me not to attend would be to jeopardize the fate of our small community.'

The fakir admonished, 'Take not as your *Bitaanah* those outside your religion, since they will not fail to do their best to corrupt you. They desire to harm you severely. One day there has to be jihad in Kashmir.'

Shah Mir responded forcefully.

'Allah does not forbid you to deal justly and kindly with those who fought not against you on account of religion, nor drove you out of your homes. Tell me, when was the last time that we Mussalmans were persecuted for our faith in Kashmir? You and I sought sanctuary here and have lived a life of peace ever since. In fact, the only evil that has come our way was when Dulucha invaded this land and caused terror and misery for everyone. There is no basis for jihad in Kashmir, which should be declared as Dar-ul-Aman – the land of peace.'

Shah Mir switched tack and asked the fakir what was really weighing on his mind.

'There is an empty ink bottle that needs to be filled,' he responded quickly. 'There is no way that Haider can be kept with his parents, or handed over to Ravan as per Rinchina's agreement, or be trained in all the faiths. Haider has to be brought up in a proper Mussalman household where he can be trained in the Islamic way of life. Bulbul is too liberal, lax and withdrawn in such matters, but I understand what Islam requires. I am duty-bound to follow its tenets – and, equally importantly, I require that the tenets be observed by all Mussalmans to the fullest extent.'

Shah Mir picked up on the fakir's brilliant thinking, reflecting recent Islamic learned discourse. Social mixing could be tolerated as a means to an end, but the fakir's ultimate goal was the total enforcement of Islam in the Valley. He himself was thinking small in the land of Dar-ul-Dawa, the house of invitation, while the fakir was thinking of Dar-ul-Islam, the land of Islam and Shariat. Haider was the key to going from Sharada to Shariat and the fakir was determined to hold the key. Bulbul had served his purpose and the fakir was the ascendant power in their community.

'We are in agreement, and you have my word that I will spare no effort to have Haider brought up as a proper Mussalman,' said Shah Mir. He was beginning to recognize that the fakir, within his limitations, could be a useful ally. Yes, he had been successful at court because of his wits, but the Kashmiris were meritorious and he could be replaced tomorrow. The fakir's strength was power and he needed that to fall back upon if required. When the fakir departed, it was with an implicit understanding that a new equation had been established.

Shah Mir knew that Rinchina had developed a deep bond with Bulbul. The Ladakhi traders would immortalize their friendship in the Song of Bodro Masjid. He decided that the best course to follow was to invite Bulbul to his small Khanqah, and when he came he honoured him. Bulbul was shown the small charity kitchen that mimicked the one Rinchina had granted him; he saw Shah Mir's charitable works and the fakir's devotion in maintaining the culture of the small Mussalman community. As a sensitive soul it moved him to tears. It was then that Shah Mir made his suggestion.

'*Bab*, you are our doorway to Paradise. There is a small matter that I most humbly seek your intercession on. It concerns our future, that of Haider. He should be brought up in a Muslim household.'

Bulbul had a soft spot for Shah Mir: it was through his suggestion that Rinchina and Bulbul's paths had crossed, and the benefit of the suggestion was plain to see. He promised Shah Mir that he would propose to Rinchina that Haider be moved to a Mussalman household as soon as was practical. He questioned as to which household would be the right one to host the prince.

'I commit that when the time comes my family would consider it an honour and a duty to do whatever would be necessary to raise Haider,' Shah Mir said humbly.

On Chander Haider's first birthday Kotarani had arranged for a celebration of the new spirit and era: universal love and brotherhood based on justice for all! The nobility had been mandated to come to the court for a grand unveiling. The Mussalmans and the fakir were there, the Buddhists were there, the Damara chieftains, and of course the Brahmins. It was the first time that the Kashmiri royalty had seen the fakir: he was tall and anorexic, with a grim visage. His long, yellow beard was in strong contrast to his knee-length, tattered, black woolen shirt. He limped slightly, supporting himself with a stick. What was striking was how bloodless and pale he was. The Kashmiris prided themselves on their fair complexion, and his ghastly whiteness made them look dark. The yellow beard was almost like a covering of pus around his face. The self-mortification marks visible on his underarms were an anathema to the Kashmiris, who treated their bodies as divine. They instinctively shrank away from him, as if he was an albino, making him an island in a culture that was all about intimacy.

Kotarani had commissioned an exciting artist, Santosh, whose skill as a sculptor was such that his work seemed to come to life. He could arouse powerful emotions and he was known to push the boundaries of the physical into the metaphysical. He was a rebel, unconstrained by social boundaries. His wife was named Santoshi – when they had married, he had taken on his wife's name in defiance of Kashmiri convention. He personally received the honoured guests and seated them in a circle around the covered piece, positioned on a rotating platform.

Kotarani had enormous respect for Santosh. Kashmiri sculptors were world-renowned and she and Rinchina had been looking forward to the unveiling. Shah Mir and his small band of Mussalman guests watched the proceedings in awe. Santoshi's forefathers had carved the Bamiyan Buddha. He dedicated the piece to them and had named the sculpture 'Six Faces'. He removed the covering with a flourish and slowly Santosh and his assistants began to rotate the sculpture. The Kashmiris watched intently as the piece, cast in bronze, revealed its six profiles. First, the familiar trinity of Brahma, then Shiva, then Vishnu; then Buddha, then Jesus Christ and finally Mohammed. The images were positioned on the corners of a Star of David. It was a double triad, the doubling of the *Trimurtis,* synthesizing the six great religious figures that were now a part of the Valley's life. But as the piece revolved, it became apparent that the back of each face was identical – and they were Shakti! Inside were the recursive triangles of the Sri Yantra; the whole piece centred on a dot, the *bindu*.

An appreciative murmur spread through the crowd.

'The external faces are different and individual, but inside they are identical and non-dual. *Pratyabhijina*, the Kashmiri doctrine of self-recognition; *antarmukhi drishti*, the sight that faces inwards; male and female fused in each piece.'

The piece spoke to the crowd's aesthetic sensibilities.

The fakir, however, had been muttering to himself during the unveiling. Sitting behind Shah Mir he suddenly stood up and before anyone could stop him, he lunged at the artist with a shriek. In his hand he held a small knife that had been hidden in his robe. It went straight through Santosh's ribs and into his heart and brought to an end the artist's foolhardy and foolish vision. To portray Mohammed, Peace be upon Him, was the ultimate blasphemy: the cultural cross-currents had hidden an undertow that had sucked the artist to his doom.

The guards fell on the fakir and took him prisoner. He was like a white wolf in his fury, and it took six men to pin him to the ground. There was total pandemonium in the assembly. The nobles had pulled out their swords and had circled the small band of Mussalmans, including Shah Mir: only Rinchina and Kotarani's personal intercession saved their lives. Kotarani had to send her personal guard, the Ekangas, alongside Shah Mir and his small band so that they would not be attacked on their return home. Slowly the assembly disbanded, the guests leaving stunned and furious. Rinchina and Kotarani knew that the murder would send shock waves throughout the kingdom, and that it represented the touchstone test of their rule. Because of his recent conversion to Islam, Rinchina in particular was under the spotlight and he needed to show where he stood on the matter. A meeting was arranged and the principals assembled in the justice hall of the fort.

Thousands of agitated Kashmiris had converged at the courthouse. The Mussalmans gathered in a separate corner, and their large presence was surprising to the Kashmiris. Anticipating the big crowd, the entire law and order enforcement contingency of the kingdom had been commandeered. When Kota and Rinchina were seated on their thrones, for the first time in living memory, each of the twenty-three ministers was in attendance. The king and the queen were decked in their royal crowns, the parasol attendants discreetly behind them. In addition, there were the oligarchs who exercised their hereditary privileges. Then there were the Damara landlords, the merchants and the representatives of the various guilds and *Samiti* communities. The Chief of police, the *Dandanayaka*, personally escorted the fakir into the court and the trial was ready to begin.

The minister of justice, the *Rajasthanadhikara*, whose title indicated that his prime role was the protection of the kingdom's subjects, gave the opening statement. Dressed in his official topcoat and wearing a wig, he was an imposing figure. His position was clear: the fakir had murdered the artist Santosh before any number of witnesses. The fakir's defence was that the artist had committed blasphemy, but this was no defence at all: artistic freedom had been violated, the rules of Kashmir's civil society had been transgressed, and death was the only adequate punishment. It was an open-and-shut case. Law and order had to be re-established; otherwise vigilantism would rule the Valley, with each person claiming the arbitrary power to dictate to others what behaviour was offensive and what was not. There would be anarchy within society if the people ceased to conform to a single civil code.

The artist's widow was given a chance to speak. She had gone mad with her grief, shrieking: 'I curse this Mussalman. What I suffer today, may he and his descendants suffer a thousand times over! May they never have the pleasures of their spouses or their children! May his sons' sons never live to see the bloom of youth! May his daughters and womenfolk turn into widows just as I am a widow today! May Rudra grant that stray dogs drink the milk from their breasts! Oh Suhdev, you let these alien absconders inside Kashmir! You paid the price, then so did the brave Kampanesa Ramachandra! Now these maneaters have turned on us ordinary folks!'

Utterly distraught and inconsolable, the woman had to be led away. Kotarani could see that Rinchina had been made very uncomfortable by the reference to Ramachandra.

It was Shah Mir's turn to speak: the Mussalman community had nominated him to defend the fakir. He had spent days with them trying to come up with a strong defence. He bowed deeply to Rinchina and Kotarani before he spoke.

'Raja and maharani, today we are here to test the core values of Kashmir. In Kashmir diverse faiths have resided based on mutual respect and the ability to exercise free choice. Religious scholars have debated with each other and the losers have honoured the winners by crossing over to the other faith. Why, just yesterday Ravan and the honourable Bulbul debated the merits of Islam. Where there has not been respect for religion, such as that shown by Harsha, it has been universally condemned. The artist portrayed Mohammed, Peace be upon Him, an unforgivable sin, and the fakir was duty-bound to avenge this blasphemy. Would the Brahmins permit an artist to slaughter a cow in front of a temple and then use the blood to paint a mural on the temple walls in the name of artistic freedom? No, the Brahmins would lay down their lives before they would permit such an act. I ask that we all condemn the artist's action because it was hurtful; I ask that the fakir's action be viewed as being one of righteous self-defence, no different than a Brahmin would do. I am the fakir's sponsor and I will not disassociate myself from him, howsoever misguided his actions may be perceived by Kashmiri society.

'But let us say that the fakir's action was wrong. Even then I would argue that the death penalty is inappropriate. In Kashmir the Brahmins are protected from capital punishment irrespective of whatever crime they may have committed. Is there no equality of religion in Kashmir? Is Islam inferior to Hinduism? Is the fakir not to have the same rights as the Brahmin?'

Shah Mir had found his voice and hit his stride: he was no longer diplomatic, he was self-righteous. He was laying seeds of doubt, building a counter-argument, taking apart the open-and-shut case. Then he played his trump card confidently.

'My Lord Rinchina, your title now is Sadar-ud-Din. Baba Bulbul gave you that name in recognition of your critical role as the first Mussalman ruler of Kashmir. Sadar-ud-Din, the leader of the Mussalman religion, cannot authorize the death of a Mussalman religious figure. Outside our gates are poised the armies of the Ghazis: today they see in you a Mussalman ruler and a kingdom where the Mussalmans live in peace, and their attentions are turned towards the plains of Hindustan. Would you have them once again turn their gaze towards Kashmir because Islam is in danger? Would you have them declare jihad against all Kashmiris because a Mussalman cleric was slain?'

Rinchina was silent and seemed to be affected by Shah Mir's appeal. However, the justice minister was not done yet.

'Shah Mir argues that the death penalty is wrong for the fakir when the fakir had no compunction in executing the death penalty on the artist. There are several other aspects to the fakir's transgressions, which need to be presented to our king and queen. I call my first witness Saras to the front.'

Kota was surprised to see Saras stand and face the fakir.

The minister continued.

'The fakir entered this kingdom on the pretext that he had come to collect herbs. I present to him three of the most common herbs and ask him to recognize and name them so we can see what progress he has made.'

An attendant showed the fakir three herbs on a silver platter. The fakir glared at the platter but was silent. The minister asked Saras to name them.

'*Bankakri* for tumours, *Kuth* as a painkiller, *Afsanteen* for liver gastritis and inflammation.' She then withdrew.

'What kind of test is this to humiliate this poor fakir?' Shah Mir protested. 'He is a Sufi. They don't seek material knowledge but manifest knowledge, knowledge of the spirit.'

'Sufi, huh?' the grim-faced justice minister ploughed ahead. 'I want to present my next witness.'

Shah Mir was surprised to see the chief of police escorting the comely boy from the charity kitchen in. He was instructed to tell his story.

The youth did not look at the fakir and started haltingly.

'It was late at night and I was in my cell sleeping when I heard a knock. I opened the door and the fakir was outside. I asked him if everything was fine. He said that he had come to talk about our relationship, describing it as a relationship between lovers.'

The boy stopped, but the justice minister prodded him. He continued hesitantly.

'He said, "In the beginning, one is desirous of becoming the pupil but in truth the preceptor seeks the pupil." He said that when he slept I would be with him in his dreams and when he would wake up and see me he would literally faint. He said that the love he had as a master for me was a hundred times more powerful than the love my mother had for me. He ended by saying that I was his destination and he wanted to make a home in my heart.'

The crowd murmured. The justice minister was doing his job with great effectiveness and Shah Mir sensed that the fakir was finished in Kashmiri society forever. Kashmiris were liberal, yes, but fiercely opposed to predatory, exploitative behaviour.

Kota intervened.

'What happened next?' she asked the boy.

'I rushed past the fakir and ran out. I did not stop running till I reached the hut of a relative of mine. I have been there ever since and have not returned back to the Khanqah.'

'There is no proof that what the youth has said is true,' Kota told the minister. 'Sufis are apt to use the language of lust-less love for the Divine, so it is not clear whether the boy understood what the fakir meant. Even if it is substantiated and found to be true, howsoever different the fakir may be, if he were punished for his interest in the youth, then Kokur would end up in jail too. Minister, this seems to be extraneous to the case. Kokur, since the artist was known to you what say you on this subject?'

Kokur was taken unawares by Kotarani's question, and he knew it was not to be taken lightly.

'Maharani and raja,' he said, 'we are simple artists. We look to our ruler for our security and protection. An artist is one-third mad, one-third genius and one-third spiritual. He does not control the forces that are his muse; instead he is controlled by them. Most of us, starting with me, are seen as non-conformist, perhaps socially deviant, even perverse. In Kashmir when we see a madman throwing stones at us, we do not respond in kind: we give the mot his space, recognizing that he lives in a different reality. Kashmir has always given its artists their space, and in return we have contributed to its culture and glory. Yet, today, we tremble in fear for our lives. Now the judgement for works of art is not fame or social ridicule or indifference but death at the hands of a self-styled censor.

'Raja Rinchina, Sher-e-Kashmir, knows that when the Buddha lived he too instructed his followers not to draw or portray his likeness. But when he died the artists began to create his image and the public found peace and serenity in contemplating these. Should the lamas have authorized that the artists who had made sculptures of Gautama Buddha be killed? Would the Buddha truly have been blasphemed by such an act? The artist in me says no to both questions.'

Rinchina interjected.

'But who are you to make that decision for the Mussalmans for whom Prophet Mohammed, Peace be upon Him, is sacred?'

Kokur drew his breath before answering.

'We artists believe that the whole world reflects the beauty of Shiva and nothing is off limits. To kill an artist is to kill a faculty of human insight that directly leads to divinity. Even if this is deemed as being off limits there is no issue of fraudulent transgression, no offence was intended and none was executed; instead it is an issue of security for us artists. Is it safe for us to practise our dharma?'

The courtiers listened to Kokur with new-found respect. Here was a person who lived on the periphery of society, coming to life only on the stage, and suddenly events had thrown him to the centre of the most gripping drama of all.

Rinchina and Kotarani withdrew into their private quarters to discuss their decision. An angry Kotarani went first.

'It is an open-and-shut case. We were witness to it. The fakir is to be sentenced to death for the murder. He has to be beheaded.'

Rinchina demurred.

'I think Shah Mir makes very good points. The fakir has to be judged the way a Brahmin would. We cannot condemn him to death.'

Kotarani was dismissive.

'Don't use our rules to justify actions against our own society. The fakir did not behave like a Brahmin who never takes a life. Now he cannot demand the same protections that the Brahmin enjoys. A murderer is a murderer, Brahmin, Mussalman or otherwise.'

'But the fakir is duty-bound to protest against a portrait of Prophet Mohammed, Peace be upon Him, that blasphemes his faith.'

'When the fakir came to Kashmir he is duty-bound to live our way of life, not impose his visitor laws on us, certainly not those which result in the murder of an innocent man.'

The two went back and forth on the issue. Kota was increasingly frustrated. 'A murderer cannot be expected to punish a fellow murderer,' she finally spat out. She saw that she had cut deep into Rinchina.

'I have made an irrevocable promise to Pandita Lakshmi that I will never ever be a party to taking a life,' Rinchina replied.

Kota weakened in the face of Rinchina's personal commitment, and she gave her final position. They returned to the hall and delivered their judgment. The fakir would be released from prison: his face would be blackened; he would be made to ride an ass backwards with his hands tied behind his back. He would be exiled from the Valley and shipped back to Kandahar, where he would be set free. There he could live with other people like himself. The death penalty would have been passed in spirit because in Kashmir a social death was far worse than a physical one: by the same token, the fakir's life had been spared, which spared the kingdom the risk of affronting Rinchina's adopted faith. The widow of the artist was to be given sufficient compensation so that she and her children could lead an honourable life even without their breadwinner. Most of the Kashmiri leaders saw this as a workable solution and one that they could live with, and praised Rinchina and Kotarani for their sagacity. One of the Damara leaders, Lone, who represented the Lavanaya clan, rushed out to share the verdict with the jostling crowd. A cheer went up, the kettledrums beating in celebration that justice, the cornerstone of Bhatta society, had been enforced. That night when Kotarani fell asleep it was with the relief that she had expelled a dangerous snake and his highly poisonous views from the Valley. But in her fitful sleep the wind rustled through the trees dotting the Valley and raced through the mountain passes to Afghanistan, whispering, 'Fakir, you have killed an innocent man ...' The guardian mountains were also upstanding in their message. Through time and space echoed the widow's curse: 'What I suffer today may he and his descendants suffer a thousand times over.'

Meanwhile, Shah Mir was selling the royal judgment to his fellow Mussalmans in the village of Malchmar.

'Look at how we won,' he said persuasively. 'The fakir walks away with his life. He was not put to death. He did not compromise on his principles. He was treated as a Brahmin would have been in the same position. Islam is not in danger; we are not in danger.'

But one young fellow, Ali, who was under the fakir's sway, spoke up. 'We have just begun to fight. We have to fight them so long as idol worship does not end and Allah's religion is not loved by all. Only then will we be secure in Kashmir.' Ali was a cavalry officer. The older people, however, did not support the hothead, and it was generally accepted that Shah Mir had done his best under the circumstances.

Ali was adamant. 'From now on the fakir will be called *Mujah-e-Awwal*, the first warrior. Others will follow him.'

Large crowds gathered on the day of the fakir's departure. When he was led out by the guards, he cut a very sorry figure. The Kashmiris booed him, shouting, 'The white wolf rejoins his pack!' Some of them had brought bags of faeces and started pelting the fakir with them. The bags burst on the fakir's face and body. He started screaming, turning his body in all possible ways to avoid the flying missiles.

'Kashmiris, I will return!' he vowed. 'And when I return you will beg to be let go, and shout to the sky that you are not a Kashmiri Bhatta!' Turning his bloodshot eyes towards the small band of Mussalmans, he shouted: 'You are not true Mussalmans! You have become corrupt and debauched alongside the infidels. When I return I will come with my pack and you will become true Mussalmans! You will drink from purity and penance as opposed to wine. Then we will punish the kafirs! We will first order them to adopt Islam; if they do not accept Islam, we will kill them! We will slay them wherever they are found! We will hunt down the royal fox and put an end to her heat. Jihad will prevail in Kashmir.'

Guhara was also present alongside her father. Unable to stand the diatribe that flowed from the homicidal fakir, something snapped inside her. She picked up a stone and threw it with all her might at the fakir. With uncanny accuracy it hit him in the mouth. He did not know from where it came or who had thrown it, but it succeeded in its intended effect. He fell silent: the only thing that came out of his mouth was the blood that oozed from his lips. Slowly, he and his guards faded into the distance.

Ali observed the whole episode, as the cavalry officer had been asked to escort the fakir to the border. When he returned to the village he announced that from that day onwards he and other devoted followers of the fakir would rename their village Persia-e-Sagheer, or little Persia. In respect of the fakir's admonitions to the Mussalmans they would impose Shariat law in the village, one that had opted out of Kashmiri civil society; while they had not declared secession, from now on the Mussalmans would operate within their own Islamic rules and laws.

It was several months later that Kotarani received a request from Ravan that they should meet. When the attendants ushered Ravan in, she greeted her brother warmly. But Kotarani was ill-prepared for what was to follow.

'I think that Rinchina has it right. This episode with the fakir tells me that what Kashmir needs is a Kshatriya mind and a Mussalman body,' said Ravan. 'We need to advance and move forward.'

'So, what do you mean, Ravan?' the queen asked hesitantly.

'I have decided to convert to Islam,' he announced dramatically.

Kotarani was shocked. She challenged her brother.

'Ravan, you are the highest-ranking Kashmiri noble to want to convert. Do you understand the consequences your actions will have for the people? How will you perform your annual *shraadha* duties towards your ancestors with Devaswami? When there is turmoil all around, there is all the more reason to stay steady and not be swept away by the winds of change.'

Ravan was not to be denied.

'From today I will be a Mussalman Kshatriya. I do not think that I am giving anything up: instead I am gaining an additional marker. I can still sit down with Devaswami and perform my filial duties. As far as the public is concerned, the security of our kingdom is my foremost duty as a Kshatriya warrior. Our greatest threat is from the Ghazis, and if we are already a kingdom ruled by Mussalman kings, there is no need to invade our kingdom.'

Kota was frantic with worry.

'Ravan, I am not sure what the personal consequences are of what you are doing.' But Ravan was adamant.

'There are no personal consequences. I will not eat the meat of a cow and I will not eat pork. Rinchina sees this conversion as highly desirable – he will no longer be perceived as an outcast or an alien. In return he has made me the prime minister of Ladakh and Kashmir. He has conferred upon me the title of Raina, master and possessor. Don't you see if something was to happen to Rinchina it would make me a figure of unity for all sides?'

Kotarani was shocked at this declaration. What ideas had Rinchina been pumping into Ravan's immature head? Even if something was to happen to Rinchina she was still the queen, Haider was her son and they were not going to be disregarded.

'Ravan, I am now even more uneasy about this step. It must have been very important to Rinchina to secure your conversion?'

'Sister, there is nothing sinister here. In fact, Rinchina shared his philosophy with me that rulers of empires cannot belong to a single faith. He told me that he is only a half Mussalman and that is what I will be. Nobody cares to read the plaque that he posted on the Awwal masjid which says clearly: "My friend for the sake of gaiety has become the observed of observers. His face claimed Islam and his hair adorned dharma. He controls both dharma and Islam and takes interest in both."'[15] Kota was surprised, "You mean that Richina's conversion is a fake story? For political expediency?"

Ravan was noncommittal, "I am not at liberty to reveal more than what the plaque says."

Kota was unconvinced.

'You cannot have your legs in two different boats. Can a woman claim that she is a unifier by becoming half pregnant with two men? What is Tukka's response to losing his position as prime minister?'

'Tukka has no choice but to do as Rinchina tells him,' Ravan retorted. 'In any case, Rinchina has very ambitious plans and sees us as retaking control of Tibet, and eventually the entire Silk Road.

There will be enough for Tukka to share in: he is a warrior; he is ill suited to be a ruler. He is still commander-in-chief of the military.'

'Ravan, to compromise on your principles is not something that you do for opportunistic gain or for power or for gaining an additional marker. Rinchina is expedient and not the right role model here. He has for sure lost Tukka in exchange for uncertain gain. Have you talked to Devaswami about this, or even to Brahma Bhatt?'

Ravan became defensive; countering his sister.

'Look who is talking about opportunistic gain! I did not marry our father's murderer. Your firstborn will be raised as a Mussalman as per the agreement that Rinchina reached with Shah Mir. Because of that Rinchina told me that he could not honour his agreement to have me as Haider's godfather. I am not being coerced; I am converting out of free choice. If Rinchina wants to reward me what is wrong with that? Brahma Bhatt is not interested in spiritual matters, and I will go and see Devaswami by and by. In any case, he did not seem to exhibit any great interest in making Rinchina a Hindu when Rinchina went to visit him. Bulbul really cares about me – he and I have established a deep bond.'

Kotarani was enraged by her own brother's bald statement, but she knew that a thousand people must have made the same statement in the bazaars. She responded nastily.

'Posterity will be my judge in marrying Rinchina, not you. I fear, Ravan, that you will blacken your name in the history of Kashmir as the highest noble who left his community for personal gain. You will not be seen as the son of Ramachandra but instead as a person who was breastfed by a surrogate who poisoned you forever.'

'Don't you ever bring up mother's milk to my face,' Ravan retorted. 'I have royal blood just like you. Let history judge me also and I think that history will judge me as a person who was not afraid to advance in his thinking. Rinchina is the temporal ruler of Kashmir and Bulbul is the most spiritual person today in the Valley; to deny these facts and instead live in the past is to be blind to the future.'

'The Mussalmans are unclean,' Kota said. 'You want to be one of them?' She shuddered at the thought of Ravan joining their practices.

'I am not going to eat beef and I am not going to commit sodomy. The rest is individual preference.'

'Ravan, I fear that today a great distance has come between us. This is not about accepting Bulbul; this is about giving up. Your action will deprive your sons and daughters, all your future generations, of the highest truths of our land! It is their right that you are taking away.'

'I did not expect this to be easy, but my mind is made up. I see no loss but only gain. Why would I lose out on the highest truths of our land if I become a Mussalman Hindu? After all, I am only adding one more Veda, the Mausala Veda, to my scriptures. If it does not work out well, I can always revert. There is nothing stopping me.'

Kotarani cut him off curtly.

'Ravan, if it was only that easy, then fish could swim backward... but I think that we have spoken enough on this subject for one day.'

With that dismissal Ravan took his leave. He left Kotarani in a state of white rage. Ravan's intended conversion had enabled Rinchina to encircle Kotarani with those who were now loyal to him. Brother and sister had been forever torn apart. What else had Rinchina promised a gullible Ravan? That he would have a shot at the throne if something happened to him thus disinheriting Chander. Kashmiri families had historically had many tributaries but for the first time a distributary had split off, never to rejoin the main stream. She sent a messenger to have Brahma brought to her; when he came she shared with him the troubling political developments crafted by Rinchina and Shah Mir.

'Bulbul and Rinchina are very close,' Brahma counselled. 'Ravan is an impressionable young man who, after the premature death of his father, is trying to fit into a world of adults. He has nobody to counter the influence that Rinchina is exercising on him. Rinchina has taken the young man under his wing, and it is understandable that the story of his convertion is a powerful one for your brother. Ravan must have felt some pressure to emulate his brother-in-law.'

'He is a turncoat to his ancestors and to his family!' Kota tried. 'He has been promised the throne at the expense of Chander and as a result he has completely lost his wits.'

'Title and power are heady stuff; he is too callow to understand court intrigues and Rinchina has found a pawn. We have to find a way to help Ravan get through this infatuation. This is an adolescent rebellion and over time he will come back to his roots.'

Kota's rage was uncontrollable.

'Rinchina went back on his agreement with me to raise Haider where he would be exposed to all faiths. He has unilaterally made a decision to ship Haider to Shah Mir without discussing with me. I will fight this decision tooth and nail and rescue my son.'

Brahma was concerned about Kotarani's distress. Knowing that it would help her to relax, he suggested that they go for a short ride and once Kotarani was astride her horse she felt better; she was bonded with her mount and being outdoors with Brahma made her feel better. The mountains had been there for millennia and would be there for millennia to come: there was a quiet strength to them, and they seemed to tell Kotarani that everything would work itself out.

'I will invite Ravan to visit us for dinner so that he can better understand his decision,' Brahma offered.

'I think it is a good idea. Save him, but as far as Rinchina is concerned I will show him that I can strike in his inner circle also.'

'How do you feel about Rinchina?' Brahma asked, concerned.

'He is a peasant by nature, a warrior by profession. He can drink and he can kill but he does have a sense of rough and ready justice.'

'Does he make an attempt to connect with you?'

'No, he is very self-centred on his goals and cares not a bit about the means. He was my death sentence, but if I passed, I would have been his death sentence. Hence we married each other for survival. We now have Chander, but beyond that we have no connection.'

'As you know, Rinchina is not my favourite, though I am surprised that Shah Mir has moved closer to him,' Brahma revealed. 'Whatever you do you can count on me.'

Brahma left Kotarani in a slightly better frame of mind than when he had come – the benefit of a true friend – but she had not cooled off. That day when Kotarani went to pray at dusk her mind was made up. She pulled out her diary and, grim-faced, wrote out her sentence on Rinchina.

Dear Mother,

Chander is my firstborn. He is from my womb. The germ plasm of each cell in him is my life force. When I married Rinchina I sidestepped his transgressions and gave him the kingdom that he lusted for. I did not give him the right to place my baby son with Shah Mir or to deprive him of his hereditary right to be the next king of Kashmir. I was deprived of your love and now Rinchina has grievously violated my innermost yearning to surround my son with all the love that he deserves. I may have rented my body temporarily, but I did not give up my maternal right, the most sacred right of any woman. When Shakti's firstborn was taken away her fury was unbounded. So is mine. I will break my marriage vows, cruel though it may be. For the first time now and forever I will not recite the protective mantras that Devaswami gave me. May Mars no longer be blocked and may it move forward on its dharmic trajectory. Your implacable daughter, ℛ

Rinchina, having ruled for nearly three years and having secured a loyal ruling cadre at the top of the kingdom, desired a vacation and left for Achchhoda lake with a small contingent led by Ali. The Mussalman cavalry had become Rinchina's personal guard, a mirror to Kotarani's bodyguards, the Ekangas. Rinchina took the opportunity to get close to Ali and accord him honours. The lake was the perfect setting to bond. Ali was still a bachelor and Rinchina encouraged him to get married as part of his advancement in court. Both sat together enjoying the gentle breeze by the lakeside. A server brought juicy watermelon slices and *husaini* and *fakhri* grapes so sweet that poets would say they were rare in heaven. Rinchina drank a glass of the Muskhabad wine but Ali was a strict teetotaller. A kingfisher rested on the branch of a nearby tree, its eyes alert, monitoring for innocent fish. A mother hen was pecking on the shore near a boat, followed by her cackling chicks. Children were splashing around in the water. At one end of the lake a fisherman was in a trance watching his fishing line. Next to him his sleepy dog watched the world with one eye lazily open while the flies buzzed around his face. Only up close could one see the faintest of ripples starting to make wavelets as the evening wind picked up. In the wavelets one could see the reflection of the trees growing on the riverbank. Rinchina walked over to the bank and saw his face staring back at him. He liked what he saw; a man who had achieved his goals and yet had more to offer the world. It was a reassuring reflection; just what Rinchina needed. After a month's restful stay, he was rejuvenated and ready to return to Srinagar.

The night before he left, a party of villagers requested an audience with him concerning a grievance. Rinchina invited them in. The head of the group, a milk woman, spoke first. Without any fear she pointed to Timmi, Commander Tukka's younger brother, accusing him of entering the village and commandeering their milk by force without reimbursing the village for it. 'So what that Timmi was worn out by the heat?' she cried. If Rinchina was truly a king of law and order and not simply a usurper, then justice must be done.

Rinchina questioned Timmi, who flatly denied the accusation. Rinchina faced the woman, demanding to know whether she was aware of the consequences to herself, her family and the village in falsely accusing one of his courtiers.

'Oh Maharaja,' she said, 'we are not so lacking in honour that we came hoping to extract a payment for milk based on a false charge. We came for justice. The payment is a pittance, but justice is priceless.'

Rinchina squirmed at the implicit insult and turned red with anger. He drew his sword and, to the surprise and astonishment of all and Tukka's everlasting horror, he stabbed Timmi. Timmi fell to the ground and, like a lion, Rinchina slashed Timmi's stomach open. The milk gushed out in a white stream, the ultimate proof of Timmi's deceit.

'Go in peace and tell the world that tyranny has no place in Kashmir,' Rinchina proclaimed.

On his return, Rinchina found bad news awaiting him. Bulbul had been taken sick and Kotarani reported that the abbess at the Buddhist monastery had passed away inexplicably. Rinchina was reminded of the promise that he had made to her, and how he had violated it with Timmi. She had warned him of the consequences of a relapse. Kotarani also seemed to be in a bad mood, and contrary to the Kashmiris' relief at Timmi's passing, she was upset that Rinchina had short-circuited the wheels of justice in order to personally execute him.

As for Bulbul, in spite of Kotarani and Rinchina's entreaties, he resisted the help of the local physicians and said that he was waiting for Rinchina's return. Having been granted his last wish, he expired peacefully. He had entered the world with nothing, he had lived in the world with nothing and he left the world with nothing: however, his universal message of peace and love was big enough for the entire world. Bulbul's passing was truly a sad day in the kingdom, as he was the beloved of all. Rinchina arranged for his burial in Bulbul Lankar on the other side of the palace.[16]

Kotarani ordered Kumara Bhatta, the greatest strategist and historian of his generation, to come from Sharadapeeth and give a eulogy to the gathered crowd of Mussalmans and Hindus. Kumara started with a recounting of the entry of Islam into Kashmir and then concluded: 'Bulbul was a paragon of tolerance and humanity. His actions reinforced the message of the Prophet, Peace be upon Him, that there is no compulsion in religion. Islam requires us to believe in the truth of the previous scriptures delivered to the prophets of different nations. He created an atmosphere of peace and harmony among all Kashmiris. He truly was the adopted son of Kashmir. Whenever we lose sight of our way, Bulbul, who now follows the other great rishis of Kashmir, will always be there to guide us back to the right path.'

The Kashmiris, both Mussalmans and Hindus, nodded in agreement. Bulbul and the rishis would always be there to guide them during troubled times. Rinchina had listened silently to Kumara. He was absorbed in his loss. He felt very alone that day.

All of these developments had been monitored and watched carefully by Udyandev and his advisers, including the Sogdian. They now felt that an opening had been created, and they could exploit it. The Sogdian was asked to be the emissary to Tukka and, so that Rinchina could not trace him, he was advised to tell Tukka that Udyandev was based in Gandhara.

Udyandev sent Tukka a message of support stating: 'While the maharaja is yet alive, you should enter the city which he is ruling, with prudence, with a view to acquire fame. Valya is enjoying the prosperity that you have earned, even at the risk of your lives, even as the tongue enjoys what the hands acquire by their industry. As Mahadeva Shiva discarding golden ornaments and besmearing his body with ashes induced snakes to coil around him, even so the maharaja, who possesses plenty of riches, is raising Valya to power and neglects you, though you belong to a high caste. Afraid of your valour, he killed Timmi simply for taking some milk, as one kills a Timi (whale).'

The message reinforced the alienation that Tukka had been feeling, and stoked the flames of fire that burned within him. Rinchina is no longer one of you,' pressed on the Sogdian. 'He has turned into a Mussalman. His best friend and ally is Shah Mir. His mentor was Bulbul. What do you mean to him? Nothing. Have you forgotten that the worst killers of the Buddhists are the Mussalmans? Yet you continue to serve Rinchina now that he is Sadar-ud-Din. Tukka, you used to be commander-in-chief and lord of Tibet. You come from the Shukalankita dynasty of Tibet. You have had Tibet taken away from you. Tukka, are you a man who will take revenge for his brother, or will you end up as a sacrificial pawn for Rinchina?'

Udyandev and his advisers had assessed him well. Tukka had been trained all his life to kill, and so his reaction to Udyandev's message was predictable. He agonized over his lifelong relationship with Rinchina but the conclusion was inexorable: in spite of his loyalty and service he was clearly expendable in Rinchina's opportunistic plan. Rinchina could not be loyal to anybody because he had sold himself to greed. He was not a Buddhist, he was not a friend, and he was not trustworthy. The die was cast. He and his band put their plan together and attacked Rinchina at Vimshaprastha. As Tukka struck Rinchina a mighty blow on the head, he fell to the ground in a faint. Tukka turned his attention to helping his friends. His anger was assuaged in killing Rinchina, and they entered the capital with the express goal of capturing the kingdom. Meanwhile Rinchina, who had feigned death, stood up. To his immense relief he saw that Valya, hearing of the attack, had come to rescue him. Assisted by his allies, Rinchina approached the rebels. Tukka and his men, now busy robbing the palace, saw Rinchina, and a quarrel broke out among them as to who was responsible for this calamitous oversight. They turned on each other and did the work that the sultan ended up finishing. Tukka was taken prisoner, chained and held so that he could not turn away. His wife was brought forth, and Rinchina ripped open her womb, swollen with child, as one would tear open beans with one's fingernails. Tukka strained against his chains to fight but to no avail.

'Ladakh's greatest traitor!' he spat at Rinchina. 'Sher-e-Kashmir, ha! A jackal can never be a lion.'

'Die!' yelled Rinchina as he impaled Tukka, lifted him high with his sword, and flung him to the ground. In life Tukka struck fear in the hearts of everyone he came across; the Kashmiris secretly breathed a sigh of relief that there had been a falling out among the Bottas.

Rinchina tried to recover from his injuries in the next few months. He had become much more security conscious and ordered a new town to be built, Rinchinapora, which was surrounded by a moat. It was previously the site of an ancient Buddhist shrine known as Buddhagira and had given the name to the town of Bodhger. He became even closer to Shah Mir, feeling that he could no longer trust the Ladakhis. His lifelong friends and family, along with Shah Mir, had always been loyal. But in the monsoon season, his head wound became infected, and as the weather turned colder his condition got much worse. As he prepared for death, in spite of Kotarani's express wishes, he formally turned over care of his son Haider to Shah Mir, appointing him as regent and instructed him to support Kotarani in ruling the kingdom.

When he felt that his life was fading away, he turned to his wife, who was constantly by his side.

'Kotarani,' he said, 'Were you truly loyal to me?'

She replied with a question: 'Did I have any choice? Did you ask me that when you came to me with your marriage proposal? Did you care to ask that when you handed over our firstborn to Shah Mir? Does it matter now?'

'Did you instruct Devaswami to not accept me?' asked Rinchina insistently.

'No, My Lord, he did what he believed was his dharma. He was not going to legitimize your rule by giving you the coronation ceremony that you desired. You were a king in name but a murderer by fame.'

'What have I done?' were Rinchina's last words. Three years, one month and nineteen days into his rule, Rinchina died on 25 November 1323. The restless warrior was buried next to Bulbul. In death as in life, Rinchina found peace only alongside his mentor Bulbul.

Three years, one month and nineteen days into her marriage Kotarani was a widow, and the kingdom was without a protector. Her heart longed for Brahma, but he was already taken and she was no Didda, a former queen who had blithely pirated married men. Next time she would be able to choose whom to marry, and the Kashmiris would scrutinize her choice of second consort very carefully.

Chaturgrantha (Book IV)
The Householder

Wave 12
The Love Birds

MANZIM stood in front of Udyandev in the fort in Kishtwar accompanied by Brahma and Yaniv. He had come to Kishtwar on the most important commission of his career: Kotarani's committee had spent months sifting through all the potential candidates, and Udyandev's name kept coming out on top. As Suhdev's brother he was next in line and brought legitimacy to the throne, but he was totally unlike Suhdev in personality, being separated from him by over twenty years in age. He had graduated top of his class from Sharadapeeth and Devaswami had indicated that had he not been an aristocrat he would have made a perfectly competent pandit, given his intellectual interests. He was handsome and had classic Kashmiri looks. He had turned down numerous marriage proposals claiming a lack of intellectual compatibility.

Saras had listened quietly to all the discussions and advised Kota that Udyan was her best choice. She reminded Kota that Udyan had been present at her dance recital, so he knew what she looked like, which was a big plus. She also pointed out that siblings were not always alike, in case Kota was worried that he would be too similar to Suhdev.

Kotarani was intrigued and, due diligence not having uncovered any character negatives, authorized Manzim, Brahma and Yaniv on their confidential overture. Udyan did not know that she had been Angaraka, which was now a moot issue, but he did know that as a widow she was *amangal*, inauspicious. For the first time in her life Kota was a handicapped suitor, damaged goods, and it was a humiliating feeling.

Manzim held aloft a painting of a couple, Shiva and Shakti, along with an astrological chart. In the most flowery language he praised Udyandev and explained that Kotarani was open to a matrimonial alliance.

'Most strange,' remarked a perplexed Udyandev. 'Here is a maharani who marries her father's murderer and the murderer of my brother; then, when she is widowed, proposes to marry the man who was instrumental in her husband's assassination. She has truly set a new low in the standards of Kashmiri maharanis.'

'My Lord, you wrong my maharani,' Manzim protested. 'She is the daughter of Ramachandra, who was loyal to your brother Suhdev to the end and gave his life on Suhdev's behalf. When Kotarani was taken prisoner she did what she had to do to avenge herself: only she, her father and the jyotish knew that she was Angaraka. It was foretold that the first man she would marry would die and so she married Rinchina.' 'What nonsense,' said Udyandev. 'Manzim, I understand that you have to fabricate stories in your line of business, but we are talking about a royal alliance here. Everybody knows that Kashmiri women are tigers, but you are telling me that Kotarani is a maneater.'

'Maharaja,' protested Manzim, 'if you truly think that I am lying, ask anybody who attended the wedding of Kotarani and Rinchina

What Kotarani was wearing: it was an all-white dress. The Ladakhis thought that it was reflective of their *katak*s, but it was really Kotarani's way of communicating to the Kashmiris that she was becoming a widow.' Kotarani's choice of white for her wedding clothes had been much talked about in the Kashmiri community as being inauspicious, and people had wondered who could have advised Kotarani to do so. The Kashmiris traditionally wore white in mourning; Udyandev had to concede Manzim's point. He turned to Brahma.

'You know Kotarani better than any person alive. I attended Kota's dance recital and remember there were stories that you were committed to each other. Is what Manzim is saying true?'

Brahma responded with a pang in his heart at the hand that life had dealt him, where he had become an ambassador for Kotarani's marriages.

'I swear on my son's head that this secret is true. I came with Manzim to vouch for Kotarani. As for us, we are only friends. We have exchanged Raksha Bandhan and I am duty-bound to be her protector.'

Udyan's questioning went deeper.

'Even if what you say is true, Kota did not honour the custom of sati. After all, Kashmir is the Land of Satisar, the Lake of Sati. Kayya, the favourite mistress of King Harsha, disgraced entire womankind by not joining the other queens in following her departed husband. Neither did Didda, and some say that Kota is following in her footsteps. Being modern is fashionable for Kashmiri women but what example of fidelity does Kota seek to set? She should have immolated herself at the time of Rinchina's death.'

Brahma recoiled in horror.

'Sati, and the ban on widow remarriage, is an abomination in Kashmir. Devaswami has ruled so emphatically. Purity cannot justify cruelty. Widows with young sons especially are forbidden to commit sati. In any case, Rinchina had converted so there was no question of following him on to the cremation fire. Would you have her buried alive?'

Udyan switched tack.

'What do you make of the story that a milkwoman is going around claiming that she was set up by Kota and her aide Saras to confront Rinchina and provoke him, fully knowing that he had a violent temper? That the milk had been offered for free to Timmi to trap him.'

'Kashmir is not only the centre of storytelling, but it is also the epicentre of conspiracy stories. How can one give any credence to such untruths?' retorted Brahma.

'Then let her stay single. After all, what is the pressure for her to marry? She is the queen and she can do what she wants.'

'If something was to happen to the queen, then Haider would ascend the throne and Shah Mir would rule in effect,' Brahma countered. 'Would you want to see that happen to Kashmir?'

Udyan did not react to the possibility but turned to Yaniv.

'I met you last at the New Year's ball. What brings you alongside Manzim and Brahma?'

'Your Majesty, the queen wants this alliance to also benefit the people of Kishtwar, the place that you now call home. Kashmir sapphires, with their velvety blue colour reminiscent of a peacock's iridescent hue, are among the most precious and coveted of jewels. Kashmir has had a monopoly on the supply of the world's most perfect sapphires: it would be easy to revive the fortunes of the kingdom if one could tap the gemological wealth that lies so close to Kishtwar.'

Udyan was intrigued.

'My brother Suhdev was a buyer but he never wore sapphires since the jyotish had told him that it was unlucky for him. How confident are you about what you say?'

'Tradition holds that the Ten Commandments given to Moses were inscribed on tablets of sapphire, and therefore it is the most sacred gemstone: the mystical Jews consider the blue gemstones as a secret message from the beyond. In Europe, sapphires are believed to be an antidote against poisons. Most intriguing is the belief that the sapphire can tell whether married couples are faithful to one another: supposedly it loses its lustre if worn by an unfaithful or impure person. In France, such evidence can be used in legal cases – the royalty of

France will come rushing to your door. The demand for sapphire is inexhaustible, only the supply needs to be there.'

'You don't believe that those regions are guarded by the most poisonous *naga*s and the snakes wear the sapphires on their hoods. The stones we do get are the ones that tumble from the eagle's nests when they capture one of the nagas to feed their young. We do not find the stones, the stones find us.'

'Such stories exist all over the world,' Yaniv responded. 'I am of the firm belief that mines can be opened and a thriving trade started via Persia into the capitals of Europe. The Silk Road will never have had as valuable a cargo as sapphires from Kashmir. I propose that I keep 20 per cent of the proceeds from the venture, the remainder will go to the maharaja and the maharani in return for providing exclusive mining rights, the labour for building the access roads and mining operations, and the associated security requirements.'

'Let me think about it,' said Udyandev sceptically, 'though I have very little interest in your proposals. But you have travelled far, so do enjoy our hospitality tonight.'

Manzim knew that his time was up. They had served up the lure of the throne, gemstones and public well-being. Now it was time for his final offer.

'Maharaja, I am grateful to the future ruler of Kashmir for granting me this audience. Before I leave, in appreciation of your consideration, I want to give you this personal gift from the maharani herself.' He placed an ivory tablet in front of Udyandev and bowed himself out of the hall, accompanied by Brahma and Yaniv.

When the matchmaker was gone, Udyandev picked up the tablet. Framed by intricate carving on old ivory was an exquisite delicate portrait of the young ingénue, Kotarani, staring directly at him with alert eyes. The profile was that of a fearless Kashmiri woman, born to rule but needing a man by her side. She was so beautiful: her finely chiselled features indicated a strength that demanded respect. He was reminded of her stunning dance recital just a few years ago and she was an alumnus from his school, a rare achievement for a woman.

How young she is! Udyandev felt a sudden empathy for her. Here was a young woman no different from him who had suffered a terrible loss but who had to rule the kingdom of Kashmir single-handedly. *Maybe we have more in common than I imagined, we both love Kashmir – and she is so regal in her beauty.*

That night when Udyandev prepared for sleep he picked up the ivory again and stared at it intently, trying to understand the person behind the image. His last waking thoughts were of Kotarani and when he was fast sleep he dreamt that she approached him, asking, 'Udyandev, do you want me?' In his dream Udyandev did not answer, but in the morning when he woke up, he handed a sealed confidential answer for Manzim to take back to Kotarani. When she received Udyandev's note, in the presence of Manzim and Brahma, Saras gave Kotarani a knife to cut the seal. She opened the note. Inside was a small verse, handwritten in exquisite penmanship:

When separate one hopes of union
When united one fears separation
You and I will achieve rapture
We need not hope nor fear.
I know that I am for you
Because I am angaraka too

A slow smile spread across Kotarani's face. Now she knew why Udyandev had resisted marrying for so long. Manzim guessed that his mission had succeeded. Brahma let out a whoop. Saras beamed, sensing the happiness that Kotarani was experiencing.

'All of you, including you, Yaniv, an outsider, have served us well today.'

Yaniv bowed his head in thanks. He knew that he now had the social acceptance that he had wanted.

'Maharani, I am loyal to this land and its people and seek to serve it anyway I can.'

Kotarani was curious.

'It is always instructive to hear from those who were not born in Kashmir. What is it that you think is unique about the Kashmiri Bhatta way of life?'

'The Kashmiri Bhattas say that their way of life seeks truth, beauty and bliss through knowledge. It gives them both worldly benefits and spiritual liberation in life. I have reflected a long time about that, Maharani. There is no other place in the world that has what you have.'

The maharani smiled. 'It is a recipe that has permitted us to be highly creative and prosperous but to preserve it and nurture it remains my biggest challenge. I am glad that you have made Kashmir your home. It is immigrants like you who enrich our culture and civilization.'

Yaniv, having received the highest compliment that one could in Kashmir, bowed his head again and took his leave with Manzim.

In Sharadapeeth the jyotish was ecstatic at the union of Udyandev and Kotarani, and paid an unprecedented social visit to Manzim to personally offer his compliments and add to the accolades that others had showered on him.

'Mated for life,' the astrologer said. 'Udyandev has such good stars. It will be a harmonious wedding and they will be together until the end. Kashmir will prosper under such a strong union.'

Astrologers were given to rhapsodies when a royal union was announced, but this time the astrologer's smile communicated relief and joy. Kokur was good at picking up the undercurrents of his society, and the jyotish's exultations, which Kotarani shared with him, gave him an idea. It was a stroke of creative genius that when Udyandev's wedding party came to the Martanda temple for the wedding ceremonies, the first *barati*s in the wedding party were a battalion of geese. Not only did geese mate for life, they were also sacred to Brahma, the Hindu Deva of creation: they symbolized a new, peaceful beginning. People, who are forbearing rather than vengeful, even to those under whom they have suffered, were referred to as *hamsa*s, or geese: it was clear that the new reign was offering absolution for the mistakes of the past and making a new beginning. The Kashmiris whispered to the Mussalman guests that Kotarani and Udyandev were signalling that they wanted their kingdom to be like *Suchi*, the abode of the geese where Brahma ruled.

The pure white geese were led by one that was cream-coloured, marching between two lines of soldiers. The geese waddled to a tank, and once they took to the water their grace and beauty lent a natural elegance to the celebrations.

The marriage rituals were performed with pomp and splendour. Tradition was invoked and the most orthodox form of the wedding ritual was followed. The first blunt question was asked of Udyan by Kota. Was he sexually potent and could he father progeny? Udyan answered ritually that he had been fed with supplements and medicines by his guru and was primed to perform his sexual dharma. All the way to the Posh Puja ceremony the Brahmins were intent on emphasizing the totally indigenous Kashmiri content but the Brahmins were not done yet. Udyandev and Kotarani were now husband and wife, but Udyandev still had to be consecrated Maharaja of Kashmir. For this investiture Devaswami had requested his two most authoritative gurus to lead the rituals. Guru Sankarsvamin and his able pupil Guru Manodadatta were the experts on this most important ceremony. It had started with Udyan commissioning a sacred scripture by Abhinavagupta and having it copied. All night long there was a grand party with music, dancing and a recital of the Vedas and the *Shiva Purana*. Prisoners were slated for release and all violence, including the felling of trees, was forbidden for the next day. Come morning the text was placed on the back of an elephant and the procession wended its way clockwise to where the consecration was to take place. The entire town had raised festal banners on their homes with the citizenry dressed in all white. Udyan donated gifts to every temple along his way. Finally, he reached Ishber hermitage where the consecration was to occur. The text was placed on a throne and the formal proceedings began.

Udyan sat on a golden chair facing east and received the inaugural bath from Devaswami, who poured water from a golden *lotta* vase held above his head while reciting mantras. The water flowed down

Udyandev's broad chest as the Vitasta did down the mountain. It made a gurgling sound of contentment harmonizing with the music that was being played in the background. Udyandev's body was then anointed; his limbs and ears were covered with gold ornaments. A double-stranded beaded thread was placed around his neck across the left shoulder and under his right arm. The head of the thread was in the shape of a serpent head and the tail was knotted to it. His hair was knotted tightly with the centrally parted ribbed hair bulging out in semicircular bunches around a compartment of lateral ribs divided in the middle. He was clothed in the finest of silks and then placed on the royal throne with a parasol covering him. Devaswami then anointed Udyan with a large tilak on his forehead. He was dressed in arm ornaments. A necklace ornament comprising three large flower-head medallions held by a necklace strap of herringbone design was placed around him. Finally, a diadem was placed on his head. It consisted of three triangular leaf designs with each leaf containing a flower-head medallion framed by scrolling foliage.

The first person to come and honour him was Kotarani, who then took her place next to him. Devaswami took a tumbler and filled it with water and held it up shoulder-high. Then he spoke mantras while pouring the water on the ground. Udyan was made to take a sword and slice the water at waist height several times. Then Kota held the sword and followed suit. All those who were attending the ceremony came and addressed Udyandev as maharaja and Kota as maharani. Kota had worn her hair smooth, encircling her head like a flattened bun with radiating ribs. She had a shawl covering the back of her hair, falling down to her shoulder and then flaring out from behind her arms on either side. She had a long lower garment with a chain girdle of tiny bells with a sash tied across the thighs, looped at the front, the end falling between the legs. Her colour was all red and starting today she was no longer afraid to be the red queen. She too had on a three-leaf crescent diadem, each leaf containing radiating foliage around a beaded medallion. Seated cross-legged on their flat throne with a cobra-head design for the back support and resting on a lotus pedestal, they were a striking royal couple. Shah Mir bowed, pledging his loyalty to the new maharaja. The ceremony was complete and Kashmir had a new royal couple.

The first royal act of the new maharaja was to grant land to the assembled Brahmins. The guests were given special gifts. Shah Mir's family in particular received many honours: his wife Layla was presented with gold ornaments, Guhara a jade necklace, and his sons Jamshed and Ali Sher received expensive *poshak*s, outfits beautifully embroidered with gold and silver threads. Most importantly, they were given dominion over Kamraj in Northern Kashmir and Maraz in Southern Kashmir. Ravan, though in attendance, had initially hung back not knowing his future in the new dispensation. He had married quietly in a small private wedding sometime back and was accompanied by his spouse. Udyandev made a point of reaching out to him and hugging him. He placed a garland of expensive precious stones around the young man's neck, so that Ravan knew that he saw him as a cherished brother. Brahma Bhatt and Sharika had also been given high honours, and Udyandev tied a small gold chain around the waist of their sleeping son. In an unprecedented gesture both the Sogdian and Yaniv were invited and honoured with gifts for their role in standing by the king and queen's family.

Shah Mir had observed the entire proceedings carefully. As an aside he commented critically in Farsi to his wife: 'The Queen is quite a free-spirited woman in her personal life. She does not conform to the rules laid down for women.'

Layla who was normally taciturn shushed him: 'The queen follows higher truths than man-made rules. Kashmiri culture is more advanced than backward Persia and it shows in the freedoms the women enjoy.'

'Nonetheless her gifts to the Mir family will show to the world that she recognizes who is the kingmaker here and who in spirit is thus the matchmaker of this alliance.' Shah Mir had already calculated the political impact of his gifts and the ascendancy of his family with the important governorships for his sons.

Finally, Kotarani and Udyandev departed for Kishtwar. After their long journey Kotarani awaited Udyandev in the bridal chamber set up for them in Udyandev's ancestral home. When the groom entered he found Kotarani seated on the edge of the bed: she had changed from her bridal garments and was wearing a diaphanous white bodice over blue silk pajamas that were pleated at the waist and narrowed around her ankles. Her hair had been loosened: on her head she wore a single ornament. Her smiling and welcoming eyes had a seductive passion that stirred Udyandev. He went up to her and took her hands in his own and sat next to her. Her thigh, touching his, trembled and radiated her body's excitement to him.

She looked at him with a small smile, not speaking a word.

'Kotarani, neither you nor I could have predicted this marriage, but I meant my vows.'

'I meant my vows also. Today is the happiest day of my life.'

'The Kashmiris are happy at our union. It will make our ancestors happy also.'

'Most men have something else on their minds on their marriage night – and yet you are worried about the public and our departed ancestors.'

Udyandev laughed. 'The night is still young, Kotarani. It seems to me that you are in a great hurry.'

Kotarani replied pensively, 'Udyandev, I have waited for this moment all my life. I have often dreamt of whom I would marry: in my imagination I would pair myself with somebody and then discard him for some whimsical reason or the other. I have to confess that when I was young I cared very much for Brahma Bhatt – but in his case, I did not have to discard him, he grew into a dear and trusted friend.'

'There is no shame in your feelings for Brahma – I too care for him as a dear friend, so we have him in common.'

'Udyan, are you comfortable that this is my second marriage and your first? Be completely honest.'

Udyan smiled, 'I was born the younger brother and I am very comfortable with being number two in life.'

'Tell me, Udyan, tell me truly how you feel inside about me right now.'

'I have always thought of myself as an intellectual, so for tonight I had planned to recite a poem about Shiva finding Shakti's tender and loving message. I feel the way Shiva must have felt

> No hook could have caught me as well as the pendant you sent me.
> You caught me like a songbird in a net.
> Your skin is softer than the petals of a flower.
> No, it was a garland of jasmine that I was putting around your neck.
> I give you my love.
> I am like a knot in the wood.
> I cannot be made into anything for anyone.
> I have to be me and someday I will be burnt.

Kotarani was touched and spoke fervently: 'The stars drove my first marriage. But now I have found my life companion and nobody could be happier than I am tonight.'

Udyandev held Kotarani as they slowly undressed each other. He then laid her on the bed. He could feel her heart beating against his ribcage and then it was his heart that began to pound in return.

Udyandev and Kotarani began their rule of the ravaged kingdom with zeal and care. Kotarani retained her sovereign power and while Udyan was given mastery of the land, the queen had her own treasury and councillors, including her private guards. Kotarani had learnt her lesson that she needed to bypass the officials and visit the villages and be connected to her people. They travelled across their vast kingdom, talking to their subjects and listening to their woes. It was clear that they faced a significant challenge.

Most of the Kashmiris were living in makeshift conditions. They were truly wretched, and several families admitted that the only reason they were alive was the charity kitchen at Bulbul Lankar. To the ones who had lost their families, Kotarani repeated her message that the maharaja and the maharani were the father and the mother of all. At one village she had a most curious run-in with a Chandala. The head

Damara, the peasants and their families had gathered to welcome the maharani. She was drinking tea when she noticed a broad-shouldered man watching her with a disarming grin on his face. He was sturdily built and had stubble on his chin. Next to him was a basket that smelled of faeces. Kotarani waved him over, but he only smiled back and made no attempt to approach.

'Why are you hanging back? Come join us. We are all one family,' she said.

The man smiled again. 'I am a Chandala. I smell worse than a skunk. I think I am best where I sit, Your Majesty.'

Kotarani stood up. ' Since you will not walk to me, I have no recourse but to come to you.' She walked up to the man and then she did the unthinkable: she sat down cross-legged, face-to-face and at eye level with him as an equal, right next to the faeces.

Neither the Chandala nor the crowd surrounding them could believe their eyes and ears. This man, destined to be a bachelor for life because of his profession – no woman would deign to marry him – now sat facing the maharani.

Kotarani had to smile back at the Chandala's infectious grin. 'I recognized you. I want to thank you – you fought alongside my father and me when Dulucha attacked the fort. Your accuracy was unbelievable.'

The Chandala's face turned red at the honour of being recognized by the queen. 'It was sport. During my off hours I practise cutting fruits such as apples by throwing stone flints. Sometimes in my village we form two stone, throwing teams and go at each other. It can get quite bloody.'

'You are an agriculturist by profession and a warrior in your spare time. If it was not for your work providing manure to the fields we would not have the best vegetables in the land.'

The man was overcome by the compliment. He doffed his cap and mumbled, 'I am just your humble servant. It is the land that gives us everything. We must protect it. It can yield us much more, double what we get today. We would never have to suffer hunger.'

'Tell me, what would you do to get more?'

The man scratched his head. 'I am a simple person and do not know much about these things, but it seems to me that people have to change.'

'It is I who needs to learn. How can we reform and double our agricultural production?'

'Maharani tell the Brahmins to work with the farmers in the fields. They were the ones who developed the irrigation schemes, they recited the mantras to increase the fertility of the land, and they taught the farmers how to plant the seeds at the most auspicious time. When the rains failed their yagna made the rain clouds appear. The farmers used to be overjoyed when their villages were granted to the Brahmins because they knew that the tribute that they paid was only a small portion of what they would gain. Today it is a completely different story: the Brahmin is totally confined to ministering his temple and he will not even walk through the fields lest he run into stinky me and become polluted.'

Kotarani was impressed. 'So what limits us is not the land but the people, and it is not the people but our social behaviour which freezes us as opposed to freeing our minds?'

The Chandala laughed. 'The only thing that I get to collect is rich people's shit from their private estates. The poor go to the fields and manure them directly. I can tell you that right now the rich are all constipated because they are frightened about the future.'

'You are a very observant man. Why do you think you will live alone and no woman will want you? Does it not limit you? You can tell the world that I said you were a very attractive man. If anybody challenges you, bring them to me and I will corroborate you.'

The simpleton's eyes grew round in wonder. 'You truly believe stinky me will find a wife? A Kashmiri father will give his daughter to me?'

'Absolutely, you will find a wife as assuredly I found my husband.'

'Maharani, you are comparing my finding a wife to your match with the king!' The man's grin broadened until it almost seemed as if his face would split. 'May your words prove to be true if not in this birth then at least in my rebirth.'

Kotarani bid the Chandala goodbye and her retinue left for a visit to Sharadapeeth. Kotarani had decided to accompany Udyandev since the last royal visit had ended in a fiasco: she was glad that she did so because the meeting with Devaswami was an extremely difficult one. Devaswami had taken Kotarani and Udyandev to task for the misrule that had occurred within the Valley. The Brahmins had moral strength and thus could be quite indiscreet in their speech. There was a warning note in Devaswami's words: Dulucha's attack had to be seen as a harbinger of the Devi's displeasure at the profligate and immoral ways of Suhdev's court. Kotarani saw that Udyandev was quite affected by Devaswami's words and he asked him to elaborate on his recommendations. He asked for more funding for the Brahmins. Suhdev had curtailed some of their privileges and Rinchina had diverted state funds to the Mussalmans, specifically to Bulbul Lankar at the expense of the Brahmins; more and more Brahmins were coming to Kashmir, fleeing from the central kingdoms and the northern countries. They had to be housed and fed. The local populace regularly congregated around the temples, but there was little to distribute. The crops that were the primary source of income for the treasury and the temples were in short supply, and prices were high. Devaswami insisted that Udyandev conduct a very expensive yagna to the Devas for the sake of the kingdom.

Kotarani, ever practical, interjected. 'Devaswami, the kingdom is desperate for resources. What should we do besides diverting precious resources conducting a yagna to the Devi?'

'Maharani, have you forgotten what you were taught? The best way to create wealth is to give it away. Act with conviction and everything else will follow.'

Kotarani did not quite know how to implement that recommendation. 'The people are dispirited and they have lost the will to live, to fight and to build a better future.'

Devaswami spoke imperiously and confidently. 'If Shakti can energize Lord Shiva, then this is a trivial social problem – you can solve it. Shivoham! Now let us go to the temple and ask her for her blessings.'

Kotarani's most challenging conversation, however, was with the Sogdian. He had asked for a private audience with her, and he had come to the point immediately.

'Maharani, I served your father Ramachandra loyally and now my loyalty is to you. I have come to warn you that the kingdom is militarily exposed: another attack is inevitable, and the kingdom does not have a commander. Lakshmaka is a Kampanesa in name only. He is always politicking in court and is never seen on the front line; his troops at the outposts have either deserted or are near mutiny. They will show a flat pair of heels to the next attacker. There are no weapons left after Dulucha's attack. You must begin rebuilding immediately – otherwise they will fall to the next adventurer. They will return to the site of their last kill. It is in their blood.'

'What do you suggest?'

'You have to correct three mistakes. First, you have to conscript all the able-bodied young men, and begin training them in earnest. Buy arms and ammunitions, and resupply your army. Second, you have to ship the new immigrants back to Persia. Their loyalty is not to Kashmir. Third, I think you have made a terrible mistake in marrying Udyandev, who is a bookworm and is the wrong king to tackle the threat that Kashmir faces. He actually ties a bell to his horse because he is afraid of the bad karma that will come from trampling the insects underfoot.' It took all of Kotarani's willpower to absorb and not react to the slap on the face that the Sogdian had hit her with. She was learning that being a queen required a thick skin. Her father had instructed her that she could always trust the Sogdian and in his one-pointed undiplomatic remarks she saw a bit of her father.

'Where are all these young men?' she asked, unruffled. 'We are so reduced in numbers – we lost 50,000 of our youth. It will take several generations to rebuild our numbers.'

The Sogdian was insistent. 'Oh, Maharani, we have to fight with what we have, even if we are down to the last man, woman and child. If you do not act, the next time you will see that a gathering of those who came to celebrate your wedding will be in the slave markets of

Turkmenistan. Please, please listen to me. I have been through this before in Persia. I am not a madman – these are not imaginary fears. I have suffered the loss of my family, my loved ones and my world to intractable zealots. It is not a question of joining them, I did nominally, but one finds that you have to toe their fanatic ways. I realized that you have to reject them totally, because there is no accommodating them. I escaped and your father gave me sanctuary. It is my personal experience that urges you to act; do not allow Kashmir to suffer the fate of Persia.'

The Sogdian's warning registered with Kotarani. *What he says is true, but what can I do?*

'As far as immigrants are concerned, you are an immigrant, Yaniv is an immigrant, Rinchina is an immigrant, Bulbul was an immigrant and so are Shah Mir and his band. They are human and no different and some will turn out to be good and some bad.'

'You have to be vigilant and be on guard against *taqqiya*. At the first sign of perfidy you will have to give them the same ultimatum that they have given: Leave, Convert or Die. You lost control of your son to Shah Mir. Why is he still around now that he has been exposed as the protector of the fakir?'

'The issue is not that black and white. I agree that he makes people uneasy, but he was also Brahma's protector. Besides he is an honest administrator. Having a Mussalman face towards Persia also serves our interest, if we can convince the Ghazis that Kashmir is not hostile to the Mussalmans.'

'Queen,' pleaded the Sogdian, 'Shah Mir is a crocodile. He is lying in wait for you, and you will have no one to fight for you. I stayed with Udyan and he is a good man, but I don't think that he has lifted a sword in his life.'

'Yes, Udyan is not a fighter,' conceded Kota, 'but a king has to have many other qualities besides wielding a sword, and Udyan has those in droves. I do not have the money to rearm. The people are starving. The treasury is empty, so my hands are tied.'

'Maharani, we cannot let ourselves be turned into slaves. You must find an answer.'

'Oh, Sogdian, you have been loyal to me. I promise I will let you know once I have decided which direction to take.'

Kotarani spent days agonizing over what the Sogdian had discussed with her. Should she have married someone else? The only options she had not explored were other kingdoms. But that would have meant leaving Kashmir to join an alien husband. Would her people have been the better off because of that? Would she have been better off? She felt her people would have seen that as subjugation through marriage and she could easily end up as one of many royal wives in a strange land. No, she had done the right thing in Udyan. She had no choice but to request Khazanchi, the head trader, to come to her. She also asked Yaniv to join her and asked for his advice on how to proceed.

When Khazanchi arrived, his generally depressed demeanour was even more pronounced: in spite of his wealth he was very parsimonious in his personal lifestyle, almost miserly. Manjari was with him and in contrast was loaded with jewellery and was a walking advertisement for his moneylending business. Kotarani could see Manjari's calculating eyes take in the court that she had not attended in many years, and then with a stiff elaborate bow she knelt in front of the queen. If Kotarani needed any validation for her intense dislike of Manjari, it was right in front of her eyes.

'Khazanchi *Mahraa*, the people are suffering,' Kotarani explained. 'What help can you provide to alleviate their suffering?' But he did not seem to hear her. When she repeated herself, which was a terrible breach of royal protocol, his response was most unsympathetic.

'The Valley has very little resources and too many people. Too many piglets and not enough teats on the sow, the people should leave the Valley and seek a better future.' Khazanchi's analogy was a breach of decorum and showed scant respect for the maharani's status.

'Khazanchi, when our kingdom was under danger last time, you extended a loan to the kingdom. We are now weak militarily and the treasury is bankrupt. I have come to ask another loan of you.'

Khazanchi licked his dry lips. 'Maharani, when I loaned money previously there was collateral in the treasury; your father was

Kampanesa and he was a man we could place a bet on. Whom should we bet on now? What is the security for a new loan? Money is now fleeing the Valley.'

Kotarani was stunned.

'Why are the Kashmiri traders deserting the kingdom?'

'Maharani, the signs are all around us. The Islamic traders now control the Silk Road. Our caravans only go just outside the Valley, and then the Islamic traders take over and keep the bulk of the profits. They have been historically restricted from entering the Valley; otherwise we would have been squeezed out long ago. These traders are carrying stories about Kashmir's natural wealth to their military counterparts. It is only a matter of time before we are attacked again, and then they will acquire the kingdom.' Khazanchi was quite unemotional in his analysis – it was all about numbers and facts.

'Kashmir has been your home for centuries. This land has made you wealthy beyond your dreams. Now when Kashmir needs you most you will abandon your home?'

'Maharani, I am not in the business of saving kingdoms. Money and gold will most assuredly leave the Valley. The only unanswered question is who will take it. Do you want me to keep the money in my home in safe keeping for the next Dulucha? By sending my money into Kanauj for safe keeping at least I am being prudent.'

Kotarani mulled on Khazanchi's words. 'No security means there is no money, which worsens our security needs; which in turn further weakens the economy. Your answer is that money and people should flee the Valley. You want to put us in a death spiral.'

'The Vitasta seeks the ocean and money seeks its own kind.'

'Khazanchi, I can read your mind quite clearly. So let us do business a different way.' She nodded to Saras who instructed an attendant to bring in a trunk. Kotarani told Yaniv to bring out the contents. It was part of the personal jewellery collection she had inherited from her mother and had been handed down for generations.

'I will offer my own jewellery as collateral and security and pawn it with you for a year. Included in it will be Suryavansh.'

Manjari drew in a sharp breath. He swooped on the jewellery before anyone else, examining each stone, caressing each necklace, her fingers like claws running over the sapphires, rubies, diamonds and pearls. Mother earth's firstborns were the most precious. These ancient heirloom jewels had no equals. Accumulated over thousands of years each piece had a story to tell. Manjari's fingers finally ended up firmly grasping Suryavansh as if to never let go.

Having satisfied herself that the jewellery was genuine, Manjari cattily remarked to Kotarani: 'There were rumours that Suryavansh was found and the rumours turn out to be true. Your father once blocked what was rightfully mine. What must he be thinking that his own daughter is now handing over Suryavansh to me?'

Kotarani stayed quiet and did not respond back.

Yaniv and Khazanchi inventoried the collection. There was haggling on the size of the advance and the interest rate, but Yaniv was able to secure half the normal rate since Manjari lusted so vehemently after Suryavansh.

But she had one final threat.

'Your Highness, you do understand that stones having rolled and come to rest with me do not generally return back.'

Kotarani stared at Manjari, like the stones, perfect in her beauty, ever glittering but soulless.

'I will take the risk that the stones might like you better than me.'

Manjari ignored the insult and snapped at her husband. 'It will take time to put such a large sum of money together but we will take their deal and bring in other partners. I will entertain our guests wearing Suryavansh,' she spat, turning towards the queen. And with a snap of her jewelled fingers she left with her husband in tow.

When Udyandev and Kotarani were together they spent time comparing what they had picked up. Kashmiri society was hollowing out from within as if subterranean termites were slipping in and attacking every vulnerable pillar of the kingdom. When Kotarani shared with Udyandev that she had pawned her personal jewellery, along with Suryavansh, to Khazanchi he was surprised, but he supported her.

'We have to lead by personal example and Devaswami's dictum was to give our money away. We have to have confidence in our convictions and these have to be based on our principles. Today you have shown a strength of character that has no equal in Kashmir's history.'

With money in hand the announcements came swiftly from the palace: Shah Mir was appointed Kampanesa and foreign minister for the kingdom. The military was told that they would receive back pay if they reported back to duty. The Sogdian was put in charge of the Ekangas and internal security, so that there were two rings of security. Part of the loan went to the farmers to plant crops for the next season. The farmers were further encouraged to maximize their agricultural produce by lowering the state taxes to only one-sixteenth of the produce. At a practical level the labour was paid to dig a bypass canal inside the city that would divert water where the Vitasta would enter the city and then rejoin it beyond the city limits. This not only saved the city from frequent floods but also improved the irrigation of the land. Kota saved the city of Srinagar from frequent floods by getting this canal constructed. The grateful farmers named the canal Kota Kol. Those who were not farmers were employed in repairing the temples desecrated by Dulucha and his followers. The Brahmins were also given a bigger future draw of the treasury, under the condition that they sent tutors to the Mussalman village. Shah Mir's approval was obtained, and the idle Mussalman youth started receiving the same education that the Damara Kashmiri children received, especially the Brahmin sciences in the fields of agriculture and husbandry.

The oligarchs and wealthy Kashmiris were mandated that if any destitute person knocked on their doors they were to feed them. From that day onwards no Kashmiri would go hungry or else the maharaja and maharani would know about it. The Kashmiris drew within themselves and bound themselves to a better future.

On Kotarani's urging, Udyandev committed personally to shoring up the security and welfare of the kingdom by announcing publicly that he would become a disciple of Devi Kali and visit Sharadapeeth on every auspicious occasion to lead the prayers to her. This was a most arduous commitment: it represented the ultimate personal dedication, and nobody had heard of a maharaja in recent times attempting to shoulder so dangerous a responsibility. Failing to scrupulously honour such a vow to the Devi meant severe consequences for a devotee.

It was a while before Kokur, Manzim and Naid met again to catch up on the gossip but this time there was cheer in the air.
'Hey, what a queen!' Kokur cheered. 'There has been a bumper crop and prices have fallen dramatically. The farmers' granaries are filled to the ceilings because they were allowed to keep most of their produce. Best of all, the queen got back her collateral from Khazanchi at the end of one year. You should have seen Manjari's face. Ooh, was she burnt. Our queen, what a tiger lady! *Wah Wah!*' concluded Kokur in appreciation. Manzim concurred. 'When I received the commission with the match of Kotarani and Udyandev I thought that I had got the biggest pay off of my life, but boys, it was nothing. I received an invitation from Shah Mir to visit him. When I reached his home he honoured me greatly with gifts and kind words of respect. He has commissioned me to find husbands for all three of his daughters, additional wives for his two sons and then husbands for his granddaughters. I have the whole clan.'

This was truly a game-changing development. The word on Shah Mir had been that he wanted to marry his daughters to men back in Persia as he had done for his two sons, whose wives had been imported. Here was the ultimate proof that Kotarani's inclusive strategy had paid social dividends. Shah Mir had made up his mind that he was going to sink his roots in Kashmir. However, there were so many 'buts' that Naid and Kokur could not blurt them out quickly enough.

Naid asked contemptuously: 'Manzim, what kind of sick thinking is this on the part of that goat face? Shah Mir's oldest granddaughter is not yet six. His sons are already married.'

Manzim chortled. 'I am the best deal maker in the business. What is age as a barrier? I can match two unborn babies if I must. Shah Mir has given me complete freedom on whatever dowry I need to offer to seal the deals.'

'He truly has become one of us. First, it was Tatiana, now that man is using his daughters to corrupt us,' Kokur sneered.

'Kokur, you are being overly melodramatic,' Manzim replied, 'but that is your profession. There is nothing sinister in a man wanting to plant his roots in Kashmir.'

'I don't care if nobody else cares,' Kokur said. 'Every wedding means that I get asked to provide the entertainment so this means good business for me too.'

'Manzim, if Shah Mir is asking you to marry his daughters to the Kashmiris, will they convert?' Naid asked. 'What about the fact that he wants you to find additional wives for his already married sons? No Kashmiri will give his daughter to a Mussalman man who is already married and has children. She cannot be a *dharmapatni*, the first wife.'

Manzim was dismissive. 'Naid, there are many noble Kashmiri families who have fewer possessions than the mice scurrying in their huts; no Kashmiri man will marry the aging daughters of destitute families because they are worse than refugees and have no dowry to offer. Have you ever thought as to why is it that in the same Kashmiri family the men are tall and well-built and the girls are short and thin? Their poor parents will gladly take an offer to marry their daughter to Shah Mir's sons. Better to be a fat and contented third Mussalman wife than to be a starving, miserable Hindu first wife.'

Naid was unconvinced. 'The fakir was shielded by Shah Mir. When one gets his daughters does one get the termite fakir too?'

'No, this is just a canard. Shah Mir has socially cut himself off from the fakir, who is now just another employee at the charity kitchen. He told me that he does not attach that much importance to religion having been persecuted by the bigots in Persia. In fact, he is even open to converting back to Hinduism. It is time for new thinking, new alliances and new relationships. This is where I excel and will make my fortune.'

Naid was envious. 'Manzim, I am without a wife, and yet here you are working to find multiple wives for your client. It is not a fair world.

If there is to be new thinking, new relationships, how about me? Find me a wife also, Mussalman or Hindu.'

'Naid, I will keep my eyes open for you, and maybe I will reduce my commission for you when I find the right person.'

'Why can't Kotarani mandate fairness and equality in our society?' Naid asked. 'I see all the other single young men like me, rolling stones on the street, with no future. The single young women at the bottom are no better off since their fathers cannot pay any dowry. Society will not act unless there is a commission. It is so unfair.'

Manzim responded firmly. 'Naid, there will always be somebody at the bottom of society, irrespective of the system that you come up with. Dowry is fair and it cements the alliance fairly: the sons get a share of the ancestral land, and the wives get their share of parental assets.'

'What land, what dowry?' Naid asked weakly. 'What alliances are we talking about? My single steady relationship is with my moneylender. My clients look down on me as I shave them, because I am of a lower caste. I feel like running away from society, but where to? In my hut, loneliness is my only companion. Now I worry that you two may desert me because you are moving up in the world and I may not be good enough for you.'

'Naid, I am not getting married, so I will always be there for you,' Kokur said, putting his hand on Naid's shoulder kindly. 'One cannot escape from one's karma irrespective of how much money one has. Look at what happened to Suhdev. One day he had Suryavansh on his chest, and poof! the next day Dulucha was ready to make halal kebab out of him. You need to flow like the river, singing as you go along – life has a way of balancing valleys with the mountains.'

Naid smiled. 'Kokur, you are always the artist and you know how to lift emotions. But I have heard an inside story from the cook that there was a major disagreement between Udyandev and Kotarani on the subject of Shah Mir. Kotarani badly wants to get Haider back, but she needs Shah Mir's assent for which she has to offer him something truly important. Udyandev does not like Shah Mir, nor does he trust him, and will not give him any more power. He says that Shah Mir is grooming Haider, his stepson, to replace him. He accused Shah Mir of holding Haider on his arm the way he holds his falcons. The cook's word is that Kotarani tried to defend Shah Mir, calling him a diamond. Udyandev countered sarcastically saying, *"Yes, Shah Mir is a diamond – a diamond that pierces the jewels around him but does not let the jewels pierce his own hard countenance.* Here we are, the king and the queen disagreeing over a person that we have handed over the military to. Should we ever trust our security to a Mussalman?"'

Kokur had to admit the veracity of the story that had been making the rounds, but he supported the maharani.

'I think Kotarani is incredibly wise. Shah Mir is a new immigrant and there is always fear that the new immigrants will do us harm. I agree that his ascent has been swift, but he is very ambitious and has a knack of sweetening even sugar cane juice. Kotarani is a unifier and yet she is pragmatic. She understands that Kashmir is about letting everyone thrive. By putting Shah Mir in charge of the army, she has presented a Mussalman to the external world where our greatest threats and opportunity for trade lie. Yet, her internal security is in the hands of the Sogdian. He also is an outsider, but will be a good balance to Shah Mir as he hates Mussalmans.'

Manzim had his own interpretation of events.

'Look, this is not complex. Kotarani is the mother of Haider and nothing is stronger than maternal instinct. Haider is being cared for by Shah Mir, according to Rinchina's express last wish, and Kotarani needs to keep him happy so that he does not mistreat her son. It is all about maintaining a healthy give and take.'

Naid pounced on a weakness he had spotted.

'Relationships! You want to talk about relationships! Take Kotarani. She cares for nothing but power and control, and this is her way of showing Udyandev that he can't have his way completely. Can you imagine that this pussy-whipped man has promised a lifelong penance to the Devi? What was he thinking?

Manzim put his hands around Naid. 'You do get down on the world, don't you? We are small people and sometimes we envy big people but trust me big people have big problems. Kotarani has gambled high stakes and certainly earned her title of being the greatest queen of Kashmir. Come, let me buy us all dinner.'

Manzim was in a gracious and expansive mood. The three friends put their arms around each other and walked up the poplar-lined path to the baker's shop. As they walked, Manzim thought about what he had not shared with his two friends. He had secured the engagement of Guhara with Raja Sapru of Bhringi. It had been touch and go but in an inspired action he had arranged for the two of them to meet at Bulbul Lankar without the elders being present. They had a good connection, and Shah Mir had enthusiastically supported the marriage since the raja was a powerful lord. Layla was ecstatic that her daughter had found the Bhatta man that she had dreamt of.

The engagement took place in Mussalman fashion with Guhara's dowry being 500 *tola*s of gold and a camel load of silk and brocade called *diha-e-shastari*, but the marriage ritual was a traditional Kashmiri ceremony. Guhara repeated each Sanskrit verse with perfect diction and understanding. An unexpected honour was the attendance of Kotarani and Udyandev, who came with Brahma Bhatta and Sharika. Shah Mir was overwhelmed at the gifts Kotarani presented to him and to the newly-weds: to Shah Mir she gave a copy of the Koran, from the royal treasury; Guhara received a pair of golden dejhoor and the Raja of Bhringi was appointed to the Department of Justice with an annual stipend. Brahma and Sharika had brought an expensive antique shahtoosh shawl for the bride.

At the end of the wedding Guhara and Raja Sapru were seated on the dais as their guests stood in a line to greet them. Kotarani and Udyandev came up to offer their blessings. Udyandev started chatting with the raja, who immediately solicited his support for a pet project of his. Guhara tried to stand up, but Kotarani waved her to relax. 'Tonight, you are the maharani and we are your well-wishers. Are you happy?'

'Maharani today is the happiest day of my life. I keep thinking that I will wake up from this dream and find myself back in Persia.'

'Persia is now run by bigots who have massacred the Buddhists, Hindus and the Jews. You are now part of the Kashmir dream, but what matters is that you have your perfect husband.'

'He better be, otherwise I will leave him and come to you for protection!'

The maharani smiled. 'Guhara, you should come and visit me even if the raja is not driving you crazy. I hear that you have become an expert in mantra chanting and it would be wonderful to hear you sing.' 'Maharani, you do not know how much the raja and I look up to you. He says that you have made enormous sacrifices for all of us even at the expense of your own happiness. Are you happy now that Kashmir is once again prospering?'

'Yes, I am very happy at the progress that is being made. There is no sacrifice too great since the people are my family and I deeply care for their welfare.'

'Will you advise me on how I can keep the raja happy?'

'I am fortunate that Udyandev is a very spiritual man and the closer he gets to the Devi the closer he draws me to him. The same can happen for you.'

'Brahma had told me once about your belief. How can I do the same?'

'It is already happening to you. Think about where you and the raja first met and where you are today?'

Guhara was struck by the maharani's insight. Yes, Bulbul had drawn the raja and her together. Kotarani and Udyandev hugged the bride and bridegroom and left.

The other guests mingled, gossiping about new developments. Some of the elderly ladies had cornered Manzim and were questioning him on what he had brokered.

'Ali Sher's daughter has been married to Lusta, the lord of the gates; the daughter of Jamshed has given in marriage to Tilakshura, who thus obtained the lordship of Bhangila. He is old enough to be her grandfather. Is this not a breach of ethical conduct on your part?'

Manzim shrugged. 'The grooms have become the recipients of huge dowries. This is an unexpected windfall for them. If the marriage works for the two parties, who are we to criticize the alliance?'

One conservative dowager commented caustically, ' The locals bear Shah Mir's daughters like garlands, but they knew not that his daughters are like life-destroying serpents of deadly poison.'

Manzim countered emphatically, 'Shah Mir has reassured his Hindu sons-in-law, saying, "*The shared pleasure offered by my daughters cements the bonds of friendship.*" His actions show that he is equal in every way to a native-born Kashmiri. Guhara and the raja's wedding has paved the way that all artificial bloodlines can be crossed to form a lifelong bond. If we bind together, our future can only get brighter.'

The dowager was skeptical and dismissive. 'Time will tell whether the progeny are the crocodile's teeth by which he will hold and swallow his victims. They are duplicitous and are not vesting into Kashmir but instead are establishing footholds for their alien manners and customs. We have to pray for our sake that Kota's firm hands maintain steady control for a long time.'

Wave 13
Governance

TO top off the good times that had come to the Valley, Kotarani gave birth to her second son, who was named Jatta Bhola Rattan. The happiness of the royal household was complete. Now Udyandev was the proud father who had a direct successor to his lineage. The Kashmiris all rallied around Jatta who was clearly the favoured offspring. The child's clothes were made of cloth woven with strands of silver thread – silver was reputed to have protective properties against invisible bad spirits. Ravan's nose was put out of joint, however, when Brahma was appointed the child's godfather; he had been hoping that Jatta could replace the loss of Haider to Shah Mir. However, Ravan's disagreement with Kotarani had ruled him out as a contender. The queen's brother had become more and more withdrawn since Udyandev's ascendancy; he no longer held sway at court and spent most of his time in his outlying castle with his wife and sons. It seemed that his only regular contact now was with Shah Mir, with whom he interacted more frequently than he did with his own kin. They often ran into each other at Bulbul Lankar; he would publicly brood about his role in Kashmir's history as he aged and often wondered whether the moving finger had moved on, or whether there was still a role for him.

 Jatta's birth launched a baby boom in the Valley. There was prosperity that had not been seen in living memory, and the public saluted Kotarani for her rule and generosity by celebrating the arrival of new babies, making up for their losses by having larger families and showing their confidence in the future. Guhara gave birth to a son, who was named Aditya. In honour of the boy, Brahma had come with Sharika and their son Bhima, bearing gifts. It was a very happy occasion for the entire Bhringi household, where Brahma was a dear friend. His own son was growing up, and he was clearly the apple of his father's eye. The guests were received in the *Bud Kuth*, the largest room in the house. Shortly thereafter, and to everyone's joy, Kotarani arrived with Udyandev with presents for the family. She found Aditya to be an absolute cherub, having inherited his mother and father's good looks. Shah Mir and his wife had also come to visit, obviously delighted at the outcome of the union. Guhara's mother snatched a few moments in private with her daughter after the other guests had left.

'Are you happy?' she whispered.

Guhara nodded, and her silent smile as she held Aditya to her breast was all her mother needed to hear.

'Keep the taviz next to you and Bulbul will always protect you,' she instructed her daughter. Guhara took the taviz hanging from her neck and gently touched her forehead with it.

'What is Raja Sapru like?' her mother asked? Guhara blushed.

'He is a good husband and says that our marriage is one of equals. Like all the Kashmiris, he is slightly crazy, but he teaches me a great deal and I am beginning to understand what makes him tick.'

The observant mother saw in Guhara's face a contented natural glow that was rare in the women of her clan and she was happy for her eldest daughter.

One unexpected consequence of Udyandev's marriage to Kotarani and Jatta's birth was that it had made the small Mussalman community in Kashmir insecure once more. Devaswami had now regained his pre- eminent position, and while he had never shown any ill will towards the Mussalmans, they felt that they had lost the gains they had made with Bulbul as Rinchina's preceptor. The exile of the fakir was still talked about and, unfortunately, Ali and his cohorts, in their ill-advised zeal to preserve the extremist principles of the fakir and emboldened by Rinchina, had taken a wrong turn in segregating their village. The Kashmiri Bhattas complained vociferously to Kotarani that when they walked through their village it felt more like Persia than Kashmir. The only language spoken was Farsi and the historic landmarks had been given Islamic names, destroying the thousands of years of historic continuity. Even the way people dressed and greeted one another was alien to them. This segregation was causing tension on both sides.

A delegation of Mussalman elders came to visit Shah Mir at his new home in Srinagar to voice their concerns. Shah Mir was at his most affable; after the initial hospitalities were over, the delegation came directly to the point: what was he going to do to ensure the safety and security of their small community?

Shah Mir smiled reassuringly. 'There is nothing to fear. We have the answer in our hands.'

The room was silent and his guests were puzzled.

'We have to integrate with the Kashmiris,' Shah Mir explained. 'Look at me and follow my example.'

Ali could not accept what was being asked of him.

'What about those of us who do not want to integrate and marry our daughters to the kafirs?'

Shah Mir was unfazed. Ali had once approached him for Guhara's hand but she had turned him down; Shah Mir had to take his hostility in his stride.

'We have Haider. He is the Crown prince of Kashmir. Kotarani may have other children and Udyandev may have become the maharaja through Kotarani and Suhdev, but any children he fathers with Kotarani cannot supersede Haider. He is our contingency trump card, and we must make sure that the prince is brought up correctly, as the great Rinchina himself instructed me to do. He cannot be allowed to have any contact with outsiders.'

The assembled Mussalmans understood and agreed. Haider's education in the madrasa would ensure that he would grow up in the Mussalman community. He would be their future in Kashmir. But even this could not resolve the immediate vulnerability that they felt in their own community. Although there was no record of a Kashmiri Bhatta ever violating a Mussalman, the fear was ever-present, stemming from a history of fanatical and prejudiced Islamic rulers in Persia and other neighbouring countries. Thus was born *Panun Fauj*, their own armed forces. The village that had seceded in spirit now had its own militia, headed by Ali. While still an officer in the exclusively Mussalman royal cavalry he had taken it upon himself to secretly train a small contingent of youth from Malchmar who could take up defensive arms if a crisis arose.

Given the peace momentum that the Kashmiris were building it was quite unexpected that when the *shali* crop was about to be harvested there was a sudden snowfall followed by a week of torrential rain. Then the sky turned red and a violent dust storm howled through the Valley. Rainwater gorged the River Vitasta and completely destroyed the paddy crop. The frightened locals whispered that their envious demons were once again on the prowl. Kotarani was informed that the price of rice had risen from 300 dinaras to 1,500 dinaras per *khara* and before long their limited food supply ran out. Within weeks, emaciated men could be seen wandering around, subsisting on walnuts, roots and wild fruits. Men and women abandoned their loved ones, each looking out for their own survival. The howling of starving babies filled the Valley and the same cry that only months ago gladdened the hearts of families now felt like a dagger. Shockingly, several babies were abandoned outside temples, their cries long silenced by hunger and replaced by a glassy-eyed stare at the horror that faced them. Whatever small amounts of silver or gold or jewellery anyone had were pawned and Khazanchi benefited from the crisis, putting up signs saying that he would buy any gold and jewellery and would pay food in return. But it was only a temporary relief: the problems of tomorrow remained unsolved.

The behaviour of the rich Kashmiris – especially those in the business community – was disgraceful. It almost seemed as if the shortage of food had made them enjoy life even more. Weddings featured ever more elaborate feasts, bordering on gastronomic orgies.

The world might have been coming to an end, but that was the ideal time for the wealthy to really show their superiority and establish their reputation for times to come. At these weddings the conversation shifted from jewellery and land to who knew whom, and to what lengths one had to go to obtain prized food items. The most talked-about wedding was that of Khazanchi's daughter, who married the son of another businessman. The publicly displayed dowry took people's breath away; it was said that Manjari's daughter had taken with her a jewellery collection that exceeded that of Maharani Kotarani herself!

When Kokur, Manzim and Naid met up it was obvious that Naid was barely keeping body and soul together. While Manzim could extract meals from the affluent clients he visited when arranging marriages and Kokur got scraps from the royal kitchen, Naid had no lifeline – his customers had completely dried up on him. Naid had always been a bit vain about his appearance: both for professional and narcissistic reasons his first act was to shave himself every morning and groom his hair meticulously. He had been a walking advertisement for his profession. But now he had completely changed: he had grown a scruffy beard that elongated his jaw and gave him the look of a ravenous squirrel. When he opened his mouth his teeth bared sharply.

'Naid, here is some rice that I was able to bring with me,' said Kokur, holding out a brass bowl. 'Eat.'

'No, no,' said Naid, his self-respect at stake. The three friends had always valued each other's independence; to be an object of charity now was too much for Naid to take.

'Naid, go ahead,' said Manzim. 'Kokur and I have been waiting here for a while; we have already eaten, this is your portion. You are getting exactly one-third, and that is fair.'

'Are you sure?' asked Naid. 'I do not take charity from anybody, least of all from my friends. I may die, but I will not lose my honour.'

Kokur assured Naid with a white lie. 'Naid, I swear by my father – you know Naid, nobody was dearer to me than my father – that Manzim and I have eaten and this is your portion.'

His conscience cleared, Naid fell on to the food. His friends watched him silently. It was painfully clear that Naid had not eaten for quite some time. What was to be done?

His body filled with sustenance, Naid said, 'Kokur, I have never seen it this bad. Even when Dulucha invaded us at least there was food to eat, we had stored and hidden it away. There is simply nothing now. People hide themselves in order to eat what food they have; if you do not hide the food you are carrying under your cloak, your own neighbours will rip it from you like vultures. This cannot last.'

Kokur was uncharacteristically anxious.

'Yes, it is very bad. Last night a delegation arrived from Devaswami to see Udyandev and Kotarani. The villages that the Brahmins depend on for food have simply refused to provide the temples with rice, saying that they have none. When the Brahmins go to people's homes to beg for food, they die of food poisoning because they are given stale, spoiled stuff. Often they are turned away, which is the greatest sin that a Kashmiri can commit. Our society is breaking down. Devaswami has served an ultimatum. His priests have to feed the Devas and Devis twice a day and there is no milk, no honey, and no fruits. He and the Brahmins are going to go on *prayopavesha* unless this situation is resolved.'

Prayopavesha was a mass fast unto death. This was the Brahmins' ultimate weapon! Any kingdom where the Brahmins died in an unnatural manner would be cursed forever. Affairs in Kashmir were taking a suicidal course.

The bile within Naid came boiling out.

'Trust the Brahmins to turn a necessity into a virtue. They are a wily lot. Look at us poor – can we also demand that we be given food because we need it for the Devas? No! Only the Brahmins have that privilege.'

Manzim listened thoughtfully, considering what was covered by professional confidentiality and what he should share with his closest friends.

'Devaswami may be many things, but the one thing that he is completely knowledgeable on is Kashmir's history. In my own family we carry the history of the families from generation to generation. I can tell you that Devaswami knows the dark secret of Kashmir. He knows that when there have been famines in Kashmir, even the nobility has practised cannibalism. Poorer families have sold their children to the butcher clan. I have it on authority that the butcher clan has sold human meat parts.'

Kokur was shocked and horrified at the revelation – the paradise of Kashmir had a stain that had recurred through its history. He felt like throwing up. But what Manzim was telling him made sense, and he was privy to the innermost secrets of the families. Snowbound for six months, stuck in the remote mountains with no food and no prospect of any external help, who knew what difficult decisions were made in the outlying areas, or for that matter inside the proud homes that rose into the skies? Naid had felt famished, but now he felt sick.

Manzim continued.

'Devaswami is a very courageous person. He is basically preparing the Brahmins for suicide rather than see them betray their moral code. His ultimatum to Kotarani and Udyandev is just a red herring to throw the scent away from his real mission.'

'I think Devaswami has a bigger problem than just the Brahmins to deal with,' Kokur pointed out. 'Hunger is demonic; the demons create hunger as a weapon against the Devas. The famine is proof that Vritra the demon has cracked Devaswami's mandala of protection and entered Kashmir. Vritra brings bad weather and famine, exactly what we are suffering.'

'What mandala? What protection?' Naid asked.

Kokur fell silent, fearing he had shared more than he should about what went on in royal circles.

'If what both of you are saying is true and you are obviously only sharing a tiny bit with me,' Naid went on, 'then clearly things are even worse than I had imagined.'

'Naid, we have been so preoccupied by the man-made calamities visited upon us that we have forgotten it is Mother Nature who decides our destiny,' Manzim stated.

Naid started giggling hysterically.

'Let me tell you what I know. I was at the Khazanchi wedding. The poor gathered in long lines, awaiting the leftovers after the last guests had departed. When they finally ate, several of them died – having been deprived of food for weeks, gorging themselves was a shock that their bodies could not bear. I was at the back of the line: the smell from the kitchen made the body scream for food, yet the mind kept saying, "Go slow". It was sheer agony.'

'The wedding is proof that our society is turning rotten and the moneyed men are to blame. Our thinking has been totally corrupted by money. The Brahmins view morals as self-discipline but are reluctant to impose moral checks on the powerful. The Ramayana is now entertainment offered by actors like me, not a code of conduct prescribed and enforced by the Brahmins for society.'

Manzim added his own take on the situation.

'One of the state elephants, which have not been fed because of the general shortage of food, died of starvation. His body had not even stopped heaving when a mob descended upon the carcass to chop it up and turn it into a meal.'

'Kotarani has to fix this problem quickly or there will be blood on the streets,' Naid demanded grimly.

Kokur nodded. 'On this issue I agree with you completely. But I do not know what Kotarani can do: she is not a miracle worker who can create food with magic. The astrologer has said that this is to be expected when there is a change in the zodiacal sign.'

Manzim was more practical. 'Let us not worry about Kotarani's problem. I am more concerned about you: we must take care of you first. I have an idea. I will introduce you to Shah Mir. I have done him many favours and he likes to please people. He runs a charity kitchen; I will ask him to give you a job there for the time being. If you are working there, at least you will be guaranteed a square meal a day.'

'But Manzim, that is a charity kitchen run by and for the Mussalmans. That is no place for Naid.'

'It is of course Naid's decision. But did Sharika worry that her child was nursed by Shah Mir's wife?'

'I am near breakdown. I need food and if you can introduce me to Shah Mir and I can get steady food I will thank you every day of my life. So what if the Lankar is run by and for Mussalmans?'

Manzim nodded his head at Naid. 'I arrange marriages between all varieties of people; each person tells me that they are different from the rest, and that they are special. You know what – they are not. We all want the same things in life. Naid, I know that I am biased because I am on commission with Shah Mir but it is good that you are rid of this prejudice towards him. Come, let us head to the Lankar.'

At the palace, Kotarani was engaged in a difficult discussion with Khazanchi and Manjari. She had asked Yaniv and the revenue minister to join her for the meeting. There had been rumours that the speculators had been hoarding food supplies and that they were in cahoots to corner the market and drive the prices even higher. Khazanchi was unbowed and unrepentant.

'Maharani, if somebody stakes ownership in a venture, they take the risk and the return. Many times, I have lent money to the farmers and I lost it all; there has been no return. So what if I balance my losses with my trading profits.'

'Have you truly lost the money, or is it merely compounding interest so that you will make even more at a later date?' the queen asked.

'Some will return the money, some won't. That is the way it is and that is the way it has always been.'

'Are you not better off if the farmers live to till the land so that you can have money in the future?' Kotarani continued.

'Maharani, I do my business in the way I know how. Your foreign minister, Shah Mir, had a theory that Persian trade should be welcomed, that it would bring peace. Well, let him now import food from Persia.'

'You know that that is not a practical solution!' chided Kotarani. 'The mountains would be hard to cross and we are short on time.' She switched tack. 'The grains and rice that you're selling to the public for their gold and silver – where did you get it?'

Khazanchi had sensed the queen's pain and distress at the desperate situation her people were in. She was weak and he was expansive in his moment of triumph. He could not resist poking Kotarani in the eye.

'When the Islamic traders squeezed me away from the north I shifted my caravans to the south, importing and exporting items with the central kingdoms. It was not as profitable at the time but I anticipated this famine. It happens every twenty years.'

'You have no fear of your maharani or your maharaja or the Devi,' inquired Kotarani icily?

Khazanchi was giddy with the power of life and death that was in his grasp.

'The maharaja is a noble soul. When he rides his horse he ties bells around its neck as a warning to other animals. He does not want to see even an insect hurt. You, Maharani, are firm but fair, and unlike Rinchina you do not believe in vigilante justice; I have done nothing wrong except to be a devotee of wealth. If the Devi is kind to me, surely you will not take offence at that.'

Kotarani turned to Manjari and pleaded: 'There are children starving across the Valley. Can an exception be made for them and an allowance released for families with children?'

Manjari's answer was as hard as the stones on her bejewelled finger.

'Maharani, the famine happened because the poor are over-breeding. I was not born into wealth; nobody gave me charity when my mother and I starved. I did not die because I did what I had to do.'

Kotarani responded with anguish: 'Manjari, you survived but there was a very important part of you that seems to have died. *Datta, dayadhvam, damyata:* Give, be compassionate, restrain yourself, is what we are taught.'

Manjari's nostrils flared.

'Compassion is the cry of the weak. Let them pray to the Devi.

Your problem is that you want to take care of people when people are happiest taking care of themselves.'

'Manjari, this is not about happiness and self-reliance. The hunger that the weak and the poor have is physical and real. Your hunger is demonic; the finery that you wear does not match the elephant hide it covers. Be careful that the weak and poor do not turn on you.'

Manjari fired back: 'Khazanchi and I can purchase anybody in this court, so we do not need sermons thrown in our face. Maharani, I am no lesser than you and if circumstances were different, would have been sitting in your place. Ignore the poor, and their problem will soon solve itself.'

Kotarani dismissed the pair and asked Yaniv what was to be done.

'Khazanchi has a monopoly until the next season's crop. He controls the food supply into the Valley. You need his cooperation, but you have to negotiate from a position of strength. If he senses weakness, he can name any price, and his greed is such that he may ask for your kingdom.'

'To negotiate from a position of strength seems difficult. Khazanchi will give up his life but not his money, and he knows his life is safe with me.'

Troubled in her mind, she went to visit Saras, who was seated in her room playing with her pets. Saras was happy to see Kotarani and offered her some tea.

'Saras, there is no food in the land. The Brahmins have gone on a fast. The public is suffering. The traders have the food, but they are holding on to it because they think that prices will rise even higher. Whether the older people and children die between now and when they release the food is not of consequence to them. If I use force they will simply stop bringing their caravans which will only leave us in a worse situation.'

Saras put her hand on Kotarani's hand and squeezed it.

'You know our need for large amounts of food is psychological. I eat very little, and when I overeat I actually feel sick. The rishis treat their bodies as holy and yet if you look at their intake it is minimal. But I think that there is something I found out that may be helpful to you.'

'What is it?' asked Kotarani.

'I was going on my regular walks through the hills. Yesterday, I followed a path that I had not taken for a while: imagine my surprise when I found that it had been traversed recently. When I walked further, I found an encampment. There must have been at least one hundred camels, all unloading grain and food, which was being stored inside a large temporary shelter. There must have been enough grain stockpiled there to feed the Kashmiris for several months. The mosquitoes and insects had been attracted by the smell of the food and were buzzing around and making a nuisance for the camel drivers and the private guard hired to protect it. Nobody noticed me and I left. I was meaning to come and tell you about it.'

'It must be Khazanchi's stockpile,' said Kotarani. 'He is obviously bringing the grain and storing it until even the oligarchs become desperate, so that he can extract the highest price.'

'Well,' said Saras, 'you can play tit for tat with him. Khazanchi is a good trader but he is not all-knowing and he does not understand the foodgrain business that well. His greed has blinded him.'

'What do you mean?' asked Kotarani.

'Come closer. Who knows who is listening when you come to visit me?'

Saras whispered into Kotarani's ear. Kotarani's eyes widened and then she started laughing.

'It is worth a try,' she said. 'Saras, you watch the world quietly and you prove to be the best teacher. You and I together will outsmart Khazanchi. If our plan succeeds, great; if not, it is time to bring out the army.'

When Kotarani returned to the palace she ordered that there would be a Maha yagna to appease Lord Indra so that Vritra could be defeated by Indra's thunderbolt. Even though the supplies were scarce she ordered that all steps be taken to secure them, including milk, honey, the sacred tulsi leaves, mint, nuts, flowers, fruits and other accoutrements. The public was invited and told that there would be free food for all at the end of the puja.

There is something about a prayer that uplifts the soul and gives hope even in the darkest of times. After the Puja was over, Udyandev announced that the storage granaries had been instructed to open their strategic reserves and give an allocation of grain to each family every day. The farther villages would have the grain brought to them. The announcement was greeted with wild cheers; the Brahmins came up to Udyandev and showered flowers on him. Udyandev took some fruit juice and fed Devaswami, who broke his self-imposed fast. The decision to open the strategic grain reserve was widely noted. It had historically been kept only for royalty, and only for the direst of circumstances. It had never been shared with the common public, for the simple reason that it did not hold enough to meet their needs.

Several days later Khazanchi asked for an audience with Kotarani. He was visibly upset.

'How can you give the grain away?' he bellowed.

'It is easy. See, you give it away, just like that!' She waved her hand, not deigning to look at him.

'A foolish gesture, but it will prove to have no value. The godowns will run out of grain in less than four weeks, and then not even you royals will have food on the table.'

'It is okay,' replied Kotarani sweetly. 'At least the people know that we are in this together and that if we run out of food we will all starve together. Moreover, I am confident that what is given away will multiply in return. The Devi will be happy that the children are being fed.'

Khazanchi stomped away. It was difficult to do business where there was violence or irrationality, but it was just a matter of time before the food would run out.

The Sogdian came to see the Maharani and reported that he had secretly picked up that Khazanchi had boasted to other traders: 'I will have the last laugh. In one month I will have the power of life and death in the Valley. I will seize the throne and food will be my weapon. I would of course need military help, but the tantrins are already in my pay and I am funding Ali's Panun Fauj and his cavalry is on my side. If I can get the Ekangas, the maharani's guard, to defect, then it is in the bag. Manjari is right, it is time to think big and lead the people's revolution! I could become the ruler and Manjari would be maharani. But I am suspicious as to what the cunning fox Kotarani could be up to?'

Kotarani nodded placidly and was not the least disturbed by the Sogdian's report. The Panun Fauj was a new development and would need following up. The Sogdian continued with a very negative report on Shah Mir. He had not paid any attention to the army, never visited the front line and ignored the needs of the troops, preferring to spend his time politicking in the capital. There was no foreign intelligence and Shah Mir had limited himself to admitting increasing numbers of foreign Sufis and other Islamic groups into Kashmir where they would head straight to the Khanqah. Kotarani was alarmed and sent the Sogdian away to find out more on this topic.

Two weeks later Khazanchi and Manjari again demanded an audience with Kotarani. She asked an interested Yaniv to observe this meeting as well.

'The Maha yagna was all a ruse! A bluff to fool me,' Khazanchi shouted. 'You just wanted to get all of the dry tulsi and mint in the Valley, did you not?'

'Why do you belittle prayer all the time?' Kotarani tut-tutted. 'It seems that our prayers have been answered. Why are you upset that we had to source tulsi and mint leaves for the prayer along with other ingredients?'

'You could not possibly have needed all of the tulsi and mint that you collected!' screamed Khazanchi. 'There is none to be found in the Valley, and it will take weeks to gather and prepare more.'

'We ended up with a surplus, but luckily, now that the grain has been distributed to the public there is space in the godown to store them along with a few other ingredients. Do you need any of it, by any chance?'

'Yes, I do,' replied Khazanchi unwillingly. 'You knew all along that the rice that I imported had to be mixed with tulsi and mint so that it would not get infested with insects and beetles.'

'Well,' interjected Yaniv forcefully, 'that creates the basis of a very successful partnership. The maharani has the tulsi and the mint and you have the rice. If the two are put together then one has a marketable product. The only question is, on what terms should the partnership be? Everyone knows that the dry tulsi and the mint are the more valuable item as the rice is a rapidly degrading asset if it gets infested.'

Khazanchi glared at Yaniv. 'What is your cut in this?'

'Nothing,' said Yaniv. 'Business is not blackmail, nor is it about leading a coup d'état: it is about sustaining society. It is your dharma that says that you need to have a long-term perspective. The Kashmiris will survive, the crops will grow again and everyone wins.'

A very angry Khazanchi, who knew he had been outmaneuvered, was nudged by Yaniv into a deal, the terms of which immediately impacted the Kashmiris. The rice would be immediately released to the public and Khazanchi agreed to keep the supply going. The price was brought back to 300 dinaras per khara. Khazanchi would lose money on the transaction, but Kotarani would subsidize the difference out of the royal treasury. When the next season's crop was harvested the state would take a higher quota than normal from the farmers, but the quota would not be an increase in the taxes. Instead it would go into filling the godowns, which would be expanded, and thus the reserve capacity would be built for the entire Kashmiri community rather than just the royalty.

Khazanchi stormed out at the end of the stressful session. Manjari, who had stayed silent, fired a parting shot at Yaniv: 'The queen has been served well by a foreign mercenary. You will see that two can play that game also.'

When they had left, Kotarani turned to Yaniv. 'Who would have thought that Khazanchi would have become so predatory and that witch Manjari would not be satisfied until she owns the whole world. Their wings need to be clipped. When money serves itself and not society, it becomes demonic.'

'They were prepared to use food as a weapon against you and the people of Kashmir. This is a crime and if we had not negotiated with them they would have caused a lot of damage. You have once again proven invaluable to me in handling Khazanchi. You will be justly rewarded.'

Yaniv felt slightly giddy at the deal he had closed: even though it did not mean much money, he was beginning to understand and implement the Kashmiri notion of lihaz; a harmonious connectivity underlying every action one took. It was harder to practise than the trader's narrow agenda of buyer beware and making an arm's-length profit, irrespective of the consequences to the other party, but it made for a better world. Maybe the self-discipline of karma was not such a bad one to operate by in this world, irrespective of whether one carried it into the next world or not?

Kotarani heard from Devaswami that normalcy had returned and that his Brahmins had given up on their threat. He did warn Kotarani however that the demons accompanying the famine would cause damage and needed to be expelled and that would need another yagna. Kotarani planned a horse ride and she asked Brahma to come and join her.

'You are very serious tonight,' he observed to her.

Kota replied, 'Brahma, we have suffered a lot and the misfortunes are unending. When I go to bed at night I am so exhausted. Sometimes I think that I will not wake up. Yet one has to keep on flowing like the River Vitasta.'

'Yes, we have truly suffered but you have defeated all the challenges that have come your way. You have displayed the strength, the people worship you as being invincible, ever captivating but never captive. What keeps you going?' asked Brahma.

'I wish the people would be more caring of each other. But it is not the queen's lot to be judgemental of her subjects. As I get older I am reminded of my father who would say that he would shut his mind and place the Devi in his heart before going into battle. He would then neither suffer remorse nor would he experience pain. I do my dharma the best that I can and it keeps me going through the worst of times. But I still wonder why?'

'Only Devaswami can answer that question,' Brahma replied, 'but I can tell you for whom we suffer. It is for our children.'

Kotarani nodded.

'Brahma, all across the kingdom families are rejoicing that they will survive and that their children will live. I really want a better world for them. As things get better Udyan and I have this dream that someday we can give Devaswami the money that he needs to expand Sharadapeeth. He believes that Kashmir's future lies in bringing in young students from our neighbouring countries; teaching and training them on the Kashmiri principles and on their return they can bring wisdom to their own people. We agree that rather than invading our neighbours or living in fear of them or sending our acharyas, this approach will protect our future.'

'I know that Devaswami sees Sharadapeeth as the beacon of light for the world. Let's put that aside for the moment. Tell me, are you at peace now and happy?'

Kotarani thought for a moment before confessing: 'I have been unlucky with my loved ones. First, I lost my mother, then my father; the stars I was born under blocked you and claimed Rinchina. Now Ravan has drifted away, a prey to his own insecurities. I have come to live with all of it with great difficulty and the unfailing help of the Devi whose presence is always there for me. But there is a hole in my heart.'

Brahma guessed the problem, 'It is Chander, isn't it?'

Kotarani was touched by Brahma's perceptiveness. He understood her so well and she opened up to him.

'Kashmir is the land of women, every child is referred to as his mother's child not the father's. I am queen, yet I am the one person who is deprived of my son. I need to see Chander, hold him. He has never experienced a mother's love or a father's strength. He has suffered even more than I have. Shah Mir, who at one time was willing to make a deal, has recently proven to be uncharacteristically obdurate and cruelly throws Rinchina's dying command in my face. I find him to be such a low schemer, always smiling and fawning even as he worms himself ahead to greater strength. Unfortunately, even Udyan, who normally will go along on every issue, has taken a strong position on Chander and says that he does not want to ever see him in our home. He says that Shah Mir is a crocodile lying in wait: he has raised Haider. Had it not been for Jatta I would find myself truly disconsolate.'

'That is uncharacteristic of Udyan who is normally so gentle and tolerant of people around him.'

'It is truly a bad situation. Brahma, I can tell you honestly that Udyan feels that Shah Mir has designs on my body. He will make allusions that Kashmir's earth is defiled by Shah Mir. You know that the kingdom's ruler is the king and its earth is the queen. The sexual allusion is most distressing for me, and it has resulted in my having to limit any personal relationship I have with Shah Mir in order to see Chander.'

Brahma consoled the maharani. 'Udyan does not suspect you of infidelity, nor is he jealous. His sixth sense is picking up that Shah Mir is crooked and he is being extra protective of you. That is all. Chander is your flesh and blood, not Shah Mir's. Irrespective of where he is, you are with him. He will come of age and will be presented to court eventually, so be patient. The time to strike is then.'

Kotarani sighed.

'Yes, that is the only way left now. But it does make me think that whenever I have given in I have regretted it. Whenever I stick with my convictions, I am strong. I must not ever give ground in future.'

'Each challenge has firmed your convictions and built your strength. The same will happen with Haider.' It was then that Brahma came up with another of his madcap suggestions. He said, 'Kota, what if I invited Chander to come to our home to celebrate the good times. I think that I can convince Shah Mir to let Chander visit Bhima.'

'So what?'

'We will make it into a boating picnic. We will take several boats with us and the only thing will be that you will be an incognito visitor and we will put you in with Chander and Jatta. Nobody will know, and certainly not Shah Mir.'

The plan worked like a charm. Bhima steered Chander and Jatta on to one of the boats and then scampered away with the others. The boats set off and Chander and Jatta found Kota in the front seated on the cushions. Chander was surprised but not upset. Kota's heart was full with happiness at the sight of Chander and Jatta. It was the first time in her life that she had seen her two sons together. They had grown into such fine young boys. She hugged Chander tightly and kissed him repeatedly on his forehead. The rowers had expertly swung the boat away from the others and it was traversing a carpet of lotuses that were swaying in the wind. She made Chander and Jatta sit on either side of her and held their hands together.

'Who feeds you?' she asked Chander.

'Layla takes good care of me.'

'Yes, she is a loving woman. Brahma uncle says that she is very affectionate.'

'She is like a mother to me.'

Kota felt a pang of pain. But she was not going to let it spoil the moment.

'Chander, I agree that next to me she is absolutely the best.'

'Why do you call me Chander when everyone else calls me Haider?' asked the boy earnestly.

'You have two names. Haider means lion-hearted. I named you Chander after Kashmir's presiding Devi Sharada whose name means autumn moon. Among her qualities is that she unites the Kashmiri people through her magnanimity and love. So your two names together mean always be fearless in showing your love.'

'I love my brother. I can play with him. If I had a sister I would not have been so sure,' announced Jatta solemnly.

'I understand,' said Kota smiling. 'Girls are bossy and demanding and that can get irritating. But trust me, girls make boys better.'

Jatta was not convinced, 'I am perfectly fine the way I am.'

Kota laughed at Jatta's pugnacity. He was so unlike his father Udyan and surprisingly Chander was the scholarly one in his demeanour.

'Chander and Jatta, you are still young and there is much that may not make sense to you. But you do accept that you are brothers?'

Both nodded their heads obediently.

'Irrespective of what people may say to you about how you are different from each other, always remember that there is common blood between the two of you, my blood which flows through you.'

Jatta spoke up brightly, 'Same blood when I fell and suffered a nosebleed.'

'Same blood if I were to suffer a cut. It is the same bloodline which has flown in Kashmir for the last 4,000 years and the same blood which overcame every handicap including the loss of my mother and my father; your grandmother and grandfather whom you never met.'

'What were Grandpa and Grandma like?' Chander asked.

The question brought tears to Kota's eyes.

'I will tell you everything I know but you should also ask that question from everyone else that you can. The stories you hear will bring them alive in front of your very eyes. They made Kashmiris proud of who they were as a people.'

'I am a Kashmiri!' said Chander.

'Me too, I am a proud Kashmiri,' piped in Jatta.

'To be a Kashmiri means to recognize that life will give you both snakes and also ladders, but the choices you should never make are the ones that are driven by fear or overconfidence, hatred or attachment. The only choices you should make are the Sharada ones, of truth and knowledge, so you should practise lifelong learning and have an open mind. The most demanding choice that you can always make with your eyes shut is the one that is driven by selfless sacrifice.'

One of the boatmen came forward to serve food. He respectfully placed large lotus leaves in front of everyone. With practised hands, each person washed the lotus leaf with a sprinkling of water. Then the boatmen brought out the picnic basket and served the food on the lotus leaves. As the boatmen passed the hot tea with savoury snacks the boys started indulging in horseplay, scooping water and squirting it at each other. Kotarani smiled. The flowing river represented liquid Shakti and was very soothing to her. The goal of life, say the Kashmiris, is worldly fulfilment and liberation. Kota silently thanked the Devi in gratitude: 'Oh Devi, tonight my heart is content and for the first time I have experienced total fulfilment.'

The boys wanted to play with the cowries, and Kota agreed. Soon the children's protesting shrieks and laughter filled the air and travelled over the waters as Kotarani got increasingly hooked with each favourable roll of the dice.

Wave 14
Goddess

SEVERAL years went by and the happy kingdom re-established the rhythm of its daily life. Kotarani and Udyan were seated in their garden one day, enjoying the vibrant flowers that were in full bloom. Jatta was pouting. The next day he and Udyan were going to depart for Sharadapeeth where their son would be admitted to the university. None of Udyan and Kotarani's arguments had convinced Jatta that he needed to go, or that he wanted to go.

Kotarani spoke endearingly: 'Precious, my *gobur*. You will make many friends for life at school. You will forget us and it is I who am going to miss you badly.'

'What friends? They will all want to tease me and say that the son of the maharaja and the maharani cannot do this and cannot do that. Why cannot I continue going to school nearby at Ishber?'

Kotarani consoled Jatta: 'Because Sharadapeeth is so much bigger. When you will walk through the library you will see hundreds of thousands of manuscripts each with the writings of the greatest realized souls of humanity. Pick Guru Gotam as your tutor. I owe everything that I know to him. He will teach you Vedic math secrets and make sure that you are number one. Besides, your cousin Bhima is at the school, and is senior to you. He will protect and guide you.'

Jatta's face brightened. He had the same relationship with Bhima that a young Kotarani had had with Brahma. He really looked up to Bhima. But he was not going to give up yet.

'You had Saras with you. I do not have anybody. Can she come with me?'

Kotarani laughed.

'Saras accompanied me because I am a girl and you know girls are not strong like boys,' she said, half joking. 'You are a brave young man, the bravest that I know of, so you don't need a chaperone. You will stay in a dormitory with other boys and it will be fun.'

Jatta was mollified that his outburst was not seen as a sign of his internal anxiety. Bhima would guide him, and it would be nice to be with the other boys. Udyan and he left to pack in preparation for their early morning departure. Kotarani watched her son disappear into the distance; her eyes were moist. It seemed like just yesterday that he was born, and in the twinkling of an eye he was off to school.

Jatta's departure created a vacuum in Kotarani's life. Her son was a bundle of energy and had occupied her every single moment that she was free from her work. However, the respite that she and Kashmir had gained turned out to be the lull before the storm and she faced challenging times once again. Shah Mir's promotion to Kampanesa by Kotarani, and his strategy as foreign minister of engaging commercially and culturally with the northern kingdoms turned out to be a colossal failure. Along with the Islamic traders, alarming news arrived in the capital that Achala, a Tartar, was amassing his troops, the Lashkar-e-Turk, for an attack on Kashmir. Achala had boasted that when he took over Kashmir he would make Dulucha and Mohammed of Ghazni look stupid. There had been absolutely no advance warning of this threat and the Kashmiris were completely blind-sided. Shah Mir's hurried and hapless peace overtures were summarily rejected. Achala was not a raider; he intended to be ruler. All that he needed to do was wipe out Kota and Udyan and their small group of loyalists, an easy target.

The maharani's council held an emergency meeting.

'The Lord of the Gates urgently informs us that Achala has entered through Herapur, the entrance station from Rajapuri,' Shah Mir reported. 'He has about 50,000 jihadis with him. Two things are worrisome. First, we have a defection in our ranks: the Raja of Mugdhapura is supporting Achala with hospitality and provisions. This has never happened before in the history of Kashmir. Second – and this is very mysterious – Achala is accompanied by a very powerful shaman. He wears a mask and seems to know everything; he knows about our battle plans and can pinpoint our weaknesses. Our soldiers are losing their nerve, stating that the jihadis have magic even more powerful than that of Bulbul, even more potent than that of our Brahmins. Achala looks to this magician for guidance on every important question.'

Kota demanded a report on the state of their defences. Again, Shah Mir's account was bleak.

'Achala has followed a different strategy than what Dulucha did. He has sent small teams to essentially cut off the escape routes out of the Valley; they know the local pathways as well as we do. We may be holed up inside our fortresses, but he has blocked every entrance and exit. He is picking off the fortresses one by one with the shaman's help. His force is not that much smaller than Dulucha's and it is highly trained. He is not burning the land, but building alliances to secure his supplies locally. He can wait us out since he intends to live in Kashmir: his strategy is to force us to confront him in the open so that he can finish us off. If we do confront him, we will at best be able to field no more than 5,000 irregulars, many of whom are ill equipped. It will be a massacre. Then he will own our land and its people.'

One aristocrat was quick to the draw. 'Shah Mir, you are commander-in-chief and foreign minister. You have lived in Kashmir for the last twenty-two years and enjoyed the highest privileges of the state for the last ten. Is this your gift to us that Shah Mir will go down as the person who handed Kashmir over to the jihadis in 1335?'

For once Shah Mir's wit failed him and he was quiet. He had risen through his talents in art and politics, but this challenge exposed his inadequacies. Faced with a colossal disaster, he realized that he had been so focused on the internal machinations of the Kashmir court that he had completely ignored his responsibilities

He bowed his head knowing that it was time to be circumspect. Kotarani sensed that the courtiers were in a state of panic and instructed them to take a break and reassemble later in the day.

Udyandev accompanied her back to their chambers. Her thoughts went back to her father. *What would he have done?* She remembered a gift that he had given her in her childhood. She used to enjoy playing chess with him when she was young: memories of her father patiently teaching her the moves flooded into her mind. On a whim she took the chessboard out from beneath its cloth cover and spread out the pieces on the floor.

The touch of the well-worn pieces was comforting. She put the pieces on the board and took away the majority of her pawns. Udyandev, Kotarani, Shah Mir, the Sogdian and a few irregulars faced the entire strength of Achala and his army. Kotarani sat down, crossed her legs and began to practise Vipashyana, concentrating her mind on the board. She felt herself enter the world of the board. Now the situation looked very different: Achala had soldiers and a shaman but he did not have a maharani. Kotarani still had something that the other side did not, Shakti, feminine power; it was a beginning. Kotarani slowed down her breathing and the battlefield began to take on a life of its own. The pieces began to move in various ways as Kotarani tested alternative strategies. Achala was determined to kill the maharaja and capture the maharani and Kashmir: what strategy would wrest the advantage from her adversary? She used the three-part principles of human choice that she had been taught at Sharadapeeth. Achala had the power, but he was also driven by *ichchha,* his desire, while being constrained by *gyan,* his limited knowledge and ignorance, which would ultimately shape his *kriya* actions. Where did that translate into a weakness and provide an opening?

Kotarani came out of her meditative state energized and relaxed. She went to Udyandev and they talked for several hours.

'I feel very humiliated that as the king I have not been able to protect my people,' Udyan admitted. 'Death is preferable to dishonour.'

'Udyan, to win needs intelligence and courage, not death.'

'I am ready for any plan and any outcome.'

'Even one that requires you to be sacrificed to save Kashmir?'

Udyan reacted sharply. 'Between you, Kashmir and me, you would be the last thing that I would want to be sacrificed. Between Kashmir and me the answer is easy.'

'Exactly', said Kotarani. 'That is the way the world will read you. The king's battle plan should reflect the thinking expected of us, but to just do that would be the move of a simpleton. The steps of the plan have to ring true but be understood only by a few, and yet there is great risk of things going wrong because Achala's shaman is an unknown.'

'What do you have in mind?'

'Udyan, you have to go into battle alongside Shah Mir. We will lose the battle and Shah Mir, brave though he will be, is likely to be killed. You will be taken prisoner and you should beg for mercy. Achala will use you as a hostage, and demand me and our kingdom as ransom. I will surrender and it is at the moment of Achala's victory that I will strike.'

'I don't trust Shah Mir. What if he defects?'

'Then you flee, because Shah Mir will not permit Achala to show you any mercy. Haider will become expendable to Shah Mir also. I will attack Shah Mir's household and regain Haider. I will send him to you for safe keeping and then surrender to Achala. Once I am with him Huli Jing will know what to do: Achala will finish Shah Mir once he knows he has had designs on me for a long time, and then I will finish him.'

Udyan's confidence rose with Kota's supreme and confident display of ultimate feminine power. He saluted her, 'Ever captivating but never captive.'

The two talked for a long time before returning to the hall where the courtiers had reassembled. Kotarani addressed them.

'Kashmiris, today we stand and fight. My husband Udyandev will lead our forces. Shah Mir and his cavalry have been given the express responsibility to guard the maharaja at all costs. We will face the enemy at Bhimanaka. We will fight with strength and attack the enemy where he is weakest. This maharani will not let what happened to us with

Dulucha ever occur again. The highest quality that we value is the courage to be a Vir: it is the foundation that every other value is built upon. I will rejoin my husband when he returns to put this *mangalsutra* back around my neck. Unless he returns victorious, he will not have a wife and I will not have a husband.'

Having spoken, Kotarani took her necklace and put it around Udyandev's neck as he bowed before her. The crowd watched in stunned silence. The maharani and maharaja were making a statement that they were prepared to separate, say goodbye and die in defence of Kashmir. A shout went up through the assembly, 'Amar Kotarani! Udyandev forever!'

Shah Mir went out into the public square and was accosted by a crowd of Kashmiris wanting to know what had transpired. His declaration was brief and to the point and was picked up and carried through the kingdom by the couriers.

'We will not desert Kashmir. We will resist to the last man, woman and child. We will win!'

The Kashmiris were greatly inspired by Shah Mir's declaration. Unlike the last time, when Shah Mir had retreated to his village, as commander-in-chief he was going to fight a fellow Mussalman; a foreign-born man was willing to make the ultimate sacrifice. The Kashmiris marvelled at him. The crowd picked him up on their shoulders and carried him to his home singing and shouting, 'Shah Mir! Amar Mir!'

The two sides assembled their respective forces in the late spring. Brahma accompanied Udyandev and Shah Mir as they led their forces to Bhimanaka, which offered several advantages to the locals. It was a narrow valley, which limited the offence in terms of its frontal assault: the archers could take positions in the gullies and among the trees, hidden from the enemy's sight. Since the battle was in the open, the enemy would not be able to use their heavy siege weapons against a stationary target – it would be hand-to-hand combat. They knew that they would eventually be overwhelmed by the larger force, but at least it gave the mouse the best odds against the cat.

When the sun rose, the Valley had never looked prettier: every inch of Bhimanaka was carpeted with flowers that swayed in the slight breeze. On one side the Kashmiris were arrayed in battle formation. The infantry was on the ground, pikes held stiffly before them, knowing that they would have to bear the brunt of the first charge. Shah Mir's cavalry of Mussalmans were behind them, the horses neighing nervously. Perhaps they were communicating to the horses on the other side the foolishness of the human race. Scattered in the hills but close by were the *tikashna*s, the archers.

Achala's forces were amassed at the other end of the ravine. Shah Mir saw the shaman signal to him as he led the charge. The horses pounded the earth beneath their hooves. As the passageway narrowed, the attackers gradually took on a V formation, creating a giant black arrow hurtling towards the Kashmiris, bringing doom and destruction. When they spotted the Kashmiris, they let out a wild yell: '*Al illah!*'

A slight clatter sounded in the back of the Kashmiri ranks. A few soldiers turned back to look. *Oh, what an ignominious sight!* Whether inadvertent or deliberate, Shah Mir's horse was backing away. On seeing him, Udyandev turned tail and started fleeing. In his hurry to run away, he had even lost his shoes and was hobbling over the rocks in his attempt to escape certain death. Shah Mir looked at the fleeing maharaja and realized that he had been handed the perfect scapegoat. 'You lotus eater!' he shouted. 'You are not fit to be a maharaja!' He signalled a retreat.

A fleeing army is not a pretty sight. The Kashmiris melted away into the backwoods in the twinkling of an eye, leaving only four people: Shah Mir, the Sogdian, the fleeing Udyandev and Brahma. The attackers howled in victory; they had their quarry in their grasp. Shah Mir ran towards his small cavalry force; his Mussalman compatriots grabbed him, one of them taking him up on his double saddle. They fought bravely to protect Shah Mir, beating an orderly retreat on their horses. The Sogdian was following Udyandev's desperate dash along with Brahma.

'You go ahead,' he told Brahma. 'I will stay behind.'

Brahma understood. He blessed the Sogdian, who shouted: 'Tell the maharani to watch out for Shah Mir. He is a crocodile who wants to eat her heart.'

Udyandev was breathing heavily and when Brahma caught up with him, he pitifully pleaded for help. Inspired by the Sogdian's sacrifice, Brahma grabbed the maharaja by putting him on his back. Brahma was strong and today his feet had wings. He bounded from rock to rock barely feeling the weight on his shoulders.

'To the river,' said Udyandev weakly. Brahma responded as if a spur had been applied. The blood began to ooze out of his cut feet, but he did not feel it. Brahma turned briefly to see the enemy was now upon the Sogdian: the jihadis had lost or left behind their heavy weapons and were fighting hand to hand with swords. The Sogdian was lethal. When one has no fear, one takes risks that an opponent cannot anticipate; he moved like a *bhand* dancer, cutting, slicing, and jabbing at his attackers. The jihadis had approached him like a pack of wolves but were reduced to a snarling pack of jackals. He was a Pashmina goat, sure-footed and precise in his moves. The jihadis circled him but each was afraid to approach: finally, with the increasing pressure from the masses of fighters that were pushing from behind, the jihadis fell upon the Sogdian. For a brief moment, the mass of bodies lifted in the centre like a waterspout, then came crashing down, never to rise again.

The distraction was sufficient to give Brahma and Udyandev a healthy lead. But the jihadis, realizing that their main quarry was escaping, let out a cry and started racing after them. Brahma reached the top of the ridge and let his momentum carry him down. There was a boat waiting in the river. The boatmen saw Brahma running towards them carrying Udyandev. Willing hands took the maharaja off Brahma's back and together the party ran to the boat. The rope holding the flat-bottomed *Paranda* boat to the tree was loosened, and the sturdy boatmen pressed hard against the banks with their long poles. Perhaps the Devi was watching, because the river currents seemed to strengthen; as the jihadis reached the riverbank, the boat turned the corner and vanished from sight. The battle had been lost, but Udyandev had escaped. Brahma, totally exhausted and bleeding, rested on the boat's carpeted floor.

A bedraggled Shah Mir returned to the fort to report to the maharani. She sat on the throne alone, listening impassively. When he finished she had only one observation.

'I gave you the responsibility of guarding the maharaja. You failed in your duty,' she said coldly.

Shah Mir could not believe his ears.

'Maharani, Udyandev showed himself a coward and deserted the battlefield. By your own declaration, he was no longer your husband in doing so. He was not worth saving,' he said contemptuously.

Kotarani was curt in her assessment.

'I understand that the maharaja ran. What I don't understand is why you did?'

Shah Mir was honest in his admission: 'If the king ran to save his life, what use was there for me to sacrifice mine?'

Kotarani was angered by his answer, and Shah Mir felt her heat.

'Kings run away all the time but you are the commander-in-chief. You have to bring victory back to the queen or else lay down your life to defend her. Now I have to rethink how the maharaja's turning tail and your foolish retreat could have robbed us of what little hope we have.'

Kota dismissed Shah Mir and asked Saras to join her.

'Shah Mir behaved exactly as I had predicted to you but I had wrongly calculated that he would put up more of a show of force. He was willing to risk his life for Brahma previously, but now he has turned tail instantly.'

'The Sogdian gave you the right input all along. Had it not been for him, the king would have been lost. Shah Mir's actions show that he is picking sides and the Kashmiris are not his chosen ones. He is turning and will use Islam to build a bridge with Achala just as he did with Dulucha.'

'Well, we will use Shah Mir's tactics and his slippery tongue to respond to Achala.'

Kotarani's pronouncement came not a moment too soon: an

emissary arrived from Achala demanding instant and unconditional surrender. He was asked to wait at the gate. Kotarani walked to the centre of the fort where the Kashmiris had gathered, addressing them with kind and reassuring words.

'Be without fear. When I became your maharani, I made the commitment to you that a mother makes to her children: your security and welfare is my prime directive. A mother will make the ultimate sacrifice for her children. Now, go home and soon there will be good news.'

The crowd dispersed slowly, fear written on every face. Kotarani sent for Manzim and surprisingly ordered that the jogi be brought to her. She also asked Shah Mir to rejoin her. Kotarani could see the stir that the jogi created as he entered the palace with his female attendants. The jogi had changed since that night long, long ago when she had secretly observed his séance. Whereas before he had projected uncertainty, he was now fiery. His shiny jet-black hair had become wiry. His liquid gaze was replaced with eyes like smouldering charcoals. His limbs, which had glistened and had lustre, now seemed to have been baked in an inner heat that emanated out of him. He projected the same power but it had gained a sinister hue. Out of the corner of her eye, Kotarani saw the discomfort on Brahma's face. She didn't care; she had to draw on all of her resources, however distasteful it may be. When Manzim arrived, she wasted no words.

'Manzim, I want you to return with Achala's emissary and act as my ambassador. Shah Mir will assist you in your mission. Take the jogi with you: he has many powers and he has consented to my request to save the kingdom. He can counter the shaman's magic. Tell Achala that my army has disbanded, that my husband has absconded. The people are panicked and ready to flee. I am prepared to submit to Achala's suzerainty; if he withdraws his army, I will meet him at a neutral place and marry him. He will receive a royal welcome as the new Maharaja of Kashmir and I will be his faithful maharani. If he agrees to this peaceful compromise, I will hand the treasure of Kashmir over to him. If not, the treasure will be lost and he will have nothing but a land emptied of its people.'

Shah Mir was beside himself. *This shameless woman will stoop to anything to keep her grip on power!* The notion that he was now reduced to being an assistant to a marriage broker made him grind his teeth. Why had the maharani become cold after he had told her that Udyandev had absconded? *It is not my fault that her erstwhile husband is a coward. But now is not the time to lose my head – I have no more options than she does. Perhaps meeting Achala will not be so bad after all. It will at least give me a head start in building a relationship with the new maharaja.* He knew which way the wind was blowing, and it was definitely not favouring the house of Kotarani.

Manzim, Shah Mir, the jogi and two attendants left the fort early in the morning and wended their way towards Achala's camp. Shah Mir's disgust at the presence of the jogi only increased when he saw Manzim's entourage – a cook and a serving woman who kept her dusky face covered with a fold of her shawl. They were accompanied by a couple of packhorses loaded with provisions. As a Mussalman, Shah Mir knew exactly what Achala's reaction would be to the nude jogi. Try as he might to avoid it, Shah Mir's eyes kept straying to the jogi's disgustingly large member. It was firm and tensile, unlike his own. But recognizing that the jogi was a young man of no more than thirty-five, and Shah Mir was approaching his late fifties, he was solaced. He also knew that the jogi would not live long and consoled himself with the notion of where Achala's sword would strike the jogi's body first.

They reached Achala's camp by evening. His guards accosted Manzim and took the group as prisoners to Achala. He was expecting them; the masked shaman was at his side. His eyes were intense as he watched every move Manzim made. The matchmaker bowed down, presenting a richly decorated sword to Achala, who did not even glance at it.

'My Lord Emperor, we come from Maharani Kotarani to extend to you the hospitality of Kashmir. Tonight, we feast; tomorrow, we talk business.'

Achala looked at the shaman, who was staring with suspicion at Manzim and the jogi. 'Son, liberation is at hand,' the jogi said firmly. 'Enjoy tonight.'

The shaman believed his magical powers to be greater than the jogi's, and he responded in fluent Kashmiri, 'Baba, this is no place for you.'

'I live in a cemetery and have no fear of death, but death has taught me to have a healthy love for life,' the jogi replied. 'Liberation is now in your and Achala's grasp. Savour every moment of life, not just the prize.'

The shaman silently turned towards Shah Mir, who bowed obsequiously and offered his greeting: *'Salaam Ale Kuum.'*

'You are no Mussalman, but a *kafir*,' Achala said contemptuously. 'You are a self-serving opportunist whose children have married the non-believers. Your cavalry fought against my soldiers – you are not loyal to the ummah.'

The shaman whispered something in Achala's ear; he instantly relaxed and changed his stance.

'Shah Mir, my adviser tells me that you have been raising Haider to be a true Mussalman, so perhaps you are not totally without merit.'

Turning to Manzim, Achala asked: 'Have you been sent to poison me just as you poisoned Dulucha's ambassador?'

'I am not in the poisoning business,' Manzim said stiffly. 'I have a reputation to keep. Your business is to conquer and rule; mine is to tie marriages.'

Shah Mir stepped in and vouched for Manzim.

'As a Mussalman I can testify this is an honest man. You have to fear nothing in the way of conspiracies from Manzim.'

The shaman whispered again and Achala once again changed his position.

'Manzim, your reputation vouches for you. So show us your hospitality tonight, and tomorrow we will talk the terms of the surrender.'

The small gathering marvelled at the omniscience of the shaman, who seemed to know everything and everybody in the Valley. Kashmiris were a credulous people and shamans and mystics were expected to have miraculous powers. The shaman left after muttering his instructions to Achala.

Manzim had a job to do. He instructed the waza to start the evening's dinner preparations. Even though it was a camp meal, it started with the mellowest of Kashmiri wines, the flavour of grapes accompanied by the fragrance of honeysuckle. Achala was Islamic, but had no prohibition against drinking alcohol. The servant silently and efficiently brought the appetizers, and it was clear that Achala liked the lamb ribs. He tore into them, ripping the meat off with his teeth. The waza kept the courses coming and the servant woman ran back and forth, keeping pace with the appetite of the diners. Shah Mir ate sparingly, but Achala had a hearty appetite. When dinner was over, the servant girl brought a plate of sweet rice pudding for dessert. This was followed with a mixture of anise seeds and betel nuts to help the digestion. Achala continued to drink copious drafts of wine, now of a bolder spicier variety. As the servant girl bent down to offer more wine, she slipped slightly. While she was able to balance the tray, she fell on top of Achala.

'A thousand pardons, My Lord,' whispered the servant girl, mortified at her faux pas.

'Are you blind?' Achala screamed. 'Don't they train slaves in Kashmir?'

The servant fell to her knees. 'Forgive me, My Lord. I am not worthy to be dust under your feet.'

She raised her head to see what her fate would be. Her eyes met Achala's; he stared back at her with fire in his red eyes and grabbed the girl by the neck. Her head cover slipped off, the jogi had brought the dusky yogini to be the server. Achala caught her by her hair with his left hand, dragging her a few yards away from the assembled group. He brought her face close to his and barked out: 'You unclean bitch! I will slit your throat. No woman dares to touch Achala.'

She faced him with her eyes downcast, then parted her lips seductively and with her eyebrows arching she softly blew warm air in his face and in a cooing voice whispered: 'I can give you pleasure such as you have never experienced before. Would you like to enter me from behind?'

Maybe it was the wine, maybe it was the jogi's betel concoction, but Achala suddenly felt he was looking at the most beautiful woman on earth. His manhood hardened immediately. This woman was all that the women of Kashmir were described to be; she made his other lovers seem like goats. Achala had been on his military campaign for far too long. He waved dismissively at Manzim, indicating that the evening was over and, still holding the washerwoman by her hair, he headed towards the tent. Out of the corner of his eye he saw the jogi smiling encouragingly at him. What had the jogi said – savour every moment? Well, he was going to savour ruling Kashmir. This servant girl was merely the first appetizer in what would be lifelong pleasure.

When they reached the tent, he flung the girl on his makeshift bed and stripped his clothes off. The washerwoman slowly removed her long scarf and then unbuttoned her short, tightly tailored blouse that emphasized the swelling curve of her breast. She then shed her lungi in one smooth movement and knelt in the cow posture of submission, on hands and knees with her face down and her hair spilling on the bed. The red and black snake tattoo contrasted with her dusky white back. Her pendulous breasts hung like mangoes on a tree branch; her round buttocks were an open invitation to Achala. He entered her from behind like a conquering bull. Then, to make the surrender complete, he reached around her with his left hand firmly and forcefully grabbing her pelvic bone, pushing deep inside and up, pounding her buttocks. She moved in rhythm with him; he penetrated her deeply, but their union was harmonic. He felt her *yoni* gripping his *lingam* like a hand milking a cow, but try as he might, he could not come. His breath became more and more laboured as he tired with the effort. The washerwoman was encouraging him, making noises: '*Dahman mar Dahman mar*, harder; push harder.' She seemed to be saying something in her native Kashmiri about the jogi and the mixture of datura and *lakshmana* that he had been fed, but Achala did not understand.

The Mussalmans have a saying: Cursed be he who makes himself earth and a woman heaven. To Achala's horror, the washerwoman suddenly swung herself up with her right arm in a circle, swivelling her body so that she faced upwards, gripping his penis ever so tight inside her padma for leverage. She supported herself on her elbows and wrapped her strong legs around his waist, pulling him powerfully towards her and the ground. Achala fell and found himself on his back beneath her. She still had his penis in her hard grip and now she was the master and he was the slave that she was riding. The washerwoman pressed her hands on Achala's chest and then began to squeeze his penis with her vaginal muscles: his last drugged orgasmic thoughts were of a corkscrew pulling his plug and blowing the top off his volcanic ejaculation. The hot lava poured out on the earth, and with each explosive flow Achala's body experienced multiple spasms. When it was over, Achala fell into a state of deep sedation. The washerwoman quietly dressed and slipped away into the night.

When Achala woke the next day, it was late morning. He felt rested and elated, as though there was nothing he could not conquer. The sun was shining brightly and the sky was blue. A crisp breeze blew through the meadow where his army was camped. He strode out of his tent. All was as it should be: his men were attending to their horses; some were repairing their weapons and sharpening their swords. In the middle of the encampment were Manzim, the jogi and Shah Mir. Off to one side of them the Kashmiri cook was working over an open campfire; the girl, hiding her face again, was serving tea and sweet bread to the group. The shaman watched all the proceedings from a short distance. When Achala approached, all stood up to greet him. The girl came to him and he accepted the hot tea, staring at her, but she made no sign that she knew him. *The houri should be grateful that I let her live.* Driven by a sense of purpose, he barked at Manzim: 'Today we do business. What message do you bring for me? Are you prepared to surrender unconditionally?'

'The maharani does not see it as surrender,' Manzim refuted. 'She sees this as a grand alliance. Her weak husband – her former husband – has disappeared into Ladakh to never return. She needs a man to help her rule Kashmir. She will always do what is right for the Kashmiri people and make any sacrifice. This alliance is what makes sense, and Udyandev does not, so she will sacrifice him like a chess piece. Nobody will give shelter to a fleeing king, and one of these days someone will bring his head to you, seeking a just reward. She will tie the knot with you unconditionally.'

Achala relaxed even more; this takeover was going to be easy.

'Will she convert to Islam?'

'She will. Her only wish now is to please you. As Maharaja of Kashmir you will have a welcome that you will have never seen. The women of Kashmir, the Kashmiri fairies, will sport with you in ways that will provide endless *leela*.'

'What about her sons?'

'You are right to ask that question. The maharani has borne two fine young men, but she is still young and strong. She will bear you many sons and they will rule the land. As for her sons, she will publicity disinherit them.'

'So far you have said the right things. What is the next step?'

Shah Mir stepped in smoothly.

'Your Majesty, the maharani has sent a personal letter to you. In the letter she proposes that she welcome you near Khir Bhavani where there is a spring and provisions. The alliance will be struck and the marriage performed there.'

Achala turned to the shaman; he nodded in agreement.

'No tricks now, right?' Achala asked. 'This woman is known for being devious and cannot be trusted.'

Shah Mir was his reassuring best.

'Your Majesty, I can personally testify that she is completely helpless. She abhors violence and her greatest wish is to bring peace to Kashmir. She will come unarmed in a palanquin, with no escort or guard but the eight carriers and her head priest, Devaswami. She suggests that you do the same. Let the partisans of Kashmir who have joined you in this battle now disband and go back to their villages; they will be the best proof that normalcy has returned.'

Achala looked at the shaman, who came over and whispered in his ear; they were obviously arguing. Shah Mir could hear broken words, indicating that the shaman was not supportive of the idea. He interjected the conversation.

'Your Majesty, in victory there has to be forgiveness and mercy. Let us make Kashmir into a demilitarized zone, free of the armed forces so the public does not have to hide like mice. If you enter the Valley with your jihadis and the partisans, who do you think will be there to receive you? Will Kotarani then willingly share the fabled treasure of Kashmir? There is no need for force when there is a meeting of the minds, an alliance of mutual purpose and a union that will breed the future rulers of Kashmir. Manzim has already told you of the plans to make your marriage into a grand celebration, one where you and your officers will partake of exquisite pleasures. Does the bee choose to destroy the honeysuckle when it can instead skilfully extract all of its nectar? If the Kashmiris have accepted you as the head of their family, as a father are you their protector or their annihilator?'

Achala thought of the sweetness he had tasted the night before, and how it might only be the beginning. He had been told about Maharani Kotarani and the catch was his. It made sense that the frightened maharani and her nervous population had been terrorized by his jihadis. There was no need to burn the land and its people. Unlike Dulucha, he was planning to stay in Kashmir and make it his base: the Maharani herself would be his figurative throne that he would mount with great pleasure. Shah Mir's temptations were stronger than the shaman's caution that Kota was clouding his thinking. The shaman was useful but he was not the ruler, and he needed to be cut down to size.

Achala addressed Shah Mir.

'I grant the maharani's request, Shah Mir, but if there is the slightest variance, you will pay with your life.'

Shah Mir bowed his head, and the deal was struck. The talk then quickly moved to tactical matters. It was agreed that the military force would be asked to withdraw just outside the Valley. A Paranda would be sent to pick up Achala, the shaman and his key officers. Manzim would dress them up and accompany them on the boat. Shah Mir would receive the wedding party at the ghat near Khir Bhavani, and then accompany the groom as he waited for Kotarani to come from Khir Bhavani. She would be unarmed, and as agreed would come in a palanquin and with only Devaswami as escort. Shah Mir would give her the Kalima and then perform the Islamic marriage.

Achala disbanded his forces. The partisans who had joined him, especially the troops provided by the disloyal lord of Mugdhapura, were disbanded and returned to their villages. He sent his core jihadis back through the pass to camp outside Kashmir proper, keeping only his elite guard with him.

The Kashmiri party departed homewards, elated at the success of their mission. Manzim especially was giddy with the alliance that he had created. Even Shah Mir, who had thought their chances of success low, had to concede that the idea of bringing the jogi and the washerwoman had worked. Sensing that he was being observed, and much to Shah Mir's chagrin, the jogi ambled closer and started a conversation with him.

'You don't like me, do you?' he asked.

Shah Mir shuddered internally. The notion of liking the jogi was enough to make his skin crawl, but he was too much of a diplomat to respond to the question directly.

'Frankly, I do not know you and you do not know me, so what is there to like or dislike? However, I am not in agreement with the deeds that you practise.'

The jogi laughed.

'Never say I am not, just stop at I am and you will be on the right path. You know you don't have to look at me if I make you uncomfortable. Tell me, how is your sex life?'

Shah Mir stiffened. The Kashmiris were disposed to talking freely about matters between man and his wife – but he was also proud, and he felt that his masculinity was being challenged.

'I am not going to answer that question. I have a large family. That is sufficient proof of Allah's kindness to me.'

'I am told that you like falcon hunting. Falcons need meat but not love. If you caress a falcon it will resist, because the oil from the fingers could damage its wings. Its identity is that it is a hunter. It may breed, but its nature knows nothing of sexuality.'

Shah Mir could feel the jogi getting inside his skin.

'Society is about morality. If sexuality is about parading around naked and midnight orgies, it must be banned and punished. Sex can be sinful; women need to be controlled so that their passions do not lead men astray. It is not about nature, but about character.'

The jogi pounced on Shah Mir's statement like a cat on a mouse.

'When you know the nature of fire, you know its proper use. Sometimes you use it for light, sometimes you use it for warmth, sometimes you use it for cooking, sometimes you use it for burning and sometimes you use it to make sacrificial offerings to God. To not know the nature of sex is to not know of all of its manifold benefits – and also its dangers. What if I said that the character of sex is that it is the most sacred of acts?'

Shah Mir knew that he was being cornered, but he was stubborn.

'Procreation is good enough for me. There is no danger in sex if you wash yourself and keep yourself clean.'

'Do you feel tired after you have sex?'

Shah Mir wanted to bring the matter to an amicable close and he was relieved that the other man had finally said something he could agree with.

'In truth when I was younger I could go many times, but yes, now I need a good sleep after it is over.'

'What if I told you that the nature of sex is that you should be stronger afterwards, full of *ojas*, vigour, and not weaker; you should, for a time, have such vitality that you feel that you are a superman. It is this difference that separates man from the animals; it is this evanescent biological force that makes sex all-powerful, not merely nature's will to reproduce itself.'

'I am not one of your illiterate villagers to be sucked in by that statement. Sex is not magic and miracles.'

The jogi seemed to be enjoying the debate, and Manzim was drawn into it, watching the two polar opposites argue.

'Tell me, how old are you and how old do you think I am?' the jogi asked.

'Young pup, I am over fifty years old,' Shah Mir said sombrely, 'and one might think you would have a sense of shame talking to somebody nearly twice your age on this matter. This is a subject that is best left to your youthful friends, who are probably on heat all the time.'

The jogi did not react to the insult.

'How would you feel if I told you that I am seventy-five years old?' said the jogi. 'I am sure that you must often fantasize that if you were to get yourself a younger wife you would regain your youth and vigour, but that is not the answer, is it?'

Shah Mir was shocked. The jogi, with his boyish body who looked no older than thirty, was in reality twenty-five years older than him! *What was the secret of his youth? Could he be telling the truth?* Shah Mir turned to Manzim questioningly.

The jogi sensed that he had the advantage.

'There is an acid fire in you that is burning you and will burn those around you. Before one orders society through moral dictates and decrees, it is good to balance the self first. Come and visit me and I will teach you how to activate your libido centre. If you want a tune-up, you know where to find me!'

Manzim chuckled.

'Shah Mir, I can vouch that the jogi has the fountain of youth and his supernatural powers are real. You should feel honoured that he has invited you; he generally keeps his distance from aristocrats, preferring to be one of the commoners.'

'Manzim, I am not Achala,' Shah Mir replied. 'The jogi's ways hold no interest for me, nor will I come under his sway.'

Manzim fell silent, but Shah Mir heard a snigger from behind him. He turned around, but all he saw was the servant girl and the cook following them. The washerwoman had her face covered and the cook was in his own thoughts, so it was hard to figure who had made the offensive sound. The conversation over, the party quickened their pace as they neared their home front.

When they reached the fort, their news was greeted with joy. Shah Mir's reputation rose immensely, and he found himself increasingly burnishing the account of his negotiations with Achala and the central role that he had played. He was referred to as the bear tamer. Kotarani gave instructions for the wedding arrangements and reception of the new lord to begin immediately. Manzim was directed to work with the tailors to make outfits for Achala and his key officers. Kotarani turned to the jogi.

'I owe you a debt of gratitude. Is there any wish of yours that is in my limited power to grant you? Devaswami will be arriving shortly and perhaps we can perform puja together.'

The jogi snorted. 'Power, what power do you have? I came to fulfil *your* desire to conquer your enemy. Forget Devaswami. Join me and follow my way. I will burn Achala and his men into ash. Devaswami can deliver nothing.'

Kotarani was reminded about the last *sammelan* that she had attended.

'What way do you want me to follow?'

'I will teach you the Kalachakra tantra which will give you mastery over hundreds of thousands of holy warriors. You will be the cakravartin, the empress and the leader of the vajra army. *These supremely ferocious warriors will throw down the barbarian hordes.* It will be the holy war to end all wars.'

'Then how are we any different from them? Their tactic is to corrupt the highest spiritual truths to seek power through unending warfare. Then we may as well join them. No, Devaswami has taught me that even if fire is burning up the universe, it is better to jump through the hoop of Kali's time than to fire up the flames further.'

'You underestimate the power of ultimate fire,' the jogi stated.

'Once ignited, fire consumes and in that lies its self-destruction because it cannot create. I feel safer riding the irresistible power of time,' Kotarani asserted. 'In any case, thanks to you Achala wants me. I can handle him, and any man who wants me, single-handedly.'

'Then you face your enemy your way, and I will go my way. Don't try to use me next time.'

His offer spurned, the jogi stomped out leaving a dismayed Kotarani behind him. There were, however, too many things to be done for her to worry about the jogi's erratic and explosive behaviour.

Kotarani arrived at Khir Bhavani the night before the wedding. It was in the small hamlet of Tulmul, and its Brahmins were considered to be the proudest in the Valley. Devaswami and the priests knew about the antiquity of the spring and the shrine, and only a few were permitted to recite the appropriate mantras and prayers that were auspicious to the Devi. Devaswami and the select priests had stationed themselves near the *kund,* the water tank housing the deity, conducting prayers all night long as Kotarani made offerings under Devaswami's watchful guidance, to the empress of the universe. Since time immemorial, the waters of the spring had been able to change colours: the priests attached meaning to the colours, with black portending extremely bad times for the kingdom. On this day the waters were milky, heralding that happy times had returned to the Valley. Obviously the Devi herself had blessed the forthcoming union.

Kota was made to step outside the temple precincts for the next ritual. Inside the offerings were restricted to milk and sugar products only, but now she was guided to pray to Kartikeya, the firstborn of Shiva, he with the divine lance. There were weapons placed in front of the deity and Devaswami made Kota pick each one, recite mantras and sprinkle holy water on them. Finally, when night fell, a small party left for Hari Parvat. There on the peak under the moonlight the yagna to Mahakali by Pandit Atal, known for his powerful mantras, was conducted. First Kota's *atma* was visualized and placed inside a small idol. Then the goddess was invoked in her warrior form; fully satiated with all of her favourite offerings, including goat's liver cooked in rice with turmeric, wine, fish and cannabis. Then the goddess's Shakti was imbibed inside Kota's atma and finally the atma was inserted back into Kota. Sexual intercourse was the fifth prescribed offering, and all the attendees understood that would happen after the marriage ceremony with Achala was complete.

The flat-bottomed boat arrived near the ghat the next morning, a mile away as prearranged. Manzim had brought the finery for Achala and his officers, and they looked truly grand in their regal clothes. However, when they boarded the royal boat a small problem had arisen: it was designed to accommodate the royal family, not an army. Achala agreed that only the shaman and a dozen of his key officers would accompany him; the rest of his corps would follow separately. It would take longer on land, but his men would arrive in time for the festivities.

The boat departed bearing its royal guest. Achala was seated in the place of honour on plush carpets, supported on either side by stuffed bolsters. One of the harem women, her face covered in fine muslin, was there to massage his feet. He and his officers were served wine, which they drank with enthusiasm despite the restrictions of their faith. By the time the boat docked, Achala and his men were in a boisterous mood. Achala leaned on Manzim's shoulder for support, his face red from the alcohol. A tent had been strung up above two thrones to receive him; Achala, with Manzim's help, drunkenly staggered towards the tent and helped on to one of the chairs, the other one being reserved for Kotarani.

A loud conch sounded from inside Khir Bhavani. The gates opened to reveal the bride, brought out on a palanquin supported by eight bare-chested men. Consistent with the agreement, the palanquin was open so that nothing could be hidden within. The palanquin was led by Devaswami, bare-chested like the palanquin bearers, who supported himself with his Shakti trident as he walked in front. Shah Mir was happy that Kotarani was dressed in black; it went with her decision to convert to Islam, and would be more appealing to Achala than the bright finery Kashmiris typically favoured.

When she wears our clothing she is one of us. Everything is going according to plan, he thought; *finally, things will settle down and there will be peace in Kashmir.*

The palanquin bearers rested their load in front of Achala, the shaman to his right; Kotarani's throne to his left. Manzim supported the maharani on her left and Devaswami held her right hand; her face was covered with a veil and she was unsteady on her feet. Nervous

Kota was led nearer to Achala, until she finally faced him. Shah Mir moved closer to begin the marriage ceremony. With a practised hand, Manzim raised the veil from Kotarani's head so that Achala could finally see what he had coveted and fought for.

Manzim could only identify what happened next as a hallucination. Suddenly Shah Mir saw Achala's eyes open wide; he looked at Kotarani and saw the face of a woman possessed. Her very skin was darkened, her tongue was lolling out like that of a mad dog and her hair was hanging loose. She must have been drinking heavily; the smell of wine was strong on her breath. Quick as a flash, she grabbed the trident from Devaswami, and before he could react she shrieked 'Jai Kali!' and buried Shakti's trident deep into Achala's heart. The shaman attempted to run, but the creature would not let him get away. She pulled the trident out and impaled him through the neck. The last sight that met the shaman's dying eyes was of the palanquin bearers pulling the supporting poles out of the royal seat to reveal battleaxes hidden beneath the cloth. Before Achala's officers could draw their swords, the axes had performed their lethal tasks. It was over almost as soon as it had begun. Shah Mir looked at the woman again, and Kotarani's angelic face looked back at him. There was a red blood-like stain on her forehead, but it could have been the powder Kashmiris used to draw the three horizontal tilak lines on their forehead. *What has just happened?*

Curiosity drove Devaswami to walk over to the unknown shaman and remove his mask; the dead man's identity took his breath away. He drew Kotarani over to the corpse without a word and she looked at his face. Even in the repose of death there was a sense of injury: it was Ravan's son, who on rare occasions had accompanied his father, her estranged brother, to court. Perhaps he was inspired to reclaim the power and glory that Ravan felt he was entitled to as the natural born son of Ramachandra, which from his perspective had been wrongly appropriated by Kotarani. Her nephew was no different from his father in his willingness to switch sides, even if it meant hitching his stars to any opportunist. No wonder, Achala had inside knowledge and his force had swelled with fifth columnists – his shaman was connected to the very top of Kashmiri society and knew everything that there was to know. Kotarani covered the young man's face with the mask. Better that he die as he had lived at the end, a confused young man who had sold his identity to such a degree that he had ended with no human identity at all.

When Achala's main force arrived, expecting to celebrate their leader's nuptials, they were instead confronted with the sight of their fearless leader and his key officers dead, their bodies twisted and lifeless among the mulberry trees. The vultures were circling the skies. At first they were ready to attack Khir Bhavani, but then they saw the figure of Kotarani on her horse and behind her the archers ready. To one side they saw Shah Mir's cavalry, which had hurriedly arrived at his express instructions. The final straw was the sight of eight men, who had walked out of Khir Bhavani bearing Kotarani's palanquin and who had carried out the riskiest part of the plan. They held their short swords in their right hands and a thick stick with a metal blunt end in their left with which they were beating the ground, making a loud staccato racket. The men approached Achala's troops, then turned around and dropped their pants, giving Achala's men the royal Kashmiri salute and shouting out, 'Dogfaces! Kiss our round bottoms. Achala! When the seventy-two virgins ask what happened to your weenie tell them that Kashmiri yonis are trained to squeeze stone lingams. Jai Kotarani, Jai Kali!'

This was the signal for Shah Mir's Mussalman cavalry to lead the charge. The Tartars had had enough; they turned and fled all the way back to Turkmenistan. Shah Mir's men were heroes as they cut down the stragglers. The story of their success, where insults were added to injury, grew bigger and more hilarious with each retelling. Even Kota laughed heartily at the thought of the royal salute and the fleeing Turcomans.

That night every home throughout the length and breadth of the kingdom was brightly lit, and the temple bells were ringing as the Bhattas celebrated the queen's decisive victory over Achala. There was food and festivities everywhere, and Kokur and his troupe went from house to house singing and dancing, the last act involving dropping their trousers to the crescent moon, the military symbol of the Turcomans. Only one home was dark: the shades were drawn on the queen's palace as if its occupants were in mourning. For days there was no news as to what had happened inside, but soon everyone's questions were answered. Udyan and Brahma had gone straight from the battle to the Amarnath caves to pray to Shiva the auspicious one. Now the conch was sounded and the fortress doors opened to welcome Brahma and Udyandev and their small entourage. The queen came out to respectfully receive Udyandev, kneeling and bowing in submission to welcome the lord of the kingdom and the master of her home. It was as if the eastern hill received the light of the full moon, dispelling all shadows. Udyandev replaced the mangalsutra around Kota's neck and she stood to join him. Kokur was behind the scenes, but as if by magic, the palace lamps lit up at that very moment.

On Udyandev's return, he and Kotarani revisited Khir Bhavani and they prayed for full seven days. Many gifts were offered to the Devi, but the one that the priests found most curious was one from Kotarani; it was a box containing an intricately carved chess set. The priests had been instructed to bury it deep in the ground next to Khir Bhavani for the Devi to find on one of her visits to the holy shrine.

That night, before going to sleep, Udyan asked Kotarani: 'Are you going to be all right after your experience?'

'Devaswami once told me that with the right training anybody could stop being human and contract into a killer,' she said. 'Little did I know that I would end up validating his dictum aided and abetted by him! Udyan, I am still shaken by the power of the Kali mantras. I went through that ghastly experience armed only with the thought of our children.'

'I too thought that the Ghazis would kill me,' Udyan replied. 'My only thoughts were for whom I loved, not about what I would lose. Would Jatta find happiness when he grows up? Would you be safe if our plan had not worked?'

'Hopefully, Kashmir will be secure now and we can build a future for our children free of fear. I did find out something interesting from Devaswami. Did you know that the jogi and Devaswami were class fellows and that the jogi was expelled from Sharadapeeth?'

'Yes', said Udyan. 'It happened before my time but my seniors relayed the story. It seems that the jogi was obsessed with wanting to gain power even at the expense of morality. He was of the opinion that the forbidden *Left Way* was the faster way of invoking the Devi, and smuggled a young woman into his room to incorporate *maithuna* ritual sexual intercourse into his practices. Devaswami was the one who discovered and reported the jogi's secret. It was a scandal that was buried deep, but not deep enough.'

'What happened to the jogi when he was caught?'

'He fled to the remote mountains where there were practices going on that were more to his taste.'

'It is troubling that the jogi is bent on securing great powers,' Kotarani said. 'Devaswami has revealed to me that he is in command of far greater powers himself, yet he never uses them except in the advancement of *vidya*, super knowledge.'

'Morality is not a prerequisite for gaining great siddha powers, but to attain Shiva one has to conquer one's infatuations across all the dimensions of human existence. The jogi seeks to subjugate the Devi, not realizing that the Devi is about increasing freedom. Wrongful arousal of the Devis' power will result in her crushing the disciple for not shaking off his profane ego.'

This talk of the jogi's ulterior motives triggered a thought inside Kota; it was time to ask her husband about something that had been troubling her.

'Udyan, tell me why you agreed to marry me. Was it so that you could achieve your vow to avenge your brother and regain the kingdom?'

Udyandev was a wise man and he understood that something had been bothering Kotarani.

'No, if that was my goal I would have gone directly for it after Rinchina's death. You came to me in my dream and I felt that you and I had something in common. We both deeply cared for Kashmir and it is a bond that not only brought us together but has kept us together.'

'Udyan, forgive me,' Kotarani pleaded. 'I do not know what came over me. Sometime I feel that ever since I became maharani everybody approaches me to own me. Except for you, Saras and Brahma, it is hard for me trust anybody. Come closer to me, please.'

Udyan embraced Kotarani and gently massaged her.

'The people say you are the greatest queen of Kashmir, ever captivating but never captive,' he whispered encouragingly and proudly.

Absorbed in the books that Devaswami loaned him, oblivious to the world around him except what he saw through his scholarly lens, full of esoteric theories about higher dimensions and yet intuiting exactly what was happening Udyan gave Kotarani much needed comfort. How brave he had been in offering himself as bait to the invader, she thought. The plan had nearly gone awry with Shah Mir's premature retreat. In the world's eyes, Shah Mir had positioned Udyan as a coward but it was he who had enticed Achala in dropping his guard. Had it not been for the Sogdian's great sacrifice, Udyan could well have been killed. Kota shivered involuntarily at the thought. She rested her head on Udyan's and then she grasped his hand; holding it tight, she fell asleep.

Wave 15
Epicentre

FOLLOWING the Tartar attack Kotarani decided to reorganize her cabinet, a move that was received well by the public. Kumara Bhatta, the head historian from Sharadapeeth, was appointed as the new foreign minister. There had been a long tradition of bringing learned advisers from Sharadapeeth into the governance of the kingdom. Shah Mir had been reluctant to give up this part of his responsibility but Brahma had supported the change, citing Shah Mir's failure to anticipate Achala's invasion and the importance of separating the two roles, since the duties of both could not be combined easily by one man.

Losing the political support of his best friend left Shah Mir with little choice. The public found the queen's call acceptable; Shah Mir was viewed as having played a major role in Achala's demise, but not as being proactive in preventing it. His sons Jamshed and Ali Sher were recognized and given important jagirs contiguous to the major forts, as well as responsibility for the forts themselves. Shah Mir was mandated to expand the size of the standing army and given the funding to achieve his goal.

Kotarani elevated Yaniv – it was an open secret that he had been appointed caretaker of the *Toshkhana*. Shah Mir found himself in the awkward position of having his popularity at an all-time high among the Kashmiris while his standing in the internal circle had diminished. To have Yaniv in control of the crown jewels maddened him. He was the most efficient administrator in Kashmir, and it was unbearable that a trader was trusted more than him. If he had deserted the battlefield, so had Udyandev. If he was not a good commander-in-chief, why keep him in that position and take away his role as foreign minister? The secret plot against Achala that Kotarani had crafted was not one that had been shared with him. Who was behind the rumours that were circulating that he was a nice person but a weak link? Clearly, Kotarani did not trust him. It must be because he was a Mussalman? He had given it his all, but now that did not count. That execrable Jew was running his hands through the gold and lining his pockets while having the pleasure of sticking his *dool* inside that gorgeous Tatiana's *kos* whom he, Shah Mir, had purchased and gifted. It was simply unbearable.

Feeling thwarted, he put Manzim to work and doggedly set about multiplying his strategic alliances within the Valley. The most formidable of these was created by the marriage of Ali Sher to the daughter of Lakshmaka, the erstwhile commander-in-chief. Brahma alerted Kotarani that by this alliance Shah Mir had obtained the loyalty of a key military subordinate; now he need not fear Lakshmaka going around him to the maharaja and the maharani.

Tilakshura, the ruler of Bhangila, married the daughter of Jamshed. He built a very successful alliance with the Kota Raja of Shamala and kept that turbulent province under his influence. He made special effort to cultivate a new immigrant group of farmers, the Chak clan, whose leader, Lamar, was a burly giant of a man and had quietly migrated into Kashmir from the territory of the Dards at the same time as him. As fate would have it, Suhdev had granted them the village of Traha, which was in the district of Kramarajya and under his control. The opposing people, the Lavanyas, especially the Damara chief Maqbool Lone, whom Bulbul had converted to Sufism, were won over with a combination of gifts and intimidation. Shah Mir also brought the people of Karala under his control and enriched himself through forceful taxes.

However, it was shortly afterwards that he made his boldest and most public move. In order to secure his possessions, Shah Mir fortified the Chakradhara plateau and showed the people that with his army his household was impregnable. While Shah Mir's role in court had been curtailed, his military power was in the ascent and none dared to oppose him. When he went out falcon hunting and the fierce birds swooped down, it seemed to the Kashmiris that Shah Mir had an aerial army that was watching the Valley waiting to prey on the weak and vulnerable.

Shah Mir suspected that his fall from royal favour was related in some way to the fiasco with Udyandev, but not knowing the forces at play, he began a campaign of openly intimidating the maharaja. He also started putting some distance between himself and Brahma, who he felt had let him down. Most troubling to Kotarani was that Shah Mir had cemented his relationship with Ravan, who had been totally ostracized by the Kashmiris after the discovery of his son's treachery. Through her sources, the queen heard that Shah Mir was planning on holding a big gathering at the mosque. Having lost the Sogdian, she requested Raja Sapru of Bhringi attend the event and report back to her.

When Raja Sapru reached the mosque, it was obvious from the number of people in attendance that something extraordinary was going on. He recognized other people – the carpenter and the stonemason were there; Kokur and Manzim, and even the Chandala were there, still sitting separately, by force of habit, in the corner of the main assembly hall. The raja had often visited the Brahmin agraharas where they were given free meals, but those were contemplative places where only a very limited number were given that privilege. Here there were thousands spilling into and out of the Lankar, carrying wooden plates in and emerging loaded with rice and huge chunks of meat. There was no way that it could be goat, the staple diet of the Kashmiris; these people could not be locals. Raja Sapru suspected that it was camel meat, which was alien to the Kashmiris. Many attendees were armed with swords, not at all what one associated with a place of devotion; they did not even seem like Kashmiris, with their long beards and Central Asian clothes. Their apparel seemed to suggest that they were recent immigrants, perhaps from Turkistan. A recent group, the Sayyids, who had entered the Valley were also present, watching everyone with a haughty air as befitting direct descendants of the Prophet himself. What had been a place of Sufi piety, had been usurped by militant men of faith. Substantial state resources were clearly being diverted by Shah Mir into the mosque to support these so-called Sufis.

There was no end to the developments that the raja witnessed. Naid emerged from within the mosque and at first the raja did not recognize him. Naid now had a full beard; he had changed his dress and was wearing a long, green shirt as favoured by the people of Turkistan. He welcomed Manzim and Kokur as if he was the host of the event, leading them to the very front of the crowd where a stage had been built. An informal militia seemed to be orchestrating and ordering the crowd; recognizing Naid, they let him through. He was clearly an important person within the mosque.

As with most public functions in Kashmir, the event started late in the evening after everybody had been fed. Once the crowd had settled down, the dignitaries arrived. Shah Mir, then surprisingly the reclusive Ravan, and finally – even more shocking – the fakir, accompanied by Haider holding the Koran. The Chandala whistled his disapproval when he saw the fakir; some of the audience joined him in the jeering, while others hushed them to stay silent.

Ravan was the first to speak.

'Kashmir's troubles began when a woman became our ruler: it invited attacks from the outside by those who perceive a female as weak. I was denied my legitimate right to succeed to the throne, and today Haider is being denied the same right. I have joined Islam, and thousands have joined along with me. Should we now become second-class citizens in our own land because we have exercised freedom in our faith?'

The Kashmiris were no strangers to sibling rivalry, and Ravan's aborted dreams were well known. Politics was in the blood of every Kashmiri, so it did not surprise them to hear Ravan ask to be made king. However, not everyone in the crowd agreed with him.

'What attack are you talking about?' one of the audience members shouted out. 'The last attack on Kashmir was organized by your own son! He was Achala's right-hand man.'

Ravan was unfazed.

'I lost my son, killed by my own sister; I will not allow anyone to disrespect his memory, nor will I forgive his killer. There is an illegitimate ruler in place today, and it is my right – and Haider's right – to take whatever steps necessary to correct that injustice.'

Raja Sapru of Bhringi stood up.

'The queen spared your son from a fate worse than death, eternal infamy,' he shouted. 'Have you forgotten Tilak, the traitorous Kashmiri, who went as a translator and eventually became a commander in the army of Masud Ghazni? He led the campaigns against his own people in India. Your son was headed to becoming even more infamous than Tilak for fighting on behalf of the Turkic enemy.'

The crowd murmured in agreement; few accepted Ravan's assertion that he had been deprived of his rights. Kashmir had evolved to the point that queens as rulers were common; the Damaras had no qualms in electing their maharaja if the blood succession did not yield a good leader; so the notion of birth prerogatives was already being questioned.

The fakir stood up, waving his fist in the air.

'Fidayeen, I am back in Kashmir. I was chased out because I stood up and protected Islam. Rinchina's acceptance of Islam made Kashmir into an Islamic kingdom forever. However, with Rinchina and Bulbul gone there is a move afoot to crush the Mussalmans. The Brahmins are teaching our youth new ways. It is unacceptable because their knowledge leads to heresy and innovation is apostasy! The level of immorality prevalent in Kashmir is unacceptable! After all, what can you expect when people pray to the Lingam? You have a beautiful maharani who rules the kingdom and uses the jogi, her sex guru, to pollute the kingdom. What is her secret relationship with her faithful dog Brahma? Is he her paramour? How many lovers has the unsatiated vixen had? Do you know how often she has sent overtures to Shah Mir that she wants to bed him? What kind of queen would covertly ask someone to arrange for the murder of her husband so that she could rest her head on his chest and yield all her loveliness to him?'

The fakir was foaming.

'We cannot be Mussalmans in name and be degraded Hindus in our customs and social behaviour!' he hissed. 'We must follow the rules Islam laid down for us to be *haqiqi* Mussalman. Our Sufi brothers are growing in number, we have our own force – Panun Fauj. They will ensure that our values and our way of life are not diluted. I have returned. This time we will fight if anyone dares to challenge me. We have to bring discipline and morality back to Kashmir. You have to choose between Koteh and infidelity and Islam and the purity of our women.' Many of the attendees broke out into cheers, pumping their fists in the air. The Kashmiris were mostly silent but the bearded Sufis were breathing fire: 'Allah o Akbar,' they cried. Some even brandished swords in the air, slashing and cutting their imaginary enemies.

The fakir continued, 'If the Hindu climbs a horse from one side you will climb from the other side. If he ties his turban one way you will tie it the other way and if the buttons on his shirt are on one side, your buttons will be on the other side. You will not only visibly oppose what the Hindu does but support what the Hindu opposes and oppose what the Hindu supports.

'For the true believer there is a vast reward that awaits them here and now. The Bhattas accumulate gold; their Brahmins imprison it in their idols. We will smash the idols first, and then liberate the gold; we will take the queen's treasure and put it to the service of Allah by giving it away as alms. It will be exactly like in the public square, maidan, of Ghazni, where one can see this trampled gold lying on the ground. It will be yours for free.'

A vast reward awaits the true believer, sang the crowd. *It will be for free.*

The Chandala stood up, demanding to be heard.

'I smell something here, there is nothing for free, even shit; I charge food to cart it away, but let me ask a simple question. Talking about dogs, will they be allowed to exist in a pure Kashmir?'

The fakir frowned.

'Dogs are a menace in Kashmir. They run in wild packs. I said that we have to clean up Kashmir – dogs would be a good start.'

The Chandala grimaced in return, speaking slowly.

'You are called the White Wolf, and you hate dogs. The Brahmin also thinks that dogs pollute. However, you want to kill the dogs, while the Brahmin, before he eats his meal, puts aside a small portion of rice, the *hoon mot*. He later gives it to street dogs to eat. Your purity does not seem to have the tolerance that Kashmir has today.'

'You are but a grain of sand in the eyes of God,' remonstrated the fakir. 'When you convert to Islam you will be equal to all your fellow men, and everyone will have to submit to the rules of Islam. You will no longer be an untouchable or a pollutant to the Brahmin. What do you care about dogs? Think of yourself.'

'I am not sure that I want to be equal to the Brahmin. He is more afraid of my shadow than I of him. However, I am a simple man, and if dogs can run free, it tells me that I am free. If not, then today it is dogs and tomorrow it will be me, anybody who is not a grain in the sand will become the white wolf's target.'

The Chandala smiled at the fakir, slightly baring his teeth at him before sitting down quietly.

Shah Mir sensed that they had lost momentum. He rose and walked to the centre of the stage.

'Today we are graced with the presence of Haider, who has grown into a fine young man,' he said slowly. 'It is a good day to remember his father, whom we call Sher-e-Kashmir. What is the central issue? The Brahmins have land, but they do not till it. What if the land belonged to the tillers? Would the tillers not work harder? Would we not all be better off? Take Naid here. He is a young man who deserves the happiness of a wife, a piece of land for his home and a simple living, but all he has is his hunger and anger at the uncaring rule that exists in Kashmir. Don't our youth deserve better? It is time for Kotarani to go and for Haider to take over. It is time for a new Kashmir, Naya Kashmir! Rinchina gave us law and order. Haider will give us social justice as befits the first true Islamic ruler of Kashmir.'

The Kashmiris did not quite understand all of Shah Mir's hypnotic speech; however, it sounded great. Somehow, they were all going to get land and they were going to get rich with free gold. Rama Raj, the utopia that existed in the dim mists of time, was here again and Shah Mir was going to be Ram! He walked back and took Haider's hand that held the Koran, raising it aloft.

'Come join me in burying the past: we have nothing in front of us but a glorious future. Allah will be our side. There will be sacrifices, but everyone will be suitably rewarded.'

The fakir and Ravan were the first two to join Shah Mir and Haider. The four of them stood holding up the single Koran. The crowd was mesmerized. Manzim watched the hushed crowd as Naid began walking dramatically up to the stage, his arms akimbo, waddling sideways like a duck.

'I want to be part of Naya Kashmir. I want land and gold. I want a wife. I want my reward. I want it now.'

The fakir made Naid take off his sacred thread and put it to the side. Then he made him repeat the Kalima after him. *La Ilaha Illo Muhammadur Rasoolullah* – there is no God except Allah: Mohammed, Peace be upon Him, is the messenger of Allah.

The bearded men in the crowd roared back. '*La Ilaha Ill Allah*!' No God but Allah!'

Shah Mir was the first to reach out to Naid. He hugged him, saying: 'From today you will be called Sheikh. You are my equal. Come join me.'

Shah Mir made Naid reach out and hold up the Koran. He looked slightly ridiculous with his thin frame on stretched toes trying to hold on to the Koran, but there was a new intensity in him. He truly believed that he was finally going to get land and be prosperous. *I will be the equal of Shah Mir. People will address me as Sheikh. It is the dawning of Naya Kashmir.*

'Waiting for the future is for sheep,' he shouted in exultation. 'The wolf pack preys on sheep. Our leader is the fakir and we will live, travel, hunt together under the white wolf's tutelage.'

Naid's first step was the breaking of the dam. The stonemason, whose work was on temples and sacred sculptures, held back, but when his brother, the carpenter, followed Naid, there was a tidal wave. The fakir was beside himself, repeating the Kalima until he was hoarse. Sacred threads were trampled on the ground as more and more Kashmiris, especially the youth, rushed on to the stage – nobody wanted to be left out. The bearded men grinned wolfishly, shouting themselves into frenzy: *'La Ilaha Ill Allah La ilaha illa' llah!'* The crowd of young men had grown so thick that they lifted the group of five on their shoulders; Shah Mir, Ravan, Haider, the fakir and Naid. The Koran was higher in the sky as the five stared up at it, as if waiting for a miracle. The crowd started spinning around in circles; someone began strumming on a santoor; then the fakir broke out into a chant and the Kashmiris hummed along with their new Central Asian brothers, the Sufis providing the chorus.

> Verily men who submit [to God] and women who submit,
> > Allah hoo Ya hoo
> and men who believe and women who believe,
> > Allah hoo Ya hoo
> and men who are devout and women who are devout,
> > Allah hoo Ya hoo
> and men who speak the truth and women who speak the truth,
> > Allah hoo Ya hoo
> and men who are patient and women who are patient,
> > Allah hoo Ya hoo
> and men who are humble and women who are humble,
> > Allah hoo Ya hoo
> and men who give alms and women who give alms,
> > Allah hoo Ya hoo
> and men who fast and women who fast,
> > Allah hoo Ya hoo
> and men who guard their chastity and women who guard their chastity,
> > Allah hoo Ya hoo

and men who remember God much and women who remember,
   Allah hoo Ya hoo
God has prepared for them forgiveness and a vast reward.[17]

The dancers were delirious, chanting: 'A vast reward, a vast reward!' Some of the Sufis had crossed their swords and were spinning round and round. The fakir, his pale face and large head dripping with sweat, tore his shirt into pieces and threw them at the crowd who fought for them as if Allah had sent them manna. Two of the spinning swordsmen fell on the ground as if convulsed by the intensity of the experience. Then the butcher rushed to join the group, carrying his meat cleaver. His immigrant family was of Saracen origin and his skin was quite dark. The fakir held his hand up.

'Butcher, in the Valley the word '*puja*' means to worship, and from today all butchers will be called *Puj*.'

The crowd roared their assent. The butcher was going to be a new icon deserving of respect.

'Slaughter those who stand between us and our vast reward!' he shouted.

It was truly exhilarating. Scores of other young men came forward, submitting themselves to being publicly tonsured and circumcised; the Naid's scissors were flying as he worked his way down the line. When the night ended, hundreds of young men had converted to Islam: they rushed back to their villages, telling their families how there would be a new order soon, and everybody was going to have land and be equals.

When Raja Sapru emerged from the mosque he saw Manzim, Kokur and Naid engaged in a fierce discussion.

'Are you sure you understand what you have done?' Kokur asked Naid.

'Do not question me,' he replied angrily. 'You always think that you are right, but now I am on the top. The Brahmins will no longer oppress us socially, economically or with their religious demands.'

'What kind of brainwashing have you undergone?' Kokur retorted, his arms in the air. 'After all, it was a Brahmin that segregated you and took care of you when you were young and caught smallpox. You would be blind, maybe not even alive today, if it was not for them.'

'You fool!' Naid shouted. 'I do not even exist for the Brahmins. The oligarchs are blind to me. When a Brahmin walks by me, he lifts his white pajamas so that he will not be stained by our reality. The fakir is not afraid of my poverty – he searches for it, he embraces it.'

Kokur was an artist – nobody was going to win a verbal duel with him.

'The fakir is a maggot. He searches the dirt to suck the blood of his victims; he is not going to turn that dirt into milk and honey. The vast reward he has for you is stolen loot.'

'One book, instead of the thousands of scriptures the Brahmins endlessly debate,' Naid countered. 'One Allah, instead of seven crore gods. No more of the Sanskrit mantras.'

'Naid, you have never read any of these books. You have no reason to fear or hate them! We don't know Sanskrit, but is Farsi or Arabic a better language for us? Don't lose your mind to somebody else's propaganda.'

Something had changed within Naid; his bitter cynicism had been replaced with belligerence.

'Don't call me Naid!' he yelled. 'You heard my name: it is Sheikh. Kokur, if I were you I would move to a different place. We are going to remove all perversion from the Valley. Purity is what we need.'

Manzim intervened.

'Sheikh, this is the first time I have heard one member of our group threaten another. Where is the *Lihaaz*? We always seek to show more respect than what we are given. Isn't this what binds us Kashmiris together?'

Naid began to shout.

'You do not understand! I am through with the past! I am now part of the brotherhood, the ummah! Manzim, you can be useful, but Kokur, this is the last time we meet as friends.'

Kokur spoke with a heavy heart.

'Naid ... Sheikh, this misguided path that you have been led on by the white wolf will only bring us tyranny. The white wolf will end up tearing Kashmir apart, just as he has our friendship; and Shah Mir, the crocodile, will feed on its carcass.'

'The fakir is a man of God! Do not accuse him!' Naid screamed at the top of his voice.

'Bulbul was a man of God who brought us together, but this fakir of your, he is an illiterate zealot and a misogynist who waves the sword in the name of religion,' Kokur responded forcefully.

Naid was frothing, 'Defaming him already! Well, now he has friends and supporters and believers! The first man, any man, who defames him will die!'

'You think it is defamation when it is the truth.'

Naid was dismissive. 'All great men who are pure and oppose injustice have to face personal attacks. We are going to build a Naya Kashmir based on equality. You are playing with your life either way, cock sucker!'

'So, this is Naya Kashmir, 'Sheikh'? You and your new friends use the mask of grievance to justify looting the Brahmins, equality to cover up mediocrity and the slogan of purity to silence every differing voice?' Sheikh responded in a calm, unemotional voice. 'Do you remember when I was starving? I had no food, and yet when I walked on the streets I had a toothpick in my mouth pretending to show the world that I was picking out the meat stuck between my teeth. Is this Kashmiri community the one I should want to belong to, a community driven by pride and not equality? Never again! I was always manipulated, told that my life was determined by my karma. Do you understand that the fakir is my chance? He gives me equality as my right. My children will have it as their birthright. Keep your freedom and keep your meritocracy. If life is not going to be equal, it is going to be very unsafe for everyone. I will have equal rights and I will not be denied, because the fakir will fight for me.'

Kokur was unimpressed.

'You need to separate the quack doctor from the real one. Equality is only Iccha. No messenger can ordain material equality – not the

Shaivites, not the Buddhists, not Islam. This is a matter of *Rajniti*, governance, not religion. You are seeing a mirage that is overpowering you. The sword creates the worst form of inequality between the oppressor and the oppressed. Already, the first casualty is your soul, your freedom. Your sons will grow up fighting the sons of their Kashmiri neighbours. An actor knows that sword fights are momentarily exciting, but it is love stories that ultimately hold an audience. This choice of yours to embrace the fakir's call is hateful and catastrophic! You have just signed a death warrant on yourself and everyone else around you.'

Naid turned back towards the Khanqah.

'I believe the fakir when he says that the sword is necessary. No justification is needed when it has Allah's endorsement. Enough, you pervert. I will return with the Fakir and some of my friends. If you are still here when we come back, it will be the last day of your life.'

With that threat hanging in the air, Naid strode back into the mosque. Manzim grabbed Kokur by the shoulders and dragged him away as fast as he could. Manzim was an expert in building alliances but his own closest personal one had just died an unnatural death.

Raja Sapru could not believe what was happening to the world. His father-in-law's speech and actions had shocked him. When he reached home, he repeated everything that had been said and done to Guhara.

'Your father has basically cast his lot with discredited Islamist opportunists – he is using the poor gullible Kashmiris as pawns to wage war against Kotarani and Udyandev, and the Brahmins have become sacrificial lambs of the Islamists. He is no different from Dulucha.'

Guhara became extremely upset and emotional.

'He is my father and I will always be loyal to him. If he has his ambitions, so does everyone else. He is no worse than anybody else at court. At least he is supporting the poor, which is more than can be said for the others.'

Raja Sapru knew that he was heading into his first disagreement with his wife.

'Guhara, this is not about political ambition. It is about tearing the very fabric of Kashmir. It is about justifying violence against fellow Kashmiris. The Brahmins were given their temple lands with the knowing consent of the rulers; Shah Mir has said that the Mussalmans have a right to take this land by force. Even if it takes a thousand years, the Brahmins will be justified in exercising their sovereign rights to get any looted lands back. What has Shah Mir done but to start a cycle of violence and retribution that will have no end? The Kashmiris accepted Islam and Mussalmans with love and hospitality. In return the Mussalmans are misusing Islam and instigating the converts to turn against the Kashmiris. Politics yes, but the Brahmins have to be off limits or else Kashmir will slide into *naraka*, the hell.'

Guhara had been married to Raja Sapru long enough to know that he was highly principled, and very stubborn. She looked up to his strength; and while she would never have admitted it to her husband, she was acutely aware of her father's failings. She knew that she would not win this battle.

She pacified him. 'I will talk to my mother. She is always honest with me and will tell me what is going on with my father and his role at the Khanqah.'

'Irrespective of her answer, what was once a symbol of our love has now become the centre of something hateful and fearful,' Raja Sapru responded. 'The fakir's mob calls themselves Sufis, but their swords are those of jihadis.'

Both agreed that it was important that they inform Kotarani of these new developments and they travelled to meet the queen the next day. They found her surrounded by others who had come to report what they had heard, circling her like a small war council. The discussion went on until the small hours of the morning. Kashmir had withstood the greatest threats externally, but this was the first time in its history that the attack had arisen from within. The tremors of the fakir's meeting had been felt all across the Valley. The Damaras were alarmed at the reports they heard and had sent emissaries to Shah Mir. He had reassured them that of course there would be no change for the Damaras, the primary landlords in the Valley; their status would be protected, and they were going to have a key role to play. However, it was important that they understood that the grievances of the people were justified, and that the ruler had to be legitimate or else the people would demand self-rule. The Damaras had understood that as long as they stood on the sidelines, this was between Shah Mir's people and Kotarani's supporters. The Damaras were experts in fishing in troubled waters – assured that they would remain unaffected; they did not dig too deep into the changes being made in front of their noses. The conclusion at the end of the all-night meeting with Kotarani was clear that the conclave at the Khanqah was a declaration of civil war against the queen and had to be dealt with accordingly.

Given the emerging threat, Kotarani felt an acute need to visit Devaswami for a darshan, accompanied by Udyandev, who was a frequent visitor, along with Kumara. Udyandev may have been king, but Kota was the favorite daughter of Sharadapeeth. The priests were older, but many remembered her. Some had passed on and there was much for her to catch up on. A special yagna was conducted for peace and unity in which 501 priests chanted the *Sharada Sahasra Nama*, the one thousand names of Goddess Sharada.

Kotarani and Kumara had a private audience with Devaswami and he received them in his library with the jyotish. After the customary exchange of pleasantries, Devaswami asked Kota what she wanted.

'Our kingdom has suffered so much. The horror of 120,000 men and women dying because of Dulucha is still fresh. Now a new threat of civil war has emerged from within. The fakir is back and has gained the active support of Shah Mir, even Ravan, who has turned traitor. The Sogdian had warned me about this and gave me his solution, which was to strike hard in the way they understand: *Leave, Convert or Die*. What should I do?'

Devaswami was quick in his dismissal.

'The Leave, Convert or Die policy is based on hate and duality and will lead to a holy war. That is not the precept that is the basis of Kashmir's civil society, which is based on lihaz.'

'The balance of power has swung in their favour driven by greed and fear. I have become the target of their moral crusade. I wake up at night afraid that our kingdom is facing extinction,' Kotarani admitted. 'What is one to do in the face of never-ending terror?'

Kumara's scholarly face was intense, reflecting his deep thought process.

'Queen, you have to fight this battle with the so-called principled puritans based on the right diagnosis. Why and how, I will expand on later, but this revolutionary threat is not to Kashmir alone but is a threat for all of humanity. The challenge to the Kashmiri way of life started in Persia at the same time that our recorded civilization did, over 5,000 years ago. These were our rival cousins, the Asuras, also descended from Rishi Kashyapa, the founder of Kashmir. They were originally the arbiters of morality and used coercion ostensibly as a pathway to purity, but in reality to drive their empire founded on materialistic pride, power, arrogance, harshness and ignorance. We separated from them and became the Devas who believed in the divine qualities of nature and its manifold diversity, with knowledge as the only pathway towards purity and siddhic capabilities. A shared, connected society, which believed in *Vasudhaiva Kutumbakam,* the world is one family, was replaced by the concept of the division of good and evil and this was propagated with wholehearted zeal because it was a useful simple concept designed to oppose our way of life.

'Matters came to a head when ten of their kings joined hands to fight a single king on our side. It was going to be the end of the Bharat dynasty, but a miracle occurred. Our king won against all odds and drove the Asuras back and further westwards. To this day, their descendants who have long forgotten about this battle of Dasharajnya are still locked in mortal combat with us.'

'You mean that this battle has been going on for over 5,000, so it is not about militant Islam but that Islam has unknowingly picked up elements of this vengeful ideology?' a surprised Kotarani asked.

'Longer than recorded history,' Kumara replied, 'and our suffering is merely the continuation of the long wail of history. Islam is the current carrier but it is not the first and will not be the last. It is the battle between those who would be masters of the earth versus those who would be masters of the universe. Persia has always represented a competitor, a partner, a cousin, a threat or an ally to Kashmir. In the sixth century King Anushirvan sent their court physician Burzuya to translate the *Panchatantra,* which has tales that are as old as one can imagine. Praise is upon the Kashmiri Pandit Vishnu Sharma for laying out the wise conduct of life, in the form of stories, which the people far prefer to our dry Brahmin lectures. The *Panchatantra* was renamed as *Kalila wa Dimna* and eventually moved to Arabia and beyond. It was valued so highly that the Persian king offered all the riches of his kingdom to Burzuya. But Burzuya opted to take the king's robe, thus symbolically sharing in his sovereignty. Persia has regressed from a seeker and beneficiary of Kashmir's truths to wanting to be an owner, not realizing that it is destroying what attracted it to us in the first place. As long as Kashmir ruled Afghanistan, we had a buffer, but when Afghanistan fell to the converted Persians their threat reached our front door.'

'If Persia has cycled from enemy to friend to enemy what should we do to face it?' Kotarani asked.

Devaswami stepped in. 'At a practical level, our values, the trinity of Truth, Beauty and Bliss – are engaged in an existential battle with their material trinity of gold, land and women. Our way of greater good connects us to the infinite generator and gives us creativity. Theirs connects them to the finite controller and makes them forcefully acquisitive. We have to protect and grow our dharmic force naturally through the strong arms of justice and freedom. The biggest sin is ignorance defined as insufficient knowledge – to stop being vigilant and ignore what we refer to as evil. The biggest trap to fall into is to kill evil, except in the rarest of rare circumstances. As a subcontracted entity, it is best quarantined if it threatens existence. The right answer is to stand for inclusivity versus exclusivity, connectivity versus the utopia of equality, purity through knowledge versus strictures and covenants, individual freedom and fulfilment on this earth versus make-believe in the afterlife.'

'It is very hard, but I can accept why you would reaffirm that our security should be tied to the highest truths without conceding the lower practical considerations,' Kotarani agreed. 'It is also important that right-thinking Muslims be protected from this contagion, which predates Islam and is using it as a carrier. Yet, how do I quarantine these jihadis and open their minds through education?'

Kumara picked up the inferences.

'Queen, let me return to the challenges of the north-west and the practical response to your individual challenge. The greatest king of Kashmir – and perhaps all of India – was Lalitaditya; he is the only ruler referred to in India as the universal monarch. His expeditions were described as the movement of the sun around the earth. He completely understood the strategic quadrangle of China, Arabia, Persia and Russia. He beat the Arabs in Sind. He made friends with the Chinese to the extent of making arrangements to provision 200,000 Chinese soldiers in Kashmir to fight the highly dangerous Tibetan Bottas. Where did Lalitaditya die? On the outskirts of Persia. Not for him the pomp and show of an armchair throne; instead he was on the front lines. Today, we still honour his victory over Iranian forces. When one compares us today with Lalitditya's time it is clear that Kashmir no longer has a meaningful forward policy. The cost of maintaining one is high, but the cost of not having one is catastrophic.'

'You are saying that Kashmir is on the front line of a long war between contending civilizations: Persia, Arabia, Russia, China and India,' Kota stated. 'This is a battle of hearts, minds, materials, manpower and military. It started at least 5,000 years ago and it may go on for another 5,000. Kashmir's front line will always be dynamic and it is for the ruler to be pushing its boundaries outwards as opposed to being hemmed inwards.'

'You are right, Queen. Frontiers are never easy to rule and manage; such a rule is not for the faint-hearted. It explains as to why Devaswami always asks you to support the yagnas and that the rishis always gravitate to Kashmir to propagate dharma. It is from here that when they had protection they took their message all the way to Japan, Korea,

Persia and Afghanistan. Did we fail Kashmir when we stopped sending our great teachers to Persia and China as we once did? Yes, they did not have protection but they should have demanded that; by ceding the ground we let a large number of our neighbours grow up on violent principles and they have now come to haunt us. Behind the sword arm is the enemy's mind. You have to win the battle at that level.'

Kota then asked the question that was troubling her the most.

'What if we do not have the strength and resources to win the military battle or the mental battle for tolerance but instead lose? This is what the Sogdian warned me. Will we have to flee? Will it be the end of the Kashmiri Bhatta?'

Devaswami stood up, collected a few devdar cedar seeds and placed them in Kota's palm.

'Migration, if it happens, is endemic to human existence; it is a brutal shock wave, a monstrous *taranga* but it can also be liberation from the shackles of a static, stultifying world view. From a Kashmiri Shaivite perspective, all forms of reality are to be welcomed. If it comes to that then one has to salute Devi displacement and say, *I am a Kashmiri Bhatta*, so let me never forget who I am and carry me to the right soil where I can once again sprout and reveal who I am – a person powered by the ultimate force of self-reliance. Our own ancestors migrated from the banks of the River Saraswati. Never forget that what can be created is infinite, whereas what can be destroyed is finite. In that inequality lies our victory. Never forget that the creators of duality in Persia were swallowed by it, and ultimately had to seek sanctuary in the diversity of India. Most assuredly, the last entity in the Universe will be the ultimate self-reliant consciousness. Shivoham!'

Kota was used to Devaswami's long responses to even the shortest of questions. She followed it up.

'Kashmir has historically been called Stridesh, the land where women rule. Where else will the Kashmiri women find the freedom and the privileges that they have here?'

'There is no secret here that we are all followers of the daughter of Tryambaka who laid down our founding principles,' Devaswami replied. 'The day the Kashmiri woman loses her Shakti is the day she loses her eminence in society and becomes subjugated. Those secrets are embodied in the dejhoor and as long as the women wear it they will have a constant reminder of what powers us. For women to have true leadership in society, they should never ever give up on the pre- eminence or the practices of the sacred feminine, which is nature's creative force. Our feminine model is not that of subjugation, nor that of equality but that of fearless symmetry. You are the living example of that queen.

'I failed you, Queen, and let Rinchina penetrate the Kashmir mandala. More encounters will follow and I can no longer guarantee the safety of the Kashmir mandala. Kashmir may regress like the Afghans and the asuras, or Kashmir can resurrect the Afghans. The cycle of time will make both happen. Queen, you have to do your duty to your people and to your kingdom and I have to do mine to the Devi.'

'You mean the Devi might leave Kashmir?' Kota asked.

'Kashmira Devi is imbedded in the land but she may stay in a form that the Kashmiris may not like. Do not forget that the barren hill overlooking the lake is empty for a reason. Many rulers have thought of building their palaces there, but have thankfully been dissuaded. It is the abode of Shikasdevi, the Devi of doom. Nowhere in India does she have a place of her own, but the Devi granted Shikasdevi a spot here in the Valley knowing that she would always be kept under control. One can ignore what we Brahmins say as folklore, but there is always truth inside our revelations; to ignore them is to proceed at one's own peril. I repeat that after Rinchina the Kashmir mandala is broken, Shikasdevi has been unleashed and I can no longer guarantee the safety of Kashmir.'

'What will happen to Chander and Jatta?' a frightened Kotarani asked.

'They will be brothers together to the end,' the jyotish replied enigmatically.

'Your words give me comfort, Jyotish,' Kota said. 'Too often the royal throne divides brother from brother. My own brother was estranged from me because he thought that the throne was rightfully his.'

Kumara had the last word.

'Queen, remember what Devaswami has said: evil or ignorance is within us, its cyclical expansion and contraction should neither alarm us nor lull us. Today, Kashmir is experiencing the expansive phase of this aggression, but it will envelop all of humanity. Some battles will be won and some will be lost, but history tells us that what the long war needs is constant vigilance. The best deterrence is forward offence driven off self-reliance that is based on knowledge and consciousness. Never betray the people, all the way down to the Chandala.'

'This has been very helpful to me,' Kota said. 'I came fearful, but I leave strong in my conviction that howsoever dark the possibilities and outcomes, inclusive diversity will triumph over exclusivity founded on coercive purity. *Vasudhaiva Kutambakam* will eventually win and the force of creativity within us, which can make us into supermen, will make the difference. I, Kota, will not swerve in fighting the long war.' The queen stood up and it was time to end the briefing. The Brahmins lined up outside all saluted their beloved queen. Kotarani was rejoined by Udyandev and they left with their retinue. Udyandev was excited about this visit; one of the pandits had taken him to the library and together they had pored over ancient manuals on vimaans, ancient aircraft designs. There was some talk about trying to replicate the design. The engines were built using mercury as the propulsive force. The drawings were pictorial and the descriptions sketchy, but they were sufficient to fire up Udyandev's imagination as he fancied himself flying over his kingdom in a celestial craft. Kota was happy for Udyandev and she remembered that the jyotish had told him that she needed to ensure that no harm came to her husband. She leaned over and squeezed his shoulder gently. It was time to face the new threat head-on and he would be integral to the mission. They would never surrender and if all was seemingly lost, still the Kashmiri Bhattas would be victorious at the end. There was nothing to fear, dharma was with them.

Wave 16
Ascent

AS Kotarani and Udyandev made their way over the mountain path back to their fort, on the outskirts of the capital city the Chandala was making his way through the fields and orchards. His forehead was bent low against a rope that balanced the load he carried on his back. His neck muscles were strung out tight, bearing the strain of the heavy pack. He held a stout stick in his right arm to help him balance his weight as he stepped over the rocks. In the distance he could see another figure walking in front of him carrying a basket on top of her head – it had to be a woman, only the women carried loads on their heads, their hips swinging gently side to side as they walked. This woman held her load with her left hand, so it was evidently not too heavy; certainly not as heavy as the load that the Chandala bore. He wondered who it was, because it was getting late in the evening and not too many women would walk alone on the pathway. She wore a red cloak, which was not a smart thing to do, as it attracted attention.

They continued to walk, bearing their loads. She was unaware that he was behind her, and he made no attempt to signal to her; there was no cause to. But after some time the Chandala's ears picked up a soft noise. Chandalas served as night watchmen because their job was best done at that time and this one had developed highly trained ears. It was gentle footsteps that he could hear and within a minute his worst fears were realized – a big black bear appeared in the clearing around the footpath and started loping after the woman, who was unaware she was the prey of this 6-foot-long beast.

The Chandala dropped his load to the ground. His mind racing, he picked up a few stones; he shouted out making a hissing sound as he threw them. Interrupted in his pursuit, the bear turned around, as did the woman. At the sight of the bear she dropped her burden, paralysed with fear; *haput*, the native bear, is a veritable terror in Kashmir. It not only kills humans and cattle but destroys maize fields, fruit trees and honey stores. Many an unsuspecting farmer has encountered a bear in his field, sitting on his haunches, uprooting a sheaf at a time and devouring the maize. This bear was about to turn his attention back to the woman when a missile smacked him on the nose; it let out a yelp of anger as another stone hit him on the forehead. A rain of stones peppered his face as the Chandala hit his target each and every time with unerring accuracy. The bear was now bleeding with the cuts. With an angry roar he started running towards his tormentor.

The Kashmiri bear fights by slapping and hitting its human adversary with quick, hard, raking blows, using his razor-sharp curved claws. He will often seize his antagonist and squeeze the life out of him while biting with his teeth. Once the adversary is unconscious the bear can move in for the kill.

The Chandala saw the bear raise itself on its haunches as it approached him. It was taller than him, and broad; snarling and with its black hair bristling, he was a fearsome sight. His eyes were burning with primal hatred at the sight of the puny man. The Chandala could smell its stink. 'You smell even worse than me,' he muttered and ran as fast as he could to the nearest tree by the edge of the footpath, standing behind its broad trunk for protection. The bear leaped towards him, but the Chandala brought his thick stick crashing down on the bear's snout. Maddened beyond endurance, the bear reversed course and swung around the other side of the tree. The Chandala dexterously threw his turban, the safa, in its face; temporarily blinded, the bear flailed at the long unwinding turban as its claws ripped into the fabric and entangled the animal. The Chandala started raining blows on its head with the energy of a man possessed. Each hit encountered solid bone. Unable to take the rain of blows, the bear fled. Just as quickly as the encounter began, it ended.

The Chandala stopped, his chest heaving with the effort and his heart pumping with adrenalin. He sat down on the ground to rest. The petrified woman came running over.

'Hey Mulberry. Don't come too close. I smell,' he said wanly.

'It does not matter to me. I am a washerwoman; I wash dirt out all day long. Are you alright?'

'What in the world do you think you are doing, walking alone and wearing a red dress in the forest? Did your mother not tell you a story that bears fancy women who wear red dresses and kidnap them to their dens? Do you want to end up like Satara's wife, who ended up as a bear's playmate?'

'We are Hanjis, boat people. Our stories are of the river and the lakes. We are not mountain folk. I went to pick up a load of washing from a new customer and was delayed.'

'Well, let me tell you that those of us who toil on the land know that bears are fierce and have their own liking. One likes apricots, the other mulberry and the third maize. Usually they come out late at night to feast, but something must have disturbed this bear for it to intrude on our path. In any case, let us head out because I do not think I have the strength to face it again.'

The Chandala helped the washerwoman pick up her load before hoisting up his own. He thought that the woman would walk ahead of him, but she waited for him to catch up to her and walked by his side. If she was aware of his smell, she did not betray it.

'You are a very brave man. You saved my life.'

The Chandala laughed. 'I guess when you see a wild animal coming at you, you fight; it is either him or you.'

'But he was not coming after you, he was after me,' the washerwoman said gently.

'We Chandalas grow up throwing stones,' he replied. 'It is the one weapon of self-defence that every Kashmiri has. When I see a bear I am trained to throw stones at it. There is no bravery, just instinct.'

'Nonetheless, I am grateful to you. Do you have relatives? Who lives in your den?'

'My relatives all died fighting Dulucha. We served as the watchmen at the gates and were decimated by his men. I was the only survivor, and I had my revenge serving under Commander Ramachandra. I live in the village of Trahagam. Which family do you belong to?'

'I live with my aunt and uncle and their brood on a boat on the banks of the Vitasta, where it bends near the rope bridge. I help out with the chores and I make a living washing clothes.'

He did not ask the washerwoman what had happened to her parents. Their generation was one of broken links, all victims of violence; it would take several more generations for the scars to heal, for families to become whole once again, for there to be a full complement of relatives at a wedding. Society had been butchered by the Turcomans and the jihadis, and it would be decades before it would be reborn again.

The two walked slowly with the practised gait of a people for whom walking was the only mode of transportation. They were of the same Valley but worlds apart. She was a water person, her world centred on the river; he was a land person, earthy and rooted in the soil. They talked about everything in their lives and they had much in common, each looking up at a society that they were at the foot of. The conversation turned to Khazanchi – the Chandala was quite surprised to hear her talk about him.

'Yes, we are related,' she said. 'Just because he gives himself airs now does not mean that we don't know his roots. Let me tell you that a long time ago we Kashmiris were mostly all boat people except for those who did limited farming. Only the Brahmins, and before them the Buddhists, lived in the caves or the monasteries. My people, direct descendants of Manu, the first boat builder, carried the massive blocks of grey limestone in the barges to the construction sites. Fruits, vegetables, maize, all the produce were traded by the boat people. Then there emerged a class of pirates on the Vitasta; they manned small swift crafts and attacked the large, slow barges, taking what they wanted and burning the boats after their pillaging. They would carry their booty to the castles that they had built on the banks of the river. All these high families that now reach up to the sky, they were all looters at one time or the other. Today, these same people are the merchants and the oligarchs. As for us, we tried to stay true to our principles and fell behind, to the point that when people see a Hanji they think they are dealing with a marine animal and not a human being.'

The Chandala chuckled.

'I suppose in my work I have no fear of pirates. I would welcome company in the outhouse, any company, but alas the pirates are too busy behaving like that bear. They want to raid the orchards and the fields rather than visit outhouses.'

'Do you like my body?' the woman asked suddenly.

'Yes, you are very attractive,' the mesmerized Chandala stammered.

'I do have an alluring body,' the washerwoman replied matter-of-factly. 'It comes from swimming constantly from a very young age. No man can resist me; I could tell you stories that you would not believe. Every evening the Hanji men come to visit my uncle, ostensibly to smoke and make conversation; they often ask me when I will marry and one of them even was bold enough to propose to me.'

'Why did you refuse him?'

'I know him – he only wants to marry me so that he can rent me out to the men on the land. Maybe he thinks that he will sell me to Khazanchi. Men think that they own women. They are so useless.'

The Chandala was shocked. 'This would be unthinkable in our village. If a man were found alone with an unmarried woman, even in the most innocent of circumstances, he would get the beating of his life. Our women's reputations are paramount to us and an asset of the entire village, not just the individual or the family.'

She laughed.

'We are from different worlds, and what makes sense in our world probably does not in your world. I am a child of the river and spend more time in the water than out of it. We stay naked until we reach puberty; when we put on our first clothing it is a coming of age ceremony. We are not as prudish as you land people, who hide your nakedness.'

'I understand nudity, but nudity does not automatically translate into promiscuity.'

The washerwoman changed the subject.

'Tell me, Chandala, what do you eat in a given day?'

'In a good year the farmers give me enough maize for three months for the work I do for them. For the remaining nine months I eat fruits and vegetables. I will occasionally catch a fish. Sometimes when there is a wedding, I may get a piece of meat from the leftovers.'

'The land feeds you. We have only the river. We eat well during the summer if there are no floods, but when the Valley freezes over for six months and longer, we only have dried fish. If we run out of fish, what do you suggest that we do?'

She continued: 'It is then that you land people who have large supplies of food hoarded in your cellars find a market for our women. Our women are sold for the sake of the children and their men, but it is the women that get the bad name of promiscuity. I can tell you the name of every man in town that has visited the boat people; you would be surprised at the names. It is supposedly about the smoke and the conversation, but it always ends up in a trade that is consummated in the back room of the boat. Some of the boat owners have even started to give their boats fancy names so that the satisfied customers can ask for directions to a particular boat whose charms they liked.'

The Chandala was amazed. He led such a simple life; nobody spoke to him if they could help it. He was all about his chores and this was a new world to him. He was afraid to ask directly the natural question that had arisen in his mind.

'Life is hard for all of us common folks,' said the Chandala. 'The farmer has his challenges and when the crops fail it gets very ugly for the land people also. In truth, at that time families have sold their daughters.'

The washerwoman interjected: 'There is some truth in that, which is why I hate it when somebody compliments me on my beauty. Chandala, have you ever wondered why Kashmiri women are so beautiful?'

The Chandala shook his head. He had no idea, certainly none concerning women.

'It is because we live in a cold, murderous climate. In every generation there is a crisis; when the food runs out, it is the ugly women who are culled. Men's caring is driven by their *kokur*s.'

He tried to steer the conversation to a more optimistic subject.

'Why don't you marry a good man? There must be a good man among the boat people. Then it is a question of sharing the ups and downs of life together.'

The washerwoman spoke vehemently.

'There are many good Hanji men and women, but they are all trapped in the system. I am going to escape – just you watch. I may make mistakes but one day it will happen. I will be a land person myself, not just the object of a land person's desires. That is why I became a washerwoman so that I could meet the land folks.'

Looking at the Chandala's torso, she continued: 'You are very strong, as strong as the Hanji men. They push the boats with their long poles against the bank which gives strength to their legs and upper bodies, but you have different muscles.'

'It comes from trekking up and down the mountain with a heavy load on my head, coming down slowly so that I don't slip. Building all that resistance in my legs is enough to make the muscles in my legs pop out.'

'What do you want out of life?' she asked him.

'I have never been asked that question before. Nobody I know asks that question – we do what we are born to do or told to do. Only once before has somebody asked me what I thought about something, but nobody has ever asked me what I wanted.'

'But you must want something. Think, Chandala, what is it that you want? A wife, a son, every man wants that. A piece of land to feed you, every Kashmiri wants that – but only the Brahmins get the grants or the *maths*, temples, from the king. The Damaras will give up their lives, but not a bit of their land.'

'I cannot really think what I want. I observe everything, but I observe in a disinterested way. I am a spectator to life. I do not think of myself as a participant except at the very edge. Wants are a burden in life; the less one wants the less of a burden one has to carry through life.'

The woman smiled.

'Do you know that you are a very handsome man? If you had a plot of land, you could marry a woman. Perhaps I would have married you. Would you not have liked that?'

Something clicked inside the Chandala's brain.

'You know, you are the second person who has said that I am a very handsome man.'

The woman frowned, her expression revealing a hint of jealousy.

'So there you are, pretending to be an ascetic, and obviously you have had an admirer all along. Who is she?'

'No, no, you do not understand. It is our queen; she said that to me.'

The woman laughed.

'The bear has affected your brain. You met the queen and she said to you that you are a handsome man?'

'You asked me to come with you, no questions asked. Now I want you to come with me. I just want to make sure that I heard you correctly: if I have a plot of land, you will marry me.'

She humoured him.

'Chandala, the day you become part of the landed gentry I will devote myself to producing sons for you. I will also have one daughter so that I can pass the knowledge of this river to her.'

'Let us go to see the queen right now,' the Chandala said, grabbing the washerwoman's hands. It would take a few days' walk, but the Chandala was not to be denied.

After a few days' forced march, they arrived at the gates of the fort. Kotarani was inside when one of her attendants informed her that there was a mad Chandala at the gates begging an audience with her; his message to the queen was that she had thought that he was a handsome man. Kotarani instantly remembered him, and ordered that he be brought in. The attendant, greatly surprised, obeyed; the Chandala wanted the woman with him to come in as well, but she suddenly developed cold feet.

'Why don't you want to come with me to see the queen?' demanded the Chandala.

'Oh, she probably won't like me' she said, suddenly bashful.

'Why would she not like you?' he asked, exasperated.

'Feminine intuition, if she said that you were handsome – and I still do not believe she said that – she will not like seeing you with another woman. Besides, she may have heard bad things about me. I have not led a sheltered life,' she said uneasily.

The attendant intervened to say that the queen should not be kept waiting. The Chandala grabbed the washerwoman's hand, and before she could resist they were walking towards the queen's chamber.

When the two of them entered the room, it took their breath away. The room was decorated in a way that they had never seen in their humble lives; both were immediately conscious of their extreme poverty in the midst of their surroundings. By force of habit, the Chandala sat down on the floor in the corner farthest away from the two chairs that were in the room, avoiding the expensive carpet; the washerwoman sat next to him, her face covered by her shawl.

Kotarani entered, accompanied by Saras. When she saw the Chandala she clicked her teeth in exasperation. She walked to the corner of the room and slowly sat down on the floor facing him. Saras quietly seated herself next to her mistress.

'You always make me come to you – even kings do not have that power,' Kotarani said. 'But first, *Wareshu*, are you well?'

The Chandala folded his hands and bowed his head low; his face purple at the honour Kotarani did him. *What a daughter Kampanesa Ramachandra had!* He would have laid down his life for Ramachandra at any time, and he knew that he would do the same for Kotarani.

Kotarani ordered *kahva* for her guests and waited until it was served. The woman accompanying the Chandala brought her cup to her mouth hidden beneath her shawl, barely daring to breathe. Kotarani made small talk, waiting for the Chandala to disclose the purpose of his visit. Finally, he found his voice.

'Oh Queen, once you told me that there would be a woman who would want to marry me. I have found that woman, but before I can marry her and raise a family, I need land. Your father told me once that the reason that the Brahmins were given land was not because of who they were but because of the goodness that they had brought the people. I am not a Brahmin, but I have served you and your father with all I have. How can I earn a piece of land so that I can have a family? I promise that I can make that land produce double what it does today, so that nobody loses. I will be a slave to that commitment.'

Kota studied his face. He looked so different from when she had seen him before: his face cleaned, his sharp Kashmiri features revealed the strength of his face. His brow was furrowed from all the thinking that he had been doing. He must have practised his words to her a thousand times.

'We do not have slaves in Kashmir,' Kotarani said. 'Everybody has freedom in Kashmir because that is the basis of human happiness. To be *swatantra,* to have liberty, is why Kashmir is the crowning jewel of the world. However, freedom does not mean getting things for free. What you did for my father was your duty to defend Kashmir. If I give you land, I must take it from somebody else. I do not use force in these matters.'

The Chandala's face fell. The laws of society were inexorable; how could he have thought that he was immune to them?

Kota watched the Chandala's face. 'You have not introduced us to the lucky woman who is your companion today and perhaps the rest of your life,' she said gently. 'May I see her?'

The Chandala nodded, totally dumb; the air had been sucked out of his dreams. Kota leaned over and gently raised the fold of the washerwoman's shawl. The two women's eyes met and for a long time they stared at each other silently. Then the queen dropped the shawl on the woman who had hurt her like no other woman that night with Brahma long ago. A woman who had played an integral role in the plot against Achala.

'Saras, it seems to me that the Chandala wants to marry a young woman to whom the kingdom is indebted. What she has done in terms of her dharma to Kashmir was beyond the call of duty; the debt must be repaid.'

The washerwoman listened, concealed within her shawl. *Oh great Queen! She harbours no vindictiveness over what occurred with Brahma, a young woman's folly; there is goodness in her every act.*

The Chandala came to life. 'What debt, Queen? What are you referring to?'

'Shush,' said the Queen. 'All women have their secrets, and this one is between your betrothed and me. The maharaja has never once asked me about my past, and you should not either. As a woman I can tell you that you have an extraordinary wife who did her dharma when it mattered greatly. Always take care of her.'

'I think my family still owns a small plot of land in a village called Sopore, a short distance away,' the Queen continued. 'I will arrange to have a paper drawn up with the royal seal transferring the land to you and your descendants forever. However, there is one small responsibility that goes with that land. Are you prepared for it?'

The Chandala nodded. He saw that the washerwoman had slipped her shawl off and was watching the queen in awe.

'Tell me your command and it will be followed, Oh Queen.'

Kota smiled. 'There is a small temple there. You know the one I mean. Make sure that you and your future generations take care of it and make your offerings to it on every festival. You must promise me that one day you will take me to that temple. Since you will now be living in the village of Sopore, I guess you will now be named Soporis. Also, from now on you will not be called Chandala; instead I name you Chand, the moon. It is the name that I gave my eldest born. May your family flourish!'

The washerwoman began to sob silently. She would be the first water person to have received a grant of land. She would be a landowner, something that one could not even dream of. She would have a husband who had saved her life. She would have respect. It was all too much. The queen took her hand and placed it Chand's, squeezing both tightly.

'Chand, tell me what gave you the confidence and optimism that I would grant you your wish for land?'

Chand spoke hesitatingly.

'My mother told me a story when I was young. She said that the Devi of fortune left the demons and went to the Devas; being fickle, she decided to leave the Devas also and went to the cows, asking to dwell within them. The cows refused, knowing of her inconstancy; but she said that no part of a cow's body was disgusting, and asked if she could live in their urine and dung which the cows agreed to. The Brahmins sip a cow's urine, hoping to be blessed by the Devi of Fortune who resides therein. Queen, I have handled so much cows' urine and dung in my life that I felt that surely someday the Devi's blessings would rub off on me!'

The queen laughed heartily at his earthy story. Chand's stories of dung and night soil were so much a part of him.

'The Devi of fortune is a woman,' Kota said, 'and she can bring wealth, but she can be fickle if she is not treasured continuously. The Hanjis are my favourite folks – simple, loving and loyal. They were part of my bridal party at my first marriage; it was they who rescued Udyandev, and they also outmaneuvered Achala's officers who wanted to accompany him. Now that one of their daughters is getting married, I want to help her choose her wedding dress. Chand, you will be taken by the attendant to be dressed. Devaswami will send us a priest and we will have a wedding that you will both talk about for the rest of your lives. Now come, there is so much to discuss, and much that I can learn from you.'

The queen and Saras took the washerwoman away. Chand could hear the three bursting with laughter at whatever confidences they were sharing, woman to woman. The attendant led him to the men's quarters. He reflected on the extraordinary set of events that only the Devi could have been responsible for. One could earn one's reward through dharma and self-reliance with a just queen, or one could plunder and pillage, led by the white wolf.

Wave 17
Polo

KOTARANI ordered that young children, including girls, be picked among the Chandalas, the Hanjis, the Mussalmans and other sections of society to attend Sharadapeeth. The aristocrats and the Brahmins expressed disquiet at what they saw as their privilege, but none opposed the queen. Kotarani also aggressively started courting the Lavanyas. Seeing that these moves had gained the queen popular support, Shah Mir countered by accelerating his pace of discontent. He opened his hand by finally bringing an adult Haider to court with him and always addressed him publicly as the king-in-waiting. Haider had grown up a deeply religious young man; he sported a wisp of a beard, had started wearing a skullcap and always carried a Koran. He would keep his eyes averted, letting Shah Mir do all the talking. Udyandev disliked Haider, but he knew that Kotarani loved both her sons equally and used Haider to send messages honouring Shah Mir and seeking to bring him back on board, but he remained indifferent.

Jatta graduated from Sharadapeeth, bringing great joy to Kotarani and Udyan, who had attended his exam where he had acquitted himself with good aptitude and attitude. The only person that Haider chose to interact with was Jatta, who had bonded with him and often made him break out into a small smile. Shah Mir had once tried to restrict Haider from meeting with Jatta but with uncharacteristic ferocity he had demanded to see his sibling. Shah Mir had not interfered again, merely referring to Haider's behaviour as typical of youngsters and hoping that he would mature in the way that was desired of him. Jatta had grown into a strapping young man, and in some ways he seemed to be the elder of Haider. He sensed that Haider was under strain from his long hours of study of the Koran, and so, on his elder brother's visits to court, Jatta made every effort to talk to him about his own adventures, alongside Bhima, all of which for Haider was a world apart.

To defy Kotarani, Shah Mir gave special attention to the Lavanyas who were ungodly: through a combination of diplomacy, favours, money and intimidation, he became their de facto patron. So when Kampana, one of their leaders, disobeyed an order from the maharani, it was understood that Shah Mir was testing the queen's resolve. Kotarani called a secret council where the minister of justice was direct with her.

'Refusing to follow a sovereign order is tantamount to rebellion and treason. Kampana should be arrested and his assets seized.'

'Seized by whom? The problem is that Shah Mir is the chief of the armed forces; it is not clear as to who will be loyal to him and who would be loyal to us.'

'Shah Mir's Mussalman cavalry is of little consequence,' Udyan offered. 'Kampana's fortress is in a very mountainous area where the horses are not of much use. It will be hand-to-hand combat. Take the Kishtwar regiment headed by Captain Avatara; they are used to mountain fighting. Avatara is young, but he is spirited and his men are loyal to me. This way the Damaras will not be involved because one can never know which way their loyalties lie.'

'That makes sense. I will put out word that I am going to visit Sharadapeeth and lead the regiment. You and Brahma stay behind so that all appears to be normal. When we reach the outskirts of the capital, we will detour and in the cover of darkness set course towards Kampana's fort. This way we will have the element of surprise.'

The mountain path was narrow and it was heavy going for a few days. Unlike the normally rocky mountains of Kashmir, this path lay over a range that was of softer material and prone to landslides. The

Kishtwaris, following the maharani and her advance party, stayed silent as they traversed the path going higher and higher, but in spite of their best efforts to avoid disrupting the terrain they heard a slow rumble. The party looked up and to their dismay saw small stones rolling down the hillside. Avatara pushed his team ahead so that the maharani would not be hurt. The rumble turned into a roar; before everyone's eyes, large rocks started rolling down and turned into a full landslide that wiped out the narrow path. The party was divided in two, a smaller force trapped in front with Kotarani, and the larger contingent left behind.

Dismay turned to horror when, from the other side of the mountain, a group of Lavanyas descended on the hapless maharani. The narrow path gave Kotarani and her small band a slight advantage, because they could hold their attackers at bay, but the archers were able to keep her main body of troops pinned so that they could not reach her. After dispatching a messenger to Udyandev, she continued the fight for another two days. Finally, she was taken prisoner and held in the Lavanya fortress on the side of the mountain. A coded message was immediately sent to Shah Mir: *The dove awaits the falcon.*

Udyandev chaired the council meeting that was attended by the mortified Kishtwar officers. An alliance between Shah Mir and Kampana did not bode well. Deciding against a military expedition, given the risk to the maharani, the council agreed that Kumara Bhatta would be given the task of initiating negotiations with Kampana. Kumara was told that he had authority to negotiate anything and everything to secure Kotarani's release. He requested that he travel alone and that only Kokur accompany him as his attendant.

There were many eyes on Kumara as he travelled across the hillside, and hourly reports of his progress were sent to Kampana. On reaching the fortress he was admitted inside and shown hospitality befitting his station. First, an attendant came and washed his feet, then he was served food; finally he was told that Kampana would meet him and he was admitted into his chamber. Dark-haired and well built, Kampana's square face exuded the confidence of a big fish in a small pond. Shah Mir had briefed him, so he was quite taken by surprise when Kumara spoke.

'Mahraa,' said Kumara, 'by obeying the orders of a female we live with our heads humbled, but you have this day made our manhood triumph. I come to you as a supplicant. It has been rightly said that the Kashmiris should adapt to changing circumstances, and change is upon us. I am here to join you in whatever capacity you deem this poor scholar can be of service to your cause.'

Kampana stared at the man.

'I thought that you were here to negotiate the maharani's release; instead you are negotiating for your own miserable interests.'

Kumara spoke humbly.

'I am intelligent enough to know that it is a failed cause. If you hold the maharani, what can possibly be of value that would justify an exchange? Once you capture the maharani, can you possibly let her go?' Kampana had to accept the logic of the argument. If he released Kotarani, she would return to recover whatever was given as her ransom and Kampana and his followers would have their heads chopped off. Shah Mir must have known that when he advised Kampana on what demands he should make. Kampana was merely a sacrificial pawn in Shah Mir's bigger game.

Kumara could see that he was making some progress and pressed on.

'Mahraa, there is one thing in which I could be of service to you. With your permission, I, your servant, will go to the prison. By reproving and consoling the maharani in turn, I will extract the secret of her treasure and give it to you, my lord. As you know, the maharani trusts me; if you give me a chance to spend time with her, I will win her confidence and see to it that she shares her secret.'

Kampana's eyes lit up. After Dulucha's ill-fated expedition, the maharani had recovered the entire treasure that he had attempted to take away. A small portion had been kept in the royal fort, but the bulk had been buried in an unknown site. Kampana could see the merit of the proposal. Let Shah Mir and the maharani play their power games; what Kampana wanted was treasure. With it, the wealth of all future Kampanas would be assured. He would be supreme among the Lavanyas, who would be supreme among the Damaras – they would be the maharaja makers. Political intrigue was a risky, uncertain business; treasure was solid, secure and everlasting.

Kampana spoke carefully.

'Kumara, I can see why the maharani picked you. You have a good head on your shoulders. Yes, the world is changing, but certain things never change. Money is one of them. I am not a bad man, Kumara; get the treasure, and 10 per cent of it will be yours.' He smiled encouragingly, wondering if Kumara were intelligent enough to figure out that once he found the location his end would be quick.

Kumara bowed.

'I will visit the maharani at dusk, accompanied by my boy who will bring my water container for my daily puja. I know that the maharani likes to hear chants at that time. I will sing the *Shiva Mahima Stotra* to her. It will put her in a good mood. I will then present the proposal to her and ask her to sleep on it. She is cautious like any woman, but I am confident that by morning she will be able to see that what I have suggested is pragmatic and the best that she can hope to negotiate. Have complete confidence in me; tomorrow you will have good news.'

Kampana was pleased. When he had embarked on this mission he had no idea that fortune would hand him not only the maharani, but also the fabled treasure of Kashmir. He would go down in history as the most illustrious Kampana, and the family name would be burnished forever. Where Dulucha had failed he would succeed. He instructed his captain to escort Kumara and his attendant to the Maharani's heavily guarded cell and then left for his own chambers. This merited some celebration. He ordered his valet to bring wine along with his favourite girl, Pyaari. Kampana had a small collection of desirable beauties. Tonight was a night to celebrate; tomorrow would bring a new taranga in his life.

Kumara, accompanied by his attendant Kokur and followed by the guards, was led to the maharani. She was in a dark, dank section of the fortress. The captain ordered the guards to pull aside the wooden bar that blocked the door. Kumara entered with his attendant and heard the door slam behind him. The maharani had her back to them; she did not move an inch.

Kokur took over. Facing the maharani he put a finger to his lips. Kumara spoke in a loud voice, for the benefit of any eavesdroppers, stating that he was engaged on a diplomatic mission to free the maharani; but that before he got down to the details he was certain that the maharani must be quite overcome by what she had gone through. He, Kumara, wanted to console her: perhaps he could recite the *Shiva Mahima Stotra* to cheer her in her current circumstances? Without waiting for a response, Kumara began the chant.

Meanwhile, with a trained hand Kokur had pulled a long cloth out of the water vessel, hanging it as a partition between Kumara and himself and the Maharani, even though Kumara had already turned his back to the Queen to give her some privacy. Kokur held the maharani's long hair and slowly cut it boyishly short with a knife. He then took some creams mixed with ash and gave a grey stubble to her creamy, smooth skin. He rubbed a different mud cream on her hands and palms to give the appearance of calluses. An expert at cross-dressing and make-up, Kokur's cast might be all male or all female and then had to play the opposite gender. He put on a long, jet-black wig and costume jewellery that sparkled as brightly as the maharani's jewels. His craft had taught him that accessories should be oversized – the audience would be drawn to the jewels and wouldn't observe the person's face very closely. Then very carefully he put on some earrings; his ears had been pierced when he was young, a common practice with the boys as well as the girls of his time.

He silently unbuttoned the maharani's jacket from behind; she had never been disrobed by a subject, but she did not move. Kokur wrapped a silk bandage around the queen's chest and tightened it so hard that she could barely breathe. Then he gave her his own shirt to wear; underneath, the Maharani's chest looked hard and flat, just like a man's. Finally, standing behind her, Kokur slipped his trousers off. He handed them over to her, and the maharani pulled them on under her dress without making a sound. When she had tightened the trousers she stepped out of her smock dress and handed it to Kokur, who slipped into it before scooping the queen's hair up from the floor and putting it into his vessel with the extra clothes. The final touch was black collyrium to lengthen Kokur's eyelashes and blush for his cheeks. Kokur sat down with his back to the door, his face slightly angled in a royal stance.

Kotarani had always been very slim, and Kumara was stunned to see how much she looked like the man who had accompanied him inside the cell. He had a hard time staying focused on his chanting, but he kept his voice steady, knowing that the guard outside had an ear pressed to the door. When he ended, he said in a very controlled voice, *'Om Namoh Shivayah, Om Namoh Shivayah*. Oh Maharani, we revere Shiva because we exist as a manifestation of his glory – nothing else matters. I have risked my life to come here to rescue you and bring you back to your loved ones. Maharani, you must part with the treasure of Kashmir as ransom and then you will be free.'

'The treasure you speak of belongs to the people of Kashmir,' Kotarani snapped. 'It cannot be used as a ransom; nor can it go into the hands of thieves.'

Kumara persisted. 'Maharani, the people do not care one whit for the treasure – what they want is you. Just think, if Dulucha had taken the treasure, would we be any worse off than we are today? Humans do not necessarily act according to principles; self-interest prevails. If you are not secure, how can the people be secure? Their security is paramount – the rest can all be replaced.'

The conversation went back and forth like a rehearsed script. The maharani fully understood her part. She could not be expected to acquiesce quickly; Kumara was patient and used every scholarly argument to reason to the maharani that paying the ransom was the best course of action. Finally, both sides agreed that it was getting late and they should rest; the maharani would give her decision tomorrow in the morning. Kumara knocked on the door and the guards came in. They saw the maharani with her back to them in disdain. Kumara bid his goodbye, but the boy was more respectful. He went around to the maharani, prostrating himself at her feet. Kokur saw the maharani touching his feet, and in his final act he patted her on the head in benediction. He could see the slightest moistening in her eyes and then with a blink it was gone. Then Kumara, followed by the respectful boy with the water vessel on top of his head, trooped out to his sleeping quarters.

While the Lavanyas slept until late morning, the Brahmins did their worship, their ablutions and their meditations before dawn, a sacred time of day for them. It was at that hour that Kumara and Kotarani made for the ramparts. The guards, lulled by the sweetest sleep that always comes at dawn, did not see Kotarani fleeing, disguised as the boy. The maharani had a surprise waiting for her at the rampart; it was Brahma, who had quietly scaled the wall with a rope that was hung to the side. His eyes ever smiling, he held his nose in mock disgust at Kokur's dirty clothes that Kotarani was wearing. Even Sharika had not been able to straighten out Brahma; he was still the same incorrigible person. But Kotarani was delighted to see him, and she knew that Brahma was jubilant to see her. The impossible plan had worked! Kotarani was the first one to scale down the rope. She was glad that Saras's diet and a rigorous daily regimen of Surya namaskars had kept her fit and lithe. Brahma followed her, supporting Kumara the scholar who occasionally needed a steady hand on his legs to keep his hold. Then the three of them scampered into the forest where Brahma had brought the key officers of the Kishtwar regiment. Overjoyed at having retrieved their maharani, they set off at a brisk pace for their camp to plan a suitable response to the Lavanyas' treachery.

The regiment bivouacked that night near a river. Everybody was tired after the forced march and the soldiers fell asleep leaving the guards to do their job as watchmen. Brahma had some private time with Kota and he noticed that her face had started revealing the faintest of wrinkles, but it only softened her beauty under the moonlight.

'Tadpole, I never thought that you would swim away from this one.'

'Kokur made it happen. Brahma, just one person like him can defeat an entire army. The very first time I set my eyes on him was when we were secretly observing Suhdev. He looked and seemed so different, and yet he turned out to be the truest Kashmiri. I can't stop thinking about him and what made him follow his dharma.'

'That day seems like only yesterday and yet a lifetime has passed. Are you happy with the choices you have made?'

'I understand your question. Brahma, I gave you my heart, Rinchina gained my body and Udyan is my constant companion. You men are competitive and would want to know what is most precious, but to me what is most important is that I made the best sustainable choice that I could, based on what I wanted, what I understood and what I could grasp. I did my dharma the best I could. I can live with my personal trade-offs because, as their ruler, the greater good of my people is the most important thing to me. What more do you want me to say? What would you say to your own question?'

'We have both been hurt very badly but our dharma makes us go on. When I look back at that day when we spied on Suhdev, I can see you have grown in confidence and conviction. I too have grown, as has my love for you. You used to follow me, but it seems that now I follow you. I have been very open with Sharika about us. She trusts me and knows that my love for you is not going to result in my disloyalty to her as my wife. She only says that we are star-crossed lovers and will meet again in happier times.'

'When we do I will finally keep the promise that I made to you. Now let us rest,' Kota said with a dimpled smile.

The maharani slept on a makeshift bed that the officers had made for her. Under the stars Brahma had gone into an easy sleep. Before she could sleep, Kotarani performed some breathing exercises, channelling the breath into her heart to relax it after her horrendous experience. She fell asleep thinking about Kokur, and in her dream she saw him back in the cell, also asleep. There was a noise at the door. Was it the guard coming in to check on the queen? Kokur was in a drugged state so he must have taken cannabis. The guard prodded Kokur, who looked up groggy and half awake. The guard was carrying his sword, but his skin was red and he was holding a noose in his other hand. Was Kotarani really dreaming?

The visitor greeted Kokur. 'What do you see in me?'

'I see Yama, the lord of the afterlife, who slays time,' Kokur replied.

The man nodded. 'In seeing me, do you see anything to fear from me or within yourself?'

'Fear is an emotion for the actor, no different than the other *rasa*s. I see nothing in me to fear except that I was born different – I am a homosexual.'

Again the man nodded his head. 'It is not an uncommon situation. Shiva, as part of his playfulness, sometimes will retain both the male and female principle as opposed to opting for one. As you are created and recreated through spanda, vibrations, a million times in a single moment, your male and female energies combine dynamically a million times also and permit you to have the greatest creativity. The Shiva-Shakti union is internal to you, whereas ordinary people have to seek this union in the opposite gender. That is why you are such a gifted artiste and ordinary humans are not.'

'How do you explain the fakir then?'

'Oh, in his case the vibrations have only ended up in agitation. But to return to you, I came to see your show and I must say that your last act was the finest. Did you not fear for your craft that you would be discovered and that the ruse would fail?'

Kokur was proud of his skills.

'I am the master of make-believe. There is none better than me. I even had the queen believing that I was the real queen.'

The man nodded again.

'If you have to go, one should go at the top and you certainly have.'

'Where are we going?' Kokur asked abruptly.

'Oh, to my place where you will wash up, rest and purify yourself and then you are off to something new. It will definitely be better than as a dragonfly. Much, much better.'

'I am a prisoner here. I do not think that it is easy for me to leave.'

'The correct terminology is that you are in a contracted state, but then so is everybody else. In fact, as I just explained to you, the common person is even more contracted than you are. You will be free in a moment if you so will it.'

Kokur was confused. 'How do I will it?'

The man bowed. 'Order me to release you from this body, and then I will follow your command.'

In Kota's dream she saw Kokur smile. His royal act had everybody taken in. First the queen, and now this man waited on his decision. He waved his actor's hand for the man to proceed and ordered, 'Yama, take me to *Pitaama*.' There was a flash of light and the next moment Kotarani observed that Kokur was floating in space: she could see him outside of his earthly body. There were guards around the corpse, stabbing it in futility. The guard who had cut his head was screaming in anger. Orders were being shouted in the distance.

Kotarani was not part of it, and yet she had complete awareness. Kokur was in space and there were his long departed father and his mother next to him. Among the welcoming crowd there were the great actors who had preceded him, giving him a standing ovation. There were others lining up to greet him, all dressed in white. It was just like the fans lining up after an especially successful performance. Kotarani saw her father Kampanesa Ramachandra accompanied by a beautiful regal lady. They were all smiling at him. Kokur's father led him to a genial-looking man and introduced him, 'This is Pitaama, your grandfather.' Kokur's grandfather patted him, 'Welcome. Bravo, we are all proud of you. Soon you will be with us in *Pitr Lok*.'

'I am dead,' she heard Kokur announce. 'What an exit!' Then Kotarani's mind went dark as the curtain fell over Kokur for the last time.

Kokur's magnificent sacrifice, Kotarani's stunning escape, Kumara Bhatta's brilliant ruse and Brahma's bravery captured the minds of the Kashmiris like nothing ever had before. It was the perfect example of what the Kashmiris believed in, one in many and many in one. Brahma and Kumara were described as the two tusks of the maharani.

The maharani was further likened to a bird that was captured in her nest and placed in a cage by the hunter. However, with the help of her friends she had flown away to freedom. She was declared to be the empress. Many actors adopted the stage name of Kokur, hoping that his magic would rub off on them, but there was only one Kokur, and nobody could quite put their finger on the secret ingredient.

After her escape, Kotarani had looked Udyan straight in the eye and asked: 'This was a narrow escape. We have faced threats before and we will face Shah Mir and the fakir together. Udyan, are you happy that you married me in spite of what people say about our marriage?' 'Kotarani, I am your *pati*, your husband, whose dharma is to protect you,' Udyan responded. 'I have not done a good job of that. I am a studious pandit and so Brahma was deemed the best person to send to rescue you. You are a great ruler and you are good to the people. I like ideas and I am free to pursue them. We each are following our own proclivities. Who cares what the people say about our marriage if we are serving the Kashmiris in the best way that we can.'

Kotarani pulled Udyan closer to her and held him tightly. She knew that she was blessed in Udyandev, and had a healthy body and mind, as she prepared for a fight to the end.

Meanwhile, Kampana had trekked over to Shah Mir's castle. Previously the scene of numerous supplicants, it looked deserted; Kampana's teeth were chattering as he described the sequence of events and the likely consequences. Shah Mir was isolated and he knew that defeat was inexorable; he had overplayed his hand and had failed. There was only one punishment fit for treason and that was death. He needed to think quickly and come up with a plan, but first he had to deal with the snivelling Kampana. Shah Mir had recognized an unprincipled opportunist in Kampana but failed to see that the man was fundamentally a coward. Shah Mir needed help himself, so there was nothing he could offer Kampana except to advise him to take care of himself until things were sorted out for the better.

As their conversation ended, Shah Mir was informed that the fakir had come to see him. When the man was admitted, Shah

Mir was surprised to see how he had changed: the man radiated power through his paleness. He was even thinner than normal and his face had the look of a vampire that never saw the sun. He was accompanied by a band of followers, all dressed in black. There was Sheikh carrying a sword, the carpenter, the Sufis, Puj – all with their own weaponry. It was Panun Fauj, a militia of sorts, and while it would not have stood up against the Maharani's army for a moment, it was a show of force that encouraged Shah Mir. The Fakir waved away his followers and sat down with Shah Mir.

'Brother, I heard the news and came to your aid. The time is ripe to go on the offensive and declare that Haider, as the new maharaja, will move to take possession of his rightful throne.'

Shah Mir eyed his guest warily. The fakir had always had pretensions of grandeur, but he seemed overly confident given the circumstances.

'Haider is dearer to me than my own boys. However, a declaration like that would subject him to grave harm. How would we back him up? Except for the small band of Mussalman cavalry, who have limited effectiveness in this terrain, we cannot count on anyone's loyalty.'

'I believe that there is a deal to be made here. I can give you what you want and you can give me what I want. You want to be the power behind Haider's throne, and I want Hind. We can both have our desires.' The fakir laughed at the sheer joy of it all.

'How do you propose to take care of the maharani, who has other thoughts on the subject? And how do you think that you will end up with Hind?'

The fakir laughed again. 'First, we must reach an understanding. Once we have it then all the pieces will fall into place.'

'What is the understanding that you want with me?'

'In matters of Shariat I rule; in all other matters Haider rules – which means that you rule.'

Shah Mir was diffident. 'So, it is exactly like it was before.'

'No, this time it will be different. My first time in Kashmir I tried to teach the Mussalmans to follow the path of strict penance, prayers and purity, but the Mussalmans kept opposing and slipping. This time

I will switch focus on the conversion of heretics, which carries higher rewards. I will set an example of the Brahmins and the rest will get the message that haram practices will not be tolerated.'

'Why are the Brahmins so important to you?' asked Shah Mir out of curiosity.

'The Kashmiri Brahmins are tough, but I will crack them in my lifetime and then I will impose Shariat all across Kashmir. Ghazni, Dulucha, Achala were not able to do that – each time the Brahmins put their society back in place. Once I control Kashmir I will work to fulfil the prophecy of the Prophet, Peace be upon Him, that the conquest of Hind be completed.'

'How do you propose to crack the Brahmins? They are not afraid of death.'

'By using the same weapon that they used against me – shame. I will slowly but steadily fill them with such shame that they will completely discard their identity. We will have them singing, *Na Bhatta, I am not a Bhatta*. Here are the rules that the Bhattas will have to live under.'

The Fakir pulled out a piece of paper and handed it over to Shah Mir, who read the document that had been carefully written by a calligrapher.

> The Hindus will not construct any new places of worship or idol temples in the territory under the control of a Mussalman ruler.
> They will not prevent Mussalman travellers from staying in their places of worship or temples.
> If any of their relations show any inclination to embrace Islam, they shall not prevent him from doing so.
> They will not ride a saddled horse.
> They will not carry swords or bows and arrows.
> They will not wear rings with diamonds.
> They will not openly sell or drink intoxicating liquor.
> They will not openly practise their customs among Mussalmans.

They will not build their houses in the neighbourhood of Mussalmans.

They will not cremate their dead.

The note concluded that if the Kashmiri Bhattas were to infringe any of the ten conditions, they were not to be protected and Mussalmans could rightfully kill them and appropriate their property as if they were kafirs at war.

Shah Mir was shocked.

'We are fighting for our survival here. The maharani is preparing for war and you pull out a note that is guaranteed to ensure our death! Rinchina won the Kashmiris over by promising justice. Bulbul won them over by his message of love and tolerance. We achieved some success by promising a vast reward starting with the land and women to follow. How far do you think we will get with this proclamation?'

'The sky is the limit,' the fakir answered.

Shah Mir could see that he was dealing with a religious megalomaniac, the most dangerous animal on earth. He got straight to the point.

'Who is backing you in all this?'

The fakir shared his secret.

'It has taken some time but the Chak clan has accepted me as their preceptor. Today they are prepared to lay down their lives for me; more importantly, they have huge numbers across the border awaiting our word. They believe in Naya Kashmir.'

Shah Mir saw the possibilities opening up again. Unlike him, Lamar Chak had kept a very low profile, maintaining his relationships with the land and the people; while Shah Mir had built alliances in court, the Chaks had expanded their own familial clan and now had sizable holdings. Physically, the Chaks were an intimidating lot. Between his cavalry, the Chaks and their external allies plus the ragtag jihadis led by the fakir, he could get the Lavanyas back in the tent and then he would have a coalition that could work.

'What caused the Chaks to make this offer?' asked Shah Mir.

The fakir spoke matter-of-factly.

'Lamar Chak is not a peasant. He and his brother had a battle for the throne and Lamar lost; when he saw Ramachandra's attitude towards Rinchina, he decided that it was safer to represent himself as a farmer. When I left Kashmir and travelled back through Dardistan, I found that his brother was at risk of losing the throne to the neighbouring Chak tribes. I brought his brother's peace overtures to Lamar and helped them rebuild their alliance.'

'What do the Chaks want? What are their aspirations?' demanded Shah Mir.

'They only want to serve me. However, some recognition for their sacrifice would be appropriate – perhaps some portion of the land that the Brahmins own could be given to them, the temple near Kupwara and its associated property. There is also some property near Trahagam we could part with.'

'The Chaks do not have a good name. They bring turmoil to the land and depredation to their neighbours. They are an amorous people and are known to steal women; there are also rumours that they have sold slaves to the traders in Dardistan. Being such giants among men, they intimidate those around them.'

The fakir laughed.

'This is precisely why we should settle them in Kupwara and Trahagam – the Kashmiris there need some intimidation. You also need to stop being so negative about your future partners. Give the Chaks land, which they want, and we can take from them what we want.'

Shah Mir understood. Lamar was a farmer in Kashmir; for him land was the ultimate prize. He would also need land to accommodate the needs of his brother's clan. Shah Mir did not believe in coincidences but it was curious how the life of the three immigrant groups – Rinchina and his Bhottas, Lamar Chak, and he – had intertwined. They had all been running away from enemies who had sought to destroy them, and gained sanctuary in Kashmir. For a brief moment he remembered the oath of loyalty that they all had taken before Ramachandra. It all seemed so long ago. He buried the memory as quickly as it arose. He returned his attention to the fakir in front of him. What was his nature? Intense, cruel, opportunistic and waving a brand of Islam which at one time he had fled from. Shah Mir had heard stories but paid little attention to them; however he needed to get to know the man better if they were to have a working relationship.

'You are the greater man today in that you bring everything and more, and yet Kotarani has money,' Shah Mir stated. 'The Damaras will sell their soul to the highest bidder, and we cannot match Kotarani.'

The fakir smiled a faint, cold-blooded smile.

'I visited Khazanchi and presented him with a simple deal. Convert to Islam and take over the mining rights for the sapphire mines. He and I are in complete agreement that there is no way that Yaniv, a despicable *juhudbazi* Jew, can have control of the most valuable asset in Naya Kashmir. In fact, Jews need to be exterminated from Kashmir. I also told him that I would introduce him to the right merchants in Persia who would give him the highest profits for his finds. Of course, he would be expected to advance financial support to our side. Khazanchi accepted the proposal. It gives him new revenues and also the satisfaction of crushing Yaniv. His wife Manjari liked it even better. She hates Kotarani. There is complete equality in birth in Islam and she responded well to that. They both accepted the Kalima on the spot. Truly everything has been ordained.'

'Maulvi, everything you have done is for the greater glory of Allah,' Shah Mir said. 'But what can I do for you? After all, you are important to all of us, and certainly living in the Khanqah cannot be comfortable.'

The fakir stroked his beard. 'I can see that you are not yet ready for the charter that I have proposed. It does not matter. Next time the list will be longer. Patience we have, and time is on our side. We will keep striking until the Sharada edifice falls to Shariat Kashmir. I will teach you to conceal, deceive and surprise. I need nothing for myself. Personally, I am happiest with my boys, shaping their young minds and building for the future when the ummah will rule the world. There is one issue though. The converted Bhatta women are known for their infidelity and for their continuing relationships with the infidels and their customs. Many of these new Muslim women visit the Mammasvamin temple. However, your daughter has sinned the most. Her husband needs to convert to Islam or else she needs to leave him and marry a Mussalman. I am told by Ali that he would accept her as his wife; she could then start a new family.'

Shah Mir sighed.

'My eldest daughter has been the biggest disappointment of my life. I place all the blame on her mother for being lax. I, of course, was focused on raising my sons. Raja Sapru will never convert, and Guhara will die before she leaves him. She has always had a mind of her own and the air of Kashmir has ruined her.'

'Then she is no longer your daughter, and no longer your problem. She is my problem, and I know exactly what needs to be done. Your daughter needs to be taught a lesson.'

Shah Mir protested weakly, 'She is her mother's favourite daughter.'

The fakir glared at Shah Mir malevolently. It was a test and Shah Mir was struggling, teetering between his daughter and the devoted family man he used to be, and the prospect of what he wanted. Slowly and irretrievably his mind buckled in to his greed. It was only a matter pertaining to a woman, thus of no consequence; a concession on it would lead to important agreements later on. They could do business together, Shah Mir running the worldly side while the fakir would be supreme in all matters concerning the imposition of Shariat. He lowered his head in assent. The fakir sensed that Shah Mir had consented to his covenant. It was always the same when he had to break a man. First, give him food, or even the throne, and once he had taken the carrot, apply the stick. He left with his mission accomplished. Shah Mir breathed easier; the man made him uneasy, almost afraid. Nevertheless, he had provided crucial support at a point when survival was at stake, and Shah Mir could now put the pieces together again.

He stepped out on to the balcony of his castle, and looked at the Valley. The falcons had been brought out for practice and were feeding. Shaheen, his prized black falcon, was circling idly in the air seeking prey. Then, spotting something, he swooped down. Shah Mir watched excitedly as the falcon teased out a houbara bustard. The bustard sped wildly; the falcon lazily gained altitude and then folded his wings for the dive. At the last moment, as the falcon came close to strike, the bustard squirted a dark liquid into the falcon's eyes. The blinded falcon fell, crashing into the ground at great speed while the bustard fled squawking angrily. The handler ran towards the falcon, to do what was necessary. In one smooth motion, the handler cut Shaheen's throat with his knife.

Shah Mir was shaken by the episode. He went inside and asked his servant to bring his grandsons to him. They were named Shirhshataka and Himda; people compared their looks to the sun and the moon. Shah Mir had to give credit to his wife: she had borne him fine children, in spite of the trouble Guhara caused. He had married his sons well and their wives had given him fine grandsons. Soon Shah Mir was wrapped up in their horseplay. His good humour restored, he regained his perspective. There was no shortage of Shaheens – where one fell, there were many others to send after the prey. What really mattered were his sons and grandsons. His grandfather had an ambitious dream for him, and he had an equally important dream for his grandsons. Blood would have to be shed so that the bloodline could prosper but that was a price that others would have to pay. As for him, with the fakir as his partner, he could once again pursue his dream.

Panchamgrantha (Book V)
Born Again

Wave 18
Descent

SHEIKH was in a reflective mood with his new Islamic friend Puj. He was seeking reaffirmation that the Islamic pathway that had opened would not prove to be a dead end. He was also testing his growing relationship with his new friend. Puj was highly persuasive.

'If you want land you have to take it away forcefully because nobody will hand it to you. If you want strength and power you have to have a clan. How are you going to have a clan if you don't have a wife? Even if you were to have a wife, as a pandit your wife will control you and limit the number of children to what she wants to produce for you. But if you can have multiple wives you can be four times stronger, four times faster. Which side do you think will win, the womanly way of Kashmir today or the manly way of Islam tomorrow? It is that simple,' he concluded triumphantly.

Sheikh tested his new friend's logic.

'You have to fight for the land. If someone gets four wives that means someone does not. We are back to the haves and have-nots. Who decides who gets and who does not?'

'The person at the top decides. He always wins, irrespective of whether one wins the fight or not. If one wins against the unbeliever, their land and women are booty. If one loses, then one can still accrue the martyr's assets and their widows. The key is to get a fast start and be at the top before anyone else. The key to gains is to never stop fighting. Most important, once you reach the top, the key is to train someone else to do the fighting so that they get the seventy-two virgins in Heaven while you plough the real ones on earth,' Puj concluded craftily.

'I made my choice because of equality but you have been at this longer and understand the game better than me,' said Sheikh. 'Conversion on its own will not change my status unless I act quickly and move to the front of this new line. The cock sucker was right that it is not about equality but about domination. In Kashmir aristocrats would fight but the peasant tilling his field would not even turn his head to glance at them. That will change now. Puj, if the key to getting what I want is to become the most terrifying convert, then let my barber's scissor be exchanged for your cleaver.'

Sheikh – accompanied by Puj the butcher, the barber's brigade, Ali and a few other armed men belonging to Panun Fauj – had embarked on a mission that had come out of the discussion that he had had with Puj. He had an important role: he was head of a group of barbers who were tonsuring and circumcising anywhere from 500 to 1,000 men a day. Any resistance and, *snip snip*, he would sterilize them. The fakir had decided that matters needed to be dealt with hastily. Sheikh was in complete agreement with the fakir that now that Kokur was gone, the jogi must also be eliminated and a message sent to the public that the laxity of Kotarani's rule would not be tolerated. There were a few others on the hit list the fakir gave him, but the jogi was number one. When they reached the Shiva temple and entered it they found the jogi seated on the cremation ground. He was in deep repose with his eyes closed, but somehow he sensed their presence.

'Who are you and what do you want?' he asked.

'I am Sheikh – and it is you I want.'

The jogi opened his eyes and looked at the armed band.

'To what purpose? The last thing on earth that you would want is me.'

'Jogi, there is no place for you in Naya Kashmir. Your magic tricks only work on the gullible, not on those who have accepted the final word of Allah. We are replacing ignorance with light. Prepare for your end.'

If the jogi felt any fear he did not show it.

'I am curious as to how you will achieve my end, when I have failed to do that all these years. As for ignorance – if you do not know yourself, everything else is worthless.'

'Self, pelf, shmelf!' Sheikh screamed. 'I belong to the greatest institution in the world. I am indebted to it. It tells me what to do and my duty is to serve this institution.'

'You only belong to yourself, which is the gateway to the universe. There is nothing higher than the universe of reality, which can provide everything. I am living proof that when one desires higher powers one will get power. But love flees power. My only salvation lies in that one day my prayers for release will be answered. But I am still not clear as to when that will happen.'

'When my sword severs your oversized head, jogi, it will bring the clarity that is missing in your life,' Sheikh threatened.

'I have been walking on a razor's edge all my life – the sword holds no fear for me. My body is my temple, but it is not me. Whosoever takes me, I become a part of them. There is power in me but not of liberation and in the wrong person I could be quite dangerous. Let not the surrender of my body result in your karmic bondage.'

The superstitious men moved back slightly, but Puj interjected, 'Sheikh, slaughter him!'

Sheikh was emboldened.

'Jogi, I do not fear you. What power do you have? Show me the strength of your God! Does Kotarani give you royal protection in return for teaching her sexual secrets? What do you do for her when the vixen is in heat and Udyan cannot satisfy her?'

The jogi laughed.

'My secrets can never be fathomed by the likes of you. I see me in you. Do you see you in me?'

'You fornicator! I see only evil in you.'

The jogi pushed harder.

'Are you still sexually frustrated?' he batted his eyes at Sheikh.

'Why are you making romantic eyes at me, you degenerate?' Sheikh shouted.

'It's a simple secret. Blink, blink, blink and see how you start smiling immediately. You will feel happier.'

'You pervert. The fakir was right – you are a fraud who peddles sex as a reward for those who follow your fake practices.'

'From what I have heard from Chand about your leader, the white wolf, he has anal problems, does he not? Why do you follow a woman hater who thinks he speaks for the creator? Surely, even you know the difference between bad sex and good sex and I am the master of mind-blowing sex,' the jogi said nonchalantly.

Sheikh swung his right hand at the jogi. He had been practicing, and Ali had taught him to aim for the neck. The jogi's severed head bounced on the ground and came to rest, his charcoal eyes gazing intently at his executioner. Sheikh looked into the eyes and he saw his own face looking back; for reasons he did not understand, he felt a shiver run up his back. He kicked the head, which went rolling away. There was nothing to it – it was so easy, just like cutting hair. He wiped the sword and then ordered the men: 'Bury him. We do not want any part of him.'

'What should we do with his head?' the men asked.

'Bury him in a sitting position and place his head on top of his sword of wisdom. Maybe that way it will knock some sense into him.'

One of the men suggested that perhaps they would be better off cremating the jogi, but nobody paid any attention to him. Sheikh had spoken, and he was the final authority. They scurried to do as they were told. Sheikh seemed to stand more erect than he once had; a certain authority had replaced the former habitual whining of his chronic loser's voice. Their job done, the party made their way back to the Khanqah, where Sheikh shared the news. He was welcomed back as a hero. The fakir smiled indulgently, stroking his beard as the group raised the executioner on their shoulders and shouted in unison, 'Sheikh, Sheikh, Sheikh! The slayer of Kotarani's sex guru.' The first task had been accomplished. It was time now for the Sheikh to clean up some more unfinished business.

Two days later, Sheikh got a report that Raja Sapru and Guhara were returning back from a visit to Sharika's home, where they had gone to celebrate Madana Trayodoshi. Udyandev and Kotarani had also dropped by briefly. Aditya had decided to stay behind with Brahma's family. While Raja Sapru and Guhara were crossing the marsh near the rope bridge on their return, they were accosted by Sheikh and his armed band. Ali was with them, but he kept his face averted from Guhara who had worn new clothes and had put a flower in her hair. Sheikh wasted no time: his men fell upon Raja Sapru and bound him tightly to a tree with ropes. When Guhara tried to intervene, Ali and a few other men caught her and twisted her arms behind her, nearly wrenching them out of their sockets. She began to sob that she was pregnant with child, but the men stuffed her headscarf into her mouth and she could not breathe. She watched helplessly as Sheikh stood in front of her husband.

'You stubborn Kashmiri Bhatta, your punishment was long in coming. I am going to cut your throat, and while you bleed to death I will enjoy your wife to entertain you – you will have the pleasure of hearing her squeals, her swansong. When we are all finished we will cut her up into tiny pieces. This will be a lesson for all Mussalman girls not to touch music or think of marrying a kafir.'

Sheikh did exactly as he had said. He signalled to the butcher, who sliced Raja Sapru's throat from ear to ear; then he strode towards Guhara. The men pushed her to the ground in front of the dying Raja Sapru and pulled her clothes off. Naid/Sheikh dropped his pants and began to rape her. *So this is what sex is all about?* If only the jogi could see him now. Guhara's resistance was futile and in her screams of agony her thoughts were of Raja Sapru. She was sobbing.

'My Raja, my Raja, forgive me!'

Raja Sapru's eyes were glassy now, but they say the ears and the brain hear for a long time. In order to stop Guhara's shrieks, Sheikh gripped her throat and squeezed it tightly. Asphyxiated, she struggled harder gasping for breath; Sheikh felt the movements increase his pleasure. As he climaxed in the instant of Guhara's paroxysm of death, he realized that Puj was absolutely correct – violence pays and extreme violence pays extremely well. The murder and rape accomplished, the band walked away leaving behind the buzzing flies and maggots to begin their task of cleaning the mess that the humans had left behind them.

Saras discovered Guhara and Raja Sapru's dead bodies when she had gone for a walk. She was catatonic as she came rushing back to the palace. The shocking news spread through the Valley as if on wings. An informal inquiry as to whether the Mirs preferred to bury their daughter themselves was met with a flat-out rejection by Ali and his cohorts – the small graveyard in the Mussalman village would not accept her body for burial. Given that Raja Sapru was Hindu and Guhara was Mussalman it created a dilemma as to which temple their last rites would be performed in. Finally, the temple of Mammasvamin was picked. It was the temple where the Jews and Hindus would pray together. Sensing that there were members of their congregation that had become Mussalmans, but still wanted to attend their Hindu temples, they had created the Turushka Bhairava or the Mussalman manifestation of Shiva. At the cremation, the only person from Shah Mir's household who attended was Guhara's mother. She prayed softly, *Forgive us without holding us accountable. Your name is Ghaffar, Ya Rab. Forgive us ...*

Sharika, who knew of Guhara's pregnancy, whispered to the Brahmin priest that a small prayer needed to be conducted for the unborn child. The Brahmin priest nodded his head in understanding – it was not the first time and it would not be the last that a great hope was aborted in Kashmir. Multiplicity arising from Diversity carried the high risk of mortality but that was the nature of the evolutionary force. Kotarani and Udyandev attended the cremation, accompanied by their guards and Brahma stood with the children. The priest handed a small note to Kotarani, which had been pinned to Raja's chest reading: *Udyandev and Kotarani the same fate awaits you. You are next!*

Kashmiris were said to be like crows: where there was one, others would gather and soon they would start cawing. But today the Bhringi clan and their kith and kin were deathly silent. Yaniv, who would frequent the temple along with a handful of other Jewish residents in Kashmir, was there with Tatiana. The Kashmiris had come to the funeral dressed in spotless white, as tradition required; Guhara's mother, in contrast, was covered head to toe in black, with a veil covering her face. Her composure broken, she rocked from side to side. Her sobs were the loudest; each wail ripped every person's heart apart. Her cries to Allah for eternal damnation for the beasts that had committed this crime could be heard across the cremation ground. The bodies had been placed side by side covered in white cloth. The Brahmin priest had laid Raja Sapru's sacred thread, twined with the string of the taviz that Bulbul had given to Guhara for her protection, on the top of the flowers covering the two bodies. The flames rose and soon the sacred thread and the taviz were no more.

19 Avian Flu

KOTARANI'S war council met after the cremation. Udyan had said that he was feeling indisposed and that she should continue without him; he just needed some rest. Kota had urged him to attend, given the gravity of the meeting but he uncharacteristically refused her. She was concerned about him and was torn on what to do, but her sense of duty forced her to leave her husband alone and go to the meeting. While Udyan's absence was noted, the council quickly got down to business.

'Maharani, this war council is without the presence of the commander-in-chief,' Brahma noted, 'because he has become a traitor to the state and he now wants to be the ruler. He has linked with the fakir and Sheikh who have become the instrument of terror in the Valley.'

The maharani looked questioningly at the justice minister.

'If we want to preserve the Kashmir that our ancestors built,' he told her, 'the maharani cannot condone the violence against an innocent woman and her husband. Whosoever is guilty should be brought to justice and punished.'

Brahma shook his head in shock at what had happened.

'As a father Shah Mir must have been complicit in permitting the rape and murder of Guhara. She was always so loyal to him. The fakir has brainwashed him and he has taken leave of his senses!'

'The snake has finally reared its head and the time has come to use the thunderbolt,' Kota said firmly.

The maharani asked for a break so that she could consult Udyandev privately before making a final decision on the next steps they should take. The council waited as she left to go to the royal chamber. Shortly afterwards captain Avatar appeared with an urgent serious message: the maharani required their attendance immediately. The group disbanded; Kumara and Brahma rushed away with Avatar. When the group was admitted into the private quarters they found the maharani very pale beside the maharaja, who was lying on the bed. She heard them enter and in a whisper informed them, 'Udyan is no more ...'

Udyan had suffered a massive stroke and on 7 February 1339 he passed away. He had ruled for fifteen years, two months and two days. He left his world that had been defiled by Rinchina and Shah Mir. Kotarani was overcome with anguish at the cruelty of his sudden death.

'Oh Lord, Maha Shiva Ratri is the night that celebrates the union of Shiva and his spouse Shakti. It is a festival of fun when children's rhymes are sung; they are given gifts and money to spend. The men gamble. Married women pray for the health and welfare of their husbands – but for me it will always be the day that Udyan was snatched away.'

The shocked group tried to console their queen. The first decision that they made was to keep the tragic development a secret for four days, as news of the maharaja's death on Shiva Ratri day would have been viewed as extremely inauspicious by the Kashmiris. A messenger was dispatched to Sharadapeeth, instructing Devaswami to come immediately, and a private cremation was conducted. This was in sharp contradiction to ritual, which demanded that the eldest son light the cremation fire of his deceased father. Each day a few more of the trusted nobility were brought into the picture; the circle was widened slowly until a core group of loyalists had built up critical mass. The maharani wanted Devaswami to stay for a while, but he pleaded that he had much to do. He would take Udyan's ashes and perform the Shraddha ceremonies for the departed soul. He also mentioned that the aging astrologer had become extremely cranky and demanding of late. Devaswami's parting words to Kotarani were that as her guru he would always be with her through her karmic journey and that the Devi would always be with the Kashmiris.

Kotarani remembered her last conversation with Udyan vividly. He had been very animated.

'As you know, I am working with Devaswami's people to design a viman. We think that we are very close to solving the problem with the mercury engine. If you and I flew over Kashmir, what would we see? Everybody is behind bolted doors, some in their huts, and others behind the mighty gates of forts. Each person defines security differently. Shah Mir sees it in capturing power while for the fakir it lies in having an ummah. For you it is in having a nurturing, tolerant state where each person is secure and can pursue their dream. I am the best example of your policy. Nobles have to stand for nobility and what we believe in and we have to do our dharma. The rest, we have to trust the Devi.'

Udyan may have been dreamy but he was right, one had to do one's dharma. It was time to go public. Kotarani assumed full powers on Udyandev's death. Much to her regret, both Haider and Jatta were passed over but the nobility had insisted; they did not want to risk the uncertainty of an untested power on the throne. Brahma's powers were expanded, as were Kumara's, and the two would now serve as the maharani's principal advisers. There was much sympathy for the royal widow: everybody remembered how she had nurtured them, and the public bowed to her. The Lavanyas saw her as one of theirs, and as a woman she was more malleable.

There were reports that Shah Mir could not tolerate Brahma's ascendancy, but he understood which way the winds were blowing and he kept his head low. The decision by Maqbool Lone, one of Bulbul's earliest Lavanya converts, to side with the maharani was an unexpected positive development and Shah Mir knew that the sympathy of the public was with Kotarani. Aged by the death of her husband, Kotarani focused on her subjects, whom she treated as having been widowed alongside her. She gave special attention to the women and had them trained in crafts so that they could work during the long winter months. *As the summer rain allays dust and heat and nourishes plants, even so she brought back prosperity to her subjects.*

Meanwhile, the investigation into Raja Sapru's and Guhara's deaths dragged on, awaiting the confession of one of the murderous bands. Kotarani was not going to make a move based on her suspicion alone against Shah Mir, the fakir and Sheikh in order to avoid a further crisis in the kingdom. The trio lay low biding their time, and little was heard from them.

Time passed and winter gave way to spring. The flocks of migrating birds returning to China and Siberia from the plains of the subcontinent filled the Valley: brown-headed gulls, great cormorants, bar-headed geese, all engaged in their annual return migration from the south to the north. They would rest at the banks of the lakes in Kashmir. The evenings were a wondrous sight: as twilight unfolded into the Valley the birds would first rise up to the sky from the marshy land where they had been feeding on the grain and tiny fish, gaining weight and strength for their onward journey and circle in the sky increasing in numbers, their shrieks dominating the landscape. Eventually several hundreds of thousands of birds wheeled in intricate circular patterns, interweaving their V formations through those of their neighbours, all without any collisions. Then as the sun dipped on the horizon behind the mountains and night quickly blanketed the hills, the birds dived downwards, flattening their wings and landing on the water, where they would float placidly. More and more of the birds would land, each seemingly very sure as to whom they wanted to have as their neighbour for the night. The sight was breathtaking, filling anyone who was witness to it with awe. If one needed proof of the hand of the Devi, surely it was to be found in watching the coordinated flight patterns of the hundreds of thousands of birds wheeling in perfect synchronization, painting broad arcs on the canvas of the sky. When darkness came, so did the silence as the birds slept, those at the periphery keeping a subconscious watch for any predators that might attempt to approach the floating population bobbing on the water.

Haigam and Hokasur were two favourite haunts of these birds, and the first reports of a mysterious illness came from those two villages. The domestic poultry had been seriously infected and was dying. The first symptoms were failing egg production and ruffled feathers; then within forty-eight hours almost all of the infected flock would be dead. Kotarani ordered the Brahmins to inoculate the villagers; with their indigenous knowledge, they were successful to a certain extent.

It was therefore not a complete surprise when news arrived that Shah Mir had been stricken with the same flu and that his end was near. Kotarani's council met to decide what needed to be done. After all, in spite of Shah Mir's treacherous behaviour, he was still the commander-in-chief of the kingdom and had a following in the Valley. After debating the pros and cons, an offer to send medical help was deemed to be the most humanitarian thing to do. The question arose as to who should go and the captain of the Kishtwar regiment was chosen. But Brahma was not happy.

'It is a mistake to send a military officer when the situation is so tense between Shah Mir and us. I will go.'

Kotarani immediately voiced her disapproval.

'Brahma, I do not trust Shah Mir. I would never forgive myself if any harm were to come to you. The jyotish has cautioned me that these people breed evil conspiracies.'

Brahma tried to reason with Kotarani.

'I have the best relationship of trust with Shah Mir even if some distance has come between us. I am also your best representative; the public will see that we care for Shah Mir. It will give me a chance to reason with him and bring him back within the fold. As far as security is concerned, the captain will be with me so there is nothing to fear. Finally, it is my dharma since I am bound by *Raksha Bandhan* to protect you.'

Kotarani's council agreed with Brahma's proposal and disbanded. Brahma stayed behind alone with the maharani. She came up to him and held him tight.

'After losing Udyandev I cannot bear the thought of putting you in harm's way.'

Brahma made light of Kotarani's concerns.

'Silly, I am going to regain Shah Mir as our friend. After all he was the one who protected my life when Dulucha invaded Kashmir.'

Kotarani held Brahma tight, not wanting to let him go. She kissed him.

'Brahma, you want to be a saviour but be extremely careful. This is not the same Shah Mir. I will see you on your return,' she whispered, and then turned and left.

Brahma walked outside where Avatar was waiting for him. The small contingent sped swiftly on their horses to Shah Mir's home on Chakradhara hill. When Brahma arrived he was surprised to see how many people were there; it was as if there was a standing army, many of whom did not seem to be from the Valley. As commander-in-chief, Shah Mir had control of the gates, and he had built a matrimonial alliance with the lord of the gates: it was obvious that the security of the kingdom had been severely compromised and that they had been flooded with outsiders, who were hiding with their local sympathizers. The people were congregating in small groups, talking in Farsi. There seemed to be a larger group gathered around a man seated in front of the door to the house. Brahma approached and was astonished to see that it was the fakir; he had heard that the exile had returned to the Valley, but assumed that he was hiding somewhere in the vicinity of the Khanqah. It was quite a different thing to see him in person. The fakir was ghastly pale, his anaemic body in need of blood. His abnormally large dome seemed to throb with hate. There was an absolute emptiness inside the fakir that made him dark to the world, and Brahma sensed it.

The fakir spoke first.

'The queen sends her faithful dog to sniff around. Have Shah Mir's enemies come to witness and celebrate his dying moments?'

'Who has put you in charge here? What is Shah Mir's condition?'

A supporter dressed in green spoke up.

'This man is our religious leader. His word is supreme here. Be careful.'

The fakir spoke again.

'You are here to see Shah Mir, but his condition is extremely bad. He has shivering fits, he is coughing badly, and his fever is running very high.'

'I want to see him. Lead us to him so that we can see what help we can provide to him.'

'That is impossible. He is in complete isolation: his family has been forcefully moved out, otherwise they too would fall victim to this grievous illness. Only I go visit him because Allah protects me.'

'Allah is great!' shouted the crowd.

Brahma was not afraid.

'We are here to see Shah Mir and we will see him. He cannot be left in the care of a murderer who was expelled from Kashmir.'

The crowd murmured and one supporter pulled out his sword at Brahma's words, but the fakir waved them back.

'Brothers, I am a wronged man. I do not even own the shirt on my back. For protecting the faith, I have to suffer in this life at the hands of people like this infidel – but Allah will grant me my reward, as most assuredly he will grant you yours.'

The crowd echoed, 'A vast reward will most assuredly be ours!'

Brahma repeated himself.

'I demand to see Shah Mir immediately.'

'I am a man of peace, sir. Why are you threatening me? Do you see any weapon on me? Even after this provocation I am willing to take one of you in. I would suggest that this young captain follow me – he can come back and give you a report on Shah Mir. Of course his life will be forfeit; not being blessed by me and not having Allah's protection, he will most assuredly contract the disease and die a horrible death.'

Avatar stepped forward.

'I am not afraid. If you have not contracted the disease, it is not communicable to humans. Take me.'

Brahma stopped him. When it came to risks he was not going to be a coward and have somebody else take his place.

'We will both go in. Tell your men to wait for us.'

The fakir smiled at Brahma's words, baring his teeth.

'It is still not too late to take the Kalima and convert. With Allah's protection you can go and visit Shah Mir.'

'Allah was not able to protect Shah Mir. I will place my trust in myself. Lead the way.'

'Do not doubt Allah or his powers,' the fakir said stiffly. 'If Allah wants Shah Mir, then it is Allah's wish and command, not failure. I am but his servant who seeks equality and morality.'

'You are no servant, instead you like playing God. The Kashmiri Bhattas call you the white wolf in shepherd's clothing and they are right.'

'You Kashmiris like your rishis to retire in caves and contemplate their navel. That is the work of monkeys and mice. Well, I am neither and not out of sight or out of mind either. I will champion the people against oppression, even if it means martyrdom.'

Brahma responded curtly.

'The rishis I know are seekers of truth and seers for humanity, personal role models of peace, morality and compassion, not murderers clothed as self-anointed saviours. Enough! We can argue outside or we can go in?'

The fakir stood up, wrapped his shawl around his body and walked inside. Brahma and Avatar followed. It was a big house and they went up some narrow, curved steps in single file. At the landing, the fakir knocked on one of the doors and they entered a room. Before they could approach Shah Mir, the fakir signalled to them that Avatar should leave his sword by the door. The captain refused, but Brahma signalled to him that it was acceptable for him to do so. The fakir took the sword in his hands.

Brahma and Avatar approached Shah Mir, who was resting in the bed with his face turned away.

'Who is it?' he asked weakly.

Brahma was quite affected by the scene and the sight of Shah Mir.

'Shah Mir, it is I, Brahma. I have come to inquire about your health. The maharani has commanded me that no stone be left unturned to cure you. The Brahmins will send their best doctors if you so command.'

'I fear it is too late,' Shah Mir whispered. 'My body is wracked with fever. My tongue is dry like parchment. I break out into sweats and there is pain in every muscle and joint.'

'It is never too late,' Brahma reassured. 'Shah Mir, you and your family saved my life when Dulucha came into Kashmir. I am forever indebted to you. The Brahmins can work miracles – but they need your permission. I have seen them rescue people who were given up for dead.'

'Brahma, it is good that you came,' Shah Mir said in a hoarse voice. 'The maharani is a good woman, even if we have had our differences. Come closer and lift me up so that I can rest against the headboard and look at you as I talk to you.'

Brahma went to the other side of the bed. He and Avatar gently lifted Shah Mir up but as they did so, the fakir suddenly tossed Avatar's sword into his hands: Shah Mir took the sword and thrust it first into Brahma's chest. Avatar tried to save Brahma with his bare hands, but the fakir clasped them from behind. Shah Mir rose from the bed like a coiled cobra and plunged the already bloody sword inside Avatar.

> *He buried their own weapon in their own bodies and thus allayed the illness of his mind. Blood issued from their heads and water came out of their eyes; their lives left their bodies and the rancour that Shah Mir had felt left his mind. Shah Mir was bathed in their blood as one bathes after recovery from illness; their two heads were like the two halves of a vessel and their wounds were like the marks of the lamp.*[18]

'Jamaat!' the fakir shouted out loudly.

The people who were hanging outside the door rushed in, led by Sheikh; when they saw the two dying men bleeding on the floor they started hacking at them with their swords. They were like hyenas, ripping pieces off their prey while the fakir and Shah Mir watched them, smiling. Sheikh, Puj and Ali, along with their cohorts, picked up the mangled bodies, carried them outside and threw them in front of the shocked attendants who had accompanied Brahma and Avatar on their mission of mercy. The terrorized attendants were made to load the bodies on horseback and, amid the jeers of Shah Mir's followers, rushed back to the maharani.

It was a stunned court that assembled for the emergency meeting. Included were the representatives of all of the Damaras and nobility and the Brahmins; in the center of the room lay the corpses of Brahma and Avatar, wrapped in white cloth. Sharika was sitting next to her husband, speechless at what had befallen him.

The first to speak was the minister of justice. It was a simple case of premeditated, cold-blooded murder; the verdict was death. Shah Mir was absent, so the maharani asked if anyone would speak to defend him. A gasp could be heard when several hands went up. There was Lusta; there was Tilakshura, even the brazen Kampana had joined in for this historic moment. Lusta was charged to present the defence.

'Lords and lady, 'I will speak as the voice of deterrence of passion. In our heat we are ready to condemn Shah Mir. But who out of us was present there when this deed happened? Let me remind all here that Shah Mir and Brahma were friends, and they each brought up one of the maharani's sons; so they are, in a way, equally close to her. The maharani has to look at Shah Mir as her left eye, just as she looked to Brahma as her right eye. Who knows what happened in the bedroom, what misunderstanding occurred, who attacked whom? Perhaps they had an argument as to who should ascend the throne. Each one forcefully represented one's ward. The best that can be said is that fate killed one and made the other the instrument. Where fate has intervened, we have no business overriding its judgement. Where fate has anointed that Haider is the future ruler, who are we to challenge it?'

'You dotard!' Brahma's son Bhima, his eyes red with grief, yelled. 'You have been corrupted by Shah Mir, as have those next to you! Shah Mir's daughters have married you and circumcised your brains. These are aliens who have entered our land! They were criminals fleeing their lands and they sought sanctuary in Kashmir. Here they have gone back on every oath of loyalty they took, broken every trust! Yet, even they are not as dangerous as you because ostensibly you are one of us and yet you are sold to them. In the guise of fairness you thwart us. Kashmir's descent into hell is beginning as we talk and dither listening to you. Retaliation is also prescribed as legitimate in Islam! An eye for an eye – if we do not act now we will be lost forever.'

Lusta spoke.

'Again, I say I understand your pain. But let us not forget that it was Shah Mir's wife who suckled you as a baby. There would be no you without Shah Mir. Let us follow the path of peace.'

Sharika spoke softly.

We are the Devas and parees, the fairies, of this land. Our ancestors have lived here from time immemorial. Nobody ever interfered or obstructed our affairs. Shah Mir arrived and then the fakir. Some groups from our community adopted Bulbul's faith of Islam and its tenets and laws. But after his death Shah Mir and the fakir have destroyed us the way a beast would. They have to be hunted down the way a beast should.'

There was a murmur in the crowd, and many heads were nodding. The sympathies of the crowd were clearly with Brahma's son and widow who were sitting next to her husband's corpse.

Suddenly there was a movement in the hallway. The crowd parted as one of the missing noblemen had shown up slightly late. It was Ravan.

He had aged in the decades since his withdrawal from court, but there was still the look of somebody that had been deprived of his right. It was in the sneer that seemed to say that he really did not care, but he did. He wore a long, white beard now. Irrespective of the sentiments that people had towards him, protocol dictated that he now was the senior-most among the attendees and had a right to speak.

'What has happened has happened. If this august assembly were to discuss all that has happened in Kashmir, right and wrong, there would be no end to it. I do know one thing: whether Shah Mir had a fever or whether he was faking it, a change has come over him. He is all but mad. You may believe that you are wronged; Shah Mir believes that he is the aggrieved party. He believes that Brahma was sent to assassinate him. He has sent me with a warning that he will sacrifice others and spare no one in the blazing fire of his anger.'

The minister of justice stared at Ravan for a long moment before he spoke.

'In my profession I am quite used to criminals making threats to undermine justice; I am also quite used to finding that truth becomes a casualty in the pursuit of justice. Very rarely are there eyewitnesses to such crimes, but it is here that one relies on circumstantial evidence. First, our Brahmins have unequivocally stated that the bird infection is very rarely transmitted to humans, but when it is, it is fatal. Ravan, you are an eyewitness to the fact that Shah Mir is alive. This is proof that his illness was faked and a premeditated plot. Second, the assassination allegation is a red herring. Brahma never held a sword in his life; he would not know how to use it. Avatar was a military man. If he had wanted to, he could have made mincemeat out of Shah Mir and the fakir. It is evident that when the three of them went up to Shah Mir's room, civil rules required that Avatar not carry his sword in with him. He must have handed it to the fakir, whom we know to have committed murder on a previous occasion. Finally, if Shah Mir is truly innocent and merely defending himself, then why this?'

With stiff steps the minister of justice walked over to the corpses. He stood in front of Sharika so that she was shielded from the bodies, and ripped one of the white covers away. A gasp went through the assembled crowd. The bodies had been mutilated beyond measure. The eyes had been gouged out; hollow holes stared out of the half skull that was cut with deep gashes. Their scrotums had been ripped. Every inch of their chests had been stabbed; but what was truly ghoulish was that there were bite marks on the bodies. The minister hastily put the white cover back on the bodies.

'The torture is a message from Shah Mir, a human turned into beast. He has shown that he speaks one thing, means a second thing and does a third thing. No man is above the law, not even Shah Mir, commander-in-chief of our kingdom. He has betrayed his trust and his duty to protect our people. He portrays himself as the aggrieved party, but every criminal denies his act. It is my duty to ask that the maharani sentence him, the fakir and Sheikh to death. Maharani, it is your duty to carry out the sentence to the best of your ability.'

The court had never seen the minister of justice so angry, but everyone had been affected by Brahma's murder. Shah Mir's apologists moved into a small circle with Ravan, knowing that they had lost the battle of public opinion. Ravan still had the last word.

'Passing a death sentence on Shah Mir is tantamount to passing a death sentence on Kashmir. The people are ready to revolt against the Brahmins; the kingdom has no commander-in-chief. The cavalry is with Shah Mir, as are the Chaks, and the fakir has assembled thousands of jihadis to swoop in and finish what Dulucha left undone. This is time to be pragmatic and reach an agreement; Shah Mir and his people have legitimate grievances that need to be heard. They have legitimate rights that cannot be trampled over.'

At that point, Maqbool Lone stepped into the centre of the room. He was a very popular Lavanya, and after Kampana's folly he had become their de facto leader.

'I have flirted with Shah Mir – as have all of us. He is an outsider, and he came in and instantly saw that we were a divided group of people. He skilfully exploited our divisions to rise to the point where now he threatens our very existence. There is a time to talk, and there is a time to fight. I am now no longer confused by what has happened in Kashmir with the arrival of Shah Mir and the Chaks and the other outsiders: they have one agenda, and that is to import their brethren from outside and take control of Kashmir. Our tolerant "live and let live" way of life is now threatened by the terror of the Fakir's way. I became a Mussalman but I am a Kashmiri first. I am proud of our culture and will not permit this alien vulture culture that feeds on death. I commit myself unequivocally to the maharani. The Lavanyas are not so bereft of power that they cannot give a fitting reply to Shah Mir, the fakir and their jihadis.'

All eyes turned to the maharani; she walked up to the weeping Sharika and held her. With pursed lips and her heart shattered, Kotarani pronounced her royal decision.

'Sharika, I ask for your forgiveness for sending Brahma to his death. I give this judgment as the guru of all classes. Shah Mir, the fakir and Sheikh are sentenced to death. Layla gave love and is deserving of all love and she will receive all support through her travails. Any and all parties who ally themselves with Shah Mir will be treated as enemies of the state; they will be imprisoned and their properties expropriated. This was an act of monstrous evil, and cannot under any circumstances be condoned.'

Ravan and his coterie turned and left without saying a word. Kota watched to see if Ravan felt any regret about Brahma, his childhood idol, but he did not show it. If he had any feelings of sorrow for his widowed sister, he did not share it.

Dearest Mother,

Today I feel the excruciating pain that hell reserves for its most wretched. Each cut that Brahma suffered eviscerates my heart a hundred times over. What must Sharika feel and what must she think about me? I bleed for her. When I saw Ravan today I wanted to ask him, 'Is the throne so important that you have sold your soul to the devil?' I wanted to see the look on his face if I had said, 'Here, take it and see if it gives you fulfilment.' Devaswami says evil is imbedded at creation and we cannot abdicate in the battle that goes on in the microcosm and the macrocosm. I am a Kshatriya warrior, and for me my dharma is to slay adharma and my pronouncement on Brahma's killers is one that I am at peace with. His death will be avenged and justice will be delivered. In fact, with his physical departure I am reconciled that as each piece of my life detaches I am coming closer to you. Now I understand what Father was preparing me for when he trained me to detach my mind, place the Devi in my heart, go into battle and feel no pain. Once I settle Shah Mir's treacherous insurrection and bring peace to Kashmir, I will bring Chander and Jatta together, talk to them about what plans they have to get married and abdicate the throne to them.

Now I only want to travel through my vast land and experience its beauty, meet the people, give them the love they have given me, visit the temples and write my journal so that you can read all about the wonders of Kashmir that you missed. The Hanjis are lovely people and maybe I will travel in one of their boats on the River Vitasta. It will only be a foursome, just Saras, Chand, who in spite of a very hard life always remains optimistic, and his shapely yogini wife. They say that I am the greatest queen of Kashmir, the empress! Who knows whether that is true, but the yogini is certain to be famous as Kashmir's Devi. She is fearless in her own unconventional way and is a great match for Chand. I find an inner purity in her and feel a oneness with her. I treat her as my younger sister and realize that she was as much a victim as I was that fateful night at the cemetery, and that she practised her dharma as best as she knew how.

Mother, sometimes I wish I had a daughter. Keep watch over me as you always do.

Love ॐ

It was war, and Kotarani sent her message out: *No Peace until Victory!*

Preparations for the final battle began. The Lavanyas took charge of the defence of the capital under Lone's supervision: there were materials to be collected, men to be trained, and loyalties to be strengthened. Shah Mir had control of Kashmir's perimeter – he had power of the gates, which meant he had the traders as well, and they would bring him all the supplies that he needed. With Shah Mir slowly preparing to tighten like a boa constrictor, Lone had to build the inner core and then expand it until the two forces met. And only one would prevail.

It was then that news came from Jayapidapura of an insurrection. It seemed that there had been a shortage of rice and the public had rebelled against the local revenue agents. Concerned for her people and worried that tension might escalate, the queen departed. She stationed herself at the fort of Andarkot to personally direct operations, but it turned out that the reports were false. The local Damara had been corrupted by Shah Mir to put diversionary pressure on Kotarani. Realizing that it was a ruse, she removed the Damara from his position and rushed back to the capital. Filled with deep foreboding, she put her troops on a forced march; but even though they travelled back with the greatest of haste it was not fast enough for her beating heart.

The maharani's absence had created an opening for Shah Mir and his people, who had attacked Srinagar during Kotarani's absence. The Lavanyas fought bravely and, step by step, they drove Shah Mir and his followers out of the city. Ali and his cavalry were not as effective in hand-to-hand fighting: the Lavanyas dragged the cavalry off their horses and captured them. Lone fought with Ali and slew him, rousing the Lavanyas and causing the cavalry to surrender.

Shah Mir, hard-pressed, sent emissaries to his feudal relatives. When victory was in sight for the Lavanyas, the forces of Lusta – the lord of the Marches – arrived out of nowhere and launched a strong counter-offensive, surrounding the Lavanyas and defeating them. Khazanchi's money had provided the right inducement at a pivotal moment in purchasing Lusta to act in favour of Shah Mir. The maharani and her forces raced for the capital, but it was too late. Kumara ran into them, having escaped through the secret tunnel with Saras, Sharika and Bhima and a few other loyalists such as Chand. However, the enemy had captured Jatta. Kumara also brought the sad news that Lone had been killed along with many other brave warriors. The capital had fallen!

Kotarani had no choice but to return to Andarkot – situated in the middle of a marshy lake and impregnable – to prepare for a long siege until new alternatives presented themselves. When the maharani and her bedraggled party reached the fort, they crossed the causeway and shut the gate behind them with a deep sense of insecurity; how long this temporary state would last before the next challenge presented itself was unknown, but for now the fortress offered respite from the encroaching dark forces.

During a lull after the battle, a triumphant Sheikh had an interesting visit: Manzim had come to him in his official capacity. A prominent Damara had offered his daughter Indrakshi in marriage to Sheikh. Manzim had addressed him most respectfully as Sheikh, with no hint of allusion to their past relationship. The fakir sat next to Sheikh, watching the proceedings and when Manzim had finished, Sheikh looked to him for guidance. He nodded his head in agreement.

'Son, the Damara understands the value of an alliance with Sheikh. But we have to do things in the proper way. The girl has to be brought to me and be educated by me, rather than the school that she is going to. When she has converted, I will draw up a proper marriage contract; only then can the marriage be consummated. She has to understand that after her marriage her proper role will be to have children. Motherhood is the most glorious of roles and deserving of respect.'

Manzim understood the conditions.

'The bride's side is eager to tie the knot. The girl is beautiful, if her education is an issue that can be remedied easily.'

The fakir smiled again.

'When the girl is brought over, Manzim, make sure that she is properly attired. I also hold you responsible to make sure that the girl is chaste. As you know our Sheikh is a chaste man and Islam does not permit him to marry a woman of loose morals. You know only too well with Kashmiri women that you can never be quite sure, can you?'

'Indrakshi is a most virtuous maiden. Her nickname is Red Apple, for she blushes at the slightest impropriety. Her parents have raised her in a way that she delights the heart with her purity of spirit. With her striking red hair she is a true beauty.'

The fakir was dismissive.

'Words, words, words, you can never trust the Kashmiris, can you, Manzim? Our way is superior. Everything is written in the marriage contract. It is there in plain sight for everyone. If either party defaults, there are automatic penalties. If the woman misbehaves, she gets beaten. Men are superior to women which is a lesson that all Kashmiri women will have to learn as part of Naya Kashmir.'

Manzim nodded politely. He could do business under any and all conditions, but the girl had to be prepared for what was in front of her. He never let his emotions get in the way of a deal; it would have been unprofessional. But he knew what had happened to Sheikh and what that might mean for the girl. She was an artist; she loved to read and write stories. Kotarani was her role model and someday she wanted to write a book about the maharani. It was going to be a very difficult situation for her. But Kashmiri girls were resilient; Manzim consoled himself that she would be fine.

Sheikh had the final word.

'Manzim, keep your commission low. If you do a good job, perhaps other commissions may come your way. Suhdev was not the only man who could have a harem. Sheikh will first take a bite of the Red Apple; but then he plans to have his fill. After all, in Kashmir, life is meant to be enjoyed to the fullest.'

Manzim looked at the man who had once been his friend – from barber to murderer, rapist, and lately moral policeman.

'You are my most honoured client. It shall be exactly as you wish.'

Wave 20
Parting

KOTA was strategizing with Kumara on what steps Shah Mir might take next. Her face was wan and there were lines around her eyes. Yaniv was also present and she had asked Tatiana and the Soporis to join them. Chand was sitting discreetly at a distance, as was his wont.

'He will declare Haider maharaja; Ravan will provide the imprimatur to that announcement and then the rest of the Damaras will follow suit. He will use Jatta as a prisoner and ask for you to abdicate in Haider's favour.'

'Is that enough to satisfy him? If I renounce the throne of Kashmir, will there be peace?'

'No, that is not the only thing that he will want. Remember, he thought that he would end up with the treasure, but it is not in the fort; Lusta took what little was found there. Shah Mir and the fakir have a huge army of malcontents under them who have been converted to their cause on the prospect that a vast reward awaits them. These people have to be driven to loot because if they don't feed the beast, they risk their discontent, which will be their end.'

'The people have suffered greatly because of the repeated attacks by the enemy.' Kotarani said grimly. 'Suhdev read Shah Mir wrong when he welcomed him inside Kashmir and provided him all facilities; I read Rinchina wrong, what if we are wrong again? We dismissed the Sogdian as a paranoid alarmist but he was ringing the right alarm bells. We were not vigilant about the loyalty of the new immigrants or about the new converts to our civilization and its values. Kumara, what if you are not reading reality right? We left the capital and fell for their ruse. We lack a military mind. I do miss the presence of my father and don't know whom to turn to. Yaniv, what do you think?'

Yaniv heaved a sigh.

'Maharani, Shah Mir has made his choice and now he will not be able to get off the white wolf. I am afraid that we have to plan for the worst.'

'You are afraid that my end is near.'

'It is a possibility we should not ignore since Shah Mir has made you the bait by painting you as what stands between the people and the vast treasure of Kashmir,' Yaniv said grimly.

'Who out there owes us a debt of gratitude that we can seek assistance from in our hour of need?' Kota asked.

Kumara thought for a moment.

'Maharani, China owes us more than it does anyone else. We have sent over 500 Bhattas, our jewels, to guide them over the last 1,500 years. They recognize their debt and in the time of the great emperor Lalitaditya they sent an auxiliary force of 200,000 men to support him in his military campaign.'

'Should we approach them now?'

'Maharani, it is unlikely that their emperor Toghun Temur, who is racked by insurgency and a rebellion against his salt monopoly, will assist us. In addition, the Delhi sultan, Muhammad bin Tughlaq, has already planted his ambassador, the Moroccan Ibn Batuta, inside the Chinese court. Someday they will help the Kashmiri Bhattas, but not today.'

'If Yaniv is right, what can I do to ensure the Bhattas are victorious?' Kota asked Kumara.

Kumara answered slowly.

'Our people's history tells us that everything that is lost can be regained. Everything that was once created can be recreated. Truth is a non-perishable asset and retaining our knowledge pathways are guarantees to our continuity, multiplicity and elevation. But I find myself believing that the better person to answer your question is Yaniv.'

'Queen, it is no secret, and it is no different from what the Kashmiris do today,' Yaniv stated. 'The Jews have survived in exile based on connectivity to their Torah, to their covenant, to their remembrance of their holy land, to their way of life. It was a revelation when I found the similarity between the Star of David and the dejhoor. I am now a Kashmiri Jew and the Mammasvamin temple is my temple. As long as succeeding generations of Kashmiris remember, understand and practise what is precious not just to them but to all of humanity, the two intertwined S's, Shiva–Shakti, universal consciousness and its connectivity with the force within you, they will survive, prosper and have victory.'

Kotarani made her decision.

'Yaniv, I want you to embark on a very dangerous mission. I want you to lead the children out of this fort. Saras, I release you to return to China.'

'Maharani, I am an old woman now and my heart is full of pain,' Saras sobbed. 'But between searching for my mother's family in the vast land of China and being with the children, I choose to accompany Yaniv. Every night, I will tell them a story and every morning they will turn towards Kashmir and salute the land of the Devi of knowledge. Even in exile, the future of the Kashmiris will be safe until it is time for them to return without danger to their homeland.'

'Maharani, who will take care of you?' Kumara asked. 'Saras has been by your side all your life.'

'Yes, she has, and she always will be. But now she will take care of what is most important to me and the future of the Kashmiris. It is she who will make sure that the children hear and remember the stories of Kashmir. Our history gives us self awareness which is our most precious asset.'

Yaniv spoke, 'Queen, I am humbled by the responsibility for this exodus.'

Kota said, 'The Valley is being swept by a taranga that is drowning our civilization. I remember you once telling me the story of Noah and how similar it was to our story of the Great Flood and Manu. Someday they will tell the story of how you were the Noah of our people and led our children to safety.'

'Kashmir gave me refuge when I needed it,' Yaniv said sadly. 'Now I have to move again. I will dedicate my life to bringing the children up. But how will we leave the fortress? Shah Mir is watching every single move that we make.'

'Yes, he is, but he is not watching the boat people who ply the lake,' Kotarani explained, 'and the washerwoman is one of them. She will arrange for a boat on a night when I will create a diversion. There is enough room for all of you and the young children will accompany you. Then Chand will take you out of the Valley by the back ways known only to him.'

'Where will we go?'

Kumara spoke up.

'Our ancestors came from the banks of the River Saraswati. Ask for the Saraswats in the south and join them and raise the children there. They will train them so that they never lose their power.'

'Maharani, what plans do you have for yourself?'

'For myself, I plan to go on a fast and secure victory by personally confronting Shah Mir.'

'Maharani, is it a wise course of action after what he did to Brahma?' Kumara asked.

'Kumara, it is more than wise. I am totally convinced that it is the only way forward. He will either give in or I will jump through the hoop of time. Either way I win. I hope that I have your blessing. Yaniv, you will need provisions and money for your mission. Come closer.'

Yaniv approached Kotarani. She reached inside her gown and took out a small box. She opened the box and Yaniv saw Suryavansh shining inside.

Kotarani spoke softly.

'Yaniv, this is my gift to you and the children. With Suryavansh, you and your descendants will become jewellers to the maharajas of the world. Use part of the income to support the children.'

Yaniv bowed his head at the command and spoke slowly.

'So you are sending Suryavansh out of Kashmir, but the jyotish had said that Suryavansh would never leave Kashmir. He was wrong.'

Kotarani spoke firmly.

'Each child is the future of Kashmir, and Suryavansh is accompanying Kashmir. Never forget what you said about the Kashmiri way – truth, beauty and bliss through knowledge and consciousness. May the Devi bless all of you and the children.'

Kumara spoke up with feeling.

'Maharani, I can objectively say that you will be seen as the greatest queen of Kashmir and in Indian history, ever captivating yet never captive. No more could have been asked for, no more could have been expected and no more could have been done. You have given us hope for the future.'

Kumara, Tatiana and Yaniv, Chand and his wife bowed and departed, leaving the maharani alone, deep in thought.

Kotarani bent her head low, perhaps so that nobody could see the tears in her eyes. She opened the pendant that she had worn around her neck. It was her mother's portrait as painted by the artist Santoshi who had given it to her. His craft had outlived him. Looking at her mother's picture, memories of her youth flooded into her mind: her father, her guru, Saras, Brahma and then her children. She felt a pang of loneliness but with it came peace. Kotarani picked up her diary.

Dear Mother,

You were without fear and set a very high bar for your daughter. Many mistakes were made before I inherited the throne. My father had trained me to be watchful of the attacks from the enemy without but we were not watchful of the inroads the enemy made within. I should have never accepted the sapphire from Rinchina and never compromised on the fakir. Their combination of sinister ambition and murderous fanaticism has betrayed the Kashmiri ethos. For the first time the common Kashmiri man is ready to kill his fellow man. I have ruled for a long time. I promise you that with me at their head the Bhattas will never surrender and the Kashmiri dream will not die.

Love 𝒦

The tears flowed slowly. Kashmir was in her heart, and her heart was in Kashmir. She saw her future in its fate; her fate in its future, as foretold ages ago, when she was at Sharadapeeth. Looking at a dewdrop, she had known the answer and answered correctly. Now she was living it.

Devaswami's sleep was increasingly marred by nightmares of a kind that he had never experienced before. He saw humans become inhuman and then subhuman as their mental development regressed. Terrible earthquakes shook the Valley of Kashmir, bringing the mountains down and raining rocks into the Valley, slamming into the ground and crushing every man-made structure like grain in a mortar. Fire engulfed the forests turning them into ash. Smoke rose in the air like a smothering blanket, blocking the sun. His eyes filled with sand from the wasted land. Day turned into night; lightning and thunderbolts searched hungrily to hunt and destroy anything that moved or stood out. Mighty stone temples became like molten wax, sinking to the ground. Living creatures were vaporized instantly, their collective souls shrieking into the ether the unbearable agony of their last moments. In many of his nightmares Kotarani would be in the distance calling out his name seeking his prayers to the Devi to save her people.

Devaswami tried to whisper his protective mantras to dispel the nightmare, but his lips would not move. He found himself paralysed, as if the Devi was determined that he be a mute witness to the destruction of Kashmir. He was the last man standing, the person who had to light the fire that would result in the cremation of the world. The angry Vitasta was a blood-red, liquid, uncoiled snake; giant boulders falling from the mountains viciously blocked its path, forcing it high in the sky; the frothing waters rose and fell in panic, roaring as they searched for a way out of the Valley where the demon forces were determined to pin it down. Then the rain fell, sharp, red acid burning the rocks, singeing whatever green grass remained on the ground. Kashmir had turned from paradise into hell. Devaswami saw the cycle of evolution begin anew. Single cells jelled patiently to form larger creatures. In the shadows embryonic monsters were beginning to emerge, mutations too gruesome to describe. Even these creatures were bound not only by evolutionary forces but by karmic laws; as they developed, they regressed back in endless loops to earlier creatures. It was the end of the Kashmiri race.

When Devaswami woke he could not move. His heart was pounding, and his limbs refused to obey his commands. Shikasdevi had revealed her *roopa* and her form was fearsome. Unchained she would grow in strength until she would strike with her apocalyptic fury. He knew what he had to do. He clambered out of his bed weakly and called for a Brahmin *chela*. The acolyte came in and saw immediately that something was not right. Devaswami instructed the young boy to make arrangements for a yagna to the goddess in the temple. Time was of the essence if Kashmir was to be saved from the wrong turn it was taking. The mighty Tripura energies had to be fused in the very mountains of Kashmir if the Kashmiris were to have any chance of long-term survival. The yagna lasted a whole week. The last step was a prayer in the temple where a dozen senior Brahmins faced Kashmira Devi holding a mirror wooden image of the Sharada idol on a palanquin. As Devaswami prayed, the Brahmins swayed the palanquin gently from side to side but always with the two idols facing each other. Having completed the deconsecrating ceremony so that the Devi could be transported, Devaswami prepared to leave. Only one final task remained. The Sharadapeeth temple bell was rung loudly. All across the Valley the temple priests stopped what they were doing. They had been trained to recognize this sound pattern, but it had never been rung before. Then they raced to their own temple bells and started ringing madly. The Devi was on the move from the Valley! The mountains recognized the sound and solemnly echoed back their answer, *Empress, we await you.*

All the Brahmins were assembled in the main hall waiting for Devaswami when he entered with the palanquin following him. There was a hush among the seated audience as he walked in. He folded his hands and began to speak.

'Today is my last lecture and I address you as *yoddha*s, warriors of truth. Terror has invaded Kashmir but we are no strangers to terror. From times immemorial when we say our thanksgiving prayer before a meal we end it by reciting *Atankahinam jagadastu sarvam*. May the whole world be free of terror. Yodhas, you have to cope with a long war. You are the representatives of the Sharada civilization, which for three-and-a-half millennium gave unmatched progress to its people. The world around us is changing and in the foreseeable future there will be two kinds of Kashmiris. There will be those Kashmiris who will obsess about the body of Kashmir, and there will be those Kashmiris who at dawn will salute Kashmir and with intense focus concentrate on its Sharada spirit. Those who are unchanging like rocks will bind themselves with this earth and fight for the land, the gold and other earthly treasures; those who flow like the River Vitasta will concern themselves with our civilization and be inspired by what has made Kashmir, the crown of Asia and the guiding light of the world. Being rooted gives comfort, whereas embracing movement brings freedom and progress. Remember our own ancestors came to Kashmir from the banks of the River Saraswati when it dried out. Do we now look back to the River Saraswati as our home?

'Kashmir's knowledge supreme is individual empowerment based on the grand techniques to the truth of *Sat*, reality, in all its manifestations. You have the key to the 5,000-year-old techniques that start with desire and take you on the Sharada pathway of knowledge and action, aesthetics and consciousness, a pathway, which maximizes human development, yielding complete fulfilment and liberation. Now I leave to ensure that the Brahmins will forever be able to perform their duties to the Devi in their holy land. When you leave, never forget that as teachers you have a responsibility to humanity that you have to fulfil. You have to teach those who seek freedom versus bondage how to realize truth versus ignorance, beauty versus hideous and bliss versus agitation. *Satyam, Sundaram, Shaktam,* our strength trinity of uncompromising truth, beauty and unconditional love. Redouble your resolve to stand for what Pandit Vishnu Sharma taught us: *Vasudhaiva*

Kutambakam, inclusivity, diversity and multiplicity, but only when there is a state of *vidya*, knowledge. I leave now to await the maharani's arrival. She needs me, yodhas, and as her spiritual preceptor I will always be there to guide her.'

The brief sermon ended. The Brahmins walked past Devaswami to get his blessing. He gave each one of them a walnut and devdar seeds. When the line had ended, he walked out of Sharadapeeth. He never looked back but steadfastly followed the ten Brahmins carrying the palanquin with the Devi ahead of him. The count of eleven moved at a steady pace accompanied by the piercing sound of the clanging cymbal.

At the mosque Sheikh was wracking his brains. The fakir was always challenging him to think big: their movement was a global one. How could he be more useful? One of his spies had come to report that Devaswami had been walking with a dozen Brahmins from village to village; he seemed to be heading to the village of Biru. Sheikh then experienced an epiphany: Devaswami was big, in some ways even bigger than Kotarani. What if Devaswami converted? Then there was the question of Sharadapeeth. Sheikh could not read and had no use for books; in any case the fakir had told him that the last word on any subject had already been written. There was no need for any other book when one had the final word. The books at Sharadapeeth had to be destroyed and the Brahmins there had to be forced into the service of the movement.

Humanity had to be brought under one law and one rule. The utopian prospect thrilled Sheikh – the notion that every single human being could be arranged like the stars in the heavens, each person moving in formation precisely according to God's instructions, was overwhelming. The fakir was the most inspirational human being Sheikh had encountered, and he agreed with the fakir that to think big one had to be radical in bringing change.

Sheikh was a man of action. With his fingers mimicking scissors in the air he commandeered his force and they set off for Varahamula. It took a full day of hard riding, but they picked up the trail easily. Soon they saw Devaswami and his band walking ahead of them. They seemed to be heading towards the mountain and it was pretty clear that Devaswami was going towards a cave. Sheikh recognized it as the Bahurupa cave, well known in the Valley. They were close enough to hear the Brahmins singing. Devaswami must have been aware that they were being followed by a group on horseback but he showed no reaction; not once did he turn back. Finally, they entered the cave and were out of sight, but the sound of the Brahmins praising Shiva reverberated through the Valley.

> Oh lords of Destruction
> Do not cast frightful and heartbreaking glances at me
> I have conquered the lords of Death
> And have attained union with absolute Consciousness
> The lords of Death cannot limit my unlimited self
> Since I am myself the towering presence of the Universe
> This frightens them
> I am all in all and have attained all-powerful identity
> Oh Lord, by your all-powerful spiritual revelations
> combined with a strong impulse of subtle vibrations of love and devotion
> has favoured my union with thee! Shivoham[19]

Sheikh could recognize the divine song, the *Bhairava Stotra Shiva Stuti* and it confused him for a moment. They were singing that he was frightened of them – he would show them who was really frightened! He thought about the group inside, and decided to hold fire; the fakir had told him that patience was important. Hours went by until he couldn't wait any longer: he ordered branches to be placed in front of the cave, and one of the men shot a flaming arrow at them. Sheikh and his men waited expectantly for the Brahmins to emerge like rats out of their holes. The fire grew in intensity: the wood crackled, and the smoke from the green leaves filled the entire front of the cave. *Any moment now it will happen.* But they waited in vain. No Brahmins appeared. Sheikh was enraged; obviously the cave had another entrance. Devaswami had escaped from the back. Just like the

Brahmins, always with a trick up their sleeve. They waited for the wood to cool down, then Sheikh led his men into the cave.

It was large, but shallow. The men looked around the rectangular room-like space, which could accommodate a dozen men. Stepping further inside, they found a small chamber where a stone lingam was visible. The space grew narrower and narrower until one could only walk sideways. The rocks on either side were smeared with vermillion. The passageway became smaller and advancing any further was physically impossible; there was no other exit. The Brahmins had simply disappeared into thin air, as if they had been absorbed into the mountain. The perplexed men came out, blinking their eyes to adjust from the darkness of the cave into the bright light. The sun stared at the men as its rays lit the dust particles oscillating in the air, billowing away from the opening to the cave. *Ulta*, reversal, was fundamental to the sun's nature: it reconverted matter back into waves as a matter of course. On the rare occasions that it happened on earth it was a cause of celebration, and the sun as witness to one such rare occurrence shone even brighter.

Sheikh knew he could not return from his expedition empty-handed. There were high expectations of him. Devaswami's mysterious disappearance might raise doubts in some minds – tongues would start whispering that he had let Devaswami escape. After all, he was a recent convert. He had to work twice as hard and achieve twice as much to demonstrate that he rightfully belonged. He told his men that they would head directly to Sharadapeeth. The men grumbled. It would be several days' hard march through the hills and they had not come prepared for a longer expedition; nonetheless, no one would defy Sheikh. His mind was set that Sharadapeeth would have to be torched, its books burnt, the temple razed to the ground, the stones scattered just as Dulucha had done. The men started their trek, the sun was burning hot, and it was with some relief that they watched it setting slowly beneath the hills. Evening would bring respite, and the men were looking forward to reaching the next village and bivouacking for the night. They were hungry, and the simple villagers would be made to show them proper respect – maybe the hospitality could even extend to some company for the night. The village headman should feel grateful that he was being given the opportunity to show some hospitality to the new rulers of the Valley, and that extended to their young women. Anything was now possible for Sheikh, and his loyal men fully intended to take advantage of the new opportunities.

As they approached the village, the men heard a scurrying and rustling of leaves and turned to see a haput bear burst upon them. They scattered instantly. The haput was attracted to the man dressed in striking green and he loped after him. Sheikh ran as fast as he could up the path, his breath coming in short, painful bursts; the bear was unfazed and came after him at a steady pace. He had patiently tracked them for a long time and was in no hurry. Finally, as if tired of the race, the bear accelerated and with one mighty swipe hit Sheikh on the back and sent him crashing to the ground. The bear pummeled him and rolled him over. Sheikh could see the bear, maddened by the heat, staring at him through his slit eyes. Fear gripped Sheikh, paralyzing him. *This cannot be happening. Life is just beginning to give me all I deserve. Is there no justice? How can I fall victim to this animal?*

It was in a primal, speechless state that Sheikh soundlessly screamed out for help, any help and all help: *Om Namoh Shivaya! Hey Ram!* and *Allah O Akbar!* raced through his mind. The bear's face drew closer and for a fleeting moment Sheikh thought that he saw the jogi staring at him. Maajae, 'Mother!' Sheikh cried out his final words and then death granted him what he had missed in life; equality and the objective chance to move up or down when reborn based on his karma.

When the news of Sheik's death broke in the capital, Shah Mir and the fakir had much to discuss.

'Sheikh is a martyr,' the fakir said. 'He was engaged in a mission and he laid down his life in doing his duty. He will be rewarded with seventy-two virgins with swelling breasts who will perform satisfactorily what they are purposed for.'

'This changes matters,' Shah Mir said. 'The Kashmiris are a very emotional people and can swing like a pendulum. We have to move fast.'

'There is nothing to fear,' the fakir stated. 'Our prey awaits us. The mouse trembles awaiting the cat. The fox shivers when it contemplates the arrival of the mighty lion. We have circled Kota, the fort, and we will capture Kota, the rani. I am confident the treasure is hidden there.'

The fakir was pleased with his clever use of language; he was beginning to pick up a few Brahmin literary tricks.

'Women trust jewels more than they trust anything else – it is in their fickle nature, which is why I am immune to them, or for that matter any temptation.'

'The woman lusts for power,' Shah Mir echoed. 'She married Rinchina for power, she disowned Haider for power, and she married and then retook Udyandev back for power. That is the key to her.'

'You must take her alive to get the secret of the treasure. No treasure, no reward.'

Shah Mir shook his head.

'Andarkot is impregnable in the centre of the lake. The people will not undertake so long a siege. Look at Lusta – yes, he saved us; but was that his purpose, or did he spot an opportunity to enrich himself? If the other side offers him a higher price, he will be gone.'

'Let me think about how to buy Lusta. You need to go on the offensive,' said the fakir.

The meeting ended. Shah Mir went on his way to meet his military forces to plan the next step in the campaign when to his great surprise his wife requested an audience with him. She always stayed in her quarters; it was his privilege to go to her. This was an unprecedented visit, and he watched her carefully when she entered the room.

Layla curtsied to him as she entered the room. As was her wont, she sat on the ground a few yards away from him with her face averted. It was a mark of respect and modesty to avoid eye contact with her master and husband. But Shah Mir could see that her eyes were red; she was obviously distraught.

She spoke hesitantly.

'Sharika asked to meet me at a safe house. She had one question for which I had no answer: did you murder Brahma?'

Shah Mir was quiet for a minute and then spoke in a reasonable tone.

'Brahma is gone. What do the circumstances of his death matter? It was right of you to console Sharika.'

'As Sharika left she said that in Kashmir one discovered one's true self. I no longer know the man that I am married to – I had my doubts as to how much you knew about Guhara, but you convinced me that you did not know the perpetrators. Now you refuse to respond to my question about Brahma.'

Shah Mir was beginning to get testy.

'You fool. Don't you understand what is going on here? This is all politics. First they thwarted me because I am a Mussalman. I did not give up, and now they want to destroy me. They have passed a death sentence on me, based on trumped-up charges. Now they are trying to attack me through my wife. Are you my equal in intelligence that you dare question me?'

Layla was not to be dissuaded.

'If you were innocent you could have gone to the maharani and defended yourself. If you are innocent why does your talk betray you? Do you know you talk in your sleep? It is your conscience speaking that you have chosen to throw your lot with the murderous fakir.'

'The fakir is pure! He believes in pure Islam, he is committed to my success! He is right that with the Kashmiris one has to conceal, deceive and surprise. Again, are you questioning my intelligence? Go back to the couch in your room; you are treading on dangerous ground!' Shah Mir screamed.

Layla turned her head and stared him straight in the eye.

'Have you forgotten what they say in Persia? If the first brick is laid crookedly, the wall will forever be crooked.'

Shah Mir could not believe this change in his wife. He spoke slowly.

'Do you understand what I just said? It was not a request; I command you. I will not tolerate rebellion.'

'It is not only you who came to Kashmir because you had a dream. I had a dream also, and my dream ended with Guhara's death. It is then that I realized that you had taken up with a *shaitan*. Sharika was right: that fakir is leading Kashmir to its doom, and you are his willing henchman.'

Shah Mir began screaming again.

'The fakir understands the need for the Kashmiri Mussalman to be distinctive. As for Guhara, I too can question you. It is you I hold responsible for breeding her rebellious spirit so that she took to music – and even dancing, I am told! I am on the verge of achieving my grandfather's hope. When I was lost in the forest and fell asleep it was Mahadevi, the great goddess of Kashmir, who consecrated me with the nectar of the words: *As long as your lineage exists, the dominion over Kashmir will be yours.* I came to Kashmir because of my dream and have worked for it all my life. I will not have you make a mockery of everything that I have worked for and everything that I stand for! Do not question my dream!'

'Distinctive yes, distinction no!' The hysterical woman would not stop. 'I knew your grandfather better than you. The great Waqur Shah was a pious and righteous man. He underwent severe penance, which enabled him to attain knowledge and a state of purity of the inner self. He received spiritual training and followed the path of truth. He held discourses with the wandering rishis from Kashmir and was amazed at their enlightenment. When he expressed his hope that you would become ruler of Kashmir, it was his hope that you would grow to be the ruler of truth and purity. What use did he have for money or power? What would he say today if he saw that his grandson had turned into a murderer in his pursuit of power? You have totally twisted your grandfather's words and wrongly interpreted them to justify your blind ambition. Just like the fakir whose pure Islam is twisted Islam.'

Shah Mir compressed his lips and then strode over to where his wife was seated on the ground. He grabbed her by the hair and began kicking her in her stomach, in her rear and thighs. His wife started crying loudly but Shah Mir did not stop his savage beating. When finally he was exhausted he threw her on the ground.

'I am of sober mind and my intention is clear,' he said in a clear voice. 'I hereby divorce you with *Talak Battah*. Your marriage contract will be honoured and all of your expenses will be taken care of during the *iddah*.'

She looked at him and without a trace of bitterness sobbed, 'Just like that, it is over?'

Shah Mir did not respond.

'Allah was thinking of me when he gave me the chance to suckle Sharika's son,' she continued. 'Little did I know then that I would have to beg for sanctuary in the home of the baby I suckled. Greed has extinguished the gratitude you should have in your heart. You are going to be a very lonely man for the rest of your life; the world now knows that you are capable of murdering even your best friend. But the world will also know that your wife had to seek shelter from the family you have most grievously wronged. Give me a travel pass, the *parpatra* so that I can return back to my family.'

Shah Mir remained silent, as though his wife did not exist. On hearing her request, he went to a corner in the room and wrote a note with flourish. He signed it and applied his seal to it and then threw it at her. With that he threw away the compass that had hitherto guided him. His wife picked up the note and painfully dragged herself out: it was the last time that they saw each other.

As Shah Mir ended his marriage, Kota's two sons were together once more in a room below. Jatta had been taken to Haider's quarters upon his capture and an armed guard was posted outside. Haider had said nothing, but it was obvious that he was happy to see Jatta, even in such inauspicious circumstances. Jamshed and Ali Sher entered the room and saw Haider in the corner reading the Koran, as he so often did. Jatta was by the window staring outside; though unarmed, he immediately adopted a defensive stance.

Jamshed was the first to speak.

'So we have the cubs. Soon we will have the lioness too.'

'Like father, like son,' Jatta retorted. 'You could not find anyone else to do your dirty work, so you had to come yourself.'

Ali Sher drew his sword.

'Corpses are meant to be viewed, not heard.'

At that moment, the fog that seemed to surround Haider was lifted.

'Stop, I say stop!' Holding his Koran, he placed himself in between Ali Sher and Jatta.

'Haider, this is not your fight!' Jamshed cried, moving closer. 'Yes, you share a mother with Jatta, but he is a Kashmiri Bhatta and you are our Mussalman brother. Join us and let us kill the kafir as the Koran instructs us to do.'

'You do not understand,' Haider protested. 'I am the Maharaja of Kashmir; when I command you to stop, I expect you to stop immediately. I am no brother of yours – certainly not in the misguided act that you are about to undertake.'

Jamshed stared in disbelief at Haider.

'Maharaja of Kashmir? You fool! You are just a pawn that the fakir and my father have used for our purpose. You seriously think that all this talk about you as the king-in-waiting had any substance?'

'I am the son of Rinchina and Kotarani. Now that Udyandev is no more, I have declared myself the lawful heir to the throne. No sword waved in my face can take that away.'

'You and who else declares you to be maharaja?' Jamshed asked.

Jatta moved forward.

'I, Jatta, son of Udyandev, endorse Haider as the lawful Maharaja of Kashmir. There is no other legitimate claimant to the throne. Stand back.'

Slightly perplexed by this new development, Jamshed took a step back. However, Ali Sher persisted.

'Out of the way, we have come for Jatta; your talk is not going to stop us. Jamshed appealed to you on the basis of Islam, and yet you side with the kafir, which is explicitly forbidden by Islam.'

Haider pressed on, his serious face even more intense than normal.

'Do not invoke Islam to mask your putrid self-interest. What do you know about Islam? Have you studied it? Did you ever care to learn about it at the foot of Bulbul?'

'The fakir has educated us,' Jamshed argued. 'Bulbul is irrelevant.

The fakir understands that the Koran should not be second-guessed; it is all in black and white; there is no need for interpreters.'

'He who considers Bulbul as senile is best off remaining silent,' Haider stated. 'Bulbul was about love and peace. Only a malignant person like the fakir second-guesses love and peace and misuses the Koran and Islam.'

'You fool!' Ali Sher chimed in. 'You do not understand the fakir. He has the power of the Jamaat; he can rally people to the cause, he can deliver numbers. You know that it is not about Islam, we know it is not about Islam, but the crowds do not. They believe that Islam is in danger; and the fakir is a master at mobilizing them. Whom do you have on your side except for the few oligarchs?'

'The only numbers that will grow if you follow the fakir are the numbers in the *kabaristan*, the graveyard,' Jatta continued. 'Our maharani can draw as many people as anyone else; only her gatherings are not about hate. As a ruler she knows that hate does not give security or progress to her people.'

'Hey, Jatta the Bhatta,' Ali Sher teased, 'do not dare to belittle the fakir – he has been recognized as our religious leader. Your words merely confirm the death sentence on your head. Kabaristan does not bother us. A dead martyr will have more rights than a living Kashmiri Bhatta.'

'I know the fakir better than any of you do,' Haider pledged. 'He should not be any one's role model, least of all one who seeks to be maharaja. My father exiled him; when I rule the Valley, my first act will be to throw him out again. He is a murderer and deserves his life punishment.'

'Your father was a murderer. Who are you to preach?' Jamshed protested.

'My father repented for his sins. I am determined to learn from his mistakes. The question is whether you are prepared to learn from the mistakes of your father.'

'My father has submitted to pure Islam unconditionally. You obviously have not, and when the Judgement Day arrives, you will be one with the kafirs.'

'I will take my chances on that. I don't need the fakir to be my saviour, nor do the Kashmiri people. Any person who waves the Koran as a manual of war is at best deficient in understanding and at worst a malcontent.'

'You know, after all the training and all the studying, you turn out to be mother's boy who would like nothing better than to suckle on her breast,' Ali Sher told Haider. 'A mother who disowned you! In Kashmir the boys are referred to as their mother's sons. You are Chander after all, and not Haider!'

'I am proud of my Kashmiri blood,' Haider said. 'I am proud of my Islamic faith. My father was asked by Bulbul to be the guardian of Islam. From my mother I learnt my duty to be the guardian of my people and maintain social amity. I will do both, and do not see a conflict between the two. I am proud that I am the first natural-born Mussalman Maharaja of Kashmir.'

Ali Sher laughed. 'What do you rule except for this small room? What action can you take as the ruler of Kashmir? Enough of this talk. Our mission was Jatta, but you have clearly outlived your utility.'

Jatta spoke. 'I love my brother and today I see that my brother loved me all along. The hate that I see in your eyes is indiscriminate. Be careful that one day you two brothers in name do not turn upon each other.'

'You talk too much like the Brahmins!' and with that Ali Sher swung his sword at Haider. Haider instinctively threw up his arm to protect himself, but Ali Sher's sword struck him fatally in the chest and the Koran dropped out of his hands. Unarmed, Jatta also fell to Jamshed's attack. Mortally wounded, his last words to Haider were: 'Brother, our Kashmiri blood flows together. *Maeja*, Mother, you would have been proud of your sons today ...'

Wave 21
Forever

MANZIM stood respectfully before Kotarani, who was seated on a small chair. Her few remaining courtiers watched the scene discreetly from a distance. The courtiers had gathered in a tight protective ring around the queen and Manzim, unlike their usual semicircle. Everyone knew Manzim's missive: Shah Mir's forces had laid siege to the fortress in the middle of the lake and Manzim was the first person to cross over the causeway in several months. Manzim had come accompanied by Puj. Thousands of eyes watched them closely from both banks. He saw that the maharani had lost lot of weight; food must have been running low, and she had clearly been sharing in the pain and scarcity.

Manzim addressed the queen respectfully.

'O Maharani, I bring you word from Shah Mir. He invites you to sit with him on the throne and enter his breast with the Goddess of Royalty, and live in his heart with the virtue of forbearance. You will gain sovereignty not only over his sons but also his life.'

The maharani responded calmly.

'Manzim, ever since I was a young girl you would worry about being given a chance to arrange my betrothal. Did you ever imagine that you would make your commission three times on me?'

'Maharani, I am duty-bound to Shah Mir and his family because I took them on as clients in a time and era that seems so far away. I am old now and have decided that this is my last assignment. I have always seen my commission as fair for practising my dharma, but I fear that I am no longer practising my dharma. Lihaz, the bedrock of our cultured society, is dead. There is no longer the intent to have a union but instead it is a continuation of war from the battlefield into the bedroom.'

Kotarani's eyes narrowed. *What was Manzim signalling to her about the intent?*

'Manzim, I understand. I too am the last person left.'

Kotarani went into a silent, deep reverie; then, as if willing herself into action, she continued: 'Manzim, I am a warrior maharani; victory will be mine in this new model of marriage. I will accept his invitation to meet.'

There was a hushed silence in the room. Nobody dared to even breathe.

Manzim picked up the thread.

'Maharani, if the terms are met, both sides can claim victory. You will seal your role as the greatest queen in Kashmir and India's history. He requests that you come with only one female attendant. Would you like Ravan to serve as your legal guardian and be one of the two witnesses? I will serve as the other witness.'

'Manzim, why the fear? After all, I am the one entering Shah Mir's den. It is not as if my suitor is coming to me.'

Manzim stayed silent. His directive was explicit: he was only an agent, with no discretion on the terms of the relationship. Puj stepped in.

'Your childhood nickname is Tadpole. You are slippery and not to be trusted, so the terms are ours. Any mistake and there will be slaughter.'

'You mean torture first and slaughter second,' one of the assembled aristocrats shouted out. 'The humane method that you learnt in Kashmir will now revert to the barbarism of your Saracen forefathers.'

The queen was unfazed.

'I will only have Indrakshi accompany me, and she will also be my legal guardian. She will know what to do.'

Manzim was surprised, 'Why Indrakshi?'

Kotarani answered enigmatically.

'We have heard about her narrow escape from a life of hell with Sheikh. Indrakshi was protected by her stars and if needed her stars will protect me.'

Manzim continued.

'My client also asks that you come dressed in transparent muslin.'

The courtiers drew their breath in sharply at the ultimate insult, but the maharani raised her hand to silence them.

'Why such a demeaning request?'

'They say that your suitors have all met with a fatal end. Shah Mir does not want you to conceal a weapon on any part of your body. He has heard a story that you are fatal as the red queen.'

The maharani spoke.

'It is truth that he has to fear, and that can never be covered. I will be naked to meet my would-be husband. Dharma will protect me.'

Manzim continued.

'In order to give immediate relief to the suffering public and establish peace in the Valley, a chariot will arrive at the fort at sundown, bearing Shah Mir's military officers; they will take possession of the fort, whose occupants must lay down their arms. They will not be harmed. The same chariot will take you and your attendant to the mosque, where the marriage will take place. When you arrive at the mosque you will sign the contract, which spells out all the terms. At the end of the marriage you will get the gift, *Mahr*, that Shah Mir has commissioned for you. Then there will be celebrations and all of us, rich and poor, can look to a bright new future.'

'Manzim, time is of the essence. I too look forward to celebrate. Prepare quickly.'

'That is the point. All the preparations have been made by Shah Mir; you have only to agree.'

Kotarani thought for a moment and simply said, 'I agree to meet him.'

'Jai Kotarani,' blessed Manzim. He bowed and returned to brief his masters on his success. The fakir was waiting with Shah Mir; after they listened to him in silence they let him go. Then the fakir spoke, his large forehead almost ready to burst.

'That immoral woman has a lust for power. She needs to be lashed. Based on Puj's report she cannot be trusted. What did she mean by claiming victory?'

Shah Mir was reminded of Kota's face when she had confronted Achala and he shuddered.

'She is capable of anything. Sometimes I wonder if she is a witch.'

'I will make arrangements that the room you will receive her in will have a *tikashna* watching her through a peephole,' the fakir promised. 'One false move on her part and you can signal the sharpshooter to let his arrow fly.'

Shah Mir was comforted.

'The arrangements are perfect. Nothing can go wrong now. You are a genius.'

'Tonight, Kotarani will be yours, and the Kota, castle, will be yours as I had predicted. We have a complete understanding of what you rule and what I rule. However, there is the matter of the treasure and assets of Kashmir – the first fifth of the treasure is mine, the remainder yours.'

'What! The people will protest. Even the Brahmins did not get 20 per cent of the treasury's assets. We will turn the Kashmiris into beggars and you know how the Kashmiri beggars are; when they ask for alms they threaten the donors that they will publicly cut their testicles off if they do not get a donation.'

The fakir turned downright nasty and vicious.

'It is ordained that the split should be such. Would you have me not follow the canonical law? Am I less than the representative of the caliph? We have nothing to be afraid of from the people. They will have to submit; soon these easily manipulated Kashmiris will not even think of their rebellious ways unless I command them.'

Shah Mir retreated.

'No, I did not mean to argue about the split and no offence was intended. The Brahmins are contemptible and need to be destroyed. You have taught me that.'

The fakir nodded his head at his chastened pupil.

'The right rules are in front of us. Our duty is to follow them scrupulously with zero deviation.'

The two men broke off; a lot of work remained to prepare for the evening's momentous event.

Kota woke up early the next morning and spent some time in yoga and deep meditation. She had chanted the *Bhairava Stotra Shiva Stuti* -the impregnable mantra shield against even the lord of death – 108 times. It was dusk when the boat arrived for her. While her officers distracted Shah Mir's men she was on the other side of the island hugging the children and Saras goodbye.

'Will you be victorious over Shah Mir?' one of the girls asked.

'Absolutely,' she said blithely. 'I have never lost against bullies and I never give up. Remember the story "Four Friends versus the Hunter"? In my case I am completely recharged by time, who is now my best friend and can burn fire much less Shah Mir!'

It was time to bid Saras goodbye. Kotarani removed the pendant with her mother's portrait and gave it to Saras.

'You gave me the most precious gift that a child could have and now I give it back to you for safe keeping. Give it to one of the girls when they grow up and tell them the story, "Monkey and the Crocodile", along with all the others.'

Saras's eyes were wet.

'Today, you look just like your mother, beautiful and at peace. Don't worry, you will outwit the crocodile just as you have every other time. He will never win your heart.'

Kota smiled through moist eyes.

'I feel stronger today than I ever have in my life.'

She turned to Yaniv. 'May you and your people be reunited with your holy land one day. Your kind act will bring great karma.'

'Queen, may you and your people stay free and safe in your sacred land. Thank you for providing me sanctuary when I needed it most.'

'One immigrant charity worker has brought such sorrow to the Kashmiri people. The other, a businessman, proves to be our salvation.'

Then Kotarani spoke to Indrakshi.

'Take my diary and protect and preserve it. The palest ink in it will defeat the reddest stained sword. Come, help me get dressed to meet my latest and seventh suitor. At his age he wants to bed me, when unassisted he cannot even get out of bed!'

Shah Mir's military officer, a Magray, took over the fort and escorted her in the chariot and on to the other side. On the mainland a curious crowd gathered around their queen. They saw that she was dressed in transparent muslin; it was a two-piece, almond white-coloured, bodice separated by a flat waist from a flowing, long gown. The muslin clung to every curve of her body. She looked regal and ageless; her bare waist was as slim as a young girl's. The antique muslin must have come from the treasury because the fabric was woven out of filaments of lotus stems, symbolizing ultimate purity. The ancient embroiderer had spaced the metallic threads so that it was almost net-like; at each intersection he had tightened a tiny silver knot no bigger than a dot. A jewel was attached to each and every knot. The holes in the net ensured that nothing bigger than a dot could have been hidden underneath the dress, but from a distance the jewels formed the pattern of the Sri Chakra, repeated endlessly around the fabric. Even though the open spaces were much wider and the dress was totally transparent, the eye was automatically drawn to the repeating patterns. The metallic thread reflected the light and gave the shimmering dress a silver glow, which sheathed Kotarani in a metallic armour of modesty. The master craftsman had taken his inspiration from *Indrajaal,* or Indra's net, and the dress reflected his execution of that famous story. The only jewellery Kotarani wore was her dejhoor. A single white iris was pinned to her chest.

Kotarani stood erect in the chariot, which was drawn by four restless horses. The crowd saw the grim-faced queen standing in the *alidha* warrior posture with just Indrakshi as her attendant. They sensed that something was amiss, and hated to see their maharani humiliated in such a way.

'Jai Kota, Fie Shah Mir!' The crowd surrounded her and followed her from the boat landing, shouting, 'Murderer Mir, Ghazi fakir'. Kota faced the crowd and bravely addressed them. Her last words were,

I invoke Omkara. Let the conch sound.
I invoke he with the lance. Let the siddhis pierce the veil.
I invoke the lion rider. Let ignorance be slain.
I invoke Shiva. Har Har Mahadev.
The next battle begins. Satyamev Jayte!

However, when they arrived at the mosque, they could see Puj and his thugs. The fakir was also present with his Panun Fauj and he let out a feral hiss. A hushed silence fell on the crowd. The Kashmiris had once reveled in voicing their opinions, but now fear ruled the air. The crowd was uneasy; things had gone too far and this was not what they had signed up. But what could they do? Puj, with a cleaver in hand, and the fakir led the maharani up to a small room in the mosque. Before entering the room Kota handed her shawl to Indrakshi. Puj was grinning and motioned to Indrakshi that she could not go any further. Shah Mir was going to get his woman tonight and Puj had been told that he would get his. It was pay-off time – free land, free women, and shortly, free gold. It felt good to be on the side of the fakir, the strong side, the muscular three 'Z's of zan, zamin and zenana versus the Bhattas' weak trinity that his Saracen ancestors had migrated towards. He had been born a lapsed Mussalman contaminated by the Bhatta thinking. The fakir had shown him the strong pathway of his ancestors and had chortled when Puj had shared his unique take on the feeble resistance opposing them.

There was fear in the crowd, but much to the fakir's irritation Indrakshi had joined the crowd who were holding hands and had started chanting to support their queen.

Oh, Greatest of Queens
Ever Captivating Never Captive
Thou art lustre in the moon
Radiance in the sun
Intelligence in man

Force in the wind
Taste in water
And heat in fire.
Without thee
The whole universe
Is devoid of consciousness
 Oh Devi
Give us your beneficence.
Shivoham! Shivoham![20]

When Shah Mir, who was waiting inside, saw Kotarani enter alone he rushed over. His arms were outstretched – whether to embrace Kota or to show her that he was unarmed was unclear.

'Welcome Kotarani. I am truly honoured.' His voice was silky smooth as he inflected the Persian intonation in Kota's name. He had worn an extremely ornamental qaba coat, for the meeting, decorated with repeated patterns of roundels containing rampant lions. He touched her possessively on her bare shoulder. Kotarani shuddered, retreating involuntarily. His clammy hands felt like a dead limp fish from the cold waters of the River Vitasta. His face, covered with a white beard, was leering like a crocodile.

Eyes lowered, Kotarani said firmly, 'My name is Kotadevi. I am not your rani yet. Have I met your conditions?'

Shah Mir looked at the vision of beauty in front of him.

'Yes, you have.' He licked his lips, she had finally submitted to him. 'There is no woman to match you in the world. You are the greatest trophy I will possess. Your dress sets off your charms magnificently. With age your beauty only gets sweeter like sherbet, to be enjoyed one sip at a time.'

'I am not a trophy and I am not sherbet,' Kota replied. 'I am Kashmir. You do not understand what this dress means. Fool, your obsession has made you blind to everything.'

Shah Mir felt constrained to ask, 'What do you mean?'

'This dress was woven to show that in Kashmir each one of us is a jewel,' Kotadevi explained, 'self-luminous and yet reflecting the luminosity of every other person. This infinite connectivity of spirit is what Kashmir is. You have sought to attach yourself to Kashmir with a double face, on one side a sweet-talking parasite and on the other a predator.'

Shah Mir seemed not to hear her; he was drunk on his success.

'Maharani, I am honoured that we are going to be attached together. You have always been good at judging the winning side, and you will be on the right side of history. From my side I have cleared all impediments. I am now single as you are, so we can be equals in matrimony. Today is the end of Kashmiri Bhatta rule and a new beginning – but it is a beginning of equality. The year 1339 will be the year of Naya Kashmir. Let me show you your dowry. It is something that you will like.'

Shah Mir picked up a small box and took out a coin. It was square in shape, unlike all the predecessor coins of Kashmir. Shah Mir proudly read out the legend on the coin: 'The Great Sultan Sham Shah-Kashmir Mint. This will commemorate our rule forever.'

'Why is it in a foreign language? Where is the Devi?' Kotadevi asked.

'What need is there for the goddess on the coins when Islam will rule? The coin should symbolize the new beginning, the beginning of the Shah Mir dynasty, a dynasty that will rule Kashmir forever.'

'For the last 5,000 years the Devi has made Kashmir a centre of enlightenment; a place where she protected all faiths, only time will tell whether tearing Kashmir apart represents progress or that you and the fakir will have suffocated the cradle of human civilization.'

Shah Mir ignored the admonition.

'I have also ordained that it is the end of history. Henceforth, Kashmir will no longer have the *Saptarshi laukika* calendar. As you know, Maharani, I was Rinchina's closest confidant and friend; to honour him, I will reintroduce the *Hijri* calendar that he was unsuccessful in implementing. Rinchina will be remembered forever.'

'Replacing our calendar with one which will be short each year by eleven days is a backward step. Our calendar is our history and your decision makes it clear that you want to destroy the roots of Kashmir. You mention Rinchina. I am here because I have a single question. Where are my sons? Where are Chander and Jatta?'

'You should not let your emotions get in the way. We are here to talk about us. Our agreement is what matters. The younger generation will now have its day in the sun.'

'The youth must have its day today. Haider Chander is the single hope of agreement that exists between us. Support him as maharaja, and I will abdicate in his favour. Beyond that there is nothing to discuss.'

Shah Mir stopped his prattle. He understood that he could not prevaricate his way through this situation.

'Maharani, Haider turned out to be a disappointment and he and Jatta were martyred to the cause. Thankfully, my sons Jamshed and Ali Sher are with us, and the Shah Mir dynasty will rule Kashmir. As I said it is the end of history, so why look back?'

Kotadevi's heart cracked when she heard the tragic news about her sons. Before her departure, Saras had given her herbs to ingest that would leave her alert but numb her to any pain.

'Jatta, Chander, Kashmir's hope dies with you,' lamented Kota. 'You monster, you have trained your sons to be murderers! The hands they lifted on my sons will turn on each other and they will suffer the same fate that you made my sons suffer.'

'Come, come, let us not be sentimental,' Shah Mir ordered. 'After all, you married Rinchina who murdered your father.'

'You talk of honouring Rinchina while you simultaneously arrange for the murder of his son, who was entrusted in your care!' Kotadevi said. 'You want to marry me while you give me news that both my sons have been murdered by you. Sick man, my condition is that the fakir must be expelled from Kashmir – you cannot have the fakir and me. Give me your answer.'

Shah Mir was acutely aware that the fakir had a sharpshooter by his side and was watching the whole scene through a peephole.

'Maharani, why do the Kashmiris create this spectre of the fakir? He has done nothing to make the Bhattas paranoid. It is nothing but sheer prejudice of a person dedicated to charity.'

'The fakir is a spider. He extends through his mouth the cobweb that grows within his heart. He traps his prey with it and eventually will eat it. The fakir sought sanctuary in Kashmir because of its tolerance – a tolerance that he is seeking to replace with virulent bloodthirsty conformance with the lure of stealing the land from the Brahmins. You can make the right choice or the wrong choice of whom to side with. What is your answer?'

Shah Mir felt that he had to show he was in command.

'I am no longer your subordinate. You tell me your answer. Do you accept the marriage proposal? Come join me? If so, the fakir waits to seal the marriage.'

'What you call joining you is *nikah mutah*, the right to rape me, for one night so that you can claim legitimacy for your rule and find out where the treasure of Kashmir is. Then you will have me murdered in the morning, just as you did everyone else!' Kotadevi snapped.

Shah Mir was stunned. *How could she know? Only the fakir and I were privy to the plan – that bastard Manzim was the only person who could have been in a position to leak it to her!* But Shah Mir was learning from the fakir, and he knew it was time to use force.

'You have always wanted power, but today I hold it. To rule, you need a man and I am willing to be generous and share my breast, my bed and my *kismet* with you. Imagine my luck; from immigrant to king. It can be yours if you join your name with my new name, Shams-ud-Din the Glorious.'

'You little man, you are so conceited that you are insecure of your shadow. I have had real men by my side, my father, Brahma, Udyandev, Devaswami. Who do you have? You had your daughter murdered. Your wife has left you and her curse of eternal damnation hangs over you. The public outside is chanting 'Murderer Mir Ghazi Fakir!'. You are now the Fakir's shadow. But new snow always falls on old snow, not knowing that it too will be covered one day. Do you seriously think that I would ever legitimize your rule? Not in a thousand years.'

Shah Mir was furious.

'What do you hope to accomplish by this foolish talk? Accept me! People are waiting outside to celebrate. We will eat a fabulous feast. We will find and grab the treasure in any case. Suryavansh cannot be hidden indefinitely.'

'The treasure is at the tip of your nose and in front of your eyes, but just like Dulucha, with your ignorance you will never find it. Feasts have little meaning for me since I went off food over thirty days ago. What you will feed off is the carcass of Kashmir since you have brought the heartbeat of the Kashmiris to a halt.'

'You have run out of options. Whether you agree or do not agree and what happens between us is irrelevant. History will record that I, Shah Mir, raped you all night, enchained you in the morning and then had you incarcerated in the dungeons. You have one choice and that is to do what I say.'

The brave maharani retorted contemptuously.

'My power arises from my free will. Your offer holds no temptation for me?'

'Your answer?' said Shah Mir obdurately.

Kotadevi turned around. She had not looked Shah Mir in the eye once because she did not want an iota of energy to be exchanged between her and him. From behind, Shah Mir expectantly watched her staring at the setting sun. The rays of the sun reflected off the jewels and the metallic threads, and the sheen covered Kotadevi in a silver blaze. The cheeks of the mountain tops were being softly kissed by wisps of clouds, the wind sighed gently between the trees and the wavelets on the lake rippled in unison on the floating lotus leaves. The Valley of Kashmir was still and it was as if Mother Nature itself was afraid to stir under dusk's lengthening shadows. The chants of the crowd, *Oh Devi, give us your beneficence, Shivoham Shivoham,* floated in the air. Then night rolled in and hidden within its folds was Shikasdevi, the goddess of doom, in the form of a python, slithering through the Valley, hungrily searching to feed on violence. Where there had been light before, now the Valley of Kashmir was in total darkness. But wait;

far away on the mountain top there was a glimmer of light. It was a candle, then another one and then more. The band of children had successfully crossed the Valley and was safely past Shah Mir's guards. *Oh Devi, give us your beneficence. Oh Devi, give us your beneficence. Shivoham Shivoham!* The crowd's chants were faster and louder and enveloped Kota protectively.

Kotadevi gently removed her dejhoor and folded her hands in front of her. The children were safe and one day her people would rediscover her in their hearts. Kumara had said that the long war would crest and then she would rise again as the greatest protector of dharma against its enemies. She would be even bigger in legend than in life and would not only be considered the greatest queen to rule Kashmir but also the greatest queen of India, and perhaps of the known world. Devaswami had promised her that she would not end up in limbo, and he would await her so that she could jump through the hoop of time. Now it was her turn, and with dharma on her side there was nothing to fear. The time had finally come to keep her promise to Brahma. That silly boy with the dangling earring who had dared to nickname her Tadpole and hurt her ever so badly had always stood by her. Guru Gotam had taught her that love is what you pay undivided attention to, and he would eternally be hers. Sharika had said that they were star-crossed lovers. The jyotish had vouched that both Brahma and she would be reborn and their karmic sacrifices would reunite them. She looked up and there was the signal, the rising moon.

'Here is my answer. I will no longer play hide-and-seek and will accept your love. Accept me and carry me to the stars.' Kota spoke firmly and then spun around to face Shah Mir.

On hearing Kota's words Shah Mir's face broke out into a triumphant smile; then he spotted the faintest of red lines appear, cut into Kotadevi's waist and her wrists with the newly sharpened knife edge of the dejhoor, which had slashed her fair skin with the full force of its dharmic mission. The flow increased and a dark red pool quickly spread around her. The dejhoor fell from Kotadevi's hand and she fainted to the floor. Taken completely by surprise, a shocked Shah

Mir drew back. He had no treasure, no queen and no satisfaction of bedding her. Instead Kota's sacrifice had left an indelible stain of disgrace to mark the violence that had birthed his rule and which begot violence in the hitherto peaceful Valley.

The door burst open: an inflamed Indrakshi barged in with an angry mob behind her.

'I am the legal guardian of the maharani. I have come to claim her.'

On 17 July 1339 Kashmir's star fell from the sky. Indrakshi was the one who supported the maharani's head in her lap during her last moments. Her tears, mixed with Kotadevi's sacrificial blood, stamped Kashmir forever and having prayed the powerful *Brahma Vidya* mantra to aid the maharani in her journey she softly crooned, 'Kotadevi! Unforgettable and immortal, *Amar Ho!*'

Epilogue

KALHANA'S successor, Jonaraja, wrote in the continuation of Kalhana's Kashmiri annals, *The River of Kings,* not too much later after Kotadevi's death:

> *As the canal nourishes the cultivated fields with water, so did the Queen nourish the people by bestowing much wealth on them. She was to the kingdom what the moon is to the blue lotus; and to the enemy she was what that luminary is to the white lotus.*

The refugee girl blossomed as she developed from adolescence into adulthood at the New England College. Having discovered that some twenty-five million Americans practice yoga, she supplemented her small income by teaching at the nearby Patanjali Yoga studio. The subject of Kashmir even reached her lecture theatre when her physics teacher gave a class on 'Quantum Mechanics and the Conscious Universe'. He talked about how his interest had been piqued as a boy in Pasadena when he discovered that the ornamental trees on Christmas Lane were devdars from this place called Kashmir where the theory and practice of consciousness was elaborated to perfection. She smiled at the thought of Devaswami walking into that California lecture hall. Sharadapeeth's legacy was arousing the interest of scholars all over the world.

The girl excelled in her studies, winning many academic honours and awards and maintained her immigrant scholarship. Her roommate and best friend from Lesotho shared her own family history from Africa, and the hope that was inbuilt in the American trinity: life, liberty and the pursuit of happiness. When she was selected to be the college valedictorian, her talk was noteworthy for its subject, 'Life Lessons from Sharada, Athena and Minerva'. Graduation day came, and when it was her turn on the stage she addressed the gathering.

'*Namaste*, I salute the consciousness within all of you. Let me start with the story of a 5,000-year-old civilization, where society's highest honour was to become a college graduate. In 1924, the Briton, Sir Richard Carnac Temple, wrote in his foreword for *The Ocean of Story*, which for its voluminous size is the earliest collection of short stories extant in the world:

"'(There is) a civilization centered in Kashmir, which was the birthplace and home of storytelling. It was from here that the Persians learnt the art and passed it on to the Arabians. From the Middle East the tales found their way to Constantinople, and Venice, and finally appeared in the pages of Boccaccio, Chaucer and La Fontaine.'"

'Yes, there once was a real Shangri La where knowledge was the exclusive pathway for a better world, where university graduates made a difference by perfecting themselves across the thirteen inner dimensions first and the material dimensions second and especially noteworthy for us girls, where Shakti women ruled. That Kashmir of Shakti needs saving today just as the Shakti of Kashmir will save the world of tomorrow.'

The graduation ceremony over, the students congregated with their proud parents and families to celebrate. There was chatter about fast-track job offers with fabulous salaries, none as loud as those coming from foreign students and immigrants, who had obtained the final stamp of acceptance in attaining the American dream. The girl's roommate's family had invited her to join them, but she felt that it was an occasion where relatives should celebrate their own success. She had learnt to be independent, and her plans would follow a different path to others. She was determined to have it all in one life, but she had to find someone very special before she began her ascent.

She returned to her apartment and changed from her black-lace graduation dress into a red Indian silk sari with a pink lotus pattern.

She had received a bouquet of flowers and pinned a red hibiscus on to the drape of her sari over the matching blouse. She got into her trusty old car and set off to the Poconos Mountains, a few hours away. The radio played Alicia Keys's *'Girl on Fire'* and she hummed the lyrics. Taking the exit for Stroudsburg, Pennsylvania, she stopped at a gas station for directions and saw a white-haired Indian filling his black Audi A8 at the pump.

'Can you guide me to Cays Road please?'

The Indian examined the girl with open curiosity. She came across as a white female, tall and strong, with the confident stance of youth and alert watchful eyes, astride imperious high cheekbones. Wrapped top to toe in a red sari and with a complexion of saffron-hued milk and a cascade of pomegranate hair falling over her left shoulder, she was a head turner. Her vehicle did not match her elegance, however. Then comprehension lit in the man's eyes. He smiled kindly and bobbed his head vigorously from side to side.

'Ah yes, from your looks you must be a student from Kashmir. Mother is waiting for you. Go one mile straight ahead and then make a right turn.'

Not knowing what to make of his remark, the girl got into her car and drove away slowly, soon entering a beautiful valley surrounded by low, green hills. On the high plateau with a commanding view of the vista below was her graduation gift, the sight of a new majestic temple, spread over 35 acres: the very first one in North America to Mother Sharada Devi!

Today, I am a Bhattarika, the girl told the resident priest. He understood instantly and led her in to do puja to Sharada Devi. Hers was a single immigrant story that had flown to America, one migration among many millions, but she had not forgotten that within her story was an entire universe. She had not forgotten that her grandmother had told her that Indrakshi was her ancestor. After the completion of the prayer the priest put a tilak on her forehead and gave her prasad. She walked out of the temple grounds, hiked up the hill and sat facing the adjoining sparkling lake. Her folded hands held tightly on to Kotadevi's dejhoor and diary which her grandmother had sent her, as had her mother before, all the way back to Indrakshi. She opened the diary at its last entry.

> Dear Mind-born Daughter of mine,
>
> If you have birthmarks on your wrists, then I am you and you are me and our consciousness is one. It means that I have jumped through the hoop of cyclical time. It means that the conch should blow and the lotus should sway even if the Long War goes on. Guru Gotam had prepared me for my exam to face two questions on life lessons that were never asked of me. The first one is what is that by knowing which one needs to know nothing else? The second one is what is that by doing that I need to do nothing else? The answers are to use Kashmir's unparalleled 5,000-year-old treasury to know and experience Shakti the supreme force within you and use it to do your dharma fearlessly. Do not subjugate yourself to any other force however sanctified or to any other objective howsoever tempting which does not sustain you eternally. Do not also confuse the body, the ego, the mind or the heart-driven urges with the desire that comes out of consciousness and gives Shakti. Dharma also means that there is a long overdue promise to a loved one that needs to be kept finally. Now you know everything and are ready to face anything.
>
> Love 𝒦

Once firmly centred on the ground, with the sun shining over her, the girl meditated on Sharada Devi. She hummed the mantra:

> *Glory to Sharada, the Power contained within the mass of vowels, the Primal Utterance who manifested as Kashmir [itself]! Glory to that Goddess of the sacred Peetha within the Land that She Embodies,*

*Who, as the personification of its very Wisdom,
Imbues her devotees with Enlightened Intelligence and Understanding.*

Her breathing slowed; then even more; ever so gently coiling the inner and outer breath within the heart lotus. The sun's refracted beams powered the girl's body with warmth and energy as if a flame was being lit within her. The sunlight intensified into blinding luminosity, then with a flash and the crack of a knot, switched into a cool silver stream that flowed up inside her and bathed her. Exactly as in her grandmother's bedtime stories, from the eye of her heart, she discerned Garuda, the mighty Indian phoenix, half eagle and half man, appear on the eastern horizon. He was speeding towards her, like a meteor, scattering the stray clouds helter-skelter, blocking the sun with his immense wings and flattening the green trees under his wake. His stern white face, adorned with earrings, had the brilliance of the fire-burning wheel of time, his wings radiated saffron golden lustre and his self-regenerating body was red mantra. His smouldering eagle eyes revealed he was the inexorable spotter and an implacable mangler and devourer of snakes with poisonous mouths and cruel minds. What the girl had really liked in her bedtime stories about Garuda was that after overcoming overwhelming odds, he had delivered the elixir of immortality to his mother. He was also the son of Rishi Kashyapa, the founder of Kashmir. It was time for the empress to unite with her first love, reconnect and save her people and unequivocally and assertively reclaim her ancestral homeland. He glided down and she hitched up her sari and mounted him. She held him firmly by the sacred thread around his neck with her left hand, while her strong white legs, bare up to the knees, gripped his powerful shoulders tightly for balance. She clasped the dejhoor on her ears and once they snapped in place felt the push of his mighty wings propel a powerful wind; the take-off generating a whistling sound of Shivoham. With Kota's diary secure in her right hand and her hair flying like a red banner, her bionic Vir took her soaring up high, over the lactating bosoms of the Poconos hills and straight back to her roots in the verdant Valley of Kashmir.

Endnotes

1. Bala Kavacha, 'Protection of the Young Woman Goddess'. Shri Bālā, daughter of Tripurā, belongs to the retinue of indigenous Kashmir Goddesses, worshipped in the *Agni-karya-paddhati*, *Devi-rahasya*, etc.
2. N, K. Zutshi, *Sultan Zain-Ul-Abidin of Kashmir.*
3. Daniel H. H. Ingalls (translator), *An Anthology of Sanskrit Court Poetry.*
4. David Gordon White, (ed.), *Tantra in Practice*, Princeton University Press Princeton New Jersey USA, 2000.
5. *Kha-cakra-pancika Stotra*, 'A Hymn to the 5 Circle Dances of the Void'.
6. Kaschewsky and Tsering quoted in Geoffrey Samuel's chapter, 'The Gesar Epic of East Tibet', in *Tibetan Literature Studies in Genre,* Jose Ignacio Cabezon & Roger R. Jackson, ed., Colorado: Snow Lion Publications, 1996, pp. 330, 376.
7. Geoffrey Samuel, 'The Gesar Epic of East Tibet', in *Tibetan Literature: Studies in Genre*, Jose Ignacio Cabezon & Roger R. Jackson, ed., Colorado: Snow Lion Publications, 1996, pp. 358-367,
8. Geoffrey Samuel, 'The Gesar Epic of East Tibet', in *Tibetan Literature Studies in Genre*, Jose Ignacio Cabezon & Roger R. Jackson, ed., Colorado: Snow Lion Publications, 1996, pp. 358-367.
9. http://www.worldwizzy.com/library/Amir_Khusrau
10. http://www.worldwizzy.com/library/Amir_Khusrau
11. Laurence Hope, *The Garden of Kama*, California: C. F. Braun & Co., 1968.

12 Laurence Hope, The Garden of Kama, California: C. F. Braun & Co,. 1968.
13 Alexis Sanderson, *Religion and the State: Initiating Monarch in Saivism and the Buddhist Way of Mantras*, Weisbaden: Harrasowitz Verlag and Open Lecture University of Tokyo, 2004.
14 Tarif Khalidi, *The Qur'an*, London: Penguin, 2009.
15 Hermann Francke, *Antiquities of Indian Tibet*, Delhi: S. Chand, Vol. 1, 1914.
16 Historians maintain that Bulbul died after Rinchina around 1327.
17 Tarif Khalidi, *The Qur'an: Sura of the Confederates* 33:35, London: Penguin, 2009.
18 Jogesh Chander Dutt, *Rajatarangini of Jonaraja*, New Delhi: Gyan Publishing House, 2012.
19 *Bhairava Stotra Shiva Stuti,* Abhinavagupta circa 1000.
20 *Panchastavi* circa 1000 Canto Four Stanza 19.

Bibliography

Bakker, Hans, 2015, Gateway to Kashmir: Paper on Saivism and the Tantric Traditions Symposium in Honour of Alexis G.J. S. Sanderson, Toronto.

Bazaz, Prem Nath, 1959, *Daughters of the Vitasta*, New Delhi: Pamposh Publications.

Bhan, J. L., 2010, *Kashmir Sculptures*, Delhi: Readworthy Publications.

Furlinger, Ernst, 2009, *The Touch of Sakti*, Delhi: D.K. Printworld.

Kak, Subhash, 2000, *The Astronomical Code of the Rigveda*, Delhi: Munshiram Manoharlal.

Kashmiri Overseas Association website KOAUSA.org

Kumari, Dr V., 1973, *Nilamata Purana*, J&K Academy of Arts, Culture and Languages.

Liu, Xinru, 1988, *Ancient India and Ancient China Trade and Religious Exchanges AD* 1-600 (1st ed.), Delhi: Oxford India Publications.

Pal, Pratapaditya, 1975, *Bronzes of Kashmir*, New York: Hacker Art Books.

Pal, Pratapaditya, 1989, *Art and Architecture of Ancient Kashmir*, Mumbai: Marg Publications.

Pal, Pratapaditya, 2007, *The Arts of Kashmir*, New York: Asia Society.

Pandit, Kashinath, 2009, *A Muslim missionary in Medieval Kashmir (Tohfatu'l-Ahbab)*, Delhi: Voice of India.

Pandit, Gopi Krishna, 2010, *Secrets of Kundalini in Panchastavi*, Kundalini Research and Publications Trust, Stamford, Connecticut: Bethel Publishers.

Pandit, Moti Lal, 1959, *The Trika Saivism of Kashmir*, Delhi: Munshiram Manoharlal Publishers.

Paranjape, Makarand and Sunthar Visuvalingam, 2012, *Abhinavagupta Reconsiderations*, Delhi: Samvad India Foundation.

Sanderson, Alexis, 2004, *The Yoga of Dying*, Handouts for Lectures, Oxford: All Souls College.

Slaje, Walter, 2014, *Kingship in Kaśmīr (AD 1148-1459): From the Pen of Jonarāja, Court Pandit to Sultān Zayn Al-'Ābidīn*, Universitätsverlag Halle-Wittenberg.

Siudmak, John, 2013, *The Hindu-Buddhist Sculpture of Ancient Kashmir and its Influences*, Boston: BRILL.

Stein, Sir Aurel, 2009, *Kalhana's Rajatarangini: A Chronicle of the Kings of Kashmir*, Delhi: Motilal Banarasidas.

Tompkins, Chris, 2014, *Sharada Sahasranama* Manuscript translation awaiting publication.

Glossary of Kashmiri Sanskrit and Farsi terms

Achkan	Knee-length, high-neck, tight-fitting, topcoat, flared below the waist
Al Illah	The God (of Muslims)
Angaraka	In astrology if Mars is in the first, second, fourth, seventh, eighth, or twelfth house
Bab	Father
Bandhan	Binding
Barati	Members of groom's wedding party
Bhairava	Guardian form of Shiva
Bhand	Folk theatre style, combining the play and dance
Bhatta	Graduate; also Kashmiri term for Kashmiri Hindus or pandits
Bhakta	Devotee
Bottas	Kashmiri term for people of Ladakhi and Tibetan origin
Costus	Medicinal plant
Dahman	Push harder; also fluids derived from a sacred place
Datura	Seeds of thorn apple which are intoxicating
Dejhoor	Woman's earring in a hexagonal shape symbolizing Shiva and Shakti union
Devadasi	Servant of the divine, also temple dancer, bayadére

Devi	Feminine equal complement of divinity
Dharma	That which sustains what is measureable
Dhoop	Incense with resin binding the combustible paste
Dinara	Copper coins
Dool	Penis
Dranga	Watch station, mini fortress
Dvarapati	Master of the entry gate
Fidayeen	Those who martyr themselves in God's name and gain redemption
Ghat	Steps to river
Gobur	Precious beloved child
Godown	Warehouse
Halal	Permissible under Islamic Law
Hamsa	Bar-headed goose, migratory bird, sometimes swan
Haqiqi	Literal
Hoon mot	Crumbs for dog
Houri	Beautiful virgin, companion of the faithful in Islamic Paradise
Iddah	Waiting period after divorce or death of husband before a woman can remarry
Indra	Hindu divine ruler similar to Zeus
Jagir	Feudal land grant
Jamaat	Congregation
Jyotish	Astrologer
Kabaristan	Graveyard
Kafir	Infidel
Kali Andhi	Black storm
Kalima	The word of Islam, recited at the time of conversion
Kartikeya	God of War
Kampanesa	Military commander
Kata	Ladakhi white silk scarf

Khampa	Martial people residing in Kham lying between Tibet and Sichuan
Khara	Unit of weight
Kol	Water canal
Kos	Vagina
Kund	Sacred water tank or pond
Kundalini	Coiled, latent, spiritual force within a human being
Lakshmana	Mandragora officinarum
Leela	Play
Mafangi	Drug addict
Mahr	Husband's dowry payment to betrothed
Mahraa	Sir
Mlechchha	Alien or foreign, if pejorative then less civilized
Mussalman	Persian form of the word Muslim
Navrattan	Nine jewels
Navreh	New Year
Nechpatri	Astrologer's almanac
Ojas	Vigour
Panun Fauj	Own army
Paranda	Flat-bottomed boat
Parees	Fairies
Pati	Husband
Pitaama	Grandfather
Pitr Lok	Abode of departed ancestors
Poshak	Clothing
Prayopavesha	Fast unto death
Raksha	Security
Rasa	Fundamental aesthetic essence
Ratri	Night
Rudraksha	A rosary made from the dried seeds of an evergreen tree
Sammelan	Gathering, including musical

Shaitan	Satan
Shali	Paddy
Shivoham	I am Shiva
Shraddha	Mourning rites
Suchi	Abode of Brahma, the creator of the universe
Talak Battah	Husband's declaration of a permanent divorce
Tantri	Chief priest at temple
Tantric	Follower of tantra
Tantrin	Militia
Taqqiya	Religiously sanctioned dissimulation
Tikashna	Archer
Tilak	Auspicious mark applied between the eyes on the forehead
Toshkhana	Treasury
Trika	Triad or Trinity
Turushka	Turkic people
Saptarshi	Seven sages
Shastras	Texts containing knowledge based on timeless principles
Shakti	Feminine cosmic energy
Shahtoosh	Fine wool from the Tibetan antelope *chiru*
Sqay	Kashmiri martial art
Vajra	Diamond or thunderbolt
Vajradatta	Thunderbolt symbol of Kundalini awakening
Vrta	Demon
Vajramukti	Thunderbolt fist
Viman	Airplane
Vipashyana	Seeing reality at its irreducible level
Wah Wah	Hear hear, expression of appreciation

Acknowledgements

THIS is Kota's story.
Amitav Kaul, movie producer and director of the forthcoming movie *The Interpreter of Maladies*, gave the story its spine. Noted Indologist, Professor Subhash Kak, Regents professor and head of computer science at Oklahoma University, has been a lifelong mentor and gave me his blessings and encouragement and breathed spirit into the story. Professor S. Sridhar, Director, Mattoo Center for India Studies at State University of New York, was unflagging in his belief that Kota needed to be reborn. Meena Sridhar, his life partner and professor of linguistics at State University of New York, was the first one to resonate with the feminine leadership quality of Kota and helped me refine it. Dr Pratapaditya Pal, the greatest curator of Indian art and to whom Kashmir owes so much, showed my story and me tough love. His detailed critique of the historical inaccuracies in an earlier version was not just a learning experience but a delight to see the master at work. Kota gained form, identification markers and period authenticity because of him. Suvir Kaul, professor of English at University of Pennsylvania, provided appropriate caution about the risks in pedagogy, when focusing on the younger audience who may lack the cultural context, while keeping the adult reader engaged.

More mentors awaited me as I traced Kota's walk. Christopher Tompkins, PhD student in Kashmir Shaivism at University of California, provided enormous help in sourcing the rich spiritual ethos that Kota was a part of. I discovered that Theresa Wilke, PhD student at University of Halle in Germany and a student of the eminent

Professor Walter Slaje had just completed her master's thesis on Kota. She verified that the dating and other historical details were in conformance with the latest thinking. Luckily, Professor Slaje had just come out with the latest and best translation of Jonaraja's *Rajatarangini*, the seminal document for historical materials relating to Kota. In the background, of course, are the works of Professor Alexis Sanderson at All Souls College at Oxford University, who has single-handedly pioneered Western thought leadership on the study of Kashmir's historical treasures.

To be a writer meant that I had to spend most of my discretionary time, spanning over a decade, living in the early fourteenth century. When I emerged from the time machine with Kota's birch bark story, Ayesha Pande proved to be a helpful guide and connected me to Beena Kamlani. As my editor, it is Beena who truly made the inner Kota shine bright. It was then that the story met its great champion in Anuj Bahri of the literary agency, Red Ink. He brought much welcomed conviction and sponsorship that Kota's untold story belonged to the world. His colleague Sharvani Pandit's subsequent edits helped ensure that Kota was always center stage and did not get overshadowed by the ideological conflicts that raged around her or that the reader did not get diverted by the equally interesting support characters. Aanchal Malhotra, also of Red Ink, was the first next-generation woman to read the manuscript. It was with bated breath that I awaited her reaction. After all, Kota's story was for her generation; and, I was relieved and delighted when she gave it thumbs up. My acid test, namely, would the reader be inspired to do something different in life after reading Kota's story, was passed with flying colors. Anuj crafted the partnership with Amrita Chowdhury of Harlequin India and in our first meeting, an always alert Kota must have felt that here comes the sun. Fiona Lappin did the final edits ensuring smooth flow and that any anachronisms or other challenges did not throw off the lay reader unfamiliar with the cultural background of Kashmir.

One last hoop awaited Kota. The merger of Harlequin with HarperCollins brought her new well-wishers. Shantanu Ray

Chaudhuri, Managing Editor at HarperCollins, took charge of the birch baton to bring Kota to the finish line. The voice from the past grew stronger because HarperCollins had been publisher of my grandfather Pandit Gopi Krishna's book – a welcome coincidence.

My heartfelt gratitude to Bidisha Srivastava for catching the errors in the manuscript. Bonita Shimray and her team came up with the stunning cover which captures the subtlety and complexity of the most important inflection moment in Kashmir's history in the last seven hundred years. Amrita Talwar shouldered the responsibility of sharing Kota's story with the world and Karthika V.K. blessed all with her munificence. Great team that always came through in the crunch.

Friends were my anchor during the difficult struggles of decoding foundational cultural concepts. Dr Nirmal Mattoo, editor of the book *Ananya* and chairman of the Mattoo Center for India Studies at State University of New York, was always un-subjugated in his understanding of what culturally a Kashmiri Pandit is about. Ravindra Nath Kaul, a seeker, helped greatly in deciphering Sanskrit words and terms and connectivity of Kashmiri frameworks with Vedic origins. Ah, Sanskrit, whose very alphabet means indestructible. What an invaluable guide it was in understanding the Kashmir of bygone times! Thanks also to Gene Kieffer, president of the Kundalini Foundation, for his talks with me on the secret supreme of Kashmir. In today's day and age, I would be remiss in not acknowledging social media friends, especially those who are Kashmiri Muslims. I could test various ideas with them and gain their understanding of Kashmir's shared history. There is certainly a strong contingent out there which believes in 'Kashmir First' in a positive way and which is proud of their historiography as opposed to the nihilist voices that get all of the headlines. I am also truly appreciative of Rahul Pandita. He is the one author who has been a trailblazer for Kashmiri Pandits in wielding the sword of Truth and has given me the confidence that Kota's story written in the palest of inks will find acceptance. To Sridhar Chityala and Sreedhar Menon, both devotees and Trustees of the first Sharada temple in North America, goes the credit for providing me a deep understanding of how far in time and space the Greater Kashmir civilization continues to survive.

Best is always saved for last. To Shiva and Dhruva, our sons, goes the honour for challenging me in my writings. I admit that when I started I was a novice. I hope that after ten years they will find the end product a worthy one. In their own way, in challenging the construct of the story, they reflect the values of excellence that are embedded in them. These are values that Sharadapeeth inculcated in Kota and nothing has changed since then for the Pandits. The Pandits are the modern-day Jeddi knights following their 5,000-year quest for the ultimate nature of reality and Kota's life story will illustrate to our smart and attractive next generation the need to have a higher purpose in life. But most of all, while the men in my family, starting with my late departed father Radha Krishan Kaul, are ones I look up to and this edition recognizes my late brother who always had faith in me, it is the luminous Pandit Gopi Krishna's writings that have always been the standard that I have set for myself. Yet, it is the women that this book and I owe the most to. Three women have reigned supreme in my thoughts: my maternal grandmother, my mother and my wife. My grandmother, Roopwanti, who indiscriminately gave all tough love; my mother, Ragya Kaul, the Jagat teacher, who taught me that a woman is not just a daughter, wife, mother or a nurturer, but a grantor of immortality; and my wife, Dr Sushma Dhar Kaul, who has been my lifelong Shakti and has been a living example of fearless symmetry and resonant connectivity.

Kota Rani's story gained resonance around the world when the first edition was published. She had said that she would jump through the hoop of time and she did! Here is offered the second edition for which Rimbik Das and Amitav Kaul designed and created the magnificent jacket book cover.

Finally, with gratitude to the many, there is reverence for the One in many, Sharada Devi, the presiding deity of Kashmira. This book is a humble offering to her, who, in the words of Abhinavagupta, unites her people through an expression of their own magnanimous qualities. May her prescription bring peace to Kashmira and the light of the autumn moon once again be celebrated in Kashmira as the auspicious radiance of Sharada Devi. May she smile when she sees both the truth and error that reside in this story and grant me the self-knowledge so that I do better next time.

Critical Acclaim

'*The Last Queen of Kashmir* leaves you mesmerized. It is a gripping and inspiring read written in a serene prose. Kota finds a place in the heart of the reader from the very beginning of the book. The author presents a riveting narrative. The book contains much for its readers. There is dance, drama, deceit, politics, love and war.' **Sushant Dhar for Greater Kashmir.**

'The mark of good historical fiction is that it should offer insights or solutions that apply to today's world. And there is a whole lot to ponder in *The Last Queen of Kashmir* – right from underlining the challenges of vetting immigrants, warning of economic destabilization through tactical cornering of markets, showing war to be a mindless ravaging of hard-constructed civilisations. And therein lies the most valuable insight this engaging book has to offer.' **Mihir Balantrapu for The Hindu**.

'The author, Rakesh K. Kaul, has provided readers an opportunity, nay a pilgrimage, into the Kashmir of distant years, recreating its richness and inviting us to get drenched in its aroma. He has skilfully weaved the complex ethos of that era into a strong and engaging narrative. *The Last Queen of Kashmir* succeeds as an acknowledgement, a celebration, of an age long gone.' – **Shreeya Thussu for Vijayvaani**.

'Wish your (@meghagulzar) next film could be a film on Kota Rani, legendary queen of 14th century Kashmir whose story is far more powerful than Padmavati.' **Shah Faesal.**

'Our history is replete with inspirational women. Thanks to Rakesh Kaul for writing the story about another great woman.' **Senior Journalist Aarti Tikoo Singh**

Critical Acclaim (contd.)

'But more notable than the literary embellishments is the historical fidelity of the narration that is sustained throughout its entirety: *The Last Queen of Kashmir* is a *tour de force* that is informative, entertaining as well as edifying.' **Vivek Gumaste for Rediff News.**

'*The Last Queen of Kashmir* will help Kashmiris realise what they were and help them regain self-recognition and self-understanding. A symbol of self-pride and to-do spirit, she ruled the land in the face of adversity.' **Saritha Saraswathy Balan for Daily Pioneer.**

'The first literary piece published in the English language that uses Kashmir's arduous literary principles.' **Chairman Ashok Advani for Business India at The Asia Society.**

'In *The Last Queen of Kashmir*, Rakesh Kaul has performed the astonishing and laudable creative feat of rescuing and resurrecting Kota Rani from the debris of history. A courageous, compelling, and inspiring story of an exceptional woman's struggle against brutal invaders and marauders, it fills a deep void in our understanding of India's medieval period.

Kaul's retelling is strong, both on facts and imagination. It is also a deeply moving tale, imbued with philosophical musings, spiritual lore, and local colour, in a unique historic-modern style, replete with a wistful-heroic rasa which, after the Mahabharata, Kaul calls *virasa*. A story that all young Indians must read, especially Kashmiris, struggling to reclaim their past.' - **Dr. Makarand R. Paranjape, Director, Indian Institute of Advanced Study, Shimla**